A T...

"On my must-read...
Ice is a perfect spr...
Xavier is a beautiful, intensely sexy hero with just the right
touch of achingly tormented soul that you can't help but
want to heal . . . Cat is a wonderful heroine, she's lovely,
strong, talented, intelligent . . . and she's fun to read."
—*The Romance Reader*

"Hanna Martine did not disappoint as she continued to
make the world of The Elementals even more intriguing."
—*Under the Covers*

"Savor the journey again and again. The characters are
deep, with multifaceted loyalties, pasts, and personalities
that drag a reader into the story . . . These books totally
rock and I cannot wait for the next one!"
—*Coffee Time Romance*

LIQUID LIES

"An amazing start to The Elementals series and one I
recommend." —*Under the Covers Book Blog*

"A different spin on the paranormal." —*Dark Faerie Tales*

"A ... orld
and ... t."
... oks

Berkley Sensation titles by Hanna Martine

The Elementals

LIQUID LIES
A TASTE OF ICE
DROWNING IN FIRE

The Highland Games Novels

LONG SHOT

DROWNING IN FIRE

HANNA MARTINE

BERKLEY SENSATION, NEW YORK

THE BERKLEY PUBLISHING GROUP
Published by the Penguin Group
Penguin Group (USA) LLC
375 Hudson Street, New York, New York 10014

USA • Canada • UK • Ireland • Australia • New Zealand • India • South Africa • China

penguin.com

A Penguin Random House Company

DROWNING IN FIRE

A Berkley Sensation Book / published by arrangement with the author

Berkley Sensation Books are published by The Berkley Publishing Group.
BERKLEY SENSATION® is a registered trademark of Penguin Group (USA) LLC.
The "B" design is a trademark of Penguin Group (USA) LLC.

For information, address: The Berkley Publishing Group,
a division of Penguin Group (USA) LLC,
375 Hudson Street, New York, New York 10014.

ISBN: 978-0-425-26753-0

PUBLISHING HISTORY
Berkley Sensation mass-market edition / April 2014

PRINTED IN THE UNITED STATES OF AMERICA

10 9 8 7 6 5 4 3 2 1

Cover photo © Conrado/Shutterstock.
Cover design by Jason Gill.
Interior text design by Tiffany Estreicher.

ACKNOWLEDGMENTS

Thank you to Cyndi Culhane, Lynne Hartzer, and Erica O'Rourke for writerly help in the developmental stages; and to Eliza Evans for her ever-insightful input on the completed manuscript.

Also, thank you to my husband, who really took one for the team and made a brave, brave sacrifice when he brought me to the Big Island of Hawaii for "research."

PROLOGUE

KEKO

"I'm not a damn babysitter."

Keko stomped after the Chimeran *ali'i*, her bare feet kicking aside old, brown leaves and crunching through patches of crispy April mountain snow. This was a shit assignment, one far below her well-deserved and hard-won position, and she'd growl at the retreating bare back of her uncle until he realized that.

"Chief, wait."

He finally stopped, one big hand on the flap of his tent, his dusky shoulders sloping under the weight of a sigh. Slowly he turned around to face her, his black eyebrows, dusted with silver, rising with growing impatience. At least he wasn't deaf. There was still a chance.

"Send Bane," Keko demanded, moving as close to the *ali'i* as was allowed by clan law. "Or Makaha. I'm the general, for fuck's sake."

Someday, after she threw down the challenge and wrested the position of *ali'i* away from her uncle, she would delegate assignments appropriate to a Chimeran's worthiness. Until that moment arrived, she would forever argue to get her way.

A gust of frigid Utah wind swept down the mountain and raced through the leafless spikes of the tightly packed stand of trees. Keko mentally reached deep inside her body, touching the heart of her fire magic, and turned up her inner heat. The *ali'i* did so as well, and wispy layers of steam lifted off the exposed skin of their torsos like wings.

"You're impertinent is what you are," he replied. He wasn't that much taller than her, but there was a reason why he'd been *ali'i* for nearly two decades. The way he commanded respect with a simple stare was unmatched. She consistently tried to emulate it.

"And difficult," he added. "But you're also my second and you're the most capable, the most skilled."

Damn straight she was. "So—"

Chief lifted a hand, his palm a paler shade than the native Hawaiian tint to his skin. "The Senatus deliberated for a hell of a long time before finally agreeing to grant the new Ofarian leader an audience. There are reasons we've kept our distance from the water elementals, not the least of which being they are historically greedy, pompous, and want to control everything. There's no one we trust more than you to shadow him his entire time here, make sure he doesn't overstep his bounds."

The flame inside her flared in frustration. "That's baby-sitting."

"It's guarding," he snapped, and she was forced to take a step back. Only for him would she do that. Chief drew himself up. "You will bring him to and from Senatus gatherings. You will explain to him the group's procedures and history, what we do and don't cover. You will keep him within range at all times and monitor any communications he has with his people."

Yes, sir was on the tip of her tongue, but she just couldn't bring it out.

"And you will report back to us everything he says or asks, and your answers. Tell us how he is different away from the meetings, if there are any contradictions to his behavior. Keep an eye out for anything suspicious. This is an evaluation period for him and his people before we consider giving them a seat around the bonfire."

"Do I have permission to kick his ass if he falls out of line?"

Chief gave her a rare grin, one that pulled at the deep lines around his eyes. "And that's exactly why we chose you to do this, Keko."

She ran a hand up and down her bare arm, dragging little

orange sparks in its wake. The mid-day sky looked heavy with snow. "What's he like? What do you already know about him?"

Chief shifted, his big feet making new prints in the old snow. "A limited amount. He is new to the leadership, having been part of an overthrow of the Ofarian government two years ago. Only after he took over did he learn his former leaders had been hiding knowledge of other elementals' existence." Chief let out a huff of breath, bathing her in a wave of Chimeran heat. "He's been pursuing contact with the Senatus for over a year. He's persistent, I'll give him that. Determined. Very serious."

"Great." Keko rolled her eyes. "Sounds like a blast." She waved a hand in the direction of the large olive-green tent she, her brother Bane, and the warrior Makaha shared. "So are we all supposed to cuddle up with this Ofarian at night and make him feel warm and snuggly so he spills his secrets?"

Chief snorted. "He's Ofarian, which means he's spoiled and arrogant. He's taken a hotel room in town at the base of the mountain. You'll be staying in a room next to his."

"What?" She would miss sleeping in the night air, no matter how cold it was. Temperature didn't mean much to her kind.

"I'm done arguing. It's an order." Stern brown eyes, the nearly black shade all Chimerans shared, nailed her in place. "Now go pick up Griffin Aames from the airport, get him to his hotel, and bring him to the gathering tonight."

Chief disappeared into his tent, the flap snapping closed behind him.

Keko marched to her tent, grabbed her small, threadbare duffel of clothes and things, and started on the two-mile hike down to where they'd parked the car. Despite her reluctance over the assignment, at least she got to drive. There were only a few vehicles in the entire Chimeran valley back home and very little need for them, but she loved getting behind the wheel. It felt so free. So very modern. So outside her own culture.

Icy wind swirled through the open car windows as she sped for Salt Lake City. She'd tied her hair back, but long, black strands still whipped at her face. This was when she loved to leave Hawaii, to feel cold new climates like this. To strengthen her magic by having to use it at all times to keep warm.

The designated meeting spot, she'd been told, was a corner of the day-use parking garage under the light pole labeled 2E. She found it, swung into a parking place, and sat. When her knee started to bounce with impatience and her belly rumbled with hunger, she jumped out of the car to head over to the vending machines perched near the elevators. Another incredible thing her people didn't have: food and drink at the drop of a coin.

A few steps away from the car she remembered the biggest rule about being seen outside of the Chimeran valley, especially in colder areas where Primaries lived: clothes.

With a growl she went back to the car and pulled out a pair of flimsy sandals with an uncomfortable strap between the toes and the lone sweatshirt she owned: a pilled gray zippered thing with "Minnesota Gophers" in cracked red and gold print across the front. At least she still had on the holey jeans with the frayed, wet hems, and one of the white tank tops she favored. Putting clothing on Chimeran skin was like scraping nails over silk. Not that she'd ever worn silk, but she'd seen pictures and had read descriptions of it in the old, dog-eared magazines that sometimes made it to the valley. The things she did for Primary comfort and Secondary secrecy . . .

Leaving the sweatshirt unzipped, she went to the vending machines and popped change into the slots, pulling out a bottle of Coke and potato chips. She'd eaten half the bag when a deep voice sounded behind her.

"You must be my ride."

Turning around, she screwed off the Coke cap with a hiss. The guy who stood halfway between her and the car wore jeans and boots and a fitted black coat with all sorts of zippers and pockets. His hair was very short and nearly as dark as hers. Thick, straight, low-set eyebrows were the most prominent feature on his face and made him seem intense and serious.

She glanced around the otherwise empty garage corner. "Don't think I am."

He nudged his chin toward her car. "Two E," he said. "Where I'm supposed to meet you. You must be Kekona."

To trust him or not? He wasn't anything like the pampered, self-important Ofarian she'd pictured. Not this militaristic-looking guy who couldn't be more than a few years older than she.

The man stood impossibly straight, as though someone had shoved a pole up his ass. "You're Secondary and I'm Griffin Aames." There was absolutely no intonation to his voice.

Oh, this guy was going to be a bag of fun.

"And what brings you to the lovely state of Utah?" she asked.

He had a really good check on his emotions. Only a slight shift of his feet gave away his frustration. "For the Senatus gathering. Was there a secret code somewhere I missed?"

And just like that, the first spark of attraction lit an unexpected flame inside her. To be fair, it didn't take much for her. For him though, there was nothing. Just a patient stare as he waited to be chauffeured to his fancy feather bed.

"No code. You just have to get past me." She lifted the Coke to her lips and took a swig, never taking her eyes off his.

A gust of wind barreled through the garage, opening one side of her sweatshirt and folding it back from her body.

Bingo. Griffin's brown eyes—lighter than a Chimeran's but still pretty dark—flicked to her chest. Flicked. Nothing more. She never wore one of those bra things—no Chimeran woman did—and she knew very well how she looked. The thin white tank top stretched over brown skin and even darker nipples. There wasn't much of her to be left to the imagination, and modesty had never been one of her strong suits.

It had been a long time. For her, at least. Maybe a month since she'd had any sort of physical contact, let alone full-on sex. And right then she was looking at the most wonderful sort of challenge, wrapped up in an olive-skinned package: the guy she'd been tasked with shadowing for the next seven days. The Ofarian with the one-note expression whose business-only walls were so thick not even hard nipples could noticeably break through them. The very opposite of who she was. The water to her fire.

He was not Chimeran. He was *kapu*. Forbidden.

But then, wasn't she supposed to find out things about him that he didn't reveal to the Senatus? Sex always seemed to bring out the hidden, no matter who was involved. She was willing to bet Griffin Aames wasn't any different. He was locked up so airtight she guessed that once those walls came down, there would be no stopping the onslaught of everything he'd tried to hold back. She couldn't wait to discover what that was.

But that was enough teasing the unsuspecting Ofarian for

one day, especially since they'd just met minutes ago. There was an art to seduction, to the chase, and applying it to someone who was not a Chimeran slathered on an extra layer of excitement. Getting around what her clan had declared to be *kapu* would be a fantastic, fun challenge. Keko folded closed the Gophers sweatshirt.

Griffin carried a structured black duffel with barely a travel scratch, and with a clearing of his throat, he swung it around to dangle off the back of one shoulder. He was an inch or two above six feet, not that much taller than her.

"I'm not carrying that for you," she said.

His eyes narrowed slightly, and she found she liked the tiny movement of his thick eyebrows. It was easy to hide expression under those things, so when they actually twitched she knew there was something going on in his gorgeous head.

"Wasn't expecting you to," he replied.

"Good. Now that we're clear on that." She circled around him to get to the car, wondering the whole time—the whole ten seconds—if his eyes had tracked the back of her head . . . or her ass.

With one hand on the door handle and the other clutching her drink and potato chips, she swept a good long look around the parking garage. No one else was around.

"Where'd you come from?" she asked as he went around to the other side of the car, threw open the passenger side door, and tossed his bag in the backseat.

"San Francisco. But of course you already knew that."

"I did."

His door still open, he planted one hand on the top of it. "Where are you from?"

She laughed, because the Chimerans had never revealed their home to anyone not born with fire. "Nice try."

When he shrugged, she found herself intrigued by the fluidity of his shoulders, how he'd suddenly broken out of his rigid mold. The straight face remained, however, along with the severe line of those eyebrows.

She folded her arms on top of the car. "How'd you know I was Secondary?"

Without hesitation, "Your signature. I can tell you have magic, that you're not a Primary human. I can feel you."

This man was infuriating, in the best possible way. She had no idea if he knew what his doublespeak implied or if he was doing it on purpose. And she found that she loved it, that ambiguity. So did the fire inside.

"Must be nice," she said, overly casually. "I wish I had that."

He cocked his head, looking genuinely interested. "Why?"

"So I can tell when I come across a Primary. I'd know who to avoid."

He looked at her for a long, long moment before saying, "Right. Of course."

He made no move to get into the car so she asked, "What do you mean by 'signature'?"

His stance relaxed some as he considered her.

"You're going to be asked a lot of questions while you're here," she added. "Might as well get used to it."

Another few moments of consideration, then he inhaled and glanced around the garage. "Hard to explain. It's a feeling in my head. Like a smell, but not really. I know you're Secondary. I just don't know what you can do."

Time for a real test. Tilting back her head, throwing him a challenging smile, she asked, "What can you do?"

He pulled out his phone and tapped the screen once. "Adine? Yeah. Salt Lake City airport, parking garage, row 2E." Griffin stood stock still. So did Keko, waiting. Intrigued. "You got 'em? Great, thanks."

Hanging up the phone, he threw a look into the corner, where Keko had previously noticed the telltale black ceiling bubble of a security camera. She'd heard the Ofarians had some reach, some pretty impressive technological skills, but to access international airport security at such quick notice?

"Okay, then. If you're looking for proof." Griffin was looking straight at her, his body never so much as twitching, as foreign, whispered words escaped his barely parted lips. Movement to her right caught her eye.

A pile of gray, crunchy snow piled up against the side of the open parking garage melted without a touch, without heat. In a slow, glittering stream, it snaked its way toward her, rolling across the black asphalt and the yellow parking dividing lines. The water coiled around her legs, up toward her hips. Once, twice, a third time around her body. Reaching, reaching, but never quite touching. A brilliant dance of water and light in the cold grayness of the garage. Then the coil of magic water receded, sinking slowly back down to the dirty surface under her feet.

The word that came to mind was . . . sensual.

Her focus snapped back to Griffin Aames. Though his expression had not changed, she knew he was grinning. Deep down, this had pleased him.

"Now," he said, so evenly she felt a distinct hum between her legs, "what can you do?"

Inhaling deeply, pulling up the fire from inside her body, she licked her lips, letting a roll of flame follow her tongue. Then she opened her mouth, showing him the spark that forever danced in the back of her throat. When she clamped her lips shut, swallowing down her magic, she gave him a look full of promise and said, "Wouldn't you like to know."

That night, Keko paced along the outside perimeter of the cage of wind encircling the Senatus gathering. She could see into it—the three elemental Senatus delegates and Griffin sat on cheap lawn chairs around a bonfire—but heard nothing. The wind barrier erased their words.

Bane and Makaha took up positions at other points surrounding the gathering, though this deep in the pitch black mountains they were unlikely to be discovered. Aaron, the only air elemental in attendance other than the Senatus premier, leaned against a nearby tree, holding the soundproof wind cage in place.

As always, Aya, the self-proclaimed Daughter of Earth, was the only elemental of her mysterious race in attendance. The dainty Daughter perched gingerly on the edge of her chair, the fire that rose from the logs highlighting the unusually lovely golden tint to her skin and the pure white shock of her hair. The green of her eyes did not reflect the firelight at all. She said so little but she was always watching and listening, always alert, and her presence never failed to intrigue Keko.

The *ali'i*, shirtless and barefoot, lounged back in his chair. The Senatus premier wore a cowboy hat and a flannel coat lined with fleece, his deeply wrinkled eyes focused intently on Griffin, who had been speaking for a long while with stiff, controlled hand gestures. Puffs of cold, white air escaped from between his lips every time he opened them.

The Ofarian was incredibly easy to look at. Keko knew power and leadership when she saw it, and it turned her on more than it probably should have.

Their flirting—however subversive it had been—ceased that afternoon and evening as she'd performed her job and explained to Griffin how the Senatus worked. The order of speaking, the presentation of issues, how the premier was voted in on five-year intervals, among other things she found boring but which Griffin listened to with an attentive ear.

Now, inside the wind cage, an argument broke out. That much was plain by the tension in the four bodies and the vehement way Griffin was talking, his gestures getting bigger, his eyes blinking less.

The *ali'i* was the first to jump up and stomp through the wind barrier. Keko couldn't look away from Griffin, who'd risen to his feet with a powerful grace. Right then and there she knew he was a fighter, some sort of soldier. A different kind of warrior than a Chimeran, but a warrior nonetheless.

As Chief grabbed Keko's arm and spun her away, she saw the premier and Aya approaching Griffin in a calm manner.

"The Ofarians are making aggressive moves to integrate into the Primary human world." The inner fire raked at Chief's voice, making it gritty and rasping.

Keko blinked, not sure she understood his anger. "And?"

"He thinks we should do the same. Rather than hiding out in our own little worlds, he wants us to figure out ways to inch the Secondary world into the Primary. And if he gains a seat in the Senatus, that will be his main objective."

A brief, alien cold swept through Keko. The various Chimeran clans spread all over the Hawaiian Islands had always been deliberately separate from the humans. The Queen had decreed that necessary over a thousand years ago when she split off from the other Polynesian immigrants. And now this Ofarian, this *water* elemental, wanted to shatter that by forcing all Secondaries to follow his people's lead?

"Why?" she asked.

Chief wiped his mouth and let out a short, bitter laugh. "Because they have nothing. The magic they once peddled to the Primaries is gone now, along with all the money it used to bring in. They go to Primary schools and are taking jobs in

Primary businesses because they have to. Griffin says it's starting to work for them but I don't know. It's dangerous. So, so dangerous . . ."

Keko agreed.

Yet she'd always embraced danger.

Looking over Chief's shoulder she saw that Griffin was alone now, gazing into the fire and dragging a slow hand between his ear and chin. She could hear the crackle and pop of the flame-consumed logs now, which meant Aaron had dropped the wind barrier.

"I want to know more about his motives," Chief told her, his voice dropping. "I want to know everything. You know what to do."

Just then Griffin looked up and caught her staring. She didn't look away.

Oh, she knew *exactly* what to do. And only a small fraction of it involved listening.

She nodded. Pure business, all general. "Yes, sir."

As the Chimerans and air elementals split off for their respective camps, and Aya did that silent thing where she melted back into the night shadows and disappeared without a trace, Keko pulled the car keys from her jeans pocket and jangled them.

"Let's go," she called to Griffin. He looked at her for a drawn-out moment before finally turning his back on the fire and following her.

Griffin was silent the whole ride back to the hotel. On the way to their rooms that were next to each other but not connected, the only sounds were his boots on the carpet and the rasp of fabric as he took off his jacket. She waited while he drew out his keycard and slipped it into the lock. When it blinked green, he pushed open the door, then froze. Turning his head he said to her, "Come in. I want to talk to you."

The *ali'i*'s orders were but a niggle in the back of her mind, a mere fly compared to the volcanic rumble the sound of Griffin's command strummed inside her. But she played it cool and sauntered past him. The door clicked shut behind her.

She'd barely made it into the little hall opposite the bathroom when Griffin grabbed her shoulder from behind, spun her around, and pinned her against the wall with a straight arm. Then his elbow bent and his body closed in.

Queen help her, she felt herself go wet, felt her whole body get switched on. Rough sex was how it was done in the Chimeran stronghold, and, as their general, it was the way she demanded it when she chose a partner.

"You're not just my driver, not just my tourist guide," he murmured, getting closer and closer until all she could see was his face. "You're their spy."

Keko arched her back, pushing her torso away from the wall and into his hand.

For a second his desire was betrayed in the flash of his brown eyes, but then his fingers dug deep and hard into her shoulder.

"You're supposed to tell them everything I say and do," he ground out. "Aren't you?"

The pulse between her legs was crazy now. The fire inside her raged. She could barely control the pace of her breath or the sexual itch scratching its way through her body.

"Well, thank the Queen you know," she said. "Now we can just get to the fucking."

Beneath those thick eyebrows his eyes widened, glowing with lust. His desire had its own color, and there was nothing he could do to disguise it or paint over it.

The moment caused his grip to slacken and Keko took advantage of it. Lunging. A forearm across his chest, she shoved him against the opposite wall. That second of surprise on his face was wonderful and sexy and a powerful turn-on.

Then she smashed her mouth against his.

Resistance lasted barely a breath, then he groaned—a great release of sound and pent-up energy that made his whole body shudder—and he was kissing her back with such force she felt it in the jump and shiver of her inner fire.

A water elemental—*kapu*, forbidden—was making her feel this way, and that made the whole thing all the more taboo, all the more sweet. He had no fire magic, yet he was burning, his lips and tongue and pressure made of heat and power.

Suddenly the contact broke and she was left reeling, empty. Griffin had taken hold of both her shoulders and had pushed her away, off of him. Her eyelids fluttered open to find his expression a swirl of confusion and base lust. His chest pumped almost violently. He looked stripped out of his skin, a completely different man from the stiff, serious, focused Ofarian she'd gathered from the airport. And he had no idea what to do with that, how to react.

Keko's lips curled up in triumph.

She lifted her hands and coiled her fingers around his wrists. Slowly, deliberately, holding his eyes with hers, she dragged his hands off the curves of her bare shoulders, sliding them over the ridge of her collarbone and down to her breasts. No bra, of course, just the thin layer of the worn white cotton tank top. She filled his big hands perfectly.

Griffin sagged, an unfettered low groan escaping his lips. Though he caught and righted himself, she'd seen it. She'd witnessed the crack in his exterior, the way this contact had freed him. She loved that almost as much as the way he was pressing his hands to her. Grabbing her with dire need. Dragging his palms over her hard nipples.

He was no longer looking into her eyes, but at her chest, at the way he was touching her. His bottom lip dropped open, and it was way too full and inviting to keep her coherent.

"Kekona," he whispered, yanking down the strap of her tank top to expose one breast. His eyes snapped back up to hers. "Now look what you started."

She was used to starting things. Back home, as general, that's how clan rule laid it out. If she wanted to sleep with someone, she had to approach them and make the offer. Of course they could refuse, but she was used to being the aggressor, the pursuer. She loved it. That power had come with her high status, which she'd fought so long and hard for.

So when Griffin yanked her closer, a claiming hand sliding around her back to spin her toward the bed, she went into immediate general mode. This was *her* scene, *her* beginning.

But just because she liked the way he'd reacted when she'd smashed open his shell, she would let him think he had the better of her. For a second. Maybe two.

When he'd gotten her close to the bed, the hand around her back moving swiftly to her ass, she wrapped a foot around his ankle, slapped an arm around his shoulders, and used his shock to whip him around and throw his larger body onto the bed. He landed with a great bounce on the mattress, his limbs going tense in defense for a brief moment, then slackening as he watched her smile wickedly.

Hands on hips, she jutted her chin at his jeans and boots. "Take them off."

He came up on his elbows. "I don't take orders. I give them."

"Funny, so do I. Tell you what, maybe I'll give you a turn."

No smile. Just a frenzied stripping. That Mediterranean skin covered all of him evenly. Born with it then, no sun lines to indicate he had any sort of time outdoors. Pity. She would have liked to trace a line between dark and darker skin with her tongue. Maybe she'd make one up in her mind and do it anyway.

She was right about him being a fighter. The hardness of his body and the lean lines of his muscles gave it away.

After he'd toed off his boots and kicked away his jeans, he leaned back on the bed and crossed his legs at the ankles. With a leader's confidence, he looked at her down his prone body, over the beautiful erection stretching up toward his belly. "You'll have nothing to tell them," he said, "unless you tell them about this. And you won't."

With a single step, her balance perfect, she climbed up and stood at the edge of the bed, her ankles bracketing his.

Whipping off her tank top, she said, "Don't want you for your words."

She thought that maybe that would coax out a smile, but any emotion he harbored came through the hot glitter of his eyes and the way they were fixated on the zipper of her jeans. He wasn't giving a verbal order, but she sure as hell was going to obey.

When she ripped open her jeans and stepped out of them, letting him know that not only did she despise bras but that she hated underwear just as much, he made a wonderful garbled sound in the back of his throat. Stomach muscles clenching, he rolled up to sit and wrapped his hands around her calves.

"Great stars," he breathed, his eyes roaming up her parted legs, across her abs and around her breasts. "You're fucking amazing."

Bending, she pushed at his shoulders, laying him flat again. The tension in her thighs was overwhelming as she lowered herself to straddle his hips, the pulsing, needy place in her body hovering just above his erection.

Taking him in hand, loving the contradiction between hard and smooth in her palm, she whispered, "I am totally telling them you said that."

Desire rattled through her body, a crazy, driving demand that wanted absolutely nothing other than for him to be inside her. She fit herself to him, making the initial entrance, then took her time working her way down. At her first curl, that first undulation of her hips, his eyes shot open and his fingers dug into the crease between her thighs and hips. He stared at where they were joined, low grunts set in time with her thrusts.

Hands planted on his iron pecs, she rode him as he drove up into her. Nothing delicate about it. Nothing remotely soft about this kind of passion.

In the back of her mind she was thinking that it was too perfect, the way they found a rhythm that seemed to mutually satisfy. Their movements were in sync, two musicians meeting for the first time who struck faultless sound on the first notes of collaboration. Like they already knew each other.

The angle was superb, where he was hitting her inside. Her fire magic was begging to be let out, building and building alongside her orgasm.

Chimeran sex was full of fire. It was a battle of wills, of flame and heat, both inside and out. Fire intensified everything . . . but Griffin was no Chimeran, and even though he was water, she feared the unknown. She feared what her body might do to him. She feared hurting him.

She feared learning firsthand why sex between two different elementals was *kapu*.

As though just to prove her wrong, he drove into her harder, the slap of their bodies drowning out all other sound. That's when she lost it, when she came with such speed and such a powerful storm that she had no time to rein in the inner fire that always paralleled her pleasure. Tiny licks of flame rolled behind her closed eyelids.

Griffin cried out and she opened her eyes to see him gritting his teeth. Chimerans loved the burst of intense heat that accompanied orgasm, considered it the ultimate satisfaction, but she could not tell if his expression was pain or pleasure. She tried to lift herself off him, to protect him from the heat that must have been immense for someone uninitiated, but he grabbed her so hard she bruised, and continued to pump her body down on his. Asking for more.

The grit of his teeth was not pain, but rather that look that men got when they loved the animal intensity of certain kinds of sex. He came with a series of groans, his whole body shaking. She took it all in, thinking that, out of all the people she'd slept with in her entire life, she'd never watched someone come with such breathtaking awe. She'd never been this fascinated. She'd never felt this satisfied.

Even after he opened his eyes and the movement of his chest leveled out, neither one of them moved. Not even a twitch. He was still inside her, her hands still planted on his chest.

"What just happened?" he murmured, and she knew he wasn't just talking about the sex or about the heat of her fire magic.

Something unseen shimmered between them. Something . . .

He reached up as if to touch her face and an invisible force slapped clarity into her brain. She pushed herself away and rolled off the bed. This was a fuck. Nothing more. She'd seen a challenge in him, she'd needed as good a release as he did, and she went after him. Mission accomplished.

There was nothing more to it. He was water. She was fire. And she had her orders.

Head on straight now, she turned around to find Griffin still lying there, muscled arms folded behind his head, one dark-haired leg cocked up. Watching her. Utter relaxation made the lines of his body soften, and there was a quiet tilt to his mouth, a warmth in his eyes, that made him seem like a new man.

And then he began to talk.

GRIFFIN

"I can't believe I'm here," Griffin heard himself say to the magnificent, naked woman standing next to his hotel bed.

When Kekona cocked her head, a sheet of straight black hair slipped off her shoulder. She was frighteningly confident in her own skin. Extraordinarily sexy.

"In Utah at the Senatus?" she asked, all casual, like nothing mind-blowing had just happened between them. Like they hadn't just fucked each other's brains out. "Or in this room with me?"

"Technically, you are in my room with me."

That could have been construed as a dismissal, but she didn't bend to pick up her clothes. Made no move toward the door. For the first time in a very, very long while, Griffin had the urge to smile. Just an urge, though; it never quite poked through.

He crossed his arms behind his head. "Either," he replied, marveling at his own truth. "Both."

She smiled knowingly behind her obsidian eyes, those things that had flashed actual fire when she'd come. For the rest of his days, he'd never be able to get that image out of his memory. He didn't think he'd ever want to.

In the back of his mind he registered that she'd spoken the word "Senatus," that the organization of the elemental races was his true reason for being here, but the vision of Kekona standing there, looking like sex itself, erased pretty much all present thought.

Not an ounce of fat on her anywhere. Taut skin in an exotic caramel shade he guessed to be somewhere between Pacific Islander and Asian stretched over some seriously sick muscles. She was ridiculously strong. Phenomenally beautiful.

But the thing that got to him most was how nonchalant she was acting, how she'd so quickly and easily ducked out of his reaching hand. That touch had meant to tell her, however stupidly, that she'd cemented a permanent spot in his consciousness. It hadn't meant to be claiming, but complimentary. She was looking down at him now like he'd waited on her in a restaurant. Didn't she just have the same experience he had? Why wasn't she completely out of her head like he was?

Oh. Right. Because it was clear that she'd had plenty of sex in her life, and he hadn't slept with anyone in over two years. Because he'd been hung up on Gwen Carroway after the destruction of their arranged marriage when she'd fallen for someone else—a Primary, no less. Because he'd thought that Gwen was what he'd wanted and had taken his own sweet time getting over her, before realizing that falling for someone because you'd been told to by a bunch of scheming traitors wasn't really falling for someone at all.

So he'd thrown himself into leading the Ofarians, rebuilding them, steering them into a new future. Work, work, work. Politics, politics, politics. No time for lovers. No desire for them, really. Until Kekona.

And what a shocker that had been.

Though he didn't want her to leave—that realization making his body tense up all over again—he knew that eventually, soon, she would.

But she didn't. Instead she came closer, causing his lungs to pick up pace. She sat on the edge of the bed and patted the rumpled bedspread. "Do you want to get a few things out of the way?"

He sat up, resisting the incessant urge to touch her. "Things. Like what?"

"Questions."

Ah, business. "Ask away."

She pursed her lips, a lovely, playful expression. "I meant do you have any for me after your first Senatus meeting, but I'll bite."

He had a ton of questions for her, none of which involved the Senatus.

"How'd you find us?" she asked.

He saw no reason not to tell her. "The Board, the old system of Ofarian leadership, had been gathering clues about other Secondary races on Earth. Scattered sightings or unproven occurrences, some cryptic references, that kind of thing. When I took over, I followed the breadcrumbs they'd been hiding." He folded his arms across the tops of his knees, knowing that the Senatus had been well aware of the Ofarians' existence for years—maybe even decades—but had deliberately avoided approaching his kind.

"I already told the Senatus all this," he added. Which meant that Kekona may have been the chief's second, but she wasn't privy to all the information her superior was. Interesting.

She didn't respond. "After the Board fell, how'd you get to be leader?"

"Ah"—he scrubbed at his cheek—"by default? I didn't know

I wanted the position when I was elected, but they voted me in anyway. I'm a bit, um, controversial."

Genuine surprise widened her almond eyes. "You didn't *want* to be leader? And your people voted you in anyway?"

Griffin exhaled, remembering how Gwen had refused the new leadership position and nominated him instead. It wasn't information he worried about sharing with the Senatus. Kekona would relay these words back to them tomorrow, and Griffin thought it might make him seem more humble. "Yes," he said. Kekona seemed sincerely confused at that, which sparked his curiosity. "How is your chief chosen?"

"The *ali'i*, or chief, isn't chosen. You fight for it. With this"—she lifted a fist—"and this." She drew a short, sharp inhale, and then expelled a small flame onto her knuckles where it danced without effect or apparent pain. With another inhale, she sucked the fire back into her body. Griffin's turn to marvel.

Kekona leaned closer. "So do you want the leadership now?"

A difficult question. The Senatus hadn't asked him this much, about his history. Maybe it was time they knew—time they understood where he'd come from to better comprehend what he was fighting for. It would give her something to report back, and in the end it could work to his advantage.

Strangely, too, he wanted to speak to Kekona's earnest expression.

"Yes and no," he answered truthfully. "I could do without the actual command, but what I want is more important."

"Better integration with the Primaries."

He nodded, not remotely shocked she'd been told what he'd presented to the Senatus just hours ago. "That's right." Shifting on the bed, he realized they were both still naked, and that while he sort of wanted to cover up, she didn't even seem to notice.

"But . . . *why*?"

This was what he hadn't told the Senatus, at least not this version, in this way. He thought that the story might sound more convincing to them coming from her, told to her by Griffin in a private setting, rather than him blathering on to three other Secondaries who wore obvious cloaks of doubt and fear.

"In old Ofarian society," he began, carefully choosing his

words, "you were born into very specific classes. The ruling class, the working class, the soldier class . . . you can guess what I was."

The way her eyes flicked appreciatively across his arms and legs made him burn like when she'd been touching him. "I can guess," she said.

"I never had any choice in what I was to become. I had no dreams except for what was given to me. No skills other than what I was prepped for, what I'd been made to tend or grow."

"Chimerans are kind of similar," she said, and by the remark she'd made about having to battle for the position of *ali'i*, it made sense.

"When I was a teenager," he went on, "I was tested, and then trained to be the sole protector of someone who, at the time, was one of our greatest assets: Gwen Carroway, our old Chairman's daughter. It was all I knew up until two years ago—her and her protection. I was eventually made head of Ofarian security."

Kekona blinked and shook her head, long strings of black hair swinging around her shoulders to brush the curves of her breasts. "I don't understand. That wasn't your dream?"

She may not have understood him, but he understood Kekona. Because she'd had to fight to be Chimeran general, she'd nursed her own dream from probably a very young age. She'd seen what she wanted, battled for it, and won.

"No," he replied. "It wasn't. But now my people have the chance to start over, to create dreams outside of Ofarian magic or structure, outside of the Secondary world. Opportunities I never had. I want that for every one of my people. I want that for all Secondaries."

Her full mouth twisted and he knew he hadn't sold her. That was okay. For now. Baby steps. Spying and manipulating was so much easier when it was done out in the open.

Kekona pulled her feet onto the bed and curled her legs to one side, getting more comfortable with him. He liked that. She was hard and muscular, a clear warrior, but there was a feminine gracefulness to her movements, and it made him hyper aware of her presence, still so close.

His hand was halfway across the space between them before he realized it. Too late. No turning back. But instead of going for her face again, which he sensed would make her back off, he fingered a piece of her glossy hair. She flinched but didn't move away.

"It doesn't catch fire?" he asked in wonder.

"Wouldn't make much sense to be Chimeran if it did, would it?"

True. "It feels . . ." *amazing.*

"What?"

He shook his head, let her hair slide out of his palm, and rolled off the opposite side of the bed. He went to his bag, ripped it open with more force than was necessary, and pulled out a pair of gray flannel pants. When he looked up, her eyes were skating over him in obvious—and wonderful—approval.

A slow smile spread across her face as she pushed from the bed and sauntered toward him with powerful elegance. The woman knew how to command a room. She didn't have to stand on her tiptoes to kiss him, soft and swift, and it was then he first tasted the zing of sweet smoke on her breath. It curled down his throat and made its home inside him, and he knew he was done for.

"Kekona," he whispered, before he could stop himself.

Her head snapped back mockingly. "Yes? *Griffin?*"

No one had managed to unnerve him, to embarrass him, in years. He found that he liked it, this reminder that he was real and not untouchable. That he was someone other than a leader, a scapegoat, a man to be feared, admired, or hated.

He cleared his throat. "Anyone call you anything besides Kekona?"

"Yes."

Suddenly, he felt very brave. "What can I call you then?"

With a lift of an eyebrow—arched and dramatic compared to his flat, thick ones—she nodded to the door that opened into the hallway. "On the other side of that, call me 'general.' But in here, 'Keko.'"

Feeling victorious and electrified, he pushed his hands into the black silk of her hair and tilted her head back. To his delight, she let him. "So this is happening again?"

"Yes." She nipped at his bottom lip. "I believe it will."

The next night, Keko let *him* throw *her* onto the bed.

It had been another grueling night session with the Senatus

around the bonfire in which he'd been asked to relay stories of successful Ofarian integration into Primary businesses and schools. The inquiries had planted hope, which, if he'd been smarter, he would have recognized as him having reached the apex before the crashing fall over the back side of the mountain. Because as soon as he concluded talking about an Ofarian man who used to do accounting for the old Board and had recently secured a job at a large Primary firm for equal pay and excellent retirement, the premier and the chief—Aya remaining oddly silent—dragged out example after example of times when the commingling had done more damage than good.

Instances that he knew far too well. Instances that had resulted in death. Twelve deaths to be exact.

So when Keko accompanied him back to his hotel room, his mood a murky, roiling cloud of frustration, he'd slammed her against the wall, his mouth claiming hers before she could speak. Spinning her around, he slid one hand down the front of her ratty, loose jeans and the other up her shirt. A smooth, willing piece of heaven, right in his grasp. His for now. She was grinning at him over her shoulder as he picked her up and tossed her onto the bed.

She gave him a wonderful fight, smiling with her jet eyes the whole time. Exactly what he'd been looking for. But in the end he let her win, because she seemed to like that. She seemed to get off on victory. When it had started he'd wanted a means through which to take out his annoyance and anger, but then as soon as he was inside her, it changed. He just wanted her, the driving velvet of her body, and the casual exchange of words and random thoughts directly after.

On the third night they didn't even make it to the bed, doing it on the floor just inside the hotel door.

On the fourth night of bonfires, the Senatus finally asked him about his story—the one he'd told Keko about growing up in the Ofarian classes, about how he and everyone else he knew had been wedged into lives they didn't necessarily want.

It had taken her a few days to relay this information to her chief. Maybe she'd deciphered the growing tension in Griffin over their past few secretive nights together. Maybe she'd actually wanted to help him. But it was dangerous to think the latter, to take the fork in the road that veered toward the personal. Still, he couldn't help but wonder.

Griffin told the Senatus about his life up until the downfall of the Board, and the other elementals were more receptive than they'd ever been to his words—at least no outward arguments or raised voices. Griffin went back to the hotel jubilant, that small accomplishment stoking his desire. With a silent folding back of the covers, he invited Keko between the sheets for the very first time. He'd expected a laugh, maybe a roll of the eyes, but instead got a slow removal of her clothes, revealing the body he would never, ever get tired of looking at. When she slipped her feet under the top sheet and lay back, the contrast of her dusky skin against the pure, starched white was remarkable and lovely, the whole process achingly slow.

With an impatient lift of her brow, he got naked under her appraisal. She made him feel like a Chimeran—full of fire and the urge to use it.

He came down over her and immediately she grinned and tried to resist, to get a leg over him, to return to their games of the prior nights, wrestling for control. But with firm hands on her forearms, he pressed her into the bed. Not hard, but enough for her not to misread what he wanted, or did not want.

"Can I just be with you?" he whispered.

Beneath him she softened, but only a little. Enough to remind him that he was leaving Utah after the Senatus bonfire tomorrow and there wouldn't be another night with her. Enough for him to know that he wanted to slow it down tonight and . . . memorize.

As he touched her—for the first time *really* touched her with care—he told her with words how much he loved the way she felt and looked, and the way she did things to him. When he finally pushed inside her and her Chimeran heat coated him, pulled him deeper in, he told her how much he loved that, too.

She didn't respond with any verbal declarations, but he hadn't expected her to. After they came, staring into each other's eyes, and he rolled off her, she made no move to leave him or the bed. That was a first. And it would also be a last. He hated that thought.

She shifted onto her side to face him, and that said more than her unspoken words.

"Thank you for not trying to make a fight out of it," he said.

Her lips rolled inward and he couldn't tell if the expression was regret or uncertainty. "It's just how it is with me."

"I know."

He stared as though seeing her for the first time. The mysteries of her people glittered around her. Her signature had made a comfortable home in his mind and being, nestling in good and tight. He would never forget it, as long as he lived.

"Do you want to be *ali'i*?" he asked, because she wouldn't respect him beating around the bush.

The answer came without pause. "Yes."

"So you'll eventually have to fight your uncle."

She shrugged. "To get where I am now, I had to fight my best friend, Makaha. I fought my brother."

"What was that like, fighting your brother?"

"My *older* brother. Bane means 'long-awaited child,' if that tells you anything about how my parents viewed him." With a rare glance down, her finger ticked at the edge of the bed sheet. "I've been fighting my whole life."

"Ah."

Looking up, she smiled, and the realization over how much he was going to miss that sight gouged a hole in his chest.

"The first time I beat two boys at once. Makaha had taken this slingshot I'd made, and when I tried to get it back Bane came over. They taunted me in front of my parents, in front of a lot of people. That's when my fire came out for the very first time. I laid them both out with my fists and finished them off with flame. I knew then that I'd be general someday."

Griffin smiled and laughed. Both happening simultaneously for the first time in *years*. Thanks to Kekona Kalani.

"Are you and your brother close?" he asked.

She seemed perplexed by the question. "As close as family is supposed to be." Which answered nothing . . . and a lot at the same time. "Bane and I share parents, but Makaha is my dearest friend. My brother in much more than blood."

They stared at each other, only a narrow strip of crinkled white dividing them. Neither moved to cross it.

They talked the rest of the night. Nothing serious, nothing about the Senatus. Just silly stories about them as kids learning how to fight, their favorite foods, how similar their parents were.

As the morning light outlined the thick hotel drapes, he took a deep breath and said, "You haven't told them about us." He didn't have to define "them."

For the first time since he'd met her, she seemed uncomfortable. "No."

"Will you? When I'm gone?"

Keko licked her lips and glanced away. "No."

He reached out then and pulled her into him, that hard body flush against his, her heat instantly enveloping him. He searched her face and found that a very different fire raged behind her eyes, one that had nothing to do with magic.

"There's something here," he murmured. "More than sex. Tell me I'm wrong."

She stayed silent.

"Go on," he urged. "Tell me."

"I can't."

Unsure what to do with this incredible victory, he ran a hand down her smooth back and held her even tighter. "I don't think I can just walk away from you. I want to see you again."

She'd never paused this long before speaking. The woman owned every single word she ever said, and she never hesitated. So when she whispered, "I want that, too," he nearly collapsed in happiness and relief.

He kissed her hard and then spouted off his phone number. "You got that? It's my private phone. I want you to call me."

She threw him the wry, cocky smile he'd grown to cherish and understand. "There's one phone in the whole Chimeran stronghold. Phone sex might be a little difficult."

It was her way of ending the connection—with a smart-ass remark—and he let her slide out of his embrace. The way she sat on the edge of the bed, shoulders all tense, bothered him, though.

"We can't," she said. "See each other again, I mean. Outside of the Senatus. I haven't said anything to them because it isn't allowed."

A sour feeling churned in his stomach. "*What* isn't?"

"Intermixing. Mating. Between the races. It's a Senatus rule. And it's *kapu* for Chimerans."

"*Kapu?*"

"Taboo."

Propelling himself off the bed, he whirled around to face her. "That's fucking ridiculous." As she bent down to snatch her jeans from the floor, he could see the words she wasn't saying all bunched up in her spine. "What?" He hadn't meant for it to come out so demanding, so cold.

"Just that"—she stamped into her jeans and pulled them up over her ass—"I never used to see anything wrong with it." She lifted her eyes to his. "Until now."

His feet ate up the space around the bed so fast he didn't remember moving. He was on her, kissing her hot and tender, and the feel of her hands on his back sent him soaring. "I'm never going to stop wanting you," he said against her mouth, and she replied with a sound so low in her throat it may have been her answering fire.

"We'll take it slow," he told her, pulling back and running fingers down her soft neck. "We'll figure it out. I'll get on the Senatus and we'll figure it out. Change things."

She nodded, stepping back, and he knew that she didn't believe him. She didn't believe either that *he* could do what he claimed, or that it would ever happen.

It wasn't hard to avoid looking at Keko as the two of them hiked through the cold, black woods to the Senatus gathering. It was impossible, however, not to feel her.

Was she doing that on purpose? Sending him those knee-buckling waves of heat that managed to penetrate his heavy coat? They felt like the strokes of her hands—the way she'd touched him all last night into early this morning. Quieter, kinder than the Keko who'd picked him up at the airport.

A fire crackled low and unthreatening within a stone circle. The premier and Aaron sat at a picnic table, talking. Chief and Bane and Makaha huddled on the opposite side of the flames. Aya had not yet arrived, but Griffin assumed she would walk out of the deep shadows at any moment. She always arrived just as the proceedings began, which intrigued him and also made him slightly uncomfortable.

He regarded the Chimerans with new eyes tonight, understanding them a little bit more. At least he knew now why Bane and Keko were so aloof to one another and why, even though she was his second, Chief always seemed to be watching her, assessing. Makaha was different, though. The shorter, stockier Chimeran warrior tracked Griffin with his black gaze. If he and Keko were as good friends as she claimed, it was possible the warrior could tell something was different about her. About how she and Griffin now acted around one another.

As Griffin stepped into the Senatus circle, the chief and the premier broke away from their people to approach him. As predicted, Aya emerged seemingly from the atmosphere beyond, her wispy white hair shining and the flames making the golden skin on her face and neck glow with warmth. The rest of her body was covered by a beautiful and unsettling tangle of ever-shifting foliage. She leisurely walked out of the shadows, as though she'd just parked her car steps away, which Griffin knew couldn't be true.

Tonight, Griffin was going to tell them everything. Through Keko, he'd seen what chiseling away at cultural walls could do for understanding on a level above a formal meeting. Talking was the key. He would appeal to the hearts of the Senatus delegates.

He was going to talk about Henry.

The muffled chime of a cell phone broke the tense silence, and the premier pulled his out of an inner pocket. He looked at the screen and swore.

"What?" Chief demanded, but the tone of his voice suggested he might already know.

Griffin couldn't name why his stomach suddenly dropped.

The premier turned and snapped his fingers at Aaron, who was immediately on his own phone, mumbling into it as he turned away.

"Where?" asked Chief.

Yes, where? Griffin wanted to scream, because his gut was telling him something horrible was about to go down.

"Where we thought," the premier replied. "She'll be stopped. Aaron's sending Madeline right now."

"What's going on?" Griffin was careful to keep his voice even, to not betray the sense of foreboding that had suddenly crashed into the silent woods. Chief and the premier, after sharing a long, silent look, swiveled their heads to look at him. He noticed, with discomfort, that Aya's eerily cool green eyes had been watching him the whole time.

"A Primary professor in Seattle," the premier finally told Griffin, "seems to have gotten photographic proof of one my own."

So that's what that sick feeling was: familiarity.

"She's been sitting on it for a while, gathering more information, writing a paper. But now she's preparing to go wide. My people found it when she posted it online in draft form."

"Stop her," Chief growled.

The premier raised a stiff hand. "We will."

All of the heat Keko had given Griffin fled in an icy gust. "*How* will you?"

The premier stood as tall as his slight stature would allow, the brim of his cowboy hat tilting back. "She's respected in her field now," he replied. "She won't be tomorrow."

Griffin's tone took a dive into distaste and frustration. "*How?*"

Another wordless look between the chief and the premier.

"Tell him." Aya's voice was small and light, fitting to her appearance. But it carried a clear command, one that the other two elemental men heeded. Her white hair seemed to move without wind. She had yet to blink, that green stare shaking and unsettling Griffin even more.

With a sigh, the premier said, "The professor's evidence will be destroyed. She will be discredited based on her current mental state." He crossed his denim-and-flannel-clad arms. "My people have the power of . . . persuasion."

Griffin wished for something to grab on to, but remained erect under sheer force of will. "Explain."

"Go on." Though Aya's voice tinkled like bells on summer wind, there was a distinct melancholy to it. "Tell him."

The premier ambled toward Griffin, the heels of his cowboy boots crunching on pebbles and snow. "If I'd wanted to," he told Griffin, "the second you found my compound last year, I could've sent a sliver of air into your ear. Into your brain. I could've woven suggestion and thought into that air. I could've convinced you of anything I wanted. Made you forget what you saw or knew. Created something that wasn't there. You get the idea. And when I pulled the air out, you never would've been the same."

Griffin's hands made cold fists against his thighs. "You fuck with Primary minds."

"We preserve our existence." Every one of the premier's words sounded dragged through cold mud.

Great stars. Griffin reeled. "Is it permanent?"

Chief answered with a mighty rumble. "Permanent for them. Perfect for us."

The statement was a bullet, tearing through flesh and bone, shredding Griffin's heart. "How many?" Then, when no one answered, he shouted, *"How many?"*

The number *twelve* flashed quick and terrible through his own mind. Twelve deaths. Twelve sets of shackles clamping him to a former life.

"Since the Senatus began? Over the centuries?" The premier had the audacity to sound bored, and Griffin couldn't help but be reminded of the former Ofarian Chairman—the one who used to give Griffin his orders. "Impossible to say. Hundreds, maybe? The dawn of technology changed everything. Made us work overtime."

"*No.*" Griffin lunged forward.

The sudden movement sent the Chimerans into motion. Chief fell back against a wall of his warriors, Makaha on one side, a trickle of black smoke curling up from his lips, and Bane looming large on the other.

Keko, to Griffin's dismay, fell in beside her brother. Her face was unreadable, but her stance was unmistakable. Defensive. Ready to attack. Standing with her people.

"No!" Griffin shouted again, the taint of old death making his muscles tight and his heart twist. "I oppose this."

The premier scoffed. "You have no right to oppose anything. You have no voice here."

Griffin flinched. Aaron pressed in tighter to his leader.

"What happens when the truth about us finally comes out?" Griffin started to pace. "And it will, make no mistake about that. You yourself mentioned technology, how hard it's made things. What then? How will we be able to defend ourselves, our very existence, when the Primaries learn what we've been doing to them? Have you thought about that?"

Aya inhaled sharply, but said nothing.

Griffin's focus darted between the Airs and the Chimerans. It had been years since he'd been in a physical fight, but the signs of an impending one would never leave his mind and he possessed strong muscle memory. The other elementals' threats against him were quiet but present.

"The truth won't ever come out." Chief's ribcage expanded and contracted. "That's why we have the Senatus, to keep that kind of thing under control. Do you understand now why we can never integrate in the way and to the extent that you want?"

Oh, he understood. He knew now that it would take a hell of a lot more than stories about young Ofarian boys to turn the tides of this mess. He looked to Keko, but she was stone-faced. No, wait. There. A squint of her eyes—showing doubt in him, fear of his opinion, blind agreement with her chief—erased all the personal good that had been forged between them. It annihilated *everything*.

"Then I'm going to Seattle." Griffin whirled on the premier. "I'm stopping this."

The head air elemental let out a mocking laugh and swept his eyes up to the stars. "I'd forbid you to do that, but you'd never make it in time anyway."

"I'm not part of you, remember?" Griffin snapped. "You can't forbid a thing. And you can't do this."

Behind Griffin came the crunch of footsteps. "It's already done," Chief said, as though the finality of his tone was the end of this issue.

Like hell it was.

Griffin roared and spun on the Chimeran. Chief was standing there like a mountain, just waiting for Griffin to come after him with a new argument, but Makaha was moving, lunging for the chief's side. Wait—no. The warrior was launching himself right at Griffin.

Fists like iron balls at his sides, thick legs pounding into dirty snow, Makaha's bare chest expanded like a balloon. It filled with magic that singed Griffin's Ofarian senses. The Chimeran warrior opened his mouth and a flame burned at the back of his dark throat.

A flame meant for Griffin. An attack.

A few years of sitting behind a desk or at the head of a

conference table did not soften an Ofarian trained from tod-
dling age to be a fighter. Griffin instantly snapped into his old
self, the one he'd been conditioned to become and often wanted
to leave behind. Fists meant nothing to this beast of a man
coming after him. Even if Griffin had a gun, it would become
ash in Makaha's threatening fire.

Ofarian spilled from Griffin's lips. He whipped out his
magic, snagging every available bead of moisture from the air,
the ground, his very skin, and slamming them all together in
his palm.

At the same time, in clear view of everyone, Makaha's ribcage collapsed, expelling the fire from within. Griffin could
see it, the barrel of flame coming out from between Makaha's
lips. The Chimeran was going to fry Griffin alive, right in front
of the entire Senatus . . . but this was *not* the way he would die,
outnumbered with no magic or power to show for it.

He flung out his water at the exact moment Makaha let his
fire loose. Chin tilted up, Makaha's eyes raged in orange and
gold. The warrior's hand grabbed fire from his mouth, a brilliant, terrifying ball in his grasp.

Griffin aimed his spear of water for that hand holding the
fireball. Aimed and struck. Makaha bellowed in surprise as
Griffin extinguished the fire burning in the other man's palm.
Griffin instantly merged his water with the moisture on the
Chimeran's skin, taking it all under his control, binding it all
together.

Then he twisted his magic.

With a roar of Ofarian words he switched the water to ice,
encasing Makaha's entire hand and making it splinter and
freeze, all the way up to his elbow.

The Chimeran made burbling, sputtering, enraged sounds,
his eyes bulging. More fire shot from his lips toward the sky,
an anguished beacon. He screamed and stared down at his hand
in terrified wonder, his whole arm shaking. He was trying to
heat himself from the inside out, but Griffin's hold was too
strong.

At last, when Griffin felt like he'd made his point, when
he'd killed the fire meant for him, he released his water.

Makaha's face contorted as he inhaled again, tapping into

his magic. Heat made a steaming glow of his body. The ice on his lower arm melted, splashing to the already muddy ground.

Underneath, Makaha's hand had gone black.

A woman screamed, and Griffin thought that it might have been Keko, as she rushed to her friend's side, her body a blur in the night. But then Bane dove through the bonfire, charging right through the flames, and took Griffin down to the dirt and wet, knocking out his wind. Pinned underneath the massive Chimeran, Griffin spit out rotted leaves and mud, and finally managed to get control of his breath.

The woman screamed again. Griffin swiveled his head and saw, with surprise, that the awful wail streamed from Aya. And that she was focused not on Makaha, but on Griffin.

The premier and Aaron came over, telling Bane he could ease off, that they could contain Griffin with the force of air. Bane refused, digging elbows and knees even harder into Griffin's body.

Griffin's head spun as he struggled, little stars dancing at the edges of his vision. But even in the chaos, he still found Makaha.

Keko knelt in front of him and the chief loomed behind his warrior. Both of her hands gripped Makaha's black one, her whole body becoming an amber glow. But Griffin knew that not even Chimeran fire could bring back to life the flesh and muscle and half an arm he had destroyed.

Griffin didn't run as he headed away from the Senatus circle a short time thereafter, so when the premier's graveled shouts gave chase, they easily caught up to him.

"You are banned from the Senatus! You hear me? You and every Ofarian in existence!"

The trees shook their bare branches at Griffin as he passed. The winter wind howled in his ears and made a mockery of the warmth of his coat.

"You will never get support from us!" the premier continued to scream. "We will never listen to you! You are on your own!"

That was the sound of failure, that heavy pounding of his boots on the uneven ground, that jackhammer of his heart, that whiz and clatter of his brain as he tried to piece together all that had just happened and attempted to figure out how he'd been blamed as the party at fault.

He was almost to the edge of the forest, where Keko had parked the car she'd ferried him around in all week. It was unlocked and he wrenched open the door, removing his bag from the backseat. He'd hike out to the main road and hopefully thumb a ride back to the airport.

Someone was running through the trees at a steady, breakneck pace as though the cold and obstacles and dark meant nothing. As though she weren't human.

Keko burst out of the tree line and charged right for Griffin. He was ready for her, ready for another attack, though he did not wish for one. She pulled up feet away, her breathing barely labored. "Makaha will lose his hand. Probably half his arm."

Griffin could have sworn that tears glistened in her obsidian eyes, but then they were gone, leaving him to wonder what emotion was real and what was not, when it came to her.

"Yes. He probably will." He had to swallow hard to get the words down.

Her rage came off her in pulsing, sour waves of heat. She was trembling, her hand shaking as she jabbed a finger into the trees. "What the *fuck* happened back there?"

He gasped. "I could ask the same of the premier. Or your chief. Or Makaha."

She recoiled. "You attacked him!"

Icy wind raked through his jacket and clothing, scraping at his already chilled skin. "I what? No—"

"You are *never* allowed to use magic as offense during the Senatus."

Griffin threw his bag to the ground. "Keko, I didn't attack. Makaha did."

"No. He didn't—"

"I saw what was coming, what he was about to do to me, and I threw the ice as a defense."

"Defense?" She laughed, that kind of hysterical laughter that often partnered with disbelief. With hatred.

"Fire was coming out of him. I saw it in his mouth. I saw it in his hand. He was coming for me, about to throw it at me. I will swear by it until the day I die."

"He birthed fire to throw it into the sky. It's a sign of frustration and warning among my people."

"Well, maybe if you'd actually told me all that instead of fucking me, none of this would have happened."

That hit home. She opened her mouth, her lips ready for a retort. Only there would be none because she knew he was right.

She slowly started to back away. "You destroyed him, Griffin," she whispered, and her voice was broken again.

He cleared his throat. "He will live."

But she was shaking her head. "You don't understand."

"So *tell* me this time!"

She glared. "He's a defeated warrior now. Disfigured. Disgraced. When we take him back to the stronghold he will lose his warrior status. He will lose his home and have to go live in the Common House with all the others who are no longer worthy. He will serve everyone above him. He will have no sexual contact. He will lose his familial rights. And I will no longer be able to have any contact with my best friend."

"*Jesus.*" The Primary invective came shockingly easy, the harsh whisper swirling between them. But she just stared at him. Challenged him. "Great stars, Keko, that's barbaric. It's medieval."

"It's Chimeran. It's how it's done."

The wind tossed her loose hair around her head. Griffin took a brave chance, moving closer. "I think you know me better than this. It's only been a few days, but I believe you know me. You know how much the Senatus means to me, how much you"—he licked his lips, cutting short that sentence. "Please understand my side, that I was protecting myself against an attack. Please. I'm asking you to take me back there and give me the opportunity to tell your chief that. To explain myself to the premier."

The formal speak sounded insincere, even to his ears. It sounded like Griffin the politician, the leader. Not Griffin the Ofarian man.

Fire consumed her eyes, and it was dangerous and explosive. "You want me to take your side? To *defend* you?"

"I would like you to come with me as I explain my side.

They won't let me back in without you. I'm asking for your help."

The silence between them grew more and more dense. "Nothing you can say to them will matter. Because to my people, Makaha no longer matters. It would be like speaking about a ghost."

The loss in her eyes was too great to be measured. She was right. An apology wouldn't mean a thing to anyone involved. Griffin would have to bear the regret on his own and figure out a new way to make things right.

"So it's over?" He wasn't talking about the Senatus.

Her expression was painfully blank. "Yes."

Then she turned and disappeared back into the forest.

ONE

Griffin's jacket had lost its scent.

For the millionth time, Keko wondered why she'd kept it these past two months, this tangible proof that she'd been wrong and Griffin had been telling the truth. And for the millionth time since he'd found her being held captive in that Colorado garage and had given her the jacket to cover up her nakedness, she held the jacket at eye level and remembered how his body had filled it out.

The black all-weather coat lined with the zippers and pockets of a soldier now smelled like any other article of clothing in the Big Island's Chimeran valley, but if she closed her eyes, she could inhale and recall his scent.

There was no point in keeping it any longer. She knew very well what she'd done. The consequences of her actions had transformed her world. She didn't need to be constantly reminded of what she'd lost. Or whom.

With a fling of her arm, she tossed Griffin's jacket over the cliff on which she stood. The warm Hawaiian wind caught it, flinging it about, but Keko easily hit it with her fire, the spout of flame from between her lips striking true. The jacket caught, dancing on the air as it burned, as it fell down, down, down, to flutter as ash into the ocean waves far below.

Take it back, she thought at the water, at Griffin. *It's yours.*

"There you are."

The male voice came from behind, drifting up from lower down the slope that dropped off into the Chimeran's hidden valley. Shading her eyes with her hand, Keko peered over the ragged face of rock she'd climbed to get up to this spot. Makaha stood where the winding trail ended abruptly, his face turned upward, the hair that was now too long brushing his shoulders.

"Do you need me?" she called down.

He grinned, and the sight of it hurt her heart. Three years after Griffin had taken half of Makaha's right arm in a storm of ice, and she was finally able to speak with her oldest friend on equal ground again, the disparity of their stations and status within the clan erased.

Because she'd fallen just as far down as he.

"Hold on," she told him. "I'll come to you."

He couldn't climb, after all.

The rock tore into her fingertips and toes as she scrabbled her way down, faster than what was probably careful. On the last few feet, she shoved away from the rock and leaped, dropping into the dirt right in front of the man who used to be one of the most ferocious warriors of the race. *Makaha*. Fierce. He'd been named well, but Griffin had snatched away that meaning, turning it into a joke.

"What's going on?" she asked Makaha, hoping against hope that it might be something of worth. Something she could use to get her status and dignity back.

His grin saddened but didn't die, because he knew very well how she felt. "Nothing. The final drums for dinner came and went and I knew you hadn't eaten all day. If you hurry there might be something left."

Scrambling for scraps after the *ali'i* and the warriors and the rest of the Chimeran people had eaten their fill. This was her life now.

She pressed a hand to her hollow stomach. She barely ate these days, but she didn't really miss it. She didn't need that massive amount of energy anymore. Not for beating clothes against rocks in the stream. Not for dragging garbage to the trucks to be hauled up and out of the valley.

"Yeah," she said, her voice hollow. "Okay."

Makaha didn't move. The stump of an arm gestured to her spot up on the cliff. "Was that what I think it was? That fire?"

She thought of the jacket's ash, floating on, and then mixing into the waves, and said nothing.

Makaha stared hard at her. He'd caught her once, a little more than a month ago, with the jacket draped around her shoulders, her nose buried in the collar. But he'd left her to her own grief, her own regrets, her own anger. Makaha's thoughts about Griffin were his own, and rightfully so. They'd never spoken directly of the Ofarian who'd hurt them both in different ways.

With a terse nod down the slope Makaha said, "Come on. Let's go be pitiful together."

He could joke because he'd accepted his status. Moved on. To Keko, the very idea seemed foreign.

Yet she followed him down into the valley, turning her back on the myriad blues and greens of the ocean that surrounded her island home. Water, water, everywhere. She would never be able to escape him.

The ground flattened out, a ring of dense foliage surrounding the great meadow that was the crux of the Chimeran stronghold. White boarded homes with tin roofs climbed the sides of the valley, their foggy windows looking toward the water in the distance, their yards little more than patches of dirt. A giant canopy made of mismatched waterproof fabrics sewn together stretched over a mass of picnic tables at the far end, the adjacent cooking fires now reduced to smoking embers. And in between Keko and the satiation of her growling stomach stood a mass of Chimeran warriors.

A flood of brown-skinned fighters streamed onto the meadow, forming lines along the green to prepare for their evening drills and exercises and prayers to the Queen. Bane appeared, half a head taller than any other, and started to meander among his men and women, hands on hips, assessing with his trademark frown.

"You know what," she told Makaha, who'd stopped next to her behind a fountain of giant banana tree leaves, "I'm not hungry after all."

Her friend heaved a sigh, but it was one of commiseration. Maybe he'd gotten to the point where he could walk in front of the warriors he'd once been a part of, but as their so recently disgraced former general, she could not.

"What are you doing now?" she asked him.

He jutted his only thumb toward the Common House, the

one-story building with the seemingly never-ending row of cracked and crooked windows that sat in perennial shadow. Almost two months of having to sleep in there, and she'd never, ever get used to it.

"Runners brought in boxes of clothing today," he said. "I'm sorting them before the sun goes down."

How long had it taken him, Keko wondered, to shake off the shame? To have been able to say that without cringing? Because her shame still clung desperately to her back, its claws sharp and deep and painful.

"Can I help?" It took a few tries to get it out.

He couldn't hide his surprise. "Sure. I'll show you what to do."

They ducked into the cool, dim Common House. Long lines of grass-woven mats covered the floor. She didn't look to the anonymous spot she'd been given right in the center of all the others. The only way she found it was when she came in late at night and all the other disgraced or unworthy Chimerans were snoring. Hers was the only mat without a body. And it was just a place to crash, nothing more.

She tried not to think about the hammock she'd strung up in her house on the bluff, the comfortable, knotted, creaking thing with the perfect view of the valley and the ocean beyond. The house and hammock that belonged to Bane now.

But every now and then, when a piece of grass from her Common House mat broke loose and scratched her skin, she let her mind drift to the feathertop mattress at that hotel in Utah, and the man who had pressed her body deeper into it. Then, just as quickly, she forced her mind back to the cold, hard reality at hand.

The back corner of the Common House had been stacked precariously with leaning cardboard boxes stamped with the name of the fake church charity Chimerans used to get donations from unsuspecting Primaries. Makaha grabbed a box, using his stump to balance it, and dumped the mass of colorful, wrinkled hand-me-downs onto the cracked cement floor.

"Kids' clothing over there," he said, pointing to a pile. "Men's by the door. Women's just opposite."

He started work right away, but Keko just watched him, a massive lump in her throat and a terrible tremble shooting through her limbs. She couldn't move, was absolutely frozen. His piles swirled into meaningless colors, his repetitive motions hammering into her brain. Frustration and humiliation pounded their awful little fists against the backs of her eyes and clogged up her chest.

No. She would not cry. But she also knew she couldn't handle *this.* Doing what Makaha had been doing day in and day out for three years, and doing it without emotion. This was not her. It would not ever be her.

Keko's feet started to back away before she even told them to. When they hit a grass mat, she turned and ran down the rows, the exit doorway a slanted rectangle of dying light in the distance.

Makaha didn't call after her, but his pity as he watched her go was like a knife in the back. He knew she would have to come back eventually. So did she, and that made her run even faster.

She burst out of the Common House and plunged into the dark under the mango trees. She didn't stop there, but went deeper and deeper into the vegetation that surrounded the central meadow. She didn't stop until she was truly alone, bracing her hands on her knees and taking deep draws of wet Hawaiian air. It would rain that night. More water.

Griffin had taken it all—Makaha's life, her life.

No, that little voice reminded her, as it had every day since her secret affair with Griffin had been revealed to a select few in her clan, and Chief had learned the truth behind Keko's planned war against the Ofarians. *You did this to yourself.*

When Keko had been captured and kept prisoner in Colorado, an Ofarian had been behind it, and she'd assumed it had been done on Griffin's order—a desperate, last-ditch attempt to weasel his way back into the Senatus. She'd planned an attack on him to retaliate, but she'd been wrong, and her war had been exposed for the awful, messy heartbreak that it was. *That* was what had stripped her of being general. *That* was truly why Chief had sent her to the Common House.

It was her fault. It was all her fault. She was such an asshole, to keep dragging Griffin into it, for blaming him. She wasn't here, hiding in the bushes from the people she used to command, because of something he did. She had to get over it. To acknowledge all that she'd done.

She had to fix it. And she had to act soon.

A great shout—a chorus that simultaneously chilled her and sent volcanic-level heat through her veins—shot through the valley. Hundreds of Chimeran voices, low and sharp, full of passion and fire and love for the land and the magic, rose up as one. She knew the chant by heart, had learned it as a toddler, and then led her warriors in it nightly—as Bane was doing now. Though she was still standing beneath the canopy of leaves, her body was mentally going through ghost motions, and making the companion movements to the warriors' call to action: the slap of the elbows and thighs, the stomp of feet, the lift of palms to the sky, and the power and confidence that came with it.

When it was over, when the chant ended on a terrific roar that shook the leaves around her, Keko released the tension in her muscles one by one. She took a great Chimeran inhale and felt the fire magic surge inside her. Its presence always managed to bring some calm. Inching forward, she parted the branches and gazed out onto the meadow.

Bane had his men and women in the traditional lines, the best, most proven along the front with him, those who were still in training and had yet to issue a challenge at the back. The last line swerved crooked just a hair, and Keko had to fight the urge to jog out and smack the offenders into straightness. They were Bane's now.

General Bane, the "long-awaited child." General Bane, who'd been her greatest motivation and the hardest competitor her entire life. It killed her to see him where he belonged, but completely *destroyed* her to know that she could stalk out onto the meadow right now and issue a challenge to any one of those younglings in the back row, and they wouldn't take it. They wouldn't be required to take it. Battles for status were mutual, and no one would ever agree to fight her, the general who'd tried to start a war over false reasons.

The general who'd violated *kapu* by getting involved with a water elemental. Her heart, the traitorous organ, turned sour and huge inside her chest.

If only she'd told Griffin about the "no battle magic during Senatus gatherings" rule.

If only he hadn't destroyed her best friend, and then asked her to take his side against her own people.

If only she could have forgotten what he'd awakened inside her.

If only he had actually been behind her capture.

If.

If.

If.

She was fucking sick of *ifs*. Chimerans weren't made like that. They *acted*. They *fought*. She was a warrior. Period. And she would fight tonight—not with fire or fists, but with words.

Beyond the lines of warriors who had now paired off and were working on stretching and strengthening drills, rose the *ali'i*'s house, a lone light coming from the kitchen window. Chief's thick silhouette moved behind the glass.

Yes, she'd made some pretty hefty mistakes, but Chief had been the one to strip her life away. And he was the only one with the power to give a portion of it back. She started toward the house. Not across the field where the warriors would see her, but around the perimeter, sticking to the cover of the trees and vines, and relying on the deepening dark of twilight.

It was dangerous to beg. It was shameful. But she didn't have any further to fall. She'd struck the bottom and bore the bruises to show for it. She had absolutely nothing to lose.

The garden behind the *ali'i*'s house was barricaded by a low stone wall, overgrown with neglect, and cool and dark at this time when day merged with night. Her uncle had been *ali'i* so long that Keko remembered the placement of each paving stone, having skipped across them as a little girl whenever she'd come to the house for personal lessons. Her aunt had lived long enough to see Keko best Bane for the generalship, but after her aunt had died, the house had fallen into the same poor, weather-worn state as the rest of the valley.

That's what happened, after all, when a people cut themselves off from the modern world.

Chief usually drank a glass of fresh fruit juice on his upper terrace in the evenings, watching the practice of the warriors he commanded. That's where he would be now, and when he came downstairs after the sun had set, she would surprise him. And she would make her final argument.

As she crossed the garden, Bane's voice echoed throughout the valley, guiding his warriors in a new series of exercises that practiced fighting at night. She blocked out the sounds as best she could as she padded along the narrow patio toward the back door. Inside, Chief ambled out of the kitchen and made his way to the sitting room on the other side of the glass door from Keko.

She frowned. Chief was a creature of habit and embraced rituals, so for him not to be up on the front balcony, fruit juice in hand, watching and nodding down at his warriors, made Keko's skin prickle with a chill. Enough that she had to tap into her inner fire and crank it up.

Her uncle, her father's brother, was somewhere in his sixth decade of living but looked only in his fourth. A little softer now but still strong. An imposing figure worthy of his title and too beloved to have been challenged for his position in all his years. That love and respect had kept her from challenging him, too, and now she stewed with regret.

Keko had been planning on it, however, and Chief had known her challenge was imminent. They'd even discussed it, because when he eventually accepted the challenge and she beat him—because she would have—it meant he was endorsing her as *ali'i.*

That would never happen now. There was only her name and her dignity to earn back.

Inside, an empty-handed Chief shuffled toward the burgundy couch with the hardened, dipped cushions. Something in the way he moved kept Keko riveted to her spot just outside the back door. She crouched, watching through the glass, her movements nothing but a whisper.

The faint light coming from the kitchen just barely illuminated Chief as he went to the wobbly end table. He paused with his hand on the knob of the single drawer, then slowly opened it. He took something out, but with his back to Keko she couldn't see what it was. Then he turned around and the shape of it was unmistakable: a tapered candle.

Chief drew a deep breath—the breath of a Chimeran, the one that used the oxygen from the atmosphere to stoke their fire magic inside, the one that expanded their special ribs. It was odd, though, because the depth of a breath indicated the level of magic you wanted to conjure, and you didn't need to take that deep of a breath to create the small flame needed to light a candle. Yet Chief's chest expanded like he was calling forth a great inferno needed at the height of battle.

His lips parted. His chest deflated. The magic escaped his body.

And no flame came out.

Not a single spark. Not even a curl of smoke. Nothing.

The mighty Chimeran *ali'i* stumbled backward as though struck. His calves hit the couch and he collapsed onto it, his normally erect and powerful body a boneless mass. His chest, empty of magic and fire, heaved. He lifted the candle to eye level and stared at the wick as though willing it to light with his mind. Then he bent at the waist and shoved a hand underneath the couch cushions, removing something hidden. Keko couldn't tell what it was until a tiny burst of hot, gold light briefly illuminated the room.

A match. There were matches in the Chimeran *ali'i*'s house.

Keko couldn't breathe, couldn't move. The earth could have opened up behind her and she wouldn't have known.

Chief touched the match to the candle, and the newly lit wick threw his distressed, hopeless, and fearful expression into terrifying focus.

Still crouching, still in a daze, Keko lost her balance. Her body tilted forward before she realized it, and her hand shot out, catching the door. The latch was faulty and the door creaked open. Only an inch or so, but enough for the sound to slice through the silent house.

Chief's head snapped up. The matchbook disappeared behind his back. He jumped to his feet.

Keko rose, too. She pushed the door open wide and ventured into the cool interior, lit by the dancing flame of the single candle. Another rare wave of goose bumps rolled across her skin, but this time she couldn't find the focus to reach for her fire and erase them.

The door clicked shut behind her. Chief was struggling to breathe, the sound ragged and nervous.

"Uncle?"

"Kekona." His hand shook and the candle flame jumped. He turned to set the taper into a holder on the end table, and the table's uneven legs rattled on the tile floor. When he faced her again, she barely recognized him. Such terror deepened the creases along his forehead and strained the lines around his mouth. He seemed pale, the silver along his temples pronounced.

She advanced slowly into the room. "You have no fire."

He took a step back. Never had she seen him retreat. Not when facing a warrior, and certainly never when confronted by one of the disgraced.

"What happened to your fire?" She heard the rise in her voice, the demand, but did not try to rein it in.

His panicked eyes flicked to the door at her back.

"I came alone," she said. That made him even more apprehensive and it empowered her to move closer. "In the name of the Queen, what's going on? What happened to your fire?"

He licked his lips, and a single whispered word dropped pitifully from them. "Gone."

"Gone." The word reverberated inside her. She would mark his claim as impossible if she hadn't seen it with her own eyes.

"It's still inside." His voice came out stressed and thin, and she barely recognized it. "I can feel it, but I can't reach it. Can't call it out. It doesn't listen to me." He touched the candle flame and it danced on his fingers like it should, then he blew it out. "But I can still manipulate it."

A great wave of realization crashed into her. "When? For how long?" When he didn't answer she lifted her voice to the level she used to use as general. "Was it gone when you denounced me for inciting a false war in front of the whole clan?" Still no answer. "Was it gone when you sent me down to the Common House and made Bane general?"

He held up a hand, but the gesture was weak. "The day . . ." his voice cracked and he cleared his throat to get it back. "The day Cat Heddig came here and exposed your affair with that Ofarian was the last day I used it. The last day . . ."

Two months ago. And all this time he'd been commanding the Chimerans. Pretending that he was still the most powerful one of them, still the most respectable. Playing the hypocrite as he stripped her of title and pride.

"Did you know something was wrong then? That something was happening to you?"

"Yes."

Keko whirled, snatching a vase holding a mostly dead flower

from a nearby table. She hurled the vase against the wall, just to the right of the *ali'i*'s head. It exploded into a million pieces, water shooting across the plaster. The acrid odor of decay plumed around them. Chief didn't budge, didn't even flinch.

"How have you hid this?" Her throat stung with the volume. "*How*?"

He swung the matchbook around from where he'd been hiding it behind his body, looked at it for a moment, then tossed it to the couch. "I'm not the only one."

Keko blinked. "What?"

"I mean"—and the harsh, slow tones of the *ali'i* returned—"that I am not alone. There are other Chimerans like me. Others whose fire has died."

She glanced at the matches, thinking that some other Chimeran would have had to have smuggled them into the valley. Someone else had to have known about the *ali'i*.

"It's some sort of disease, Keko. I don't know why it strikes, or who it will hit, but the numbers are . . . growing."

She pressed the heels of her hands to her forehead. "A disease. And you've been able to hide this how?"

He looked to the candle, and then down at his fingers that had held the flame. "There are some Chimerans, healthy ones, who know and who . . . help us. Give us flame when we need it."

"Cover for you." A subtle, secret passing of fire from one hand to another. And it had worked. "Who else? Who else is afflicted?"

He shook his head. "You can take me down, but I won't betray the rest."

What a fucking deceiver. "So you'll protect and hide others exactly like you, but throw your general, your own family, into the Common House."

"Two completely different things. You made a terrible mistake. And you broke *kapu*."

"I know what I did. But at least I'm admitting it." She advanced toward him. One step, then another. "Who. Else."

Chief just shook his head.

"I see. So in keeping their secret and by not sending them to the Common House, by not exposing their ultimate weakness, they protect you, too."

His silence was answer enough.

"It doesn't matter." She waved a hand. "I don't want them."
I want you. I want to be ali'i.

"It's been going on longer than you think," he said. "Longer than I'd imagined. Maybe going back to the Queen. This thing . . . it's not new."

It was horrifying information.

It was useful information.

She started to back toward the door, her bare feet going toe-heel, toe-heel on the tile that now felt like ice.

"What will you do?" Chief started to follow. When she did not respond he cried out, much louder, "What will you do?"

She looked to the bank of smudged windows overlooking her aunt's dead garden. The moon hadn't risen yet and it was so very dark outside. It was the same within.

"I came here," she said, "to actually beg you to give me another chance. That's not what I want now."

"What do you want? Do you want me to accept your challenge? Do you want to be *ali'i*?"

Her life's most precious dream, wrapped up and handed to her.

Except that Chimerans never wanted anything that couldn't be fought for and won with sweat and power and magic, and this, to her surprise, was no different.

Her gaze found the small black lava rock that he wore on a rope around his neck—the very stone that the great Queen had picked up the day she'd grounded her canoe on Hawaii and declared it her people's new home. Keko had wanted to wear that rock her whole life, to feel its scratch on her skin and its weight against her chest. To know the Queen's power and hold her blessing.

Looking at it now, Keko thought something entirely different, and she stood there for a long time, trying to wrap her head around it. Trying to figure out what it meant.

The great Queen had had a purpose in bringing her Polynesian people to this string of islands over a thousand years ago—a worthy purpose. A heroic purpose. The first Chimerans had loved her for it, and had followed her willingly across the ocean. Keko knew now that she, too, needed a purpose. She wanted her race to look up to her not because it was required, but because it was desired. She would not get that through begging. She would not get that through blackmail or trickery.

The only way was to earn it.

Yes, she could challenge Chief right now, and she would win his position, but it would be false. Yes, she could expose his lies, but that would also expose other innocents who would in turn be cast out, and where was the honor in that? She would assume power over a stricken people, carrying with her this terrible secret of their affliction. How would ascending to *ali'i* now do anything to help them?

When she was *ali'i*, she wanted power and glory for all her kinsmen, not less for others through no fault of their own. She wanted strength, not scandal.

The lava rock moved on Chief's chest as he breathed. Waiting for her to speak. To decide.

Every night since Keko's fall, she had prayed hard to the great Queen for her blessing, for answers, for explanation, for a way out. And tonight, it had finally been given.

"What will you do?" Chief pleaded.

Personal revenge was a single sentence away. Except that rash, emotional decisions had destroyed her in the first place. She'd done enough damage. Now she needed to heal.

The Queen—through the events of this night—had finally given Keko the answer. And Keko embraced the sacrifice that it required.

She lifted clear eyes to the *ali'i*, feeling absolutely sure of herself for the first time in months. Maybe years. "Thank you, Uncle."

Turning, she went for the door.

"For what?" he shouted at her back. "For *what*?"

He couldn't come after her, she knew, or he'd risk the clan knowing he'd allowed her audience. Let him wonder. Let him fear. It was powerful fuel.

She slipped back into the night, the answer she'd wanted and all Chimeran power in her hands.

TWO

"I don't like it, *sir*."

Griffin hated when David called him *sir* in private, but of course that's why David did it: to show his ultimate displeasure with his leader and best friend when no one else was around.

Griffin stared down his head of security. No room for friendship right now. The two men had managed to draw solid lines between personal and professional, and it had served them well in the five years of Griffin's Ofarian leadership.

"Don't have a choice," Griffin replied. "The Senatus premier invited me back to a gathering after three years. Me. Not an Ofarian contingent. I'm not walking in there with my cabinet behind me and a row of soldiers along the flanks."

David made a frustrated face and pinched his lips between his fingers, staring out the windshield of the car in which they sat on a sloped South San Francisco neighborhood street.

"Not after we just narrowly dodged a war with the Chimerans," Griffin added, much quieter. "Not after what happened the last time the Senatus invited me to sit around their fire."

Thinking of fire made him think of Keko, as always. He shook his head at his lap, still unable to believe how she'd suddenly reappeared in his life two months ago . . . and then had disappeared again, leaving him unexpectedly shredded.

Three years apart from her, he discovered, hadn't cut into any of his want.

Griffin unfolded himself from the car and David followed, pushing out from behind the steering wheel. "Fine. You'll come with me," Griffin said over the roof. "Gwen'll meet us there. That's it. That's all I'm bringing."

David ran a hand through his curly blond hair and nodded tightly, knowing there would be no further discussion on the matter. "I'll make sure you're safe, that all the roads to the gathering are clear."

Their eyes met, smudging that line between personal and professional. "I know you will."

David jogged around the hood and hopped up onto the sidewalk. The mild winter day was punctuated by music streaming from an open window. A Primary man washed his car in his driveway. A couple walked their mutt, heading for the two Ofarian men. The working class neighborhood was where Griffin had grown up, and it smelled and felt the same. Wonderfully the same.

He let the couple and the dog pass by before saying to David, "They're throwing me a peace offering. As they should. The Chimeran chief owes me a massive apology, I owe them a first-person account of Keko's capture, and then we'll be back on even footing. I hope."

David grinned. "So you're saying it's good that your ex-lover has a jealous, angry streak?"

Griffin laughed ruefully, and it hurt. Thinking of Keko usually did.

"Are you ever going to tell me what happened three years ago?"

David had been with Griffin in Colorado two months back when they'd discovered Keko being held captive by one of their own, and the revelation of Griffin's previous liaison with the Chimeran woman had come to light. But Griffin had never spoken of the awful misunderstanding that final night three years ago around the Senatus bonfire. It would only undermine his already tenuous position among his own cabinet and his Ofarian detractors, who still possessed a powerful voice.

An image of the mighty Makaha, reduced to sagging in the snow and dirt, half his arm black, his mouth open in a scream, assaulted Griffin's memory. Followed quickly by one of Keko, and her horror and shock and disgust. And then her back as she'd turned away.

"Maybe someday," Griffin replied.

After the incident, he'd appealed to the Senatus many times, but his stance that Makaha had attacked first fell on deaf ears.

So he'd given up trying to make contact, but had not given up on his dreams. He still desperately wanted to be part of the Senatus, but he realized now that he'd rushed the process before. He'd barged in waving his opinions like flags, but after witnessing their fractured system and lack of true communication, he knew now that he needed a new approach. He just didn't know what that was.

David may have been more right than his joke intended. The chance to move forward with the Senatus had risen from the ashes of any possible future with Keko. Ash. Yeah, that's what they were now. Griffin tried to see that as a good thing.

"Will Kekona be there?"

Griffin shrugged, feigning ignorance by checking his watch, but he remembered all too well what Cat had told him after she'd returned from Hawaii two months ago: Keko's generalship had been given to Bane. He also knew that that action would've destroyed her. And there was nothing he could do about it.

As he caught David watching him, he knew that no amount of nonchalance would fool his friend, but that David would also never press for information Griffin wasn't willing to give.

Griffin peered across the street to the picture window of the second-floor apartment, alive with the flicker from the TV. "You sure you want to sit out here tonight? Call up Hansen to be on watch. This is beneath you." He said that last sentence with a grin.

"Nah. I'd rather handle it myself. Kelse is working late anyway."

Griffin understood. Back when his main job had been the safety of Gwen Carroway, the woman everyone had thought would be the next Ofarian leader, her protection had been his life. He'd hated handing over the responsibility to anyone else.

"I'll be just a couple hours. Want me to bring out leftovers?"

"Hell, yeah." David patted his gut as he ambled over to the bus stop bench across from the Aames's apartment. Perfect sight lines in all directions.

Griffin shouldn't need all this protection in his own city, his own childhood neighborhood where he was about to have Sunday dinner with his family, but after the assassination attempt by Wes Pritchart five years ago, and the detractors that had since grown more vocal once his "relationship" with a Chimeran had come to light, they couldn't be too careful.

Griffin jogged to his family's building and inserted his key, the same one he used to wear around his neck when he was young and his parents had been away on duty. Inside, the same stairs still creaked. The same carpet still welcomed him into his parents' place, only now it was flattened and darker with permanent stains.

"Hey, Pop."

Griffin's father sat wide-legged on one of the couches making an *L* around the TV. He looked up from the baseball documentary whose volume was cranked all the way up to compensate for the driving beat of the music pumping from his sisters' room.

"Griffin," Pop said with a nod toward the TV. "You'd like this. All about the Yankees."

Griffin grimaced and chuckled. He loved baseball, hated the Yankees.

Pop lifted a beer bottle to his smiling lips. "I think your mother could use some help."

Nothing like a visit home to remind you that you aren't leader of the Ofarians in every way.

"Sure," Griffin said, sliding around the pinch of furniture cramped into the tiny living room. How his parents had raised nine kids in here, he'd never know. But they'd stuck to their "Keep Ofarians Strong By Population" creed and had never once complained.

Until Griffin had helped overthrow the old Board. Until he'd been given command. Until his father had to take a position in a Primary security firm to pay the bills. After that, the issue of struggling Ofarian classes and touchy Primary integration sat right in the middle of the dining room table along with the mashed potatoes and pork roast. Pop thought that being born into and serving in the Ofarian soldier class was the greatest honor ever, and its reduction in numbers was a slap in the face. He never missed an opportunity to tell Griffin as much.

But then, Pop had never been an assassin.

Despite Griffin's difference of opinion, they were still his parents.

Griffin leaned into the kitchen, where his mom was

spooning green beans into a big bowl. "Hey," he said, smiling. "Need help?"

She looked up, her cheeks pink from the warm kitchen and hard work. She had the exact opposite coloring of Griffin and his father—her blond hair just starting to gray at age 52, her pale skin barely showing her distinguished wrinkles. "Hi, baby."

The endearment never failed to make him happy, even though she was only seventeen years older than he was.

She added, "Could you go tell Henry and your sisters that dinner is in fifteen?"

Down the short hallway, Griffin rapped on the door to his sixteen and seventeen year-old sisters' room, which positively vibrated with the music's bass. When no one answered, he cracked the door open. Meg, the older one, was teaching the younger, Eve, some sort of dance routine.

"Fifteen minutes," he shouted. "And turn that down. I could hear it on the street." They stopped moving, and Meg gave him a classic eye roll. He pointed a finger, grinning. "I could give you *nelicoda* for that."

As he suspected, the threat of dosing her with the chemical that neutralized water magic did nothing, just made her roll her eyes even more dramatically as she reached for the volume knob and twisted it down.

"Close the door, will you?" Eve said on his way out.

"Not a chance," he replied.

The door to Henry's room—which had once been Griffin's room, along with two of his brothers—was slightly ajar, and Griffin pushed it all the way open. The twelve year old was perched on the edge of his bed, playing a handheld video game.

Griffin lingered in the doorway, unnoticed. "Hey, you. Whatcha playin'?"

Henry finally ripped his eyes from the screen and looked up. "Griff!"

The kid was a mini-Griffin: thick, dark hair that could never be anything but super short, and brown eyes hooded beneath eyebrows that he would have to get used to being teased about. He dove back into his game, thumbs flying, elbows twitching up and down.

"*Armed Battle 4*," Henry said. "Wanna play me? Bet I can kick your ass."

"Language, dude." Griffin crossed the carpet to ruffle his littlest brother's hair. He peered over the small shoulder at the game screen. Humans destroying other humans and aliens that looked nothing like real Secondaries. Guns and knives and chain ropes. Blood and body parts everywhere. Death and glory in the form of points.

I won't tell anyone. I swear.

I didn't mean to see that.

Please don't. Oh, God, no. Please don't. Please don't kill me.

Three different Primary voices. All saying essentially the same thing. There'd been nine more who'd never gotten a chance to say or plead for anything before Griffin had taken their lives.

"No, thanks," Griffin managed to get out, trying to seem as casual as possible. "Hey, can you turn that off for a second?"

Distracted, Henry kept playing, the sounds of death and dying stabbing into Griffin's brain. His hand shot out, knocking the game to the bedspread. Henry slowly turned to Griffin, and the look on the kid's face was nothing like the playful defiance Meg had given him. He looked petrified, and Griffin felt guilty.

"Sorry." Griffin ran a shaking hand through his hair. "I, uh . . ."

"'S'okay."

Brothers born to such different generations. Henry gazed up at him with nothing but pure adoration and his own heartfelt apology, though he'd done nothing wrong. Griffin sank to the bed and wrapped an arm around the shoulders that had yet to widen into the Aames shape. The boy was still pretty scrawny, all knobby knees and long limbs, but he was on the verge of change. About to come into his body—and his water powers.

The first of the Aames family who didn't have to become a soldier because the Ofarian class system dictated it.

Be an advertising executive, Henry, Griffin wanted to tell him. *Be a writer or an engineer or a janitor. Be something no one tells you to be, and don't be afraid to go into the Primary world to do it.*

Griffin held his brother tight, sending his dreams and wishes through the embrace.

"Um. Griff?" Henry's voice was muffled, and Griffin realized he'd wrapped his other arm around the kid and had curled Henry's face into his shoulder.

He let Henry go. "Sorry," he said again.

The answering grin was pure joy, pure pride. Henry stood up, then dropped into a fighting stance Griffin recognized from Ofarian-sanctioned practice sessions, meant to prepare kids for soldier testing and training. "Want to help me on something? Captain Hansen says I've got promise, but I need help on my form and I need to practice, and Meg and Eve just ignore me, even though they're both really good already. Please, Griff. You're the best fighter we have."

Maybe once upon a time.

Sliding his hands to his knees, Griffin said, "I'd rather help you with—"

"Math." Henry heaved a great sigh as he came up out of the stance. "I know." He went to his desk and fiddled with a familiar orange textbook. "It's kind of embarrassing, you know, to be Griffin Aames's brother and be one of the worst in training."

"I'm sure that's not true." Griffin tried not to let this revelation mess with the filter he'd applied to this boy who had such incredible promise. "I know someone who could make you a genius, though. You're already smart, but she could send you to the top of your class in math, teach you things about computers you never even knew existed."

Griffin had been looking for ways to bring Adine, the half-Secondary tech wizard, further into the Ofarian world, and he saw instruction as a possible natural progression. Henry seemed to brighten for about one-point-two seconds, then his face fell, because when you're twelve, how could math or computers ever compare to being able to throw your opponent and disable his weapon?

Henry shrugged, dejection making the corners of his mouth turn down. He started to throw some punches at an invisible foe that did indeed need some practice.

Griffin rose to his feet. "Dinner's almost ready."

"Pop says you're going back to the Senatus tomorrow."

Griffin's eyebrows lifted. Pop had told Henry that? Probably with a side of opinion and a whole helping of doubt. He heard the skepticism in Henry's voice, echoed straight from Pop's words, and vowed to change that attitude toward the positive. When Henry's future—and that of *all* the Ofarian kids in that generation—shone brighter than any Ofarian's before him, Griffin would finally lean back and exhale in satisfaction. But not until then.

"I am," Griffin replied.

"Pop says—"

Griffin's phone rang, and the vibration made him jump. So few people had access to his personal number, and those who did knew he had dinner with his family every Sunday and that it was cherished time. He pulled the phone from his jeans pocket, stared at the unfamiliar number, and warily answered. "Yeah?"

So strange, to recognize someone's breath, the light, sharp inhalation before speaking. Even the pause was achingly familiar.

"It's me."

As though she were standing right there turning on her magic, a wave of heat washed over him. He fell sideways into the wall, realizing he'd been longing to hear from her these past two months and dreading it at the same time.

Behind him, Henry took up the video game again, and Meg cranked up the volume on the same song she'd played a million times already. In the living room, Pop shouted futilely for silence over the TV.

"Just a second," he murmured into the phone, pushing off the wall and weaving back around the living room furniture toward the front door. Pop threw him a worried, questioning look and Griffin waved him off, miming that it wasn't anything. When really, it was everything.

Out in the stairwell, Griffin shut the door on the noise. His toes stuck out over the edge of the very top step and his heart was clobbering the hell out of his ribcage. He closed his eyes and just listened to her breathe on the other end, waiting. It sounded like it was raining where she was, raindrops hitting glass.

"Keko," he finally said, opening his eyes.

"I always liked the way you said my name." When they'd been wrapped together in wrinkled, damp hotel sheets, talking until daylight, her voice had sounded much the same. Wistful. Gentle. Feminine. He'd liked the way she said his name, too.

Odd that in the timeline he was running through his head right now, he skipped right over the last time they'd seen each other—two months ago when she'd bolted from that house in Colorado, believing that he had been behind her kidnapping. Hating him.

"You destroyed one of my trucks," he said, referring to her escape, how she'd spewed a fireball at one of his vehicles and then stolen the other.

"I also tried to start a war." So matter of fact. Still the trademark Keko confidence, but with a layer of sadness underneath. A twinge of regret.

It unsettled Griffin to hear something so unlike her. He lowered himself to the second step. "I know why you did it."

She laughed, a short, bitter sound. "So sure of yourself, are you? That you were the face that almost launched a thousand ships?"

He plucked at a stray carpet fiber between his shoes. "You were still angry with me for what happened with Makaha. You felt I hadn't paid for it, that I wasn't sorry. You wanted to make me sorry." When she said nothing and let the rain in the background provide the soundtrack, he added, "And you were as angry as I was about the way things between us ended."

"I don't want to talk about that."

Then what? he wanted to ask, but didn't. A long silence followed, but he would've sat there all night, as long as she didn't hang up.

"Do you still talk to Gwen?" she asked, the question surprising him as much as her abruptness.

"Of course."

"I'm not . . . jealous . . . of her anymore."

His heartbeat picked up speed. His head tried to wrap around the fact that Kekona Kalani had used the word *jealous*.

"Were you ever?" he asked.

She sighed. "Not the first night we were together. Or the second. But when you told me about her, how you two were once supposed to get married and that you were still working together, I felt . . ." Keko trailed off, and Griffin thought that maybe it was because she didn't actually know any words for those kinds of emotions. It had been obvious to him she was used to going through life with two speeds: on and off. Everything else in between wasn't worth a glance, let alone a thought.

His head dropped, and even though she couldn't see him, he shook it. "You never had any reason to be jealous. She and I . . . what we were supposed to be . . . it wasn't ever . . ."

His turn to scramble for descriptors.

"What?" she said.

"Love."

The word hung there. Maybe it could have been love once between him and Keko. When they'd parted in that hotel room, when he'd held her hand as she drove him to the Senatus meeting site for the last time, it had seemed like love might have been an exciting, easy road to begin to travel together. But now?

The divide between them was too great. Years and distance and near wars and ugly cultural mishaps, not to mention their separate races, had filled it in with nothing good. The chasm had just gotten deeper and wider the longer they'd been apart.

"I hear you're getting what you want," she said, tonelessly.

I don't have you. The force of the unexpected thought almost pitched him forward down the stairs.

"And what's that?" he asked.

"The Senatus. I'm sure this one will go better than the last. I won't be there to distract you."

"Keko—"

"You said that if I hadn't fucked you, none of this would've happened."

Breath hissed out between his teeth. "There were two people in that hotel room. Two adults. Makaha still came after me. Even if you'd told me about the magic rule, I would've defended myself. No use rehashing it."

"But I think about it a lot." The way her voice turned distant started to frighten him. She didn't sound like herself at all. "When I roll over in the Common House and see Makaha sleeping, half an arm thrown out to one side, I think about how I could've served him better."

"Great stars, Keko. The Common House?" He remembered

all too well her description of the place, what it meant—or didn't mean—to Chimeran society. Griffin had called the concept barbaric. "They sent you there?"

"Chief did, yeah. He told the people I was wrong about my reasons for going to war. He didn't tell them about you." Keko cleared her throat. "Doesn't matter anymore."

Now she definitely scared him. Being general had meant everything to her. More, maybe, than the Senatus meant to him. She'd been on track to be the next chief.

Through the line he heard the continuous pelt of rain, then the honk of a car horn and the *swoosh* of it driving through a puddle on pavement.

Griffin jumped up. "You told me there was only one phone in the Chimeran stronghold."

And Cat had told Griffin that there were only two or three vehicles in the whole Chimeran valley on the Big Island. No paved roads.

"Where are you?" he demanded.

Still no answer.

"Keko, why are you calling? What aren't you telling me?"

"I figured out how to serve my people again." Her voice drifted high and far away. She sounded eerily at peace, strangely at ease for all that she'd been through. "I'm calling to say good-bye to you."

"Good-bye? What the hell is going—"

"We've parted on such shitty terms too many times, Griffin. Just this once, this very last time, I wanted it to be good."

Panic enveloped him. "Wait—"

She hung up.

He stabbed the redial button, but it just rang and rang and rang.

THREE

One hour northwest of Madison, Wisconsin, there was nothing except the sword of the rental car's headlights slashing at the skeletons of the cold, late-March forest, a sky heavy with stars, and the Senatus.

Griffin fidgeted in the passenger seat as David swerved the car through the hilly, dark countryside. Griffin's knee bounced and one fingernail scratched consistently at the underside of his thigh. Anxiety drew down the corners of his mouth. His vision was a bullet shooting into the night, all his other senses hyperaware, desperate to pick up something—anything—that might clue him in as to what was about to happen.

Keko had called to say good-bye. Why? Why now? What the hell for? What was she going to do?

"Got your game face on, I see." From behind the wheel, David threw a wry, obvious glance at Griffin's twitching leg. "Might want to check that before you walk in there."

Griffin immediately stilled and sank deeper into the seat, but didn't respond. He hadn't told David about the phone call from Keko. He'd stewed about it all last night—not getting a wink of sleep—and the entire travel to the Midwest. He couldn't've called the chief even if he'd wanted to. Griffin's sole connection to the Senatus was the premier, and he didn't want to press his luck by asking how to contact the Chimerans directly. He also didn't want to compromise Keko—whatever it was she'd gotten involved in now—because he had no idea what the chief did or did not know.

And he still had no idea what he would say or ask when he finally came face to face with the head Chimeran.

David glanced into the rearview mirror, fingers tightening on the steering wheel. "SUV coming up fast behind us."

Griffin swiveled in his seat. The headlights of the massive black truck flashed twice. He glimpsed red and blue on the license plate: Illinois. Gwen, driving up to meet them from her home in Chicago.

"This it?" David braked and pointed at a sign for a private campground, the CLOSED FOR THE SEASON tag dangling from a pole.

Griffin double-checked his GPS for the coordinates the Senatus premier had sent him earlier that day. "Looks like it."

David steered the car off the two-lane paved road and onto a gravel drive. The bones of bare branches stretched for them as they slowly rolled past. The drive seemed to go on forever, slicing deeper and deeper into the forest, until it finally opened up into a small clearing, a shuttered shack at one end, a ring of stones surrounding a giant, unlit bonfire at the other.

They parked next to two other vehicles, their headlights illuminating the premier and Aaron, the chief and Bane. No Aya as far as he could tell. Gwen swung her giant SUV on the opposite end of the line.

The signatures of Secondary magic zinged through Griffin's mind. David ground fingers into his forehead, indicating he was feeling it, too. "At least we know we're in the right place," he said.

Gwen and David were waiting for Griffin to move, but he just sat there, peering out the windshield, memorizing the scene and the players' placements.

The premier and the older air elemental Aaron huddled on the right side of the fire pit, the white vapor of their breath puffing out, and then dissipating. The premier, dressed in jeans and a bulky plaid flannel coat lined with fleece, still wore the same cowboy hat Griffin remembered from three years earlier. Short and slight, he shifted from foot to foot, stamping in the cold.

To the left stood the two Chimerans. Shirtless, shoeless, muscular, and powerful as all hell.

"Showtime," Griffin said, and David killed the engine. The headlights died, then Gwen's quickly followed, throwing the gathering into blackness.

Griffin unfolded himself from the car, heading for Gwen. It had been two months since he'd seen her, and though he wanted to pull her in for a hug, he didn't.

"Thanks for coming," he murmured instead.

She kept watchful eyes on the Senatus. "Of course. It evens the playing field for you."

No one would dare speak their native languages with Gwen present. As a Translator, a rare genetic trait, she was able to pick up any language in an instant. Five years ago, that skill had changed the Ofarian world.

David flanked him on the other side, chuckling. "You ready for some Grade A groveling?"

Griffin didn't want groveling. At least, not entirely. Maybe two days ago he would have been satisfied with a heartfelt apology from the chief because it would have meant a step in his desired direction. Not anymore. Now he wanted answers about Keko, but it was forming the questions that scared the shit out of him.

So many secrets had come to light since the last time he'd been in the presence of the Chimerans. So many more still buried.

Griffin's mind whirred with a racket of magic signatures, and an intense churning of political analysis, strategic planning, and general nervousness.

"Chief," said the premier in his flat Canadian accent, "a little light and heat, if you please."

The symbolic lighting of the bonfire, calling the Senatus to gather. Griffin approached the ring of stones, his two most faithful Ofarians at his back. This would all be new to them, since last time he'd come here he'd been alone.

In the moonlight, he watched Chief bestow a regal, respectful nod to the premier, then give a curt, authoritative gesture to Bane, pointing at the piled logs. Bane, massive and glowering, stomped forward. It was difficult to look at him; he reminded Griffin of Keko so much—the same tint to their skin, the same dramatic arch of their eyebrows, the mixed Hawaiian heritage enhancing all their best features. Bane drew a Chimeran breath, the expanse of his muscled chest widening even more. He bent forward at the waist as he released his magic, a great and forceful spurt of gold and sunset flame shooting from between his lips. It struck the logs, which instantly caught fire.

Then, slowly and deliberately, Bane lifted his dark eyes and pinned Griffin with a hard stare. One that wouldn't break under anything less than a tank driving between them. A quick ripple of flame flashed across Bane's irises, and tendrils of smoke drifted out from between his lips.

"Whoa," David said at Griffin's shoulder. "You see that?"

"Yeah," Griffin muttered.

"Maybe the war isn't over. Thought they called you back here to bow down and apologize."

That's why the premier had, Griffin thought, and maybe the chief, too, but Bane's warning had something to do with Keko—clearly personal and full of the very answers Griffin wanted. As he stepped into the stone ring, the fire's heat struck but did not warm him.

The premier craned his neck to take in the other Ofarians, assessing. "Only two. Where's the third? The one I asked you to bring, the one you found in Colorado."

At the mention of Colorado, David and Gwen shifted in confusion. Griffin hadn't told them about the premier's request because he knew he couldn't fulfill it.

"I don't know where he is," Griffin replied. "He took off over a month ago. He tends to do that."

The premier gave him a squinty-eyed glare from underneath the brim of his cowboy hat. "He's Secondary. Elemental. He is spirit to my air, to your water. He should be here."

Griffin stroked his chin. "Yeah, well, there's really nothing I can do about that. Sean's his own man, he's not Ofarian so I have no control over him, and he's had a shit life."

"I think you should find him."

"Maybe he doesn't want to be found."

The premier wanted to say a lot more, but he pressed his already thin lips closed.

Time to change the subject. "I want to thank you, Premier, for inviting me back," Griffin began, adopting a more formal tone. Turning to the chief, carefully avoiding Bane's continual stare, he added, "And I feel I should apologize, on behalf of my entire race, for what one rogue Ofarian did to your general."

"*Former* general," Chief barked.

It took immense effort for Griffin to hide his immediate reaction.

"Gentlemen," said the premier, removing his hands from the crooks of his elbows and holding them up in stern warning, "we'll begin discussions on the issues at hand when the Daughter of Earth arrives. Not before."

"Good." Bane's voice rumbled and crackled like an inferno taking over a building. " 'Cause there's something I want to say to him." He pushed out from behind the chief and started for Griffin.

Flashbacks to Makaha. Flashbacks to Keko's too-late statement about not using magic in an attack.

Griffin planted his feet. Ready, if it was called for, to do it all over again.

"General," the chief growled.

"Peace, Chimeran," boomed the premier.

Bane kept coming.

Griffin stood his ground, dying to scream: *What's happened to her? Fucking tell me already!*

Bane pulled up three feet away, his bare chest heaving, but not filled with Chimeran breath like Makaha. He nudged his chin into the deep shadows wedged between the trees. "I want to talk to you. Privately."

David, Griffin's head of security, jumped all over that. "Not outside the protection of the gathering."

Griffin held up a hand but didn't unlock his stare from the Chimeran general.

The chief appeared beside Bane, and Griffin could not read his face. It seemed to shift from worry to hate, desperation to fear. Griffin understood none of it.

"*Gentlemen.*" A sharp reprimand from the premier.

"No harm intended," said Bane to Griffin. "Just words. It isn't Senatus business."

The premier crossed his arms. "Up to you, Ofarian."

Without hesitation Griffin turned to David and Gwen. "I'm going. Alone."

"But—" Gwen began.

"It's not a discussion. Make sure we're not disturbed or overheard."

After sharing a long look, his two oldest and dearest friends fell back. When it came down to it, they had no choice in the matter. Maybe on another night he might regret ordering them to do something they so clearly didn't like, but not on this one.

Bane headed off into the forest, the chief following, Griffin picking up the rear. He didn't let himself think about how he was being drawn away from formal protection, didn't let any sort of fear trickle in. His goal and a thousand questions propelled him to trail after the two wide, Chimeran backs stomping barefoot through the frigid forest. When they'd gone deep enough into the trees that the bonfire light didn't reach and only the moonlight rained down, Bane stopped short and whirled on Griffin. Got right up into his face.

"She'll die," the general snarled. "All because of you."

An invisible monster drove its great taloned fist right into Griffin's stomach. "What's happened?" He could barely get the words out.

"What's happened?" Bane slapped his own chest, the sound violent and thick. "What's *happened*? You've destroyed her is what happened."

Griffin ignored the tingle of water magic, that sword of ice, begging to be released. "I did no such thing."

Bane lunged. The chief was suddenly between them, pressing hands to Bane's chest, pushing him backward. "General." There was surprise in the chief's voice. Also censure. Surprise that Bane could or would be so emotional about the sister who'd bested him in the past, and censure because the crazy rules of Chimeran society didn't allow him to show such concern.

The chief turned around to face Griffin, and looked at him for a long, long time.

"Tell me," Griffin demanded. "Great stars, just tell me. She called me and I"—he struggled mightily with how much to say, how much to reveal—"I don't know what to think."

The chief's eyes widened. "She called you? When?"

"Yesterday afternoon. She didn't say anything, only good-bye. Where the hell is she?"

"It should come from you, Chief," Bane said.

By the strain on Chief's face, Griffin knew that the head Chimeran did not want to tell him. That this little separate powwow had been Bane's idea, and that if the chief did not talk, Bane certainly would.

With a long, slow sigh, Chief reached up and removed a thin, plain rope from around his neck. On it was strung a black rock no larger than a quarter, lumpy and nondescript. Griffin had noticed it before—it was the only thing he'd ever seen the chief wear on his torso—but he'd never given it much thought.

Now the chief held it out to Griffin.

He didn't take it, didn't even touch it. "What is it?"

Chief remained as even keeled as Bane had been dramatic. "It's the symbol of the new Chimeran lands, of the islands that would eventually become Hawaii," he said. "When our Queen first set foot on the Big Island, she picked up this very rock, held it up, and declared that she'd finally found our new home. That was fifteen hundred years ago."

Behind the chief, Bane folded his big arms.

"And?" Griffin prompted.

The chief regarded the rock with a dazed sort of wonder as it swung on its rope. "The Queen brought our people across the ocean from Polynesia in search of one thing: the Fire Source. The food our powers need to breathe and exist in this world. It is pure, raw fire magic. She felt it call to her from the other side of the water, and bade her people to follow her to find it. This stone is the symbol of her quest. Of her love for her people. Of her leadership and bravery and selflessness. She is a goddess, in our eyes."

So much to learn. And the Ofarians had once thought they'd known everything . . .

"What does this have to do with Keko?"

Bane came to the chief's side and they exchanged a serious look. Chief looped the rope back over his neck. "Keko is trying to succeed where our great Queen failed."

Dread nearly took Griffin off his feet. "What do you mean, 'failed'?"

"The Queen knew the Source was somewhere on the Hawaiian Islands. She could sense the raw magic but didn't know where it was, how to get to it. All she knew was that if she could find it and tap into it, she and her people would know more power than they ever dreamed." The chief glanced away.

"She spent her whole life searching. When she finally found it as an old woman, it destroyed her."

Griffin swallowed several times to try to get moisture into his mouth. "And you . . . you think Keko is going after the Source."

"We don't think. We know."

"How?"

"She left a note in my house. Yesterday morning before sunrise. Bane was with me when we found it. And Keko was gone."

Griffin started to pace, soggy leaves parting beneath his boots. "Why?" he asked, but as soon as the word escaped his lips, he knew the answer. It made him nauseous.

"If she finds the Source and brings back the raw magic," Bane said, "she will be greater than our Queen. Higher than *ali'i*, higher than any Chimeran in any of the island clans is allowed to dream. It will erase all her shame and make her into something new. She'll be untouchable."

"But you said the Source killed the Queen."

Chief licked his lips. "That's the belief, yes. Legend says that she did find it, that the power was hers for one brief moment before it destroyed her. It's why no Chimeran has gone searching for it ever again. Because we don't believe it was meant to be found. That we may borrow its magic from afar, but death will come to anyone who touches it."

Great stars, *no*.

"Why didn't she tell anyone else?" Griffin asked, a thought coming to him. "If all she wanted was glory and the chance to save face, why didn't she announce what she was going to do to the entire Chimeran valley? Wouldn't this kind of thing give her major status?"

The chief looked down, suddenly and strangely silent.

Bane jumped in. "She is desperate and depressed, Griffin, a lethal combination. Claiming to go after the Source would only bring her more scorn. We believe in proof, nothing less. Valor and strength that can be seen and tested. She's on a suicide mission with no promise of glory at the end. Only a chance, and a very small one at that."

"So she has nothing left to lose," Griffin snarled, turning away so he wouldn't have to look at the Chimerans as he thought it all through.

"No," Bane said. "She doesn't. And it all started with you."

"What do you want me to do about it now, three years apart and with her gone?" Griffin snapped over his shoulder.

No response. Because Bane didn't know. He was sick with worry over his sister—even though he wasn't officially allowed to feel such—and he'd chosen to take it out on the man who was easiest to blame, even if the blame wasn't entirely Griffin's to shoulder.

Griffin got it. And he couldn't say that he wouldn't have done the exact same thing, being in his position.

The story made sense in his mind. His heart didn't want to believe it, but the terrible squeeze and aching in his chest told him that it was true.

If Keko had taken off from the Chimeran valley yesterday morning, by the time she called Griffin she could have gotten to some town with a phone. Their conversation had seemed so cryptic at the time, but made a world of sense now. She'd known exactly what she was doing, what she'd wanted. What she had to do to get it. She'd sounded like someone saying good-bye when they knew they would never come back.

Goddamn it, why was the chief so quiet? Did he feel *nothing* for this woman who'd given him years of service and was of his own blood?

Griffin spun in an uneven, frustrated circle, scrubbing cold hands through his short hair. Did he wish he hadn't known? Did he wish she'd never called him? Was there anything he could do?

"Keko will—" Bane began, but that's as far as he got before the earth ripped open a short distance away and a voice poured out of its depths.

"THIS WOMAN MUST BE STOPPED."

The voice crackled up through the forest, shaking the bare trees and making the stars go blurry. It was made of a million sounds at once: angry as fire, ethereal like a whisper, melodic like bells.

In the distance, Griffin saw the other Secondaries around the bonfire mobilize, scrambling for the forest, running toward the sound. Running toward Griffin and the two Chimerans.

In the foreground, a sapling shivered and tilted to one side, crashing into another. Under the moon, at the very edge of where the firelight reached, an irregular circle of cracked mud and scrubby brown grass *shifted*. He stumbled backward, out of its circumference. The ground churned as though in a blender, rocking and spinning and turning in upon itself.

The air and water elementals coming from the bonfire finally reached him, skidding to a stop when they noticed what was happening.

From the hole in the earth, dirt and roots and stones crawled on top of one another. Grass and mud wound around an invisible form, piling higher and higher, until it assumed the shape of humanoid legs. Clay and sand pushed up and around the legs, forming a torso. Branches shot out to form arms, little twigs for fingers. The dirt rounded atop the neck to form a head, and yellow-green grass sprung up from the scalp, curling around the face that started to appear decidedly female.

As the small nose pushed out from the round cheeks, the eyes turned otherworldly green, and the hair transformed to white wispy silk, he recognized that face. Aya. Daughter of Earth. Not completely of the natural world, but not entirely human either.

By the stunned and silent expressions shared by everyone around the broken circle, no one else had ever witnessed such an appearance of an earth elemental. Not even the premier. Before, she had always simply walked out of the shadows on human legs to join them around the fire.

"Listen to me." Aya's voice tumbled back into a normal register, closer to the feminine tones Griffin remembered from years earlier.

She turned to Griffin and the Chimerans, the movement incredibly fluid. As she did so, her body changed, solidified. Her skin turned the warm brown of a tree trunk, then shifted to the burnished tan of sand, only supple and humanlike. A foot made of roots pulled free from the clinging earth. By the time she set it back down it was solid, her toes curling over the mud. Leaves wove themselves around her body, cloaking her in a loose garment of glistening brown. The more Aya moved, the more human she appeared. More human than the last time Griffin had seen her, as though she'd developed further into this body, if that was even possible.

She raised a twig arm, and the leaves and flowers at the tip shifted into fingers. She pointed one at the chief. "Kekona Kalani must be stopped."

The chief blanched under the weight of Aya's declaration, his mouth going slack, his shoulders slanting toward the churned-up earth.

The premier pushed ahead of the Ofarians. "What did Kekona do now?"

Aya's green eyes flashed with an inner light that reminded Griffin of deadly ice. She answered the premier but kept staring at the chief. "Kekona seeks power to change the world."

Bane shoved forward. "That's not true."

"No?" A very human lift of pale eyebrows. "Kekona is looking for the Fire Source, the root of Chimeran magic. She thinks it's harmless—*you* think it's harmless—but that root is buried deep in the Earth's core. It's part of the foundation of this world, and the Chimerans have only been allowed to borrow it. If the Source is disturbed in any way, it will alter life. It will create death. If Kekona touches it, fire feeding fire, she could destroy continents or create new ones. Massive destruction that the Children of Earth would have no way to counter."

The silence that fell over the wood was as ominous as Aya's words. More revelations, more shock. And by the horror and distress and utter paralysis making twisted masks of the Chimerans' faces, this was something not even they knew.

And Keko was already gone.

"The Children of Earth guard the Source. It's one of our many duties, to keep the power sacred and safe, to protect it from disturbance and to protect the Earth from its wrath. I'm telling you now, if you do not find Kekona and stop her, my people will hunt and kill her, just as they did the last woman to lay claim to what was not hers."

The Chimerans shared a look. "The Queen," Bane whispered, reaching big hands up to clasp around the back of his head.

The premier thumbed back his cowboy hat. "Kekona has caused enough problems for the Senatus and for all Secondaries. She must be dealt with."

"No," Griffin protested, because Keko's own people had not. "Don't."

Aya turned to him. The top of her white hair barely came

to Griffin's shoulder, but her presence was massive. "Don't what?"

"Just . . . don't kill her."

Aya's eyes flashed green again, but in a different way. Griffin couldn't pinpoint exactly how.

"She must answer for her actions outside of Chimeran law," said the premier to Aya. "Will you allow us to go after her?"

After several long moments, Aya ripped her eyes from Griffin to consider the premier, and though there was no wind among the trees, her leaf cloak and spider-webbed hair undulated. "I could return to my people Within now, tell them what's happened, and give the order to hunt."

Griffin wanted to object again, every muscle in his body straining forward.

"But a thousand years ago," Aya continued, "there was no Senatus. No cooperation between our races. I'd hate to erase something we've built so determinedly without careful consideration. Can I trust you, Premier, to find Kekona before she reaches the Source and give her suitable punishment?"

"You can, Daughter. Absolutely."

"Wait—" Bane started.

Aya nodded, ignoring the Chimeran general. "If you don't succeed, if Kekona reaches the Source, she is ours and there will be no compromise. Agreed?"

The premier shoved his hands in his coat pockets. "Agreed."

"You don't want a war with us," Aya added with a glance at the earth under her feet. "We will swallow you."

Bane growled, a lick of flame passing from eye to eye. Why wasn't the chief saying anything? Why was he just standing there, looking like he'd been bound and gagged?

The premier raised his voice. "Kekona will be found and stopped. I'll immediately appoint a search team to get to Hawaii, and Chief can assign a Chimeran scout as a guide."

The chief ground fingers into his temple. "Let me think about this—"

"There is no 'thinking,'" the premier began, and the two men devolved into an argument over how exactly to go about the search. Griffin might have been mistaken, but it seemed as though the chief was actually trying to steer the premier away from going after Keko.

Damn his culture. Damn the rules of status.

Griffin stood there, a cold that had nothing to do with the weather seeping into his bones. They were going about the search in the wrong way. They weren't properly taking into consideration their quarry. They were forgetting about Keko's determination, her drive. Her spirit.

"Wait. Stop." Griffin grabbed the premier's arm and spun him around. A dangerous move since he still wasn't part of the Senatus, but he wouldn't be ignored. Not now.

The premier looked at Griffin's hand upon his arm, then slowly raised his eyes. "Things sure have gotten more compli-cated since you showed up, Ofarian."

Griffin released him but refused to look away, refused to back down. Yeah, maybe a lot of shit that had happened recently could be traced back to him, but if they were going to blame him for starting it, then he should be the one to bring it to an end.

"Keko will not be hunted and trapped like an animal," he said. "Being chased by strangers who are intent on stopping her will only feed her purpose. Don't you get it? She will fight and fight and fight until she gets what she wants, and she won't stop running until she gets to the Source, if only to prove her-self. Bane?"

The Chimeran general nodded haltingly. "He's right."

"What are you suggesting?" the premier asked.

Griffin licked his lips, stood tall. "Let me go after her. Alone."

"Why you? Because she was your lover?" The premier sneered at that last word. "How do I know you won't help her?"

"Because the Senatus means more to me." He nodded at Aya. "And the protection of the Source, the earth itself. I want Keko brought in as much as you do. Let me prove my loyalty."

Keko's life meant most of all, but he couldn't say that. Not when the premier eyed him so warily. Let the Senatus leader think Griffin wanted revenge for her trying to start a war. Let them all think whatever the hell they wanted, as long as it would allow him to get to her first. As long as it would allow him to save her life.

"I'm telling you, if she knows she's being hunted, you'll never find her. I have the best chance. I am water. What better way to fight a fire?"

"I second this." A most unexpected endorsement from Aya. Griffin looked over at her, and there was that look in her eyes again. Something . . . unsaid. Something meant only for him.

"Chief?" prompted the premier.

In the span of his pause, the chief drew two breaths, neither of which brought forth fire. "I agree with what you think is best." He bowed his head, and Griffin could not read his face.

The premier came toe to toe with Griffin, his voice low and authoritative. "If you find Kekona Kalani and bring her to me before she finds the Source, before she causes any more trouble for any of our races, I will know you have the Senatus's interests at heart. If you do this, you will win your seat among us."

FOUR

Away from the dispersing Senatus, after retreating deep into the darkness of the old-growth forest, Aya folded herself back into the earth. With an aching sense of loss, she let go of her human body and merged her being with the land, returning to the true form of a Daughter of Earth. The borders between Aboveground and Within blurred and then disappeared.

It was getting harder and harder to do. One day she'd no longer be able to transform back and forth like this. But she'd made her choice, and she gladly lived with it.

Through rock and dirt and clay she rolled. Around and under and through a great maze of roots and aquifers, she sent herself digging. She knew the layout of Within as well as the minute details of her human skin, and she followed the striations in the earth like a road map. She searched for her home, hidden in the earth's crust by the planet's oldest magic. *There*. She found it, burrowing faster and faster to reach it. The feel of the earth around her was beginning to suffocate and press in.

She couldn't wait to be free. She couldn't wait to live in a house, with windows that allowed in the breeze, and windows that permitted light, and a door that let her come and go easily and of her own accord.

With a final push, she thrust herself through the walls of her abode. The rock and clay opened, ate her, then spit her into the small, open space beyond. Her body was made of quartz and minerals, sand and magic, and it landed unceremoniously in the center of her doorless cave.

Though she'd just been human, and the transformation into Daughter of Earth had sapped much of her energy, she reached for her human form again. Pushed away the parts of her that belonged solely to the earth. The golden brown skin she loved smoothed out the hard angles of rock. Proud white hair tickled her shoulders. She curled onto her side on the clay floor, her short legs pulled up to her chest.

As her evolving human lungs expanded, she gasped for air. Always this shock, the first time breathing Within. The constant trickle of oxygen was just enough to sustain human life, and also just enough to be torture. It was meant to remind the Children of their original forms. It was meant to remind them that humanity and the Children had once been one being.

All it did was reinforce Aya's belief that she well and truly belonged Aboveground.

Normally it only took a short time for her to become accustomed to the dense, dark surroundings, but now she couldn't seem to take a steady breath. She was coughing, choking. Then something scraped down her cheek and landed with a plink in the clay, then another and another, and she realized she was crying.

Her tears solidified as they escaped, turning into tiny, rough diamonds. So many. Until she was surrounded by their glitter and could take no human joy from them.

This must be what betrayal felt like.

It had been only months since she'd last seen Keko, since the two women had last propped their feet up on a rock by a wintry mountain stream and spoke haltingly of things that the Chimeran woman probably found mundane but that Aya thought of as fascinating. Cars and ice cream and games, and those soft things you pulled over your toes when they were cold. Keko always made Aya smile with her frank descriptions and honest opinions. Especially when it came to men.

The last time they met, shortly after Keko's rescue in Colorado and right before her war against the Ofarians was called off, she'd finally spoken to Aya about Griffin. Even though Keko's words had been harsh, the expression on her face had been wistful and soft, and it was crystal clear to Aya—even though she was still learning about human emotions—how the Chimeran woman truly felt about that Ofarian man.

Over the years, since their first chance meeting in the forest the night Griffin had maimed that Chimeran warrior, Aya had come to relish their sporadic, solitary talks. Keko must have, too, because she often sought out Aya after Senatus gatherings. Though Keko was not human, she'd managed to teach Aya much about humanity and Aboveground.

And now Aya had sentenced her first true friend to die.

Another great shudder wracked her body. For a moment she doubted her choice to evolve because humanity hurt far too much. Then she forced herself to think of Keko, who loathed self-pity, and pushed herself up to sit.

It was going to be all right, she told herself. Griffin was going after Keko. Griffin would find her and bring her back safely. Griffin would keep the Source intact.

And Griffin would win a seat among the Senatus, laying grounds for Aya's supreme plan—a plan with which the Father would never agree.

She'd been sly, just now before the premier, to make him think she was on his side. Just like how sneaky she had to be to make the Father think she still agreed with him and the ways of the Children.

So much duplicity. If she were caught before her evolution into human was complete, she would face the ultimate punishment. Something worse than death.

Please, Griffin, she silently begged. *Find Keko and bring her back. Appeal to her heart, because I know that deep down, hers belongs to you.*

A crack splintered open the cave wall. Aya rolled unsteadily to her feet, kicking dirt and clay over the diamond tears to disguise them. A tiny glowing root pushed its way through the short crack, pulsing with an energy she knew intimately and had once loved more than her own life.

Daughter. The Father's wordless voice emanated from the root. *Come to me and report.*

Brave Queen. Good Queen. Mighty Queen. Show me your secrets. *Grant me redemption. Make me worthy. Help me earn back my name. Guide me to help our people. Above all, award me mana, your spiritual power.*

Each word matched the beats of Keko's heels as they struck the moist earth. Each syllable made a prayer. Each footstep moved her closer to her fate. Her faith guided her.

At the end of this road, even death would be a prize worth winning, because the people who had shunned her would know what she'd tried to do, how she'd attempted something as significant as becoming the Queen herself. If death came, Keko's name would be spoken with breathless wonder and respect.

If she lived, she would lead. If she lived, she would hear words of admiration with her own ears and see awe with her own eyes, and she would know that she'd earned it.

Keko had been walking northwest through the coastal rainforests near Hilo, Hawaii for nearly two days. She slept through the cool, rainy nights curled up against trees, protected by the arch of massive leaves. She drank from streams and pools, and nibbled on the food she'd stolen from the stronghold before sneaking away under the cover of night. She avoided lights and Primary homes and civilization, sticking to the remote natural areas.

She wanted her actions to match the Queen's as closely as possible. No Primaries. No modern conveniences or roads. No assistance. Only heart and determination. Only love for Chimeran magic, Chimeran ancestry. When Keko came into the Queen's legacy, she would touch the Source clean. Absolved.

And then she would succeed where the Queen had not. She wouldn't be Chimeran if that kind of stature didn't make her fire flare with anticipation and longing.

Keko hunted for something very specific: a signpost left behind, a marker from the ancients. Over the course of her life, the Queen had carved thousands upon thousands of prayers into lava rock all over the Big Island. These prayers called out to the Source, asking for guidance. Almost all of these prayer carvings had gone unanswered, left to bake beneath the sun for future generations to question, but one had actually worked. It was that rock that Keko sought.

Travel was slowgoing, traversing the hilly landscape somewhat inland from the water, weaving in and out of tall, straight trees that bent in one direction under the constant force of the ocean wind. Keko took her time, analyzing the Queen's legends, making sure she headed in the right direction. She didn't fear pursuit.

Chief wouldn't try to stop her because even if she succeeded and earned the Queen's name, he would be healed. Bane, out of duty and because of Chimeran rules, would be forbidden to search for her. She wondered if Chief would tell Bane about the disease, then decided no. He would want to protect himself. Chief would let her brother think Keko weak and stupid and desperate.

She put the two Chimeran men out of her mind, because there simply was no point in thinking of them. No going backward, only forward.

But the problem with not thinking about her brother and uncle meant there was more space and time for Griffin to slink in. It happened in the most unlikely of places, following random, unrelated thoughts. Memories and images of Griffin, sliding into the blank minutes of her life.

Griffin, kitted out in soldier gear, stalking into that Colorado garage where she'd been held prisoner. His pale-faced shock when he realized she was the captive. The desire that still floated behind his frustration and anger.

The open set of his mouth as she pressed her hands hard into his shoulders, pinning him down. Riding him until they both came with their eyes wide open.

The way he'd slowly run his hands and eyes over her body that last night in the Utah hotel. Memorizing her lines and curves. So many parts of him had been lost to time and she wanted all those details back. She should have memorized him, too.

Suddenly she wished she hadn't burned his jacket, for reasons that had nothing to do with the wet weather.

It was raining again, though it looked like it might pass over quickly. Keko turned her face to the sky and let the new droplets hit her cheeks and closed eyelids. Water, water, everywhere, each strike a little bit of Griffin.

She'd been right to call him. A paralyzing doubt had overtaken her the seconds before she'd dialed, but the moment she heard his voice she knew she'd done the right thing. Only now did she realize she hadn't actually apologized for the whole war thing. Words like that didn't come easy for her, but maybe Griffin understood.

Or maybe he didn't, and she'd succeeded in making everything worse by not spewing out all the things she longed to say. Now she'd never get to, and it was that loss of a chance that hurt the most. He would never know how much she regretted blaming him for her capture, how ashamed she was of her subsequent actions.

She wondered if he would think her quest foolish. The stern Ofarian leader, the Senatus hopeful, might appreciate her desire to take back what had been lost, to lead her people in her own right. But the man who'd murmured to her in bed about new chances and dreams for his race, *that* man would sympathize with her need to find the Source, no matter the cost—even though she would never be able to tell him the reason why without compromising innocents. It created a heartrending polarity.

Keko realized her feet had stopped walking right in the middle of a macadamia nut tree farm. He was doing it again. Griffin was making her veer off her path, steering her mind in directions it didn't need to go, and he wasn't even here.

With a violent shake of her head, she gritted out "Stop it!" and exorcised Griffin for good. She'd said her good-byes, and that was that.

FIVE

"I already know you don't like it," Griffin said, pulling out his old soldier's vest from the back of the closet and tossing it on the bed, "so don't even think about calling me 'sir.'"

David scowled from where he leaned a hip against the blond wood dresser. With a hand scraping through his hair, he turned his head to look out the long bank of windows framing the slope of Hyde Street, Alcatraz hazy in the distance.

"No backup," David muttered. "No nothing. It sucks and it makes me look like a shitty head of security."

"No, it doesn't. Not when I'm ordering you to stand down. Not when, technically, no Ofarian knows where I am or what I'm doing. If anything, I'm the one who looks shitty, but I'm okay with that. Hell, I'm used to it."

David pushed off the dresser, its legs scraping an inch on the hardwood floor. "At least let me put up some soldiers in Hilo. In case you need them."

Griffin threw a small backpack onto the bed to join the vest. "Absolutely not. The second Keko suspects I'm there for any reason other than to stop her from throwing herself into a volcano or whatever the hell it is she thinks she's gonna do, she'll put up a massive fight or she'll vanish. No soldiers, David. Just me."

"Fuck." David gave Griffin his back and stared out the window, arms tightly crossed.

Griffin understood David's frustration. After all, Griffin had had David's position once. The major difference was that Griffin had just barely tolerated the old Chairman, while David was a brother in all but blood.

Gwen came into the bedroom holding a small cardboard box. "This just came for you." She squinted at the PO Box return address. "From Adine?"

He took the box but didn't open it, just tossed it next to his vest.

"What is it?" Gwen had never been one to mince words. Sometimes the Ofarian woman reminded him of a diluted version of Keko.

Griffin glanced at the box, debating whether or not to say. Which was dumb because there were no two people in the world he trusted more than those in the room with him right now. "Signature sensor," he said.

Gwen reached out and tapped his forehead. "Is yours broken?"

He ducked away from her touch. "It's, ah, something Adine has been working on for me. Something other Secondaries might be able to use. Something that enhances our own abilities."

Gwen glanced at the box. "What do you mean?"

"It should, if it works right, be able to track signatures long after a Secondary has left a scene. Like a trail."

"Adine can *do* that?"

Griffin shrugged. "Something she's been playing with. Mixing technology and magic. I asked her to do this for me on the side, but by the way she jumped on it, I wonder if it was something she hadn't already been pursuing. Which might scare me if it wasn't Adine."

The half-Secondary woman had no magic of her own, just an otherworldly brain when it came to anything with wires or code or technology. The Ofarians had saved her life, then had got her settled on her own two feet in the Primary world, so Griffin got a pretty steep discount on her otherwise astronomical price of services.

"Kind of like what Kelsey is doing with medicine and magic," Gwen said.

At the mention of his doctor wife, David finally turned around. He scanned the sparse items laid out on the bed: the vest and the box with the sensor, a long knife in a leather holder, packets of freeze-dried food, a small first-aid kit, sturdy boots, and a single change of clothes.

"The vest still fit?" David smirked. "You've been behind a

desk for the past five years. Got a little soft around the middle."

"Asshole." Griffin pulled on the vest. Far too many emotions accompanied the drag of the lightweight mesh over his T-shirt. All those pockets that had once zippered in tools of death.

When he had to let out the side straps a notch, Gwen said, "Aw, you're not soft. Just old."

"Great. Thanks." Griffin was grateful for the tiny bit of levity.

The three of them stood within a companionable silence, letting their mutual past settle into the cracks of the situation. It wasn't the first time they'd said good-bye, but each time carried its own feeling, its own baggage. It wouldn't be their last either.

It reminded him of another recent good-bye, and why he was doing all this in the first place, making his friends' faces pinch that way.

David's phone rang. Looking at the screen he said, "It's Kelse," and ducked out of the bedroom.

Griffin watched him go, then removed the vest and folded it into the backpack.

Gwen eased down to sit on the edge of the bed. At one time, years ago, Griffin would have given just about anything to have her sit there as a prelude of something else to come, but now it just gave him a bittersweet feeling.

"It has to be me, Gwen."

She raised her hands. "I know. Did I say anything?"

He threw her a questioning, sidelong look.

She sighed. "I think I know a little bit about taking on something huge, something only you can do. I get it. I see all the strings dangling out there—Kekona and the Senatus and the Ofarians and the Fire Source—and I get how you're the one person able to tie them all together." He threw the leather-wrapped knife into the backpack. Gwen bent down, getting in his direct line of vision. "I also know how hard it is, what it feels like, to be jumping around trying to get all the ends of those strings in your hands when all they want to do is fly away."

Griffin stilled and met her sympathetic eyes. He still loved her, but in a much, much different way than before. "Thank you," he said.

With a slap to her knees, she stood. "So what did the cabinet say?"

He whistled and shook his head. "Exactly what you'd think they'd say. Divided along the typical lines. One loves the idea of revenge, going after the woman who tried to attack us. The guy who has been against the Senatus from the get-go now loves this idea—show them we can get things done better than they can, clean up their mess, et cetera. Others want me to just butt out. My supporters are the same." He yanked the zipper around the pack. "But none of them know the real reason why I'm going."

"Because you want her back."

"What—" He blinked. Several times. Then glowered. "No."

Gwen looked at him with her special brand of patience and authority. She had the power to stand there all day. "I don't think you're being honest with yourself about your relationship with her."

"Because there is no relationship. There never was. It was just sex."

She crossed her arms. "Really."

"You wouldn't understand."

Her eyebrows shot for the ceiling. "I wouldn't?"

With a grimace, he turned away. "It's weird, talking to you about . . . her."

"Try me."

Afternoon was turning to evening, and he had to get to the airport. He didn't have time for this, yet he continued. "I can't sit back and watch her do something this idiotic. This selfish. I don't want her to cause anything like Aya described. I don't want to see her hurt. Or end up dead. Despite everything, despite how we hurt each other and what happened in Colorado and what she tried to do to us, I don't believe she deserves this. If I can stop it, if I can help her survive, I will."

This time he hated the sympathy in Gwen's brown eyes, so he hurriedly added, "And then there's the Senatus. What it could mean for the Ofarians if I bring Keko back."

"Right." Gwen sighed, pivoting toward the door with a roll of her eyes. "The Senatus."

"She's worth more," he blurted. "More than her mistakes."

Gwen stopped and turned back around. "I fucked up, too, Griffin. We all fuck up."

Griffin hid his wince, because not even Gwen knew what he'd done to Makaha. And maybe it was time to admit that that had been a colossal fuckup. That he should stop trying to rationalize his way out of it.

"Thank you. I kind of needed to hear that." He slung the backpack over one shoulder. "Are you going back to Chicago?"

"I'd rather stay here and wait for you, if you want. If you need me, it's easier to get to Hawaii from here."

"Stay," he said quickly. "Please."

"I will. I'll have Reed fly out here, too. Just in case."

Once upon a time Griffin would've hated to have heard that, but now it gave him peace. "Good."

She laid her hand on his cheek. "It's been a really long time since I've seen you smile. Or laugh." Thought lines dashed across her forehead. "Did I do that? By pushing you into leadership after we took down the Board?"

That was Gwen, humble to the core. *She'd* been the one to destroy the Ofarian Board. "You didn't push me. I could've said no."

Her hand dropped. "But you didn't. And that's what makes you a spectacular leader. Because you took on something that scared you."

"No." He shook his head. "I just want what I want, what I think is best. I'm stubborn and maybe a little bit selfish, not spectacular."

She cocked her head, her blond ponytail swinging. "What do you want more? Keko or the Senatus? Because you can't have both."

He already knew that, but that didn't make it any easier to hear. He searched Gwen's face, thinking how to respond. "I want Keko alive so she can give herself another chance in life. But when it comes down to it, I just want what's best for Henry."

Gwen smiled, but it was tight-lipped and small. "See?" She sighed. "Spectacular."

The road to the Chimeran stronghold on the Big Island of Hawaii was exactly as Cat Heddig had described: a treacherous, rocky, barely discernible dirt line carving up through the thick trees and undergrowth somewhere on the island's easternmost section. By the time Griffin swung the rented four-wheel-drive

SUV into the cluster of three decrepit, turn-of-last-century buildings meant to disguise the entrance to Chimeran land, his teeth ached from being consistently jarred and his stomach felt queasy from all the twists and turns and dips to get there.

Standing in the middle of the dirt road, just outside a poor excuse for a convenience store, was Bane and another male Chimeran warrior. Bane's massive arms were crossed over his bare chest. The other warrior, shorter and leaner, had a black tattoo of whorls and lines covering one shoulder, and wore a band of white beads around his neck.

Griffin stopped the SUV in the road, the grill just feet from Bane's unflinching stance. Griffin slid out from behind the wheel, leaving the engine running. Instantly, Secondary signatures assaulted his mind. Bane's was nearly overwhelming, a steady thrum of power lacing itself through Griffin's awareness. Much like Keko's. He wondered if their family blood had something to do with the strength of their magic, if it had contributed to their rise to the top of their people.

"Bane," Griffin said, not stretching out a hand for a shake because the larger Chimeran hadn't unfolded his arms.

"It's 'General' to you," said the other Chimeran, stepping forward.

"Ikaika," Bane murmured, not removing his stare from Griffin. "It's okay. He's here for Keko."

The warrior named Ikaika looked as surprised at Bane's response as Griffin felt. The two Chimerans exchanged a look, and a wordless understanding seemed to pass between them. As Ikaika nodded, falling back again, Griffin studied him.

Not only was Ikaika smaller than Bane, his signature was far weaker. A thready, stuttering pulse that merely teased Griffin's senses. Odd.

"Get in," Bane gestured to the SUV. "I'll drive."

As Griffin hoisted himself into the passenger seat, Bane gave him a hand signal telling him to wait, and the two Chimeran men went into the convenience store. The Hawaiian sun shot down between billowing puffs of silver clouds threatening rain, hitting the grimy windows of the store, but Griffin could still make out the Chimerans' silhouettes. Bane was talking, Ikaika's face lifted in rapt attention. Finally Ikaika nodded, hands going to his hips.

Then Bane touched him. Even through the darkened window, even only in silhouette, the embrace was a powerful thing. No, embrace wasn't a good word for it. Griffin stared, fascinated and curious. Bane's hand went around Ikaika's neck, and he pulled the warrior to him. As their foreheads and noses touched, Ikaika also slid his hand around Bane's neck and they each took a deep, simultaneous breath.

The separation was a slow process, but by the time Bane marched out of the store, his shoulders had resumed their tense position and the familiar scowl was back in place. Griffin had to look away, out through the windshield, because at that moment Bane reminded him far too much of Keko.

Bane threw the SUV into drive and it took off with a jolt past the three vine-covered buildings. He pitched it over a steep edge and followed some kind of pseudo-road that Griffin never would have been able to find. Finally the land flattened out a bit, the foliage parting over the windshield, and Bane stopped the car with a violent jerk. Griffin unclenched his fingers from where they'd been wrapped around the door handle.

Bane's hands made fists on his thighs. "I want you to help Keko."

"I am," Griffin said. "I will."

"No." Bane swung his head toward the passenger seat. "I mean, I want you to help her find the Source."

Griffin reached for the door handle again, feeling as though they'd taken another sudden dive down that steep road. "I . . . don't understand. I'm supposed to bring her back before she gets to that point."

Bane shook his head. "That's what Chief wants. Self-preservation and all that. Imagine what would happen to his position if Keko succeeded and she waltzed back into the valley with the Queen's treasure."

"But what Aya said—"

"*No.* There's got to be a way for Keko to get to the Source."

The desperation in Bane's eyes, the tension in his body, was alien and worrisome, huge and alarming.

"How you acted toward me at the Senatus," Griffin said, "getting all pissed off that I'd driven her away—"

Bane snarled. "I had to, in front of the *ali'i.* In front of all the others."

Griffin pinched the bridge of his nose. "Okay, you need to tell me what the hell is going on."

Bane rolled his eyes toward the driver's side window. "No, I don't. I need you to help my sister get to the Source and bring back the magic. If I could go after her myself, I would. But I can't."

None of this made any sense. Did Bane want him to take part in some sort of coup? Griffin refused to be used like that. He turned in the seat toward Bane, stabbing a finger at his own knee for emphasis. "Look. I'm here to stop Keko from killing herself. I'm here to prevent potential massive devastation to the earth."

With a growl, Bane threw open his door and jumped out. He slammed it shut with such force it sent the car rocking. Griffin had no choice but to follow, stomping after the general as he descended a twisting, jagged path down into the valley. They came around a bend and the whole Chimeran stronghold—the place hidden from all other Secondaries for over a thousand years—opened up before him.

The sight matched Cat's description perfectly: the sagging, white-boarded homes with the tin roofs stacked up the mountainsides; an enormous, rippling tarp covering a collection of picnic tables; the ocean sparkling in the distance; and the great meadow the center of it all. The one thing Cat hadn't mentioned was the long, one-story building at the very base of the mountain, just opposite the field.

Griffin stared at it, hearing Keko's disgusted voice on that fateful night three years ago, describing what would happen to Makaha. "That the Common House?"

Bane stopped walking. "Yeah."

Is Makaha there now? Griffin wanted to ask. *Can I see him? Can I talk to him?* Knowing full well he could not. Griffin's presence in Hawaii was secret, known only by Bane and the chief—and now, strangely, Ikaika. Hopefully someday he would be able to meet Makaha's eyes and personally express his regret, to talk with him man to man and not enemy to enemy, but today was not that day.

"Chief's waiting," Bane barked, and took off again.

They circumvented the field and entered the back door of the only house perched on the edge of the wide area of grass.

Inside it was damp and sparsely decorated, all the furniture basic, uncoordinated, and warped. The chief, wearing a troubled look, sat at the dining room table. He kicked out a chair for Griffin.

"I need to get going. She's already got a two-day head start on me." Griffin hoisted his pack farther onto his back and did not take the offered seat. "Tell me everything I need to know. And fast."

He sensed Bane's presence at his back, the general's overwhelming magic signature filling the room. All that Bane had just said in the car—and had not—pressed against Griffin's awareness, creating questions he couldn't ask.

The chief folded his hands on the table, the tips growing white from the pressure. He looked at them as he spoke, his voice hoarse, as though his fire had dried it out. "She will have headed northwest, along the coast. On foot. Her note said she was following the Queen's path."

Griffin scratched at his cheek and chin, nodding. "And she'll want to do it exactly like the Queen did. No vehicles. Nothing the Queen didn't have. That's good. Tell me about this path."

The chief fingered the stone at the base of his throat. "Legend says that the Queen had failed to find the Source after searching this island her whole life. Finally, in her old age, she gave this rock to a man she designated *ali'i*, told her people that she belonged to the Source now, and if she was truly meant to find it, it would guide her to it. Then she took her longtime partner and left this valley.

"Thirty-two days later, her partner stumbled back. He was old and weak, and he told the story of how his Queen carved her final prayer to the Source onto a stone in a small, dangerous valley along the coast. She carved it all throughout the day, the two of them fell asleep in each other's arms, and when he awoke, she was gone. He guessed that sometime in the night the Source had answered her prayer and had guided her to its location. He searched but he never found her, and he assumed she was successful."

"And no other Chimerans ever went after this stone prayer," Griffin said, "if it supposedly revealed the Source's location? Wouldn't that be the prize of all prizes?"

The chief frowned. "Until Aya told us that thing about her

people killing the last woman who went after the Source, we've believed that the fire took the Queen for its own. Before he died, her lover declared that no one should ever go after the Source, because to do so would be to claim yourself greater than the Queen. She is our goddess, so no one ever has. Until now."

Greater than the Queen. *Keko, what do you think you're doing? What did you bring upon yourself? And why do your uncle and brother want such different outcomes?*

"I'll bring her back safe," Griffin said to the chief. "The Source will remain untouched."

He heard Bane walk away, the Chimeran's signature trailing after him, the sound of the glass panes rattling in the back door as he made his exit. But Griffin didn't go after him. If the general refused to give him any answers about his cryptic plea, Griffin didn't owe him anything in return. Keko's life was Griffin's goal. His sole purpose.

The chief's gaze drifted over Griffin's shoulder and out the window that framed an overgrown garden. "Yes," he murmured, almost to himself. "I'm sure it will remain untouched."

And Griffin didn't know what suddenly bothered him more: the troubled, conflicted look in the chief's tired eyes and the anxious bounce of his knee, or the fact that his Chimeran signature was essentially nonexistent.

SIX

Griffin hiked out of the Chimeran valley on the opposite side from which he'd arrived. Even if he'd wanted to hop in a car and close the gap between him and Keko with an engine, there was no way even the best four-wheel drive could have managed on this landscape. It wasn't vertical, but pretty damn close. He had to pay smart attention to where he put his hands and feet, the land soft from rain, the vegetation sometimes giving out and making him slide.

This terrain had probably been kid's play to Keko. Her stamina and strength were already something incredible, a gift of her Chimeran blood, but she'd also grown up here, among the birds with their strange songs, and the ferns and vines that looked injected with steroids. A dangerous advantage for her to have, and he dared let himself worry that maybe he'd underestimated how far ahead she'd gotten.

But then, he had a damn good advantage over her.

When he was well away from the valley, heaving for breath on top of a rise that swept back down to the stronghold and even farther away to the ocean, he unzipped his pack and pulled out Adine's sensor. A slim silver piece with a screen larger than most smart phones, it fit perfectly in one hand. He flicked it on and the screen jumped, coming to life as it slowly scanned and displayed in uneven, colorful circles the altitude pitches of this mountainous land. Red for the tops of the hills that faded into dark blue at sea level. A jumble of hills and crags, canyons and bodies of water.

He could feel the faint tug of the signatures of the collective Chimeran population far off to his right. There, on the screen, in blinking, shifting white, a graphic cloud echoed what he sensed.

Also, a thin, faint, white streak smeared northwest across the screen, zigzagging through the concentric, colorful circles, traveling down the slopes and back up again. Away from the valley. Away from the spot in which he stood now.

Keko.

He could not physically sense her signature anymore, but it was right there in brilliant clarity, in a visual form no Ofarian, or anyone else, had ever laid eyes on before. The perfect trail for him to follow.

He realized, with a cold feeling, that if this kind of technology should ever fall into the wrong hands, it wouldn't just be Adine who would be compromised. Every Secondary would be vulnerable. He'd have to get her assurance that this particular device—since he had been the one to commission and pay for it—was the only type of tracker in existence.

But . . . one situation at a time.

Griffin stared at the device and memorized Keko's path, intermittently dropping the screen to look up and match the digital signature trail with the topography spread out before him. Once he had it committed to memory, he turned off the tracker and stashed it in his pack.

He would never catch up with her on foot. Not with her physical ability, not with her two-day lead and knowledge of the landscape, and not with the day's light starting to die.

But he'd close a good chunk of the distance if he used his magic.

He opened his mouth and filled it with Ofarian words. He threw out his arms, tilted back his head, and opened up his whole being to let his magic take hold. The language of his ancestors, the one that had originated on another world somewhere up among the stars, spun through him, taking his human body. It sank into him, shifting the molecules of his hair and bones and organs to water, to the element that defined his people.

In fiction, Primaries called magic "power." He remembered that the first time he'd heard that term as a boy, he'd found it odd. But that was before his body had changed, before he'd actually wielded water and discovered how truly special he was. As soon as he matured he understood the synonym for magic as "power," because that's exactly how he felt. Powerful. It had never changed for him. Using it this time in the wet Hawaiian forest as a thirty-five-year-old was as humbling and wonderful as the very first time in his parents' living room at age thirteen.

Opening his eyes, he looked at his arm, a translucent, shimmering appendage that defied the rules of this world. To transform his body entirely into water was simple and demanded little from either himself or his magic, but he needed his clothing and he needed what he carried on his back. That was a different process entirely, and it required an awful lot.

Digging deep, as deep into his powers as was possible, he centered his concentration, and then *pushed* his magic outward. It shot out from the confines of his body, stabbing into the cotton threads of his clothes and the nylon strands of his pack, and the many solid pieces of the contents inside. He changed everything, from Adine's signature sensor down to his scant camper's food.

Everything, water.

But with gravity and the steep up-and-down terrain dotted with more types of plants than he could ever hope to know, pushing a flow of water overland wouldn't be the best way to go. Unless . . .

It was risky—it would drain his energy even faster; it would put him in danger of losing his magic altogether—but in the end it would help him the most.

He weighed the options. Chance losing Keko *and* the Senatus, or chance kissing his water magic good-bye.

It was a no brainer. He was strong. He was centered. He was steadfast. Catching up to Keko would keep her alive, give him the Senatus, and create a better future for Henry. Magic was nothing, in the grand scheme of things. Being Ofarian meant more than magic; Cat Heddig had taught him that. If he had to let it go, so be it. The end absolutely justified the means.

So he became vapor.

The magic tugged hard at his senses and his control, but he took hold of it, quick and firm. His body and belongings divided, dissipated, rising up from the earth. Water to steam. He'd only done this a handful of times in his life—the risks of going to vapor were impressed upon young Ofarians very early—but the skill came back easily. It was the energy he worried about. So what was he doing hovering around navel-gazing for?

He grabbed a gust of wind and rode it. The invisible force yanked him from his hilltop and whisked him northwest. Over the steep drop of the land, across the open space, above the trees. Cutting his pursuit time in half, maybe even more.

Still, he wished he had an air elemental with him to speed things up, to direct traffic so to speak. As it was, he had to ride the existing air currents, expelling even more energy to keep himself on track to follow Keko's trail.

But that wasn't even the toughest part. It was keeping himself together. That was the danger of this form. If he spread his vapor too thin there was the threat of it snapping, coming apart. Separating. And if an Ofarian in vapor form lost control of his molecules, too much space coming between them, there was no getting them back together again.

The most tame Ofarian campfire stories described water elementals regaining their bodies after going vapor only to find their magic was gone. The most evil, the most disgusting, had Ofarians coming back into human form without limbs or heads.

That wouldn't happen to Griffin. He refused to believe it would. He was leader of all Ofarians. And his purpose was paramount. Not even all the powers of the universe—this one and the next—could deny him that. He didn't fucking care if that was arrogant. He had to believe it. He had to put his trust in it.

As a cloud of steam, he crossed streams and soared over tree canopies, darting through leafy sugar cane farms and scaring feral cats. The drain on his energy taunted him. He could feel it seeping away, his magic and his will squeezing every last bit out of every last drop of strength before he reached for the next. But he was gaining ground. If he was lucky, he'd catch up to Keko before nightfall.

Then all of a sudden he lost the trail, one hill looking too much like the other, the vapor form messing with his awareness. He had to go solid again, had to check the signature tracker, or else he'd be doing even more damage by heading too far in the wrong direction.

He hated to do it, to waste energy on retransformation, knowing he'd have to turn vapor all over again, but he did it, coming back into his body on the edge of ranchland, ten or so cows lingering in the distance. It took longer than he'd thought, and when he swung his pack around his body and ripped open the zipper, the tracker wasn't fully operational.

He panicked, muttering, "No, no, no! Come on, work!"

He zapped it with more magic, pulling out every last particle of water from its surface and innards. When he turned it on, it took a long time for the screen to flicker into color, even longer for it to register his own signature and the dragging line of Keko's residual path. The images were patchy, and blinked in and out. The device vibrated oddly, like it was struggling to work. Quickly, he memorized what he saw on the screen. Turned out his aim was only a little bit off, and he made his course correction, committing to memory her new direction.

Next time he came back from either water or vapor form, he feared the sensor would not work at all. Never had any tech felt so unstable or glitchy in his hand. Usually Ofarians had to expend extra energy to transform not-living articles, but he'd never had to worry about tech not working after re-transformation. Perhaps it was the specific mix of magic and technology that Adine had used. Perhaps Ofarian powers didn't play so nicely with whatever it was that she'd injected into the circuitry.

He'd have to bring that up to her when he returned to San Francisco—no doubt her genius mind could come up with a solution—but for now he had to make the blip of information it fed him count.

He turned to water, and then vapor again, his magic trembling with exertion, and headed back out, riding the air. He zoomed around the dark slashes of twilit trees. He curled around wind-wracked bushes bursting with flowers. He rode as many correct currents as he could, and had to fight against others to keep on his designated path. Push and pull, push and pull.

In the middle of the night he could feel his magic dying. Lowering himself to the ground he assumed solid form. He collapsed in sleep for a few hours, shoveled food in his mouth to build up his strength, and then started out again. Broken daylight just cracked the horizon.

He hadn't wanted to be right, but he was—the tracker didn't work at all. But he remembered which direction Keko had gone. And he liked to imagine that he could feel her now, that he was getting close enough for his own Ofarian senses to do their thing.

He also took reassurance in knowing that she had to rest, too, and that she didn't know she was being followed. If he slept four hours to her seven or eight, and wrung as much water magic out of his body as he could, maybe he could catch up to her when night fell again.

But that single dose of food and brief rest wasn't nearly enough, and his magic only lasted a few hours. His molecules started to shift midair and he had to drag them along like dead weight. In the last few miles, the burn on his psyche and the ability to hold his form together became simply too much. He had to choose: continue to try to hold his vaporized body together and push just a little farther with no guarantee what it would do to his human form, or turn himself solid and go on by foot.

Before he could decide, he lost his grip on the vapor, the last finger of control releasing the final bit of magic. It happened above ground, before he had a chance to lower himself and find his feet. His body coalesced, its solid form sucking in the vapor, and then he fell, snapping through branches and bouncing off huge, arching banyan tree roots, to hit the ground hard.

He tried to get up but he had hardly any energy left. Breath sawed in and out of his lungs. His sight wavered. Every muscle protested movement, but Griffin ignored every complaint.

He hauled himself up, leaned against the banyan tree and got his bearings, and continued after Keko on foot. Weaving, weak, he needed every yard, every step, every inch. He had to keep moving.

And then, when dusk came, he finally sensed her.

She was a prick of light in the corner of his mind, a low and steady buzz setting into his blood, pulling him forward. Though his feet were leaden, he pushed on because there was a good chance her signature could go cold, and without the tracker he'd lose her.

She was moving slowly, methodically. So carefully that even in his exhausted state, he closed some distance between them as dusk gave way to night. As he drew nearer, the sound of a waterfall grew louder, obliterating the otherwise eerie silence that cloaked Hawaiian nights.

He trudged into a thick stand of giant ferns that looked positively prehistoric in scale and shape. Pushing aside the drooping fronds and charging forward, he almost pitched himself into a steep ravine, the dramatic drop-off ending a hundred feet at the stream bed below. Moonlight filled the space between one side of the ravine and the other; it was deep but not so wide across, maybe thirty feet. Peering to the right, it seemed to empty into the violent ocean a good mile or so away. To the left, it carved a big slice out of the dramatically sloped land, but the deepening darkness hid just how far up it went.

On the opposite side of the ravine, scaling the nearly vertical pitch hand over hand, was Keko.

She was a spider, the way she climbed so easily. A spider who breathed fire. Every time she released her hand or bare foot, a quick, brilliant fireball exploded from her mouth, lighting her way, showing her where to grab next. Griffin watched the scene play out in flashes, like an old-time movie, until Keko finally hauled herself up over the lip of the ravine and rolled to her feet.

Keko. Great stars, he'd found her. He'd found her and there was this chasm yawning between them. If he'd had any strength left, he could climb down and then back up in pursuit. If he'd had any magic left, he could swirl into vapor and reform as solid right in front of her on the other side. But he had neither, and though the ravine wasn't all that wide, it was too far to jump.

Across the ravine, the moonlight played with her skin and settled into the crevices between her muscles. He was just close enough to see it all, just far enough away not to reach. She wore a tank top, loose, frayed denim shorts, and a pack that crossed over one shoulder, the strap lying diagonally across her back. She was sweating, glowing, breathing hard.

And then she turned around. Stared across the open space. Stared hard . . . right at the spot where Griffin crouched behind a fern.

"I know you're there." Her voice burned through the darkness. "The question is, how many of you there are, and whether you think you can actually stop me."

True to Keko, she did not back into the shadows out of sight, but instead came right up to the cliff edge—facing her unknown hunter. The dark hid the fine details of her face, but he could picture her challenging expression, her intense glower.

Griffin pushed aside another fern frond and showed himself. "It's me," he said, echoing the simple declaration she'd given him just days ago on the phone. "Just me."

A terrible pause, filled with silence and the consistent, pleasurable thrum of her signature. He'd never forgotten its song, the way it meshed so well with his mind. Even when he'd come upon her as a captive in that garage, even when she'd been flaring with rage, he'd been unable to deny how the thing she couldn't even feel herself affected him. It was a layer of connection between them that she'd never truly understand.

Even across the ravine he could almost hear her mind working, considering, questioning, weighing what to do, how to respond.

"Use your fire as light," he said. "I'll prove it."

Another pause, and inside it he feared she'd run. Then he heard her draw a breath—a Chimeran breath, the kind he so vividly remembered Makaha taking—and a gorgeous stream of sunset gold fire spouted from her lips, arcing up and over the ravine, drawing a hot, crackling, radiant line between them. Her mouth closed but the firelight remained, and in that brief moment he witnessed a world of emotion cross that beautiful face he hadn't seen in two months.

Disbelief and joy. Distress and relief. Resolution and doubt. Then shock. Then fear. Then a clench of her jaw and a narrowing of those lava black eyes, and a reappearance of that anger he knew so well.

She always managed to send him tilting.

Griffin stood his ground, the rainbow of fire hitting its apex and starting to come down right for him. This flame arrow could easily kill him. He had no water magic left to fight it. No strength left with which to dodge it. He had nothing but his own courage, his own purpose. He had to believe that Keko, whose people valued physical strength and bravery above all, would not kill a person in such a way.

The fire's heat slicked over his skin, getting closer and closer. He took his own deep breath, standing tall, staring across the void at Keko. Those fathomless eyes, as dark as the deepest part of the ocean, pierced him.

The fire died. Sputtered out mere feet above his head.

Something else charged through the twilight between them. Something old and familiar. Something he'd missed terribly.

He opened his arms. "It's just me, Keko."

It had been only a second of darkness, and he already ached for the vision of her face.

"How'd you find me?"

"I'm Ofarian."

She let out a sound of derision that carried effortlessly through the quiet Hawaiian landscape. "Goddamn bloodhound. Forgot about that."

He doubted that.

"You should be at the Senatus gathering." He remembered that tone of voice from the garage. The low one, the threatening one. The one that made clear she wouldn't be anyone's prey.

So that was it, why she'd followed the Queen's footsteps at this particular time. She'd thought the chief would be gone at the Senatus and wouldn't find her note until he returned. And she never, ever expected Griffin to get involved.

"I was," he said. "Chief and Bane told me you'd disappeared."

Even in the silent darkness, her surprise was evident. "What did they say?"

"Give me some more fire. I want to see your face."

She laughed. "Not a chance."

"You know it's just me."

Tiny, twin flashes of flame sparked and died, and he knew it was annoyance manifesting in her eyes, but that was the extent of light she gave him. "What. Did. They. Say."

He knew what he could tell her, and what he shouldn't. He knew what might make her pause, and what would send her sprinting in the opposite direction so fast he'd never have a prayer of catching up.

He said, "They told me, in secret, about the Fire Source. That you were going after it."

It took her a long, long time to answer. "Did they say why?"

"They didn't have to. Once they told me the story of your Queen, I figured it out."

He hoped that was cryptic enough to satisfy. She didn't supply any more.

"Why are you here, Griffin?"

"I'm going to sit. I'm not going anywhere. Don't run, okay?" He let his knees give out, let his ass hit the dirt. His body released a grateful sigh. If she were to run, this would be the perfect opportunity.

"Why are you here?" she asked again.

"When Chief and Bane told me you'd gone," he slowly replied, thinking through every word, "I knew they wanted me to go after you. To bring you back."

She laughed again, and it sounded like sorrow.

"Let me finish. Chief wants me to bring you back because he doesn't want you to find the Source and rise above him. Bane wants me to find you because you're his sister and he's worried. Your fucking clan laws won't allow him to go after you himself."

It was the truth. At least part of it. The part she might actually buy. There was so much more—and so much he didn't understand himself—but dumping it on her all at once was the absolute wrong way to go, not when she was poised to take off from the starting blocks and he was exhausted. He couldn't mention the Senatus's demands. He couldn't even mention what Aya had told him about the Source's danger. She would despise the first and scoff at the second, thinking that Aya's warning was just a ploy to get her to back off.

He added, "But that's not why *I* came."

She still hadn't moved, her body a dimly lit statue at the lip of the ravine. "So tell me."

The stars were incredible out here, he thought, then realized that he couldn't be sure if the stars he saw were actually those in the sky or the ones sparkling at the edges of his vision.

"I came for you." Fatigue had a way of pulling out the truth.

"No, you didn't."

"You don't deserve this end. Throwing yourself into the Source in the hopes that it might give you a name after your death. It's fucking stupid, Keko. I'm just going to say it."

"And what if that name is 'Queen'?"

"Pride is internal. So is strength. Everything else is bullshit."

"You're such a fucking boy scout, such an Ofarian, always

thinking you know what's best for everyone else. You're not Chimeran. You couldn't possibly understand."

"I understand you want to lead. Remember when you told me that? I understand that your one dream is gone, and you think this is the only way to get it back."

"You don't know anything." It came out sounding sad and detached, which was unnervingly like how she'd sounded when she called him. "Because you were given what you never really wanted. You were just handed my dreams."

Ah, now he got it. She was resentful over what he'd told her in the Utah hotel room about how he'd reluctantly taken the Ofarian leadership.

"That would never appeal to you, though," he said, "just being given something that big. It's not in your blood. You'd still find something to fight for. But this . . . *this*"—he waved a hand around the ravine—"is not worth it."

"You are fighting, too. Don't tell me you aren't. All that stuff you told me about, the class system and such, how much you love your people. That's why you want the Senatus—"

She cut herself off and the warm Hawaiian night suddenly went frigid.

"That's it. The Senatus sent you to stop me."

"No." The denial came too easily.

"Don't fucking lie to me. You have some sort of deal with them, don't you?"

This was going south, fast. To admit to that would only lose her. In more ways than one. To deny it would at least buy him some more time. And that's exactly what he needed.

"You're wrong, Keko. I'm here because I want you on this Earth. I'm here because there are ways other than dying to get what you want."

She said nothing, but he knew she still didn't believe him. Suddenly he was grateful she'd refused him any more light, because he couldn't be certain what his face showed.

"You know why I think you called me?" he asked softly, his voice easily carrying.

"Enlighten me."

"I think it was your way of asking for help."

"Ha!"

"You've never had to ask anyone for help in your entire life.

You don't even know how. But you were lost and sad and you knew I would come for you if I thought you needed me."

"I don't need you."

He could have imagined it, but her voice tripped over the word "need."

"No, maybe you don't need me. But deep down, you're glad I'm here. You're relieved your phone call worked."

She started to back away and his stomach sank. He tried to find his feet but his strength wouldn't let him.

"You're not going to catch me." She toed farther away from the ravine edge, her dusky skin melding with the darkness. "You're not going to stop me. This is my name. This is my fight."

"Keko—"

Then she turned and ran into the night forest. No amount of calling out brought her back.

SEVEN

Time worked differently Within.

Though days had passed Aboveground since the Father had
summoned Aya to report on the Senatus gathering, she just
now carved her way through the earth toward him. He would
never comprehend the time differential. She could show up
next year and he would never know. His existence was beyond
days or nights, his awareness so entirely different from the
humanity Aya would one day adopt.

Arriving at the center of the Children's world, deep in a
secret place below the surface, she expelled her earth form into
the maze of dark tunnels surrounding the Father's home and
assumed her chosen human body. Here, the Father's energy—
his influence and power, and the ancient history of her race—
pulsed up through the floor and radiated out from the walls.

She also felt the completely different kind of human presence trickling down from the world above. It had a magic of
its own, and it got stronger and stronger the more human she
became. It called to her. Begged her to finally release the form
of a Daughter of Earth and become a real-life guardian angel
for their sister race.

Soon. Soon. She had a plan to see through first, and it relied
on Griffin Aames.

Aya walked slowly through the caverns, the walls glowing
with lights emanating from stones placed at intervals. Sons and
Daughters moved about, their rock and mineral bodies making
the whole place seem to undulate. Down one passage she
glimpsed a human man, his pale skin smeared with dirt, his
eyes huge and hollow and bright against the black of his soiled

body. He dragged a small brush over the walls, never missing a spot, cleaning away crumbs and pebbles. Then he bent down, scooped the debris into a bucket, and shuffled off down the shadowed passage to deposit it somewhere unseen.

And so would go his days from now until his cold, lonely death.

That man had chosen to evolve. He'd stood before the Father—as Aya had done not so long ago—and declared he wanted to embrace humanity over being a Son of Earth. The irreversible evolution complete, he'd taken his desired place among the humans. But instead of working to protect and help them, as was his responsibility, he'd caused death. His mind had snapped. He'd attacked a woman, and then took her life.

Sometimes the evolution did that, the permanent shifting between races too much for a single body and mind to handle. When that happened, offending Children were brought Within in their human forms to live out their punishment. What punishment was worse than being denied the very world you'd longed to be a part of?

If the Father discovered that Aya had revealed the Children's true form to the Senatus by unfolding from the earth right in front of them, she could suffer the same fate before she ever discovered the depth of personal connections. Before she knew human touch. Before she knew passion.

Placing her precious human hand to her chest, right over the steady, beautiful thump of her human heart, she drew a shaky, thin human breath and continued on.

At last she came upon the Father's chamber. The great cavern, the very heart of Earth, would make scientists drop to their knees with tears in their eyes. The passageway leading into the cavern ended abruptly, the ground disappearing sharply into nothingness. Utter blackness extended below and above and to either side, but directly in front of her, across the chasm, was the Father.

No longer made of anything human, he'd chosen his form thousands upon thousands of years ago, and this was what he'd become: a great wall of rock, an abstract face in the stone and mineral that rivaled the height of some of Earth's tallest buildings. Though he had no eyes, he saw her. Though he had no ears, he knew what she said. His body was intertwined with this planet, his limbs a system of millions of roots that stretched to all corners of existence. Even now they grew, pushing through ore and rock, forever expanding.

This was what she might have become, should she have chosen to remain a Daughter, and should she live as long as he.

Come forward, Daughter.

No mouth, but his words invaded her mind.

Giant chunks of rock and earth broke free from unseen walls amidst a symphony of cracks and rumbles. The pieces flew in from the shadows—above and below and from both sides—and barreled toward Aya. They slammed together at her feet, fitting into a puzzle to create a hovering walkway that extended out from the passage opening.

She stepped out onto the ragged, mystical bridge and made her way to the end, bare toes just inches from the edge. There she stopped and lifted her face to the awe-inspiring, paralyzing being above. She told him about Keko and the threat to the Fire Source.

Aya spoke English from her human mouth, because the Father understood all forms of Earth's communications. "I debated whether to order Kekona Kalani hunted right then and there, the moment I discovered what she was doing, and the threat to the planet and to its people, but in the end I felt diplomacy was most important."

Why?

"We've spent over a thousand years monitoring Secondary actions, keeping them in our eye and under our thumb. They still need to think we are on their side, and if I ordered a Chimeran put to death we'd end up separated from them, maybe even at war. We wouldn't be able to track how they interacted with humans. We wouldn't ever know if humanity would be threatened before it was too late. I had to make sure they still trusted me and the Children. I had to make them believe I was holding their interests and concerns to heart. That's why I gave them a chance to go after Keko first."

The Father did not respond. He usually didn't, unless he had something specific to say.

"I'll warn Nem," Aya said. "If Keko finds the Source, he has permission to destroy her. If that happens—and I don't think it will—the Senatus will at least understand we made appropriate compromises."

It hurt to say. She used that pain to relay the story in a way that would appease the Father. She used those feelings to lie, lie, lie. All for the benefit of humanity, she told herself.

In truth, Aya had been struggling to find a way to get Griffin accepted into the Senatus, since the air elementals and the Chimerans stood so firmly against him. Griffin believed as she did, that the Secondaries had to find ways to work themselves into the human world—an opinion the Senatus hated. A viewpoint the Father opposed. After all, the Children were tasked with watching over humanity, their sister race. Once Secondaries started arriving on Earth millennia ago, that watchfulness had included keeping magic separate from human life.

Before she chose evolution, before she'd been assigned to the Senatus, Aya had believed as the Father and as all other Children do. Then she'd tasted life Aboveground and felt in her heart there had to be more. Her opinions had changed, but she had to pretend they hadn't.

And now Keko's crazy and reckless act had presented Aya with a previously unseen opportunity.

Griffin would bring Keko back alive. He would keep the Source from causing massive global destruction and he would earn an equal seat among the other elementals. Aya would gain her needed ally on the subject of integration. Griffin would be able to work ideas on her behalf and she would not risk punishment Within.

It was precarious. But it was worth the chance.

Aya spun through the earth, a drill made of magic and life, churning her way through the plates below the Atlantic Ocean. If she were Ofarian she could travel by water, but the Children were only tied to solid earth and what grew out of it, no more. It was the reason they were charged with guarding the Fire Source but could not touch or manipulate it.

Still Within, she located her island and arrowed northeast toward it. Her island. Her secret, special place in the human world.

As she breached the surface and burst out from the rock and dirt, even the weakest rays of the sun sent a welcome warmth cascading over her body. She unfolded from the ground as a mound of limestone. Her limbs rolled out and away in miniature avalanches, her fingers extending from stacks of pebbles. Lumbering to her stony feet, she pushed humanity into her extremities, lifting her head, feeling the first brush of hair over her shoulders.

For the first time ever, the transformation was painful.

Here on the edge of the world, standing on a windswept cliff on the northwest coastline of Ireland's Aran Islands, Aya felt the sting of the cold, the slice of hard, sporadic rain. She ripped a thin sheet of limestone from the cliff face and whipped it around her naked body, the rock moving according to how she commanded—like fine, beaded fabric—its protection from the elements stemming from her power.

The ocean below was a churning mass of hard gray and bitter anger, the air salty. She drew in breath after breath and waited.

Soon, after her evolution was complete, she wouldn't be able to just appear here, where she valued the pristine natural beauty and the utter solitude. She would have to take an airplane, and then a train, and then a ferry. She'd have to drive a car to find this general area, and then hike on her two feet to this very specific place.

She wondered if she would actually ever do that, or if this spot would become nothing more than a wish and a memory. For now, however, she would keep these moments of freedom and sparse sun and clean air.

The ground suddenly rumbled and she lost her balance. One arm shot out to grab at the limestone, and her fingers shifted form to meld with the stone and keep her from pitching over the edge into the water below. She held fast, her head swiveling to her left, toward the source of the rumbling.

Six feet away, the cliff face bulged outward. A gray, blocky leg kicked free, a heavy limestone foot coming down. A second leg followed. Then a torso peeled away, making the new arrival at least a foot taller than she was. The arms were the last to form, thicker than hers, decidedly masculine.

Nem's human body came to him extremely quickly, and when his facial features smoothed out they retained none of the strain Aya now carried after her transformation. His skin didn't have a more natural hue yet, still desperately clinging to the burnished silver-gray from which he'd just emerged. His hair made high, faint tinkling sounds as the shining white strands brushed together in the wind. It would be a year or so before he appeared human enough to walk among them. He had, after all, only recently chosen to evolve.

Nem looked down at himself, watching his human body fill out its shape with an equal mix of curiosity, awe, and disapproval. The last thing to fully transform was his right arm. It shifted from stone to plant, the length of it a thick green stem, his palm the great black circle forming the center of a sunflower. Long, delicate yellow petals shot out from his palm. Then the wind grabbed and ripped free those petals, leaving only five, which became his fingers.

A sunflower petal tore off and slapped against the cliff face, becoming lodged in a crevice. The others whipped away to Aran Island places unknown or to bob on the undulating waves below.

Nem flexed his new fingers, making a concerned face at the stiff movements.

"You still do that?" she asked, releasing her rock hand from the limestone. "With the sunflower?"

"It helps the transition," he replied, flipping gold and silver eyes up to hers. "It keeps me calm. It releases some doubt."

She sighed, her eyes briefly closing. "I didn't ask you to choose evolution."

He looked bewildered, but since he'd only just started to experience basic human emotions, he wouldn't even understand what he was feeling while in this body. Not for a while yet. "But we're to be mated."

"We *were* to be mated. That was before I made my choice."

He frowned at the arm that had been the sunflower. One finger pressed to the bare skin on his chest, then slid down over his belly. She'd done that, too, back in the beginning. Back when her body was new and strange.

Not having control over his emotions yet made them all readily available and apparent, playing in vibrant color across his face. "I evolved to have you. I did this so that our Son or Daughter would have our combined strength and guard the Source after I am human."

"I can't give you an heir anymore. I'm too far along for that. My body can no longer carry a Child of Earth." And until their bodies were fully compatible again—human to human, not human to Child—mating was out of the question. She was secretly glad for the time and space that disconnect would put between them, because now that she was more human than Child, she was beginning to understand what it meant to want someone else for something other than mating.

"The Source needs a guardian after my evolution." His voice was rising, his frustration growing, his confusion and inability to fully understand the differences between the worlds heightening the stress of everything.

"Then you need to find another Daughter as mate. Quickly." To Aya, the whole thing was very sensible.

"But I want you!"

The sharp shout bounced off the rock behind her and came back to hit her in the ears a second time. She jumped. Instantly a look of horror crossed his face, followed by a tense gathering of the skin between his eyebrows.

"I'm sorry," he said. "I feel like that was inappropriate somehow."

His fists uncoiled from where they'd gathered at his sides. The aggressive forward tilt of his torso pulled back. His wild eyes searched the ground at her feet.

Aya exhaled, admittedly a little scared, a little thrown. When she'd been at Nem's stage, she remembered screaming in the confines of her home Within. Screaming so no other Child would hear. It was only when she went Aboveground that she didn't have that panic or fear. That's how she'd known she'd made the right choice. Nem, however . . .

He straightened his shoulders, calmed himself. "Why did you ask me to come here? It's a long way from where I ought to be."

She was grateful for the return to matters at hand. "I know, but I couldn't go to Hawaii. If she saw me . . . if he sensed me . . ."

At Nem's utterly confused look, she stepped closer, meaning only to comfort. She caught a glimpse of the magnificent-looking human he would become, and she stopped her advance, because that felt entirely *wrong* to think.

"The Source may be compromised," she said.

Humanity escaped him. Just vanished. His skin crackled

and went solid. Limestone pushed out of his skin, then he seemed to realize what had just happened and he snatched back the human form.

"You called me *away* from the Source to tell me this?" He started to twitch, to pace.

"As I said, I can't go there. Too much is at risk."

She told him everything that had happened at the Senatus—everything but her own agenda.

"You *let* her go after the Source." His voice was very dark. "When you know what damage she could cause."

Aya folded her hands in front of her, the short cloak of pebbles swinging around her body. "No. I made a strategic move to keep our position solid within the Senatus. I have every confidence in your ability to protect what your line has always kept safe."

Please believe me, she silently begged.

Nem planted his hands on his hips. "Are you as confident in this Ofarian? That he'll capture her before she finds it?"

Aya shrugged. "Does it matter? We have the advantage and the victor's spoils, no matter the outcome."

He started to shift on his feet and she knew he longed to dive back into the earth. Maybe he wouldn't recognize what showed on his face just then, but she knew very well what it was.

Intent to harm. Murder.

She came forward to calm his frenetic movements with a hand to his arm. He stopped instantly, his eyes snapping to the place where they touched, human skin to human skin. The first time for him, likely. The second for her, after a brief moment of contact from Keko over a year ago. His dewy lips dropped open and he swayed on his feet. Aya removed her hand.

"I need you to promise me," she said, "that you will not go after Keko before she reaches the Source."

"What?"

"I need you to promise me that you will let this play out, that you will let Griffin do what he must do. If he fails, if Keko finds the Source, then she is yours, but not until then. I need your word. I need you to understand what I'm asking. *That's* why I called you here."

Nem inched away until his back struck the limestone. His skin started to shift on its own, silver-white cracks smearing over his shoulders and around his waist.

"You've changed," he said.

"That's what happens when you evolve."

"I didn't mean your body." As he said it, his gaze swept from her face, over her shoulders, and down her torso. His mouth slackened when he came to her breasts. His brow furrowed when his gaze skimmed over her bare legs and the covered junction between them.

She didn't quite understand her revulsion, only that she didn't care for this very human reaction from a man who wasn't entirely one yet. It made her feel uncomfortable. Unwelcome. Unsafe.

She knew of human mating, how it was done, the physical aspects of it. But Nem knew nothing, only what his human body was telling him. She didn't want that with him. Not one bit.

With a gasp, Nem glanced down at himself, down to the place between his own legs. Uncertainty twisted his features. Then anger. His head snapped up and he pinned her with a severe, glittering stare.

"I didn't mean your body," he repeated. "I meant your mind. What's happened?"

She started to panic and desperately tried to maintain her composure. "I don't know what you mean."

He pulled himself away from the cliff with a hard *clink* of broken rock and a dusty shower of pebbles. "Is it that air elemental?"

Her stomach felt funny. "What?" And her voice sounded odd. Too breathy, too scared. Too out of her control.

Nem advanced another step, but she couldn't back up or else she'd go over the cliff and into the waves. Oxygen dwindled, like she was trapped Within again.

"That's what I thought," he said, nodding.

Aya tried desperately to recover. "What air elemental? What are you talking about?"

"The new one the premier brought in recently to wipe the minds of humans. The man with the curly hair."

The only way Nem could possibly know about that particular air elemental was if Nem had been in Canada last month when the premier had summoned Aya to his race's compound.

Now it was her turn to advance, anger and fear roiling through her body. "You *followed* me? To a private meeting with the Senatus premier? The Father will have you locked Within—"

"You won't tell him." Nem's voice dropped, and she'd never heard him sound so utterly human. "Because then I will tell him how you revealed yourself to the Senatus. How you compromised the secrecy of our entire race. I'll bet you didn't mention that part to the Father when you told him the rest. You made the mistake of telling me."

"You wouldn't."

"And then I will tell him that once you become human, you will not be interested in mating with another human, but a Secondary, an air elemental. That, above anything, will see you trapped Within until you wither and die as flesh and not of earth. Alone."

Aya's entire body shook with a rage and frustration that was completely new to her human mind.

She tried to fight it, but that air elemental's face stabbed into her vision. His haunted, distant pale blue eyes, the hair Nem described . . . She'd only seen him that once, over a month ago, but the memory taunted her with a need and want she didn't know how to hide or react to.

She thought she knew this new world. She thought she knew how to live within it. A Son of Earth had proved her wrong.

"It seems," Nem said, turning away and speaking to her over one broad shoulder, "that for once in our existence, we have reached a mutual understanding."

He punched a fist into the limestone, half his arm instantly disappearing. Then he stepped through the cliff face, the earth swallowing him easily, gracefully, to return to the island place Aya could not go.

EIGHT

Hiking on three hours' sleep. What rest Keko didn't get was counterbalanced by the constant reminder that Griffin Aames was on her tail.

Griffin. Who had come to the Big Island to stop her.

Another shudder passed through her body, and it was like food or water, giving her energy. Nothing like a good, angry chase to push her onward.

Nothing like the knowledge that the Queen's prayer was so close.

Her pace was slower than it had been yesterday, but it was still a good one. She was still moving. When she'd left him, Griffin had been absolutely wiped. Even in the darkness, even though he was trying his best to hide it, she'd seen the steep slant of his shoulders, and heard the wheeze and fatigue in his voice. He'd probably passed out on that ridge last night. But as soon as he woke up, he'd cross the ravine and hunt her all over again. She would be stupid to discount someone of his determination and focus.

She had to keep moving.

She ate the last of her granola bars as she trudged on. She was desperate for water, but she didn't want to backtrack to the stream she'd crossed a few hours ago. Although backtracking could possibly throw Griffin off, her time and resources were running out. She would press on. She was fire, after all, and fire didn't need water.

She hadn't been fooled by anything Griffin said to her—did he really think she believed he was here for any reason other than the Senatus? For anyone but himself?

He, however, had been fooled by the chief.

It made sense Chief would send Griffin after her. If Keko did find the Source and survive, if she brought back the cure, she would be venerated above the Big Island *ali'i* and all the other island chiefs. She'd be above the Queen. Of course Chief wanted Keko stopped before that could happen. He had other Chimerans covering his weakened ass, after all, and could still live as he had been.

Griffin could go on thinking she was doing this solely for the glory. That was fine by her. He already thought her hot-headed and stubborn and brash. As long as he never knew the real reason. As long as he never found out about the wasting disease. The head Ofarian could never discover a weak link in the Chimeran race.

Bane, though . . . Bane's motives puzzled her. Messed with her mind. Made her heart feel oddly tight.

There was no room in Chimeran society for familial ties once a person began challenging others to establish their place in the ranks. Bane and Keko had long since ceased being brother and sister, even before she'd ever beaten him for the title of general. So what the hell was he doing? Why would he ask Griffin to find her and bring her home safe? Unless Griffin had misread him.

Unless Griffin was lying. Again.

Both were possible. Neither changed her mind.

The ground was soft from rainfall this close to Hilo. It was pointless to try to keep dry. The damp just kept coming. She was starting to miss the scent of the air within the valley, the smoke and smell of the erupting Kīlauea volcano that occasionally drifted to them.

Thick clouds pushed quickly inland, a line of clarity drawn just off the coast where it was tauntingly sunny and dry. She changed her route, finally angling toward the water. There, a little farther northwest on the Hamakua Coast, she would start to look for the geographical markers the Queen's lover had described. She tried not to worry that the landscape had changed too much.

Movement behind her. A shuffle of leaves, a crack of branches. Small but noticeable, odd and out of place. She whirled.

A flash of dark in the distance. A man sliding behind a tree. Griffin.

She ran.

Didn't matter how tired she was. Didn't matter her tongue was sticking to the roof of her mouth. She ran, sprinting through the underbrush and around the hills. She ran, away from the man who would stop her from doing the one good thing in her life she was meant to do. She could hear him pursuing fast. He called her name more than once, and then all she heard was the pound of her bare feet on the uneven earth and the slap of her pack against her back.

She zigzagged, trying to throw him off. The curves around the hills were wide and she followed them left and right instead of taking a straight line that would show Griffin her path. It seemed to be working, because the sound of his pursuit died off. Her breath sawed in and out of her lungs. If she was tired, then she must have seriously worn down the Ofarian.

A few more sprinted steps to prove she'd lost him, and then she finally slowed down. Finally let herself jog. A dormant volcano rose straight ahead, its cone shape now covered in green. She'd head that way and not stop running until night. It was in the opposite direction from where she needed to be, but tomorrow she'd veer back to the water and get her bearings. Tomorrow she'd—

A hard, giant something slammed into her from the right side.

She had no time to react. Just barely enough seconds to whip her head around to make out Griffin's snarl so close to her face. Then his arms and legs clamped around her, snatching her feet from the ground and tossing her up and over his body. Together they sailed through the damp air.

She hit the dirt and bounced, rolling a little uphill, hitting a massive root, then tumbling back down. The momentum let her find her feet again, and she whirled to see Griffin also recovering from the impact, transforming his fall into a shoulder roll, and then popping into a crouch.

Keko dug deep, drew a Chimeran breath, and spit fire into her hand. Let it burn and crackle and glow with its own life. As he eyed her weapon, she scanned the desolate, windy surroundings, searching for other Secondaries—his backup. No one visible, but she could make out his path, tracing how he'd managed to cut her off. She'd zigged and zagged too much and he'd merely taken the shortest distance between points A and B. A dumb mistake.

Returning her focus to the Ofarian, she noticed with satisfaction the heaving of his chest. He wore no shirt, just a lightweight vest with pockets and zippers.

At his side, one of his hands flexed and curled. Like he was getting ready to arm himself with his own magic.

"I'm ready," she said, finding a firm stance, giving the fire a good burst of flame. "Not like Makaha. And I won't miss."

He didn't flinch at mention of the man he'd maimed. "I'm not here to fight you."

She nudged her chin in the direction from which he'd attacked her. "Where are the rest of them? Are they on their way, now that you've found me?"

He started to raise his hands, but she snapped out a sword of flame in warning and he lowered them.

"I told you," he said. "There are no others."

"I can think and run at the same time, and I came to the conclusion that you're lying. The only reason you'd be here is for the Senatus."

"Or you." His response came so quickly.

"Or the Senatus," she repeated.

He shook his head at the ground, his hands resting on his hips. His body was the complete opposite of hers: loose and unafraid. Unaffected. She refused to be taken in by that. He wasn't going to get her to lower her guard.

"Three years," he said to the dirt. His dark hair was shiny with sweat and rain.

Then those brown eyes flipped up to hers under the canopy of his furrowed brow. That look—the way *he* looked—made her suck in a breath. Made her fire actually falter on her fingers.

"Three years you had my phone number and you never called. I thought you hated me, and when I first saw you in that garage in Colorado I thought I'd been right. And then there was something else. I saw the truth deep in your eyes. I saw in your eyes what I heard in your voice when you finally did call me days ago. That, Keko, *that* is why I'm here."

For a split second she was tempted to let the fire go. Instead she touched her palms together as if in Primary prayer, spreading the flame between her hands.

Griffin watched her, but not in fear. Respect maybe, but not fear. She didn't know which she wanted more.

He said, "You think all you're worth is what you can prove to others. I came after you to tell you that I think you're worth much more."

"This is all I have left."

"Bullshit." Griffin lifted his arms, let them slap to his sides. "Do I look like I came from the Senatus? Wouldn't I have an army behind me?"

She peered over his shoulder again. Still no movement among the trees. No shapes of soldiers.

"If they wanted you," he said, "they'd come for you. Make no mistake about that. They wouldn't send just me. Think about it."

She did, and then she lowered one arm, letting the flame on it die a green death.

"I'm thirsty," he added with more than a little exasperation. "Can I have a drink?"

Her throat tightened in a similar want. She licked her lips.

"I'll need magic," he said, then waited for her to give a shallow nod of permission.

The Ofarian language was still as gorgeous as she remembered, all flowing words that ended too soon. She cringed, hating this reaction. Despising even more how she watched with wonder him using his magic.

The air around his head started to dim and shimmer and coalesce. He was taking moisture from it. Whipping it together to form droplets, churning it into a little spout high above the ground and aiming it toward his mouth. Dropping back his head and opening his mouth, the floating funnel of glistening water poured itself inside. It trickled out of the seam of his lips and trailed down his chin. He wiped his mouth with the back of his hand.

"I'm worried about you," he said. "I'm already tired of this chase. I'm tired of being scared for you."

"You're not scared."

She stared hungrily at the empty space in the air where the water had been.

"I'm not?" His thick eyebrows lifted. "I left my people for the first time ever and crossed an ocean to talk you down from the ledge, knowing I'm the only one who could do it. There's a tad bit of fear there, yeah."

That didn't affect her. Nope. Not at all. "You can't stop me. You'll try, but it won't work."

He threw a pointed glance at her hand. The one she thought still owned fire. The one that no longer did.

Her lips parted, ready to take in another Chimeran breath.

Griffin came closer, his shoes silent on the ground, his presence consuming. "Are you thirsty?"

She narrowed her eyes in suspicion, forgetting to rekindle the fire at the mention of a drink.

"It's a simple question, Keko. No underlying objective."

So why was he staring at her mouth?

"There's a stream—" she began, but Ofarian words overlapped hers. That beautiful water language drowning her out. Pulling her under.

Griffin's image went blurry as the air in front of her swirled, then shifted to a sheet of undulating water hovering at eye level. It rolled into itself, forming a long, liquid thread that danced and glistened before her. The sight of it made her stomach tighten and her throat clench in need.

"Open wide," he murmured.

Standing at least six feet away, after a long chase across brutally uneven Hawaiian land, and he still had the energy to tilt the magic water toward her. Still had the ability to do things to her with his voice. It was just water, but it was also so much more. There was so much in his offer. So much in her acceptance.

She wanted to fight her thirst—told herself to fight it. The next stream was somewhere around here, and this was the windward side of the Big Island where rain was aplenty, but in the end her body's need won out. The weakness she'd been ignoring all morning craved attention. Maybe fire didn't need water, but Keko's body did.

Keeping watchful eyes on Griffin, she parted her lips. Tilted back her head. When the first cool drops hit her tongue, her eyelids started to flutter and she had to force them open. She gulped down the water, lifting her hands below her chin to cup and drink even more.

The way Griffin watched her reminded her of their very first meeting that day in the airport parking garage. Outward watchfulness, a carefully constructed shell that hid a machine of assessment and calculation and . . . desire.

She quickly severed that line of thought, snapping her jaw shut against the water. It splashed on her chin and chest and she stepped away, almost tripping on a root in her rush.

"Better?"

It had been years since she'd heard that tone in his voice. That ravaged, hoarse quality he'd used when he told her he'd never stop wanting her.

She shook her head, rattling out her anger and wits from deep inside, pushing them to the forefront. She would not be swayed by whatever it was Griffin Aames was trying to use on her. Her purpose was far, far more important than sex. Greater than any lovers' past.

"Yeah." She would not say thank you. "This was not a victory."

He let out a half laugh and shoved a hand into his short hair. Whenever he'd met with the Senatus during that week they'd spent together, he'd arrived around the bonfire carefully groomed. Even when he'd come to "rescue" her in Colorado, wearing full-on soldier gear and a scowl, he'd looked like a million dollars. Now, with that vest pulled over his bare chest, sweat and rain and streaks of dirt making lines across his olive skin, his hair poking up at overlapping angles . . . he looked like a billion.

"Never claimed any victory," he said. "You just looked thirsty."

She glanced in the direction of where she believed the Queen's prayer to be hidden. "I'm going now."

Lips pursed, hands coming to those slim hips, he nodded. "And I'm following."

She released a growl of frustration to the billowing sky.

"You know I will, Keko."

Yes, she did know. Her panic was a living thing now, swimming throughout her body, slashing at her gut, pulling out her worry. Griffin *couldn't* follow her. She couldn't risk him ever finding out about the Chimeran disease, not when he was shadowboxing, looking for the perfect way into the Senatus. Not when it put her people at a serious disadvantage against his.

She couldn't risk being this close to him again, not when her heart and soul were so raw, when she was at her lowest point.

But . . . this was her land. Maybe if she let him get a little closer—if she let him think she'd given in, that she was softening to him, willing to be swayed—he'd get sloppy. Then she'd lose him so fast he'd never be able to track her.

She tightened the strap of her pack that ran diagonally between her breasts. "I'm not slowing down for you."

"Don't expect you to."

And then he smiled.

Griffin woke up because of the warmth on his face. When he'd fallen asleep stretched out on the wet grass, legs crossed at the ankles, hands tucked into his armpits, he'd been cold but determined to suck it up. Unwilling to give Keko any sort of ammunition against him.

As his eyes cracked open, he stared into the dancing flames of a small fire built only a few feet away. Its heat coated his pebbled skin and he resisted groaning in relief. On the other side of the fire, just beyond its circle of light, was Keko.

She sat on her heels, her back to him, head bowed toward the hands in her lap. Perfectly still. The fire and her presence confused him.

She easily could have taken off while he slept. She'd been the first to fall into sleep, her body tucked into a nest of tree roots, curled away from his sight. Only when he knew she was out did he let himself rest, knowing he could wake himself up after a few hours. And here she still was.

Silently, he came up to his elbows.

She hadn't spoken to him all day as she'd set a blistering pace northwest toward the coast. But then, he hadn't asked anything of her, just stared at her back, trying to figure her out. They'd stopped when the light died.

Now he looked at her back again, only under entirely different circumstances. It was quiet here, calm. Every now and then the fire would flare, sending light to graze her back in a loving stroke. Her white tank top was one of those that looped around her neck, exposing her defined delts and lats. Her long black hair was pulled over one shoulder. She wore jean shorts that made her ass look like a denim-covered heart. The shape of her, motionless for once, was intoxicating.

The way the firelight played across her skin made him think that he could see the magic inside her.

She was whispering something, the hush of it mixing with the breeze. It was another language, spoken so softly, and in a gentle tone that he'd never associated with Kekona Kalani. He longed for Gwen to sit at his side and translate for him. Just as quickly he changed his mind, because this moment of solemnity and peace was so unique and mesmerizing that he wanted to enjoy it for what it was. The puzzle was part of the appeal.

The whispers stopped. Keko's head lifted slightly, her gaze going into the trees and brush.

"Thank you," he said.

She didn't jump, which told him she'd likely already known he was awake. Her hands slid to the ground near her hips and she looked over her shoulder at him, her hair swinging in shadow, nearly touching her waist.

"For the fire," he clarified.

"You were shivering." Flat tone, flat eyes.

He wasn't fooled by her act of generosity. She would still try to lose him. She'd make him think she was acquiescing by having him tag along, maybe even try to seduce him so he'd nearly die from orgasm, go all moony-eyed, and then she'd disappear. He knew those games and wouldn't fall for them. But he didn't have Adine's little toy anymore, and he had to keep her as close as possible for as long as possible. Let her think him dumb and malleable, if in the end it gave him an advantage. If it allowed him to keep a close eye on her.

She slid her legs out from under her body and sat perpendicular to the fire, hands wrapped around her knees. Great stars, her legs were long, that caramel skin such a gorgeous color.

"What were you doing?" he asked.

"Praying."

He didn't know what surprised him more. The fact she'd answered so quickly, or the nature of her answer itself. "To whom?"

She looked confused. "The Queen. Of course."

He sat fully up. "The Queen who died when she found the Source. She became a deity after that."

Her eyes narrowed, her face just above the tips of the flames between them. "Yes."

"So what do you pray for?"

Keko answered slowly. "What people usually do. What do you pray for, Griffin?"

He sat cross-legged. "I don't. We don't. Ofarians give thanks and pay homage to the stars twice a year, but we don't have a god or goddess that looks out for us. We don't have religion."

"Yes, you do."

"Huh?"

"What you just described. It's religion. You believe the stars gave you your magic, right?"

He swept a long, arching look across the sky that was slathered with twinkling lights. "Not exactly. Ofarians came from somewhere out there, somewhere else in the universe. Our magic came from our home world, but it's the stars we can see as we stand here on Earth. So it's the stars we acknowledge."

"You have rituals? Things you do and words you say that you believe make you stronger?"

"Yes."

Her hands left her knees and slapped lightly back down. "It's religion. Yours is less tangible, but no less a faith."

Now this was getting interesting. "Less tangible?"

"Well, yeah. You worship something that doesn't actually give you power, but a substitute."

"We don't 'worship' the stars."

She acted like she hadn't heard him. "But we worship the woman who gathered all the Chimerans together from all across Polynesia and New Zealand and Southeast Asia. She dreamed of the 'land of raging fire' and took us across the sea to find the wellspring of our power. Here. We owe her everything. She was real." Another light slap to her knees. "Tangible."

"Huh. I'm not sure I follow you."

She flicked her eyes skyward. "We came from up there, too, you know."

Griffin couldn't hide his surprise. "No. I didn't know." Still such little knowledge about the other elemental Secondaries. Did it frustrate the other races as much as it frustrated him?

Pulling all her hair into one hand, she started to braid it. "In a meteor shower, the story goes. There was something in what came through the atmosphere, something that affected portions of the population in the South Pacific. Something that mixed with the fire magic that was already present in the Source, and it changed some of the people."

Absolutely fascinating, but Griffin couldn't find his tongue to tell her so.

Now Keko swung her legs around, too, sitting tall on her hips, her white tank top nearly glowing in the night. "That's what the Queen did. She found all of us, scattered over hundreds of places and islands, and brought us together. Taught us how to use our magic. She only wanted what's best for her kind. It's why she searched for the Source in the first place, to make us all stronger." Keko licked her lips. "It's why I've asked her to bless my purpose now."

"And that purpose is . . . ?"

She almost answered. Almost. Keko opened her mouth, took a short breath, then changed her mind, lips pressing shut.

"You want to be a goddess," Griffin said.

Keko's eyes glittered like black diamonds. "No."

"But you want to lead."

"You know I do."

With a hard pang he realized this was the easiest they'd spoken in three years, since the final time they'd been alone in that hotel room. Easiest, but also the hardest, because so much of what he'd told her was lies.

Every time she brought up the Senatus and he had to deny its involvement, he felt an invisible knife gouge into his heart. And every time he had to pluck that knife out and ignore the doubt and pain welling in its place, because Keko's life and safety—and the protection of the Source—was worth more than the truth at this point. He would deal with the truth later. When she could listen and actually *hear* it.

Picking up a stick, he poked at the fire. It flared more than his poking warranted, and when he glanced up he saw the flames reflected in her penetrating eyes.

"So your Queen brought all the Chimerans to these islands. Did they make the great migration with the Primaries, when the other cultures settled here?"

Another burst from the fire, this time without him touching it at all. "Someone read the tourist brochure."

He rolled his eyes. "Is that how it happened? Did you cross the ocean with them?"

Again she lifted her eyes to the stars, as though consulting the objects he still wouldn't name as deity, no matter what she said.

"Is it some sort of secret?" he pressed.

She lowered her chin. Met his eyes. And it took all his strength not to react to the intensity of her direct look, not to let her see the shiver that shook his spine.

"No. I guess not," she said. "No orders or *kapu* or anything like that."

"So . . ."

She fidgeted with something on the ground, shot a blank look into the shadows, looked anywhere but at him. "So, yes. We came over with the Primaries."

Holy shit. He couldn't hide his excitement. "You were at one time integrated with them. Lived together."

"That's what the tales say, yeah."

"What happened?"

"What do you think happened? When we came here, so close to the Source, our magic increased. The Queen became more powerful. We scared them and separated ourselves."

It was a different time then, he told himself.

"They made up stories about us. How we lived in volcanoes and made them spew ash and fire. How we demanded sacrifices. How we held power over the common people."

"Sounds a lot like some of the Hawaiian folktales." Yeah, he'd read the tourist brochures, and anything else on old Hawaii he could get his hands on, once he learned where Keko lived.

She looked half amused and half annoyed. "Or maybe the folktales sound like Chimeran history. Stories and legends are usually made up to try to explain real things that you don't understand."

"True." He frowned in thought. "So explain the Chimeran name. Isn't that Greek?"

She shrugged. "We didn't call ourselves that. The air elementals gave us that name a long, long time ago, and it stuck."

"Ah." He poked at the fire some more, glancing up now and

then to see her face through the flames. The wood was wet, but that didn't matter when a Chimeran controlled the blaze. "You've been separate from Primaries all this time?"

She bobbed her head from side to side. "Not entirely. Here and there some women have left the valley—if they're runners or lookouts or something—and came back pregnant. My grandma was one of them. Japanese athlete, she said. She was sent to the Common House for breaking *kapu*."

Some blood intermingling in her history and she was still as powerful as the rest of her clan. Interesting.

"The Chimerans seem to have held on to a lot of the old ways," he noted.

Her brow wrinkled. "We've had to, being isolated like we are."

He considered her. "Do you agree with that?"

Her bottom lip partly disappeared as she chewed it. "Are you trying to politic me? Out here after you chased me down?"

He sighed. "Just trying to learn about you. Just trying to understand."

"We are who we are, who we've always been. And this is how we'll always be."

I wasn't talking about the others, he wanted to say, but didn't.

"This status code," he said, "this thing Chimerans have about ranking yourselves through fighting and physical proof, has it always been like that?"

Her back stiffened. "I get what you're doing."

"And what is that?"

"Trying to get me to question my own culture. You're still trying to stop me from going after the Source, only this time with words."

No point in denying that. He changed tactics. "So the old ways, way back when you lived with the Primaries, were based on this system of learning how to fight, and then climbing the ranks?"

She started to rip out her braid, fingers like claws scraping through the black strands. "No, that was the Queen's idea. For the Primaries, for the ancient Hawaiians, once you were born into a class you couldn't ever move out of it. She didn't like that. When she divided us from the humans, she changed the rules."

"Which have stayed the same for, what, a thousand years or so?"

She eyed him askance. "Or so."

"And you're okay with that?"

She came to her knees in a quick, smooth movement. Her torso loomed above the points of flame, looking like she was growing out of the fire. Maybe she was. "What are you suggesting? That I just leave my people?"

Brilliant, Keko. Bravo. He opened his arms wide. "If the shoe fits. If you're unhappy, if they've shunned you, you have the right to leave. You don't have to stay there and live with their scorn. You aren't alone anymore. This isn't a thousand years ago. Hell, it isn't even a hundred. You can walk out of that valley and survive in another place."

Like San Francisco.

That thought made a fist and punched him right in the chest. He tried to ignore it, but the ache, the longing, was too great.

"I can't do that," she said, but he saw the conflict marching across her face.

He put every last bit of heartfelt conviction into his voice. "Yes, you can. If you are unhappy, change your life so you can be. If you don't like the way things are with your culture, leave. By sticking around in that valley and living in that shithole of a Common House because someone told you to, you're only reinforcing what you hate. You're giving them power over you, and I can't believe that you, of all people, would allow that. It's a different world out there now, Keko."

Flames flickered in her eyes, but he saw them for what they were: a mask over her sorrow.

"God, you're so arrogant!" she spit. "You think you have all the answers but you don't know anything."

"So tell me!" Now he was on his knees, leaning closer to the heat. "Dying for personal glory is so old-fashioned, so selfish. This isn't the fucking Middle Ages where you run off to slay the dragon to win the prince. If you think I don't have the answers, tell me what I need to know so I understand."

She rocked to her feet and glared down at him. "No."

"Why not?"

Backing away, out of the firelight, she was almost taken by

the darkness before she lowered herself to the ground and stretched out on her side, giving Griffin her back.

He still kneeled there, watching her, until he heard her say, faintly and into the black of night, "Because I don't trust you."

NINE

"How do you know you're heading in the right direction?"

Keko didn't turn around, didn't even slow down, when Griffin's voice came up behind her. His eventual arrival had been expected. She hadn't even bothered to disguise her path.

The first, predawn chirps and squawks of the birds had awakened her. After putting out the fire and taking the ash and smoke back into her body, she'd struck out for the coast without a glance backward.

"Because I know." She threw the words over her shoulder as she sidestepped a fallen tree, half rotten.

She wasn't Ofarian but even she could tell she was approaching a place of legend, as though the old magic was calling to her. Excitement mixed with the fire dancing in her belly.

A landmark from the Queen's lover's tale appeared on her left: a slope of land that looked like a woman's body arched up in ecstasy. She would follow that to a specific ravine and waterfall, splash her way to the ocean, then scrabble around a rock ledge lining the harsh coast to find the Queen's hidden cove and her final prayer.

"The chief told me about a prayer."

Griffin didn't sound out of breath today. He sounded strong, alert. Focused.

"What did he say?" Keko asked, feigning boredom.

"That the Queen carved something into a stone in the evening, and in the morning her lover woke up to find her gone. There're a whole bunch of holes in that story. Care to fill them in for me?"

The thing was, a little part of her wanted to tell him. An

even bigger part of her had actually enjoyed their heated discussion last night about religion. She could hear the skepticism in his voice—about what she was doing and about the Queen. Though he'd been fed lies about her true quest and seemed to be eating them up—as she wanted—his cynicism about the Queen bothered Keko greatly. If he would know nothing else, he would know the correct history about the woman Keko revered, religion or not.

"When the Queen split the Chimerans from the Primaries," she began, "she moved them all around the Big Island trying to find the Source."

Griffin fell into step beside her, but she didn't look over at him. She just kept talking, her eyes on a specific place ahead where the land dropped dramatically down to sea level.

"Wherever she moved she carved prayers into the lava rock, pleading with the Source to reveal itself. It never answered, but she could feel it, dream of it. She tried thousands of different prayers and thousands of different pictures, trying to find one to make the Source acknowledge her."

"What were they of?"

How could he watch her and still walk a straight line? It was disconcerting.

"Mostly people. Chimerans. But she tried animals, objects, ancient symbols from the old world."

Griffin reached up to lift a branch that dangled across their path, but Keko's arm shot out to get there first and lift it up for herself. After he went under and she let the branch snap back, he looked at her with odd amusement. She turned and walked on, making him catch up again.

"The prayers are still there, you know," she said.

"Yeah? Where?"

She shrugged. "All over the island. The state protected all the petroglyphs—that's what the Primaries call them—and they put up signs about how no one really knows what they mean. You can walk right up to them, I heard. In the middle of golf courses and resorts and stuff."

"Wow. But not the one we're headed to."

"No, not the one I'm going to." She let that switch of words sink in, then added, "The others are all in huge groups. This one is alone, hidden. Her final prayer. The one that worked."

"This man, this partner and lover of hers, said that the Queen found the Source, but how did he know that since she was gone when he woke up and he never actually witnessed it? How do *you* know that? How can you be so sure?"

Keko stopped and turned on him. "Because the Source killed her and made her a goddess. It gave her back to us in the way it wanted her to serve."

He made a sound of disbelief that she wanted to snatch from his throat. He kept running his big hand between ear and chin, over and over again. It took him a long time to speak, and when he did she wished he hadn't. "What if she really fell into the water and drowned? What if she tripped down the side of a cliff and snapped her neck at the bottom?"

She narrowed her eyes. "It won't work, what you're trying to do. Trying to discredit my beliefs."

"I'm trying to make you think in another way. I'm not going to stop either, until I know you've given this up." He let out an exasperated sigh. "You're relying too much on faith."

"I would say you don't rely on it enough. I remember that about you. How you know exactly who you'll be talking to before you enter a room, exactly what you're going in there for. You draw road maps between every possibility and make planned detours to get your way. You won't do anything if it's not planned, not considered a million different ways."

"Because I have to. It's my job, my responsibility, to think that way."

With every moment that passed, the closer he seemed to draw to her. He was like a magnet and she couldn't pry herself away. She could feel herself losing focus when she could least afford to. If she couldn't tear herself away from his nearness, she would have to use their proximity. Manipulate it. Bring him in closer to throw him off guard so she could find a window and escape through it.

Keko leaned in, tilted back her head. "I also remember what you're like when you let it all go. I remember, so, so vividly, Griffin, how your walls cracked and you just . . . surrendered."

For a moment she thought he'd gone Chimeran, because the heat that flashed in his eyes was potent and nearly visible.

"It was the first thing I thought when I saw you," she went on. "That I wanted to break that cardboard leader into a million pieces. You were my delicious, forbidden challenge, and I knew I was going to love seeing you crumble. I knew I was going to love seeing you strip down and get into what you truly wanted."

Though the air was moist and Griffin was made of water, his voice sounded scratchy and dry. "And did you love it?"

"You know I did."

She'd forgotten she was supposed to be using this situation and these words for *her* benefit. She'd inadvertently neglected her original intent. Her honesty had just slipped out because he—even after all these years and across their great divide— could still make her crumble, too.

Stupid, stupid.

He shifted on his feet. Just a little movement, but enough to break the spell. Enough for her to nudge herself back a step. Once she'd done that, her whole body turned and she walked away.

He followed a few seconds later. This time he trailed in silence.

When she came to a steep decline peppered with rock and tricky soft ground, and flagged by the telltale landmarks, she pointed. "I'm going down there."

At the bottom trickled a silver line of a stream, twisting its way to the ocean. Follow that, and she'd find the hidden cove sheltering the Queen's prayer.

Griffin came to her side, peering down. "Where you go, I go."

At midday, she finally scrabbled over the last part of the treacherous, jagged lava rock shelf that paralleled the ocean, and stepped into the Queen's hidden place. It was little more than a crevice in the island, a narrow fissure carved by water and wind over millennia, bordered with steep green land, carpeted with vegetation, and divided from the sea by a small stretch of black sand.

This was where she'd find her fate. This was where she'd discover how to heal her people and vault her name into the heavens.

"Are you sure this is the place?" Griffin asked.

All morning he'd never trailed more than a few feet from

her. Not when lowering themselves down to the stream bed. Not when picking their way over the slippery banks. Not when clinging to the rock ledge along the ocean. Now he jumped down from the rock, landing on the sand right next to her.

"You can't feel it?" she said.

The shimmering black sand clung to her toes and the soles of her feet. Peering down the length of the little valley, she found another landmark the story mentioned: a promontory of rock sitting halfway up the cliffside that looked like a face. The nose was worn and the chin shallow, but it was a face. Somewhere below that, in a bed of *pahoehoe* lava rock that rippled like frozen, smooth, black water, the Queen's prayer would be waiting.

"I do feel . . . something," Griffin said, and when she looked over at him, he was frowning. He stared off into the tangle of trees and brush between the beach and the prayer.

She smiled. "See? Told you the—"

He lifted a sharp hand, his eyebrows drawing together as he squinted hard into the valley. "Not the Queen," he whispered, impatient. "A signature. A Secondary signature."

Keko swept a long look over the small valley, the whole thing easily spread out and visible to her eye. The place was untouched, virtually impossible to get to unless you shimmied along the rock ledge like they had. The surf was white and angry against the beach, admitting no boats.

"No one's here," she said.

"That you can see," he murmured cryptically, his eyes flitting from side to side.

"Then let me get what I came here for and we can get the hell out of here fast." She was about to correct herself, to backtrack and say "I" instead of "we," when she realized exactly what he'd revealed, what signatures he was talking about.

Senatus backup. Other Secondaries—more Ofarians? Air elementals?—come to help him keep her away from what she needed to do. Fuck *that*.

"You asshole." She spun and took off running, but not before she saw the shock on his face.

"Keko, wait!"

No way was that happening. She sprinted, her toes digging in the sand, her thighs pushing her off the narrow crescent of beach and onto firmer ground. Her arms swung ahead, slapping aside branches and leaves, making way for her bullet of a body.

Behind her Griffin was shouting her name, crashing after her. He'd have to take her down again, and even that wouldn't stop her. She'd crawl for the prayer with him clinging to her legs, if it came to that.

"Keko, stop!"

Then there was nothing but the wind in her ears, and the sting and scrape of bark and leaves on her skin as she flew. She could see the land just below the face in the rock now, the patch of lava rock tilting toward the ocean that would hold the prayer. She could see the lone, gnarled *Acacia koa* tree pushing up through a crack in the rock, bending over the prayer, its canopy sheltering what had been carved by the Queen's hand.

Almost there. Push. Run. Charge.

The valley rumbled. The ground shook, branches and flowers and hanging fruits vibrating against the wind. She momentarily lost her footing, stumbling to one side before correcting herself. All she could think was: What sort of magic was Griffin loosing at her back? What were his minions doing to try to stop her?

And finally—how would she humiliate them all when she succeeded?

A cloud of birds dislodged itself from a stand of red flowering *ohia* trees off to her right and took to the sky.

Another terrible rumble. Except this time it didn't come from behind. It originated in front of her. Near the prayer. She could see it plainly now, the flat rock of the histories, the thing her people had been forbidden to search for but which was now hers.

The earth was angry, its shaking tossing her from side to side. The Senatus would have to do more than that to get her to turn away. A Chimeran warrior woman was hunting. Didn't they know nothing could ever block her from her quarry?

Distantly, she realized that Griffin had stopped shouting.

Keko reached the edge of the patch of lava rock and launched herself onto it. If she could just touch the prayer, the Queen would protect her. The Queen would bless her.

Thunder emanated from beneath her feet. It wrinkled the

rock, flowing toward the prayer, making the great tree over it shudder and tip.

Then the tree itself moved.

The trunk straightened, lengthening, like a man unfolding to stand from a crouch. The bulk of the tree swiveled toward Keko, its dome of branches becoming tens of waving, threatening leaf-tipped arms. A face shifted among the boughs. A man's face, snarling and menacing, its eyes gold and silver, its amorphous mouth open in a soundless scream.

Keko skidded to a stop, the lava rock tearing into the pads of her feet.

The tree's trunk cracked up the middle, becoming legs that ripped free from the earth, dislodging chunks of rock and sending Keko falling backward. Immediately she scrambled back to her feet.

The treeman was coming for her, his great strides eating up the space between them, each step grinding rock under the tangle of roots that were his feet.

What magic was this? Ancient Hawaiian she'd never heard of? The Queen's? Elemental?

A great bough swung toward her, sweeping away everything in its path. Crackling, crashing, rumbling. The movement was lumbering and heavy, but coming fast.

She drew a Chimeran breath, but the bodily shock of hitting the ground and the narrow window of time only allowed her a shallow inhale. Deep enough to let her release a small stream of flame, though, and she spewed it at the bough coming for her. The tree was wet, however, its bark damp from the ocean proximity and the perpetual rain, its leaves unable to light. That shouldn't have mattered to her magic, which meant he was doing something to parry her flame. The bough arm kept coming at her. Then another joined the attack.

She'd be crushed if she didn't run, so that's exactly what she did. She sprinted toward the edge of the valley, where she could use the steep sides, maybe climb above the tree. Then she'd make her way back to the beach and onto the narrow rock ledge. The treeman was too large and couldn't follow her there.

A terrible screech filled her ears—one that sounded vaguely like her name being pushed through a grinder made of rage and vengeance. Did this thing *know* her?

Keko refused to panic. Chimerans didn't fight this way, didn't run—this was a new enemy, a new challenge—but she would find a way to defeat it, to get around it. There was no chance, however, to stay still enough to catch her breath. No chance to dig for her fire and let out enough to burn away and eat through the damp of the tree and whatever magic it was using. Fire knocked against the inside of her chest, begging to be let out. To do what it was meant to do.

For the first time ever, she wished Chimerans had been taught ways to defend themselves other than with fire and fists.

A powerful gust of air came at her back, the suck of forces that told her another bough arm was coming her way. The treeman had closed the distance between them.

"Keko! Keko!"

A man's voice this time. A voice she knew. A voice that created more conflict than ease.

She couldn't see Griffin but she could hear him drawing closer, the sound of her name getting louder. He was coming for her like the treeman. Working together? An attack from both sides? This awful creature was part of Griffin's larger plan, maybe. A last-ditch effort to turn her away. His chase and his words had failed, so he'd summoned this thing. Or maybe it was a soldier of the Senatus, sent for her because Griffin had failed. Who knew what sort of magic the premier had access to? And Chief had hid so much from her, why not this?

The great splinter of tree boughs filled her ears and she knew it was close.

She veered to one side, changing course, trying to throw off the treeman, but his bough caught her in the back of her left shoulder, tearing across her skin, making her howl with pain. Sending her body airborne.

She flipped midair and hit the ground hard, skidding. Dirt and sticks wedged into what she knew to be a bad laceration across her upper back and shoulder. Gritting her teeth against the pain, she rolled to her side. The valley winked, and she could vaguely make out Griffin's shape through the vegetation, sprinting toward her, a giant knife clutched in his hand. A two-pronged attack then.

It only made her more pissed off.

She would *not* lay eyes on the Queen's prayer only to be

destroyed by a magic being that could be leveled if only she could get enough fire. She would *not* fail her people because Griffin Aames wanted to sit gabbing with other elementals around a campfire in the middle of nowhere.

Biting back the agony, she flipped onto her raw back. Her knee felt wrenched, too, though she hadn't known when that had happened. With her back pressed to the ground, she looked up. The treeman—massive and trembling with rage, that strange face among the leaves twisted in determination—loomed over her. He looked more man now, each terrible limb delineated in powerful muscles made of razorblade bark. Every bough arm pulled back, some ends making fists, others sharpened into spear-like points. He was gathering his strength, intent on smashing her, pulverizing her into the earth.

If she was going down, she was going down with her fire.

And she'd take Griffin with her, because she could plainly see him now. He charged through the last barrier of brush. Toward her. Mouth open in soundless fury. Blade shining in the blast of sunlight that shot down from the parting clouds.

Keko found her breath, took control of her heaving chest, and inhaled. Deep and long, the kind of breath that tasted of death. Fire magic built inside and shot up her throat. It dared her to use it. Despite the chaos, despite the danger, it brought her peace.

Oh, Griffin, she thought in the moment the fire touched her tongue and she scrambled to her feet. *For a few days we were magical.*

The boughs with their clubs and spears were descending, descending toward her.

She brought her hand to her mouth and fed her palm fire. Dropped her arm back to throw.

Griffin planted a foot on a chunk of tilted lava rock and launched himself off it. His body soared, making an arc. His face twisted with murderous intent, the long knife in his fist.

She released the fireball, arm and shoulder muscles screaming from the injury and the force of her pitch. Both targets were in range and scope: Ofarian and treeman. They would feel the power of her burning weapon.

Griffin's body hit the apex of its curve and came down. Only not on her. Not anywhere near her.

He slammed into one of the legs of the treeman high up on

the thigh, and held on in a three-limb clutch. The arm with the knife stabbed downward, piercing the bark that was somehow now half flesh. The treeman howled, boughs pulling up.

It was too late. Too late to realize that Griffin was helping her. The fire had already left her hands and was catapulting toward the treeman's leg. Toward Griffin.

"Griffin!" she screamed.

He was holding on to the knife handle with both hands, the blade dragging down and through the treeman's strange flesh, when he looked up and saw what was coming for him.

The fireball hit.

Griffin fell. His body struck the ground, crumpling at the feet of the treeman. The stink of burned hair filled the air.

One of the treeman's boughs shaped into a human hand as it plucked out the knife from its thigh. A piercing wail—a shriek not born in this world but delivered through the mouth of one of its strange, awful creatures—drowned out all other sound.

The treeman was shuddering, stiffening. Its movements turned jerky and rigid as the human parts of him surrendered to the tree. It bent forward, cracking branches pressed to the leg that bled a mixture of red human blood and a clear, viscous substance. Its screams faded, trickling out through the tips of each leaf.

Keko could *see* the human part of him leaving the tree, moving down from the top of the canopy as though the man were being sucked into the ground through the trunk. The legs jammed back together, the trunk bulging outward as the tree expelled the inhabiting humanity into the dirt. The roots shivered, clamping to the ground, burrowing down.

With a final sigh, the treeman went perfectly still. It was no longer any sort of a man, but just a tree. A gnarled, twisted *Acacia koa* tree half bent into itself, with a pale, bulbous, jagged scar running down the right side of its trunk.

Griffin lay sprawled at its base.

Worry and panic overtook Keko. But it was the anger and confusion that set her feet to the earth, sprinting over to him.

He lay on his back, heels kicking into the ground, hands covering one half of his face. The one visible eye was squeezed tightly shut. He bared his teeth, sounds of pain leaking out from his throat.

In a terrible flash she was reminded of the story of the Ofarian man who'd wandered into the Chimeran valley a quarter century earlier. How her people had set him aflame and sent him back to the mainland permanently scarred to serve as a warning. A living, breathing KEEP OUT sign.

Brave Queen, what had she done?

She hated this concern, this fear over having injured someone. It was such a foreign feeling and it completely threw her off guard. Chimerans weren't supposed to question their victories. They were just supposed to have them.

Then she finally noticed the thin but constant stream of water that poured out from under Griffin's hands. It trickled over his temple and ear and right cheek. The sounds of his pain lessened, his lips closing over his grimace, the tension in his body slackening. Finally his visible eye opened, blinking up at her. He peeled away his hands.

The water had washed away the dirt on one half of his face. He had been struck, but not full-on as she'd pictured or feared. The flames had grazed a bit of his temple, taking a small section of hair near his ear. There was some blood and bubbling of skin, too. He'd scar, but the quick application of water had helped, and the whole thing was much, much smaller than his entire face melting off, as she'd imagined.

"Griffin . . ." She had absolutely no idea how to react. How to deal with or show the relief and shock and turmoil that raced through her. She fell to her knees a safe distance away—because her legs simply gave out and because she didn't want to be close enough to touch him. "What the *hell* . . ."

He struggled to his elbows first, then pushed up to sitting, his long legs bowed out in front of him. He tested the tender, oozing spot on his head and looked up at her from under his lashes. "Good thing I wasn't expecting a thank you."

She pressed the heels of her hands to her eyes. She was just so . . . confused.

"Hey," he said. "Are you okay? Are you hurt?"

The hands came away. "Huh?" Dimly, she thought that maybe she had been injured in the fight, but nothing could get past the image of Griffin attacking the treeman in her head.

He eyed her questioningly, and she ignored him, turning instead to look at the bent and inert *Acacia*.

"What was that thing?"

"My best guess?" he said haltingly. "A Child of Earth."

Her head whipped back around, and she could feel her stupid hands trembling from one shock after another, coming like blows to her body. "You think . . . you mean . . . that was *Aya?*"

No. No way. She'd spent many hours talking with the small woman with the golden skin and wispy white hair, and those sparkling green eyes that owned both unimaginable depth and attractive innocence. Keko had actually enjoyed those moments, speaking with someone on a level that did not involve Chimeran politics or sexual desire. She had felt the kindle of friendship, of caring and interest on an entirely new level, and she would have sworn that Aya had felt the same.

"No." Griffin, too, frowned at the tree. "I don't think that was her."

Keko pressed fingers to her throbbing forehead. "You must be right. I *hope* you're right. It felt male to me."

"It did to me, too." A dark look swept over him that spoke of anger, which didn't make much sense. None of this did.

A distinct, thudding pain began in Keko's shoulder and started to shoot down and across her back, but she had no time for it. No brain space left to address it. "I didn't know they could do that, change themselves. In all my years at the Senatus, I've never seen that. And I've only ever seen Aya."

Griffin's face was blank. Too blank.

"Have you?" she asked.

"I saw . . . something similar."

"From Aya?" Keko rocked to her feet and the world gave a little lurch. "Is that how this happened? You were at the Senatus and saw her do something similar? And then you two banded together to come after me? Was that treeman part of—"

Her body and head felt strange. Pockets of numbness and pain traded places, sending her mind reeling and making her tongue feel thick.

"That's not what happened—Keko?" A familiar face appeared before her. Concerned dark eyes capped by straight, dominant eyebrows. "Are you okay?"

Why couldn't she see Griffin clearly? Why did he sound so far away?

"Keko?"

The sky tilted, turning on its side. Weird. And then she was flying. No, not flying. Falling. Falling from where she'd just shot up into the clouds. She toppled sideways, knowing she was about to hit the ground but unable to stop herself.

Something caught her, and it wasn't lava rock or wet Hawaiian sand. She was cradled on her side, the embrace around her both firm and kind, dusty and sticky. Grit scraped against her legs and side, and she was surrounded by a scent that was decadently familiar.

"Shit. Shit, shit, shit." A voice in her ear. A voice she'd heard in her dreams many, many times.

He was touching the skin on her shoulder and back in places just outside the borders of her pain. Those hands she knew, too.

"Keko, stay with me. Can I get you to sit up?"

He jostled her body, pulling her up as she tried to find her core muscles to help him. She couldn't do it on her own, couldn't remain upright no matter how hard she gave herself a warrior's order. Griffin propped her uninjured shoulder against his chest. More swearing, but she didn't mind because it gave her something to focus on.

The sound of a zipper, and then a rustle of fabric. A distinctive *gloop* of packaged liquid, and then a rip of plastic.

An icy, breathtaking, unbelievable sensation hit the wound on her back. It spread out, dug in. It was water, she realized, but also something more. Water and sparkling magic, making its way into her body.

His voice again, murmuring words in that language she loved.

She started to feel stronger in slow increments, and with that strength came recognition and memory. This man had come here to stop her from saving her people. She twitched, tried to pull away, but she was still weak and he held her fast.

Then his face appeared in front of hers. That beautiful, beautiful face of a man concerned. Frightened and determined. *That* was the face she knew.

He was not her enemy, but a healer. He was healing her fire body with his water.

As power and ability slowly marched its way back into her muscles and bones and blood, she couldn't break her stare from his face. Couldn't look away as visible relief softened his features and full awareness bloomed inside her mind.

He exhaled so deeply his chest went concave. "You're back. You scared me."

His hand pulled away from her shoulder and when he brought it around to her front she saw what he held in his palm: a foggy bubble of magicked water that wobbled between his fingers. With easy movement, he set the bubble on the earth and released it into the dirt.

"*I* scared *you*?" Keko blinked at the wet spot. "What is that stuff?"

He picked up an unmarked bag made of thick plastic, now empty. "Ofarian water magic blended with Primary medicine. Something our head doctor has been working on for years. Experimental still, but promising." He shifted, walking on his knees to get a better look at her back and shoulder, and whistled. "Very promising."

In the Chimeran valley, if you got injured you lugged yourself down to the stream, slapped water over your wound and pretended you didn't ache. The greater the pretender you were, the more you were respected. Pain had always been part of the process, but now, feeling this incredible care and healing so soon, she questioned the good in holding on to that kind of pain. In pretending.

She questioned the shame she should be feeling in allowing Ofarian water magic on her body—the shame she *should* feel, but didn't.

"Are you going to tell the Senatus about that stuff?"

"Yes." No hesitation. "Eventually. Maybe someday the Primaries, too."

Of course. All part of his big plans. Which she'd thought she'd known so well but now couldn't stab with a fork.

"It speeds up healing," Griffin said, deftly switching the subject away from the Senatus, "but doesn't immediately cure. The Child got you good. A nice, deep laceration that's still open. Can I bandage it?"

She was aware she was staring, wide-eyed, like a fool. Annoyed with herself, she ripped her gaze away and looked straight ahead.

"It needs it," he pressed, knowing full well she was debating jumping up and heading over to the prayer as though this whole violent interlude had never happened. "Otherwise it'll get dirty and infected."

"Fine. Sure."

Out of the corner of her eye, she could see his twitch of a smile as he pulled off his vest. Bare-chested, he unzipped another pocket and pulled out sterile packages of large bandages and tape.

"Any more of those water magic doohickey bags?"

"Nope."

He pushed her hair to one side and the way he touched it, fingers slow and sliding, reminded her of how he'd looked at it back in the hotel room—with marvel. Now it was with purpose, but he still lingered. She grabbed the knotted black mass of it and held it out of his way.

"You got my only one," he added quietly, then pressed a bandage over a particularly sore spot. She refused to hiss or acknowledge the pain.

His sole bit of healing magic, that he could have used on his own singed head, and he'd used it on her.

"Maybe you should turn back now," she said, "so you can put one on that burn."

He ripped off pieces of tape with his teeth and laid them over her skin with care. The second she felt him finish, she popped to her feet, amazed at how stable she felt, how much the pain in her back and shoulder had ebbed. She watched him rise, slowly, still bare chested, his vest hanging loosely from his hand. Though he stood still and patient, there was worry in his eyes and a certain tension to his muscles.

Looking over his head where the ocean surged into the small canyon, she tried to piece together everything that had happened since she'd stepped onto the beach. Turning, she went to the tree and placed her hand on the scar Griffin's knife had given it.

"The Children want to stop me, too," she said. She sensed Griffin come up behind her. "Did they learn about me from you?"

"No."

"Chief, then."

Griffin didn't respond to that, but instead said, "I don't know any more about them than you do. I don't know why they did this."

As he came around to place his own hand over the scar, just below her own, she saw the frustration and bewilderment on his face. The kind you couldn't fake or hide.

Her hand slid from the bark and she stepped back, suddenly feeling drained. Suddenly realizing all that had just happened. "You helped me, Griffin."

"Yes. I did." His brow furrowed. He came closer, erasing the space she'd just given herself. "You couldn't see that's what I wanted from the moment I sensed him?"

"I . . . no. I thought you were trying to stop me from getting to the prayer. I couldn't let that happen."

"You need to stop and listen, get out of your own head sometimes. That kind of thinking could have gotten you killed."

"I could've sworn you were coming after me."

She thought of Makaha, how Griffin had sworn that her friend had attacked, too. Look how wrong Griffin had been. She gulped down bile made of personal disappointment.

"Maybe if you'd listened," Griffin said, "you would've known the truth."

"I saw you were trying to help me too late. I couldn't stop the fireball."

"I know that. I saw it in your face." Griffin's gestures were curt. "And I know you were just trying to protect yourself, but you have got to stop thinking that you're alone. It worries me. It saddens me. This whole thing is not about whether I'm for or against you. It's not that black and white. I know that's how you've been raised, what you're used to, but that's not how it is with almost everyone else in the world. Sooner or later you're going to have to realize that."

"But I thought—"

"Keko, I know." His eyes closed briefly on a deep sigh, and when he opened them, they were wet. "I understand you."

TEN

Keko turned away from Griffin's dirt-streaked body and that patch of bloody skin between his ear and eye that would always remind her of what he'd just done for her. Very deliberately she walked toward the stone prayer. As she picked her way up and across the broken and upended slabs of lava rock, Griffin's voice struck her back.

"You're not still going on with this, are you?"

"What's it look like?"

He made an exasperated sound. "Like idiocy."

The prayer was so close.

"You need to rethink things." He was coming after her again, not running but with quick, purposeful footsteps.

"I came all this way. I'm not turning back now. Please don't try to stop me."

"Jesus, Keko." He caught up to her, grabbed her arm and spun her around. He'd put his vest back on but hadn't zipped it. She wriggled free from his grasp.

"Can't you see now why I came to Hawaii? I'm not going to leave you alone because *that*"—he jabbed a finger at the tree—"can't happen again. And since this attack took both of us by serious surprise, you should be prepared that it might."

She drew back, insulted. "You think I can't take care of myself?"

He lifted his palms to her. "I know you can. I know that. Just"—one of those hands shoved into his hair and gave it a good tug—"you don't really want to throw your existence away to something like that, do you? Life can be so much more than what you've made it out to be. So much more than what your culture has allowed you to have."

If only he knew exactly what she was doing for her culture, he might understand. And for the first time, she actually had the urge to tell him so. Because this argument of his—this belief in her hubris and selfishness—was starting to do far more evil than good.

"I just want you alive, Keko."

She turned away, because she was starting to believe him.

A few steps more, and at last she gazed down at the carving made by the Queen's own hand over a thousand years ago. The slab of lava rock tilted sharply to the left now, the treeman's uprooting creating a pile of disturbed ground right next to it, but the image of the carved person was still clear. A figure made of simple, clean lines, arms bent at the elbow in supplication. Tiny brown leaves and golden seeds and little piles of dirt clung to the shallow grooves. Keko gently blew them away.

"What does it mean?" Griffin's voice was soft, inquisitive.

Keko frowned at it. "She is asking the Source to reunite her with her element. Her final wish."

He moved closer to her side. "You said this thing told her where it was located. Can you read it? Do you know where the Source is?"

When she glanced up at him he wasn't looking at the petroglyph, but scanning the canyon in a measured soldier's way, wariness painted across his face.

"No. I can't." A feeling of unease and hopelessness skated down her spine. "It doesn't say anything about where the Source is." She dropped to her knees and frantically scraped away all the vines and dead brush and leaves from the waves of lava rock immediately surrounding the prayer. "There's nothing more. Nothing more here."

Griffin waved his hand, gesturing her to come to him. "Then I think you should get up and we should get out of here. We don't know if that thing will come back. Or if he'll bring friends."

"No." She reached out and placed a hand over the figure's body, and suddenly realized what she must do. "I have to carve my own prayer."

"What?"

"The Source answered the Queen's final prayer in her hour of desperation, when she wanted it the most. I have to do the same, and there is no time more desperate than now. This was *her* prayer. I have to carve my own."

"We should really get out of here."

"We?" She met his eyes. "I'm not asking you to stay, but I'm not leaving either."

Keko searched around and found two rocks, one that had been broken into a point that she aimed against a new lava slab. She used the wide edge of the other rock to make the first chip. It fell away and she breathed with satisfaction and growing excitement.

She carved for a long time, echoing what the Queen had drawn and whispering prayers and pleas to both the Queen and the Source. Griffin paced at her back but did not otherwise try to dissuade her.

As the day's light began to leave the canyon and her work was thrown into shadow, Griffin's silent worry had reached fever pitch. She didn't allow herself to feel the same, because if the treeman had wanted to come back and attack, he would have done it by now.

"It's dark," Griffin said, as if she couldn't read the sky. "We're stuck here until morning. I don't trust even you to negotiate that ledge at night."

Keko unfolded her legs and gave her back a good stretch, the tightness in her wound making her feel alive, not halfway dead as before. The two rocks she'd used to carve her prayer were well worn down, as was she, but the prayer was complete.

"I'm staying here tonight."

He rolled his eyes. "Well, I hope glory is worth it."

She tilted her head to one side, and then the other, stretching her neck. "You keep assuming I'm doing this for me."

His pacing stopped. "You're not?"

She met his shocked stare with her even one. "No."

She could sense his question before he asked it.

"What are you talking about?" When she didn't answer, he dropped his voice. "What the hell do you mean?"

But Keko just shook her head and looked to the indigo sky. "And now we wait."

The answer had come to her as she'd chipped rock into rock. The legend said that the Queen had carved her prayer in daylight and the location of the Source had been revealed under the moon. Keko would sit here and watch the rock until the same happened to her. And she had every bit of faith that it would.

"Keko—"

"I didn't ask you to stay, Griffin."

He regarded her for a long time before lowering himself to the lava rock on the opposite side of the prayer, making himself comfortable by sitting on a balled up T-shirt he pulled from his pack.

They sat in silence, until the moon came out and the prayer came alive.

At first she thought it a trick of her eye—an aftereffect of the wound and the pain, coming on the heels of days of being chased. Fatigue, hunger, desperation, all pounding into her brain.

But no. The air above the prayer—her prayer, not the Queen's—sparkled. Tiny winks of blue light hovered in space a couple of feet above the rock, growing in number and density with every passing second. Keko scrambled to her feet, heart hammering.

The chest of the basic figure she'd carved glowed blue-white. The figure was her, Keko, bearing the Queen's treasure. Crowning her effigy, twinkling in stasis above the rock, were hundreds of little lights, like stationary fireflies.

The answer—the location—was in there. Somewhere.

The euphoria of the magic, of the Source actually acknowledging her and answering her prayer, died. Keko began to panic and scratch at her arms.

"But . . . what does it *mean*? How am I supposed to figure this out?"

Griffin's knitted brow smoothed and he slowly rose to standing. "I think I know."

She grabbed his arm above the elbow. "You do? Tell me."

He tore his gaze away from the lights and looked at her with frightening calm.

"It's a star map," he said.

Her grip on him fell away and she whirled back to the prayer, trying to see what he did. "A star map? How do you know?"

He just looked at her. And looked. "Because I know the stars. Every single one of them."

Their conversation from last night came roaring back.

"It seems to me," he said, coming to her side, his hand waving just above the floating pinpricks of light, "that if the Chimerans came from the stars, too, in a way, that the stars would be the ones to guide you in the end. Maybe they have something to offer your people as well, not just the Ofarians."

His words were drifting around in her head, bouncing off her desperation and adding to her confusion. "But what am I *looking* at?"

He pointed to the glowing blue-white spot on the figure's chest. "That's the Source. Positioned under certain stars, at certain angles right now. It would have been a different configuration for the Queen, all those years ago. Maybe back then, since she used the stars to guide her people across the ocean, she knew how to read them."

"I . . ." It was too conceptual for her, too outside of any way of thinking she'd ever been exposed to, and it wasn't clicking in her head. She turned her face to the sky and all she saw was a maze of light. She was so close. So close. And now this?

She looked back at Griffin, whose expression was watchful and utterly frustrating.

"Can *you* read it?" she asked.

He nodded.

Excitement spiked in her heart and made her fire flare in anticipation. "Well? And?"

He crossed his arms over his chest. "How about a trade? I decipher the star map and you tell me why you are really doing this."

She went cold. "What?"

He nodded to the place where she'd sat to do her carving. "What you said earlier, about how this whole thing wasn't really about you. I can help you, but I need to know what I'm contributing to. You can understand that, can't you?"

With a snarl of aggravation she swiveled away to stare into the darkest point of the canyon. The star map glowed at her back, sending diffused blue-white light into the reaches.

Of course she understood what he was asking. She'd want the same thing. You never got something for nothing. Only she didn't think she could give him what he was asking.

"The star map is fading," Griffin said behind her. Not taunting, not demanding. "If you want to go it alone, you could memorize as much detail as possible now, and then probably plug the points into a computer program to find the general location."

At that she turned back around, pushing aside all her insecurities, all her self-doubt. She couldn't afford to let him see that. "I don't know how to use a computer."

The subtle parting of his lips was the only thing that told of his surprise. He cleared his throat. "So you need me."

Coming closer to the star map, looking down into the mess of floating lights and the brilliant, tempting X that marked the treasure, she knew she'd never be able to memorize all that detail.

"I want something more," she said.

"Name it."

The space between them screamed with tension.

"*If* I tell you," she began slowly, "I want your word that you will never repeat a word of it. Not to Gwen, not to your dog, and absolutely never to the Senatus."

"My god," he whispered, "what is this about?"

"Your word, Griffin. What I could tell you would never hurt me—I'm far beyond that and I wouldn't care if it did—but it would destroy others. It would compromise all Chimerans in the eye of the Secondary world. It would create huge rifts among my people and the island clans, and that scares me more than anything."

As he stared at her she knew immediately that he would never agree to such an oath. All that she'd just said would steer him away from agreeing to her terms. In fact, it had probably churned up even greater determination in him to discover it on his own, without her stipulations. It had *always* been about the Senatus and the Ofarians to him. It had never been about her or her people. What she'd wanted or believed in had never factored into his role or objectives—

"Done," he said. "I swear."

All breath punched out of her lungs. "What?"

"I told you"—he inched closer, making the space between them even more pressurized—"I'm not here for them. I'm here for you."

How on earth had she pegged him so wrong?

"The stars," she blurted, because she knew how much they meant to him. As much as her Queen. "Swear on your stars."

He drew a breath. By the twitch of his hands at his sides, she thought he might touch her, but he didn't.

"I swear on the light of the stars, the power that brought the Ofarians to Earth and that which I hold dear, that your secret is safe with me, Keko. I will never use it against you or for my own gain. I will never tell another soul."

Brave Queen . . .

And then he repeated it in Ofarian. She couldn't understand the words but she knew what he was saying, could almost see the oath that his strange syllables and beautiful phrases wove around them both.

She covered her face with her hands. She couldn't help it. It was all so overwhelming. So unexpected. Every motivation and emotion she'd assigned to him now felt false.

"Do you believe me now?" he asked quietly, and she knew he wasn't asking about the oath.

Behind her hands, she nodded. If he were here for the Senatus—at their order or to wedge himself into their ranks by using her—he never would've agreed to this. He could be lying, but the stars . . . they were his religion, whether he recognized that or not.

She looked at the star map, whose brilliance had faded somewhat. Soon it would be gone, but Griffin had it all stored away in his head. Exactly what she needed. But could she actually give him what he wanted in exchange? Could she tell this ambitious man about the disease that was weakening her people? Her *leader*?

"I need time," she said. "I need to think."

He reached out to take her hand. Looking down at where her fingers were clasped lightly in his, she added, "I can't think straight when you touch me."

He let her go.

The most startling thing about waking up was not realizing she'd fallen asleep in the first place. Dawn smacked Keko's eyelids open and she came awake with a gasp. Sitting up, she felt the tug on her shoulder wound and the gouges in her skin from where rocks and branches had bedded down for the night.

Immediately she looked over at her carved prayer, sitting there sort of ugly and harsh next to the time-weathered one made by her Queen. The starlight magic was gone. So was the glow in the figure's heart. All that was left was the map and knowledge in Griffin's head.

He appeared before her then, as though she'd called out for him. The faint light coming over the ocean cast his body in silhouette.

"Morning." His voice sounded like he'd had lava rocks for breakfast. "We need to get going. Light's coming up."

He zipped up his vest—over a black T-shirt this time; it must have gotten chilly overnight—threw his pack over his shoulder, and turned his face to the relentless ocean. That's when she saw the dark smudges underneath his eyes, the drawn line of his mouth, and she knew he hadn't slept at all. Had probably paced the whole night, scanning for the return of the earth elemental, standing guard.

Keko pushed to her feet and dug into her pack for something to eat but came up empty. A little plastic cup filled with hard pebbles of who-knows-what was shoved into her hand. She looked up at Griffin.

It was different now, in the growing daylight, knowing that they each had something the other wanted. Knowing there were secrets. Knowing they were connected in even more ways.

She saw his conviction, his oath, in his tired, red rimmed eyes, and felt the anguish of an unmade decision wrestle in her gut.

"Freeze-dried soup," he said. "Not good for much but energy. I'll add water if you'll heat it up." He ripped off the top seal of his own cup, spoke Ofarian to drag water from the air, and poured it into the little containers.

She dipped fingers into the muddy-looking soup and added heat. Steam curled up from the water that plumped the powdered pebbles into things resembling vegetables and meat.

"Careful," she said, handing him his cup. "It'll be hot."

"I like hot," he said. "Remember?"

Too much. She started off toward the black sand. "I can

walk and drink at the same time." She downed the hot liquid in a few quick gulps.

"You okay today? How's the shoulder?"

She waved nonchalantly, pulling out a dull twinge of pain. "Fine."

They made it up and around the ledge, their backs sliding along the uneven bluffs, their feet shuffling precariously over the sea-sprayed rocks. Finally they stepped down into the stream bed that shot back up into the island.

"Here's what I'm going to do." Griffin blocked her path upstream. "There's this thing the Ofarians use in all our businesses, the ones we don't want Primaries to know about. It's called waterglass, and we combine a consistent flow of shielding magic with water and run it between two panes of glass in the windows. I want to cast something similar over us, use it to disguise our movements."

"You're worried about the earth elemental."

"Yeah. Neither one of us knows anything about them. Who that one was, how Aya is involved, how he found you . . ."

The mention of Aya made her feel uneasy.

"The way he appeared," Keko said, "it was like he came from the ground and pushed himself up into the tree. Took it over. And when you stabbed it—"

"He left the tree. Went back into the earth. I noticed that, too."

"You think he could find us again?"

Griffin nodded, hands on hips. "I can use mist to cloak us as we move up the stream bed, until we climb out of this ravine and get out of the natural areas. The mist will throw him off, if he's looking or following. I would've used it last night except he already knew where we were and it just would've drained my energy."

"So we get out of the stream bed, and then what?" She raised an eyebrow. Before, she'd expected to have a travel course and a plan of action when she left the stone prayer, but now her travel was entirely dependent on the knowledge and route in Griffin's head. Maybe she could get him to reveal something more. "Which direction?"

His eyes narrowed, fully aware she was trying to needle

information from him without actually giving up any of her own.

"Toward civilization. Back into the modern world," Griffin said.

That made sense. "He can't get to us in the cities, not without walking in as a human, like Aya did. There's too much man-made stuff all around. Too much below the surface. That would be my guess."

Griffin scratched at his face, dark growth shadowing his cheeks and jaw and neck. "Exactly. I'm wondering, though, why he came after you in the canyon. Why not attack when you started out? Why even let you get that far?"

She looked at him quizzically. "How would he have known what I was doing?"

The pause before his reply was long. "I have no idea." He frowned. "You'll have to stay fairly close to me when we're inside the mist. It's harder to maintain at a distance, less effective."

Exactly how close? Because being this close to him already was rather unnerving. "But if the earth elemental comes back, wouldn't you be able to feel him coming?"

"Not until he was practically on top of us. Or below us, as it seems. Now come closer."

She moved to within six feet and he threw up a veil of nearly invisible mist, wrapping it around them like a blanket. Its surface caught the light at certain angles, making tiny rainbows.

Concentrating, he shook his bent head and waved her in. "I need you closer."

Three feet.

He visibly relaxed, the strain of the magic lessening and the faint shimmer of mist tightening around them. He lifted his chin, met her eyes. "Perfect. That's good."

Try as she might, she couldn't look away. "He can't see or hear us?"

"Shouldn't be able to. I've never done this before."

"A virgin, eh?"

Griffin cleared his throat and swiveled, facing upstream. "Just keep near me."

Keko wanted to resist the order out of habit and pride, but

as he started to negotiate the stony, irregular bank of the stream, she couldn't help but notice how his ass and legs looked in those shorts, and thought, *No problem, sir.*

As they walked, she could hear him murmur in his language every now and then, altering the mist, testing it. His voice sounded as tired as the droop of his eyes and the downward slant of his shoulders made him look, but he never said anything about fatigue, never complained.

Midday they came to a small waterfall, tucked into where the land shot upward and sloped far back, stretching all the way to the majesty of Mauna Kea. Here they'd have to climb out of the ravine in order to hike to the road and thumb a lift into the nearest town, but just the thought of scaling the rocks at that moment pulled on her shoulder wound like a hundred-pound weight. This weakness was abhorrent, but she knew she had to listen to it or else risk more serious injury.

Griffin was also peering up at the climb, his thumbs hooked through loops on his vest. They lowered their heads at the same moment, catching and snagging each other's gazes. Now would have been the perfect time to lose him. He wavered on his feet. Caught himself. If she pushed herself up those rocks right now, even in his weary state he would follow. He would follow until his legs snapped off.

"A short rest?" she said, shouldering off her pack.

He regarded her, then stretched out a hand to create a narrow divide in the sheltering mist, parting it like it was made of silk. He touched the element like a lover.

That was the way it was with him. Griffin, the unmovable Ofarian leader with the iron gate pulled down over his life, who'd been frenzied and borderline harsh when they'd fucked in exactly the way she'd demanded, was the very same Griffin who could smooth his hands down her skin in the way he touched the mist right now.

For a brief moment in time, *she* had been his element.

No matter how strongly she told herself to look away from him, she couldn't. That lack of control took large bites out of her concentration.

"All right," he said, pulling back his hand and letting the mist close. He removed his pack and vest and carefully set them at his feet, but did not sit. "I can use the waterfall to power some of the magic while we take a break. Won't drain as much energy from me."

With a simple Ofarian word, the mist veil arched up to merge with the waterfall. It domed outward to encase the tumbling water and the wet rock ledge on which they stood.

Keko stared at him and his beautiful magic like an idiot. A weird, unwelcome emotion bubbled up from inside her, and it had nothing to do with fire.

She couldn't believe that the two of them were standing alone together near a hidden Hawaiian waterfall. She couldn't believe that Griffin Aames had come here specifically to keep her from doing what she most wanted to do, but then had sworn on his beloved stars to give her information to help her move forward. He was far too beautiful and far too frustrating for her own good. And even though she desperately wanted to, she still shouldn't trust him.

Mighty Queen, this was all so fucking confusing. But nothing more so than the fact that she still wanted him.

She remembered the day he'd stalked into the garage in Colorado, how suddenly and powerfully he had made her *feel* again after three years apart. How she'd tried so hard to shove her want and need aside, to project an air of steel toughness, and what the aftermath of that rejection had made her do.

This man was like war to her: dangerous and exciting, strong and deadly. He carried emotion on his back like a weapon, hitting her with blow after blow. Sentiment weakened her, weakened all Chimerans. She couldn't afford that. Not now.

With a nod to the shallow pool frothing at the base of the waterfall, she said, "You mind if I take a quick dip? I think it'll wake me up."

Something shifted in his expression, and she recognized it for the desire inside herself that she was really shitty at hiding. She'd never been one for pretending, for covering things up. In the Chimeran valley you said and did what you wanted, and the outcome of those words or actions made you what you were.

But Griffin . . . Griffin threw everything out of whack.

Wanting or needing to fuck was one thing. Carrying around a soul-deep passion, a severe longing, for another person—and not just their body—was so foreign to her. By the look on his face, maybe it was strange to him as well.

He was pretending, too.

She flicked open the snap on her frayed jean shorts. Griffin's eyes dropped to the motion, his jaw tightening.

"I still can't be too far away from you to keep up the spell," he said.

"Then sit right there on the edge of the pool. Turn your back if you want. Or don't."

She let her shorts drop. Griffin's expression turned pained, his eyes squeezing shut as he turned around. "I know what you're doing."

"You're a smart man. I'm sure you do." She pulled off her bloody and tattered tank top no longer remotely resembling white, then reached over her shoulder to rip off the bandage.

Naked, she stepped down into the pool and sank into it, surrounding herself with his element. Loving the coolness of the water as it lapped against her hot, hot skin.

"I'm in," she said, lowering herself enough for the water to make a wet line across the tops of her breasts. "You can turn around now."

He didn't.

ELEVEN

Conflicting thoughts battled inside her head.

I want you.

I doubt you.

Go home.

Stay.

Turn around and watch me.

To drown them out, she threw water over her shoulders and dragged it down her arms, scrubbing off the dirt and sweat, making her fingertips hurt.

Griffin sat cross-legged, facing away from her, on the lip of the rock. His wide back heaved with a sigh. The damp black T-shirt pulled tightly across his torso, and she could see nearly every muscle delineated underneath.

"It bothered you," she said, taking a chance with this topic of conversation, "to find me in that garage naked."

His dark head dragged slowly back and forth. "You have no idea."

"Because everyone could see me?" And here's where she took an even greater chance: "Or because you still wanted me?"

Another sigh. "Both."

"For a long time, I thought it was hate."

"No." A quick response. "Not hate. Never hate. Confusion, though. Confusion over why you were there, why you were being so hostile to me when I had no idea what was going on." He barked out a cold laugh. "And a hell of a lot of frustration. Because you'd never left my mind in three years. Because I never expected to see you again, and suddenly there you were. Captive. Taken by one of my own behind my back. Naked and angry and all up in my face, exactly how I remembered you. I gave you my coat because I couldn't stand looking at you. You were too much for me, for my senses, after all that time away. You instantly kick-started everything back into high gear, the way it once was. For me at least."

Keko hadn't realized she'd stopped washing until he finished, completely frozen by his words. When her hands resumed movement over her body, they worked slowly, as though pushing through mud.

He turned his head, giving her his profile. "And you?"

Her arm paused over her chest as she considered how to answer. "I felt vindicated at first. Seeing you proved I was right about you and your people." She scoffed at herself. "At least in my own head, for a time. I remember being so mad at how good you looked, how you never took your eyes off me, how you made me put on the coat like you owned me or something."

"But you did it. You put it on."

"Because I thought that if I did, you'd continue to think you had power over me, when really it was me trying to turn the tables. And because"—*oh boy*—"for the first time ever I was aware of other people looking at me, and I liked your eyes on me the best. Yours were the only ones I wanted, even after the way we'd ended, and that realization made me insane. I didn't know what to do with it, how to react."

Slowly, gracefully, he leaned back on his hands, his triceps and lats making all sorts of gorgeous waves under the thin layer of the T-shirt. The mist above rained down sparkles in his nearly black hair.

"This is the first time we've talked about it," he said. "I didn't think we ever would."

Beneath the water she rubbed at her legs and feet, because she didn't know what else to do or say.

"So I understand your behavior in the garage," he said, "but I still don't get what happened right after. The war and all."

Two months ago she'd been so *sure* he'd been finagling his way into the Senatus by capturing and using her. She'd been *positive* that he was orchestrating a war between Ofarians and Chimerans. Her soul had been shattered by his callousness with Makaha. Her heart had been destroyed by his coldness to her after they'd left the bonfire, and then three years later in that garage.

"I think you do get it," she said. "I let myself want you, and when you didn't want me in return I came back at you the only way I knew how: fighting, war. I'm not saying it was right. Standing here now, looking back at how I'd been trained to think, it feels so foolish. So dangerous. I deserved my punishment."

"Who said I didn't want you?" His voice rose. "I knew what I was to you in the very beginning and I didn't care. I went into it willingly."

"And what do you think you were to me?"

Another humorless laugh. "Come on, Keko. I'm a man. I may be horny as all fuck when I'm around you, but I still like to think I can cling to a chunk of my brain when I'm inside you. You already told me I was a challenge to you in Utah, someone for you to do to pass the time. Something forbidden. Maybe even something to secretly get back at the chief for making you watch me."

"All that is true."

"It was true, in the beginning. But that last night in the hotel room? I thought I might've become something special to you, if only for a little while."

"You were."

He went perfectly still, a half-drawn breath exaggerating the deep V of his torso. She'd never been so attracted to a man's back before.

"Were?" he asked.

"Were," she said. "I don't know what you are now."

It occurred to her that maybe he was baiting her as much as she was baiting him. Each trying to pry out information from the other without revealing their own hands. Maybe she should grab on tightly to that and not let other, more physical, demands try to steer her in other directions. Except that those demands were making her thighs tremble with need beneath the water, and she couldn't resist slowly running her hands up and down them.

"What are you doing?" For someone who could transform himself into rain, his voice sounded so very dry. "To your body. Right now."

Her hands froze halfway up her thighs, water sloshing around her chest and upper arms. "I'm washing."

"Where?"

The urge to touch her own nipple with one hand and push the other between her legs nearly sent her underwater. For a moment she could have sworn she felt him in liquid form sliding over the part of her that was quickly going slippery. Or maybe that was just her imagination, her fantasies, breaking through the barriers of reality.

"Griffin . . ." It came out plaintive. Hot. An entirely different sound than she'd wanted to give him.

It meant the balance of control had shifted again. He'd unknowingly taken over and she was slipping. He was affecting her, turning her on, and . . . Brave Queen, she didn't want him to stop.

He pushed off his hands and shoved them both into his hair so hard she thought he might be digging into his skull. "God, I know. I know. Don't answer that."

With terrible effort, she lifted her hands from the water, the dripping as it hit the surface loud and strangely sexy. She'd started this—this advanced form of flirting that got her naked within four feet of him—but now she wasn't entirely sure how to finish it. Or even if she should.

Because no amount of sex was going to erase what she was feeling. How dumb she'd been to ever have thought that a physical release could drive away unwanted and burdensome emotion.

Cupping water in her palms, she poured it over her shoulder, trying to focus on getting her wound clean, but instead only noticing the slow, cool tease of the narrow streams as they trickled over her skin—as they made dancing paths down and around the swells of her breasts. She pressed her finger to one lazy droplet, tracing it downward, until she grazed her nipple.

A tiny moan of pleasure leaked from her throat.

A louder one rumbled from the chest of the man sitting on the rock. "Ah, fuck it. Just tell me."

Turn around. See where my hand is. Where I want yours.

But to say it felt far too intimate, which was odd since her mouth was trained for boldness.

"I'm trying to wash my back." She was fully aware of how

dumb that sounded, how romantically manipulative, but since she'd been conditioned to own what she said, she let it hang there.

His back straightened. "Don't strain yourself. The wound could open up again and bleed. Here, let me help."

Yes. Her hand tightened on her breast, the nipple hard in the center of her palm. She held her breath, wanting him to turn, to strip out of those clothes, and slip into the water right in front of her. Wanting his hands on her. Her eyes drifted closed with the fantasy, with anticipation.

Then something did touch her—something cool and wet and refreshing—but it wasn't Griffin.

Her eyes flew open to see the waterfall pulling away from the rock face, defying gravity. Scant droplets turned to a steady shower as the small waterfall poured over her spot in the center of the pool. She stood up, rising above the surface, and let the water rain down, flattening her hair down her back and sluicing over every inch of her body. It beat down upon her, cleaning her and making her feel impossibly dirty within the same second.

She felt Griffin's presence within the water that cascaded over her, even if it wasn't *him* exactly. Smiling, catching a mouthful of water, she looked over at him. He sat motionless, his back still to her, hands on his knees. His magic literally surrounded her.

Just like when he used to move inside her, and she and her magic had surrounded him.

"If you can't see me," she said, "how do you know where to send the water?"

"I can always feel you. Remember?"

Oh yes. She remembered.

The thought of it pulled her out from under the enchanted waterfall and sent her feet sliding across the slippery stones at the bottom of the pool. Toward him. The surface of the water only touched her mid-thigh, and when she reached the edge of the pool, she was markedly aware of her nakedness. She was Chimeran, where the body in all its faults and beauty was revered and never shamed, but just then, standing behind a clothed Griffin as he stared ahead at the curtain of mist enclosing them, she wanted to be *noticed*. By him and only him.

Standing this close, she observed things about him she never had before. The series of short white scars above his left elbow. The freckle above the neckline of his T-shirt. It nestled in a paler strip of skin that seemed to have been exposed by a recent haircut.

The urge to reach up, run her hands over his scalp, twist his head around, and claim his mouth with hers was so powerful she had to clasp her hands behind her back.

"I'm done," she said.

He jumped and swiveled, only to see her standing naked and dripping not two feet away. The magic waterfall slapped back against the rock, sending a brand new splash across her bare back. The mist veil wavered. He pinched the bridge of his nose with one hand and made a face like he'd been kicked in the gut.

"Didn't meant to scare you." She cocked her head. "I thought you could feel me."

As his hand dropped, he looked into her eyes. "I thought I might've just been imagining you getting closer."

"Because you wanted me to be?"

His Adam's apple made a long, slow undulation in his throat. "Yes."

To his credit, he never once looked away from her face, and she found that more erotic than almost any brand of touch or kiss or dirty word.

The waterfall splashed and gurgled behind her, a soft, tantalizing sound.

"Your turn to get in?" she asked. "I promise I won't look."

His eyes searched her face for two seconds, and then three, and then she lost count.

Suddenly he popped to his feet, towering high above her, her eyes level with his knees. Quickly, nearly frenzied, he whipped off his shirt, not caring that it landed in a puddle. Keko felt her breath catch, her fire flaring in response to the sight of the stunning, sweat-streaked chest above. Then he pushed his hands into the waistband of his shorts and shoved them and his underwear down. They pooled around his ankles and he just stood there, gloriously dirty and naked.

And undeniably hard.

With the tiniest of shrugs, it was as though he dared her to take him all in. He seemed to say: *See what you do to me?*

"How very Chimeran of you," she said.

The excitement of seeing him again in this way swept through her body, cranking up her desire to a wild blaze. Heat pulsed below her skin and small tendrils of steam curled around her body. The sight of the steam made his nostrils flare and she couldn't deny how much she enjoyed his reaction.

Before, three years ago, they'd grabbed each other and fucked whenever they'd had a moment alone. A swift attack, hands everywhere, quick and furious penetration. Intense, fiery orgasms. Now, however, they were just . . . looking.

He threw a pointed glance at his erection. "The second I get in that cold water, this'll die."

One corner of her mouth curved upward. "I can help with that."

She turned, sinking shoulder deep into the water and resting her back against the rock. Taking a Chimeran breath, she stoked her inner fire and released all of it through her skin. The water instantly warmed, but she had to keep feeding it heat because of the waterfall.

She lifted her face up to Griffin. "Bath's ready. You don't want to touch me though, unless you want to get burned."

"Maybe I do."

But as he stepped down into the pool, he gave her a wide berth. To remain true to her word not to look, she gave him her back and set her forearms and elbows on top of the rock.

She wouldn't look, but she would listen. And she would imagine.

The sound of him moving through the water, the rasp of his hands over his skin and the stubble on his face, the trickle of his element through his hair, made her desperately want to be Ofarian. To give up her fire just for a minute. She would swirl all around him, tease him, taste him in new ways.

Maybe that was exactly what he was doing to her now, because the easy touch of the water surrounding her body suddenly felt different. Controlled. Absolutely sensual. She closed her eyes and gave herself up to it, imagining that it was actually Griffin's liquid fingers slowly coiling like rope around her ankles and calves. Moving up, up, up to the parts of her thighs that made her quiver with want. Running back and forth across her clit. It was Griffin's liquid hips that lapped against her ass. It was Griffin's liquid hands that slid around her ribcage and stretched for her nipples.

The water promptly stilled, as no churning pool of water below a fall ever should. The seductive ebb and flow over her body receded, and she bit back a small sound of anguish in the wake of its absence. The mist still shifted and shimmered overhead, but it was the complete silence, punctuated only by Griffin's harsh, ragged breathing, that had her spinning around in the water.

He was a hard statue made of bronze and dripping with the element he owned. Any tease or denial had vanished from his eyes. His mouth was set with clear intent.

"Turn off your fire," he growled. "I'm coming for you."

Griffin couldn't stand it any longer. Being this close to Keko, seeing her body and the way she gazed up at him with longing and magic and heart in her eyes, had shoved him right up to the edge and finally tipped him over and off. Now he was falling, and the only thing to stop him from crashing was her.

There would be no talking himself out of wanting her. There would be no rationalization. No thinking about why he'd come to Hawaii in the first place. Only her. Only Keko, and the torrent of desire and emotions she sent rocketing through him.

If she told him no, if she pushed him away now, he would go, but she'd never been one to tease. If she wanted something, she went after it, and right now he was sure she wanted him as much as he wanted her.

He stood there, waist deep in the pool, as she slowly turned around in the water. The dreaminess in her eyes slayed him, because he knew he'd been the one to put it there.

He gave his order. He told her his intent.

That mouth—that gorgeous, lush mouth—parted. He watched the rose glow painted over her skin start to fade as she toned down the Chimeran fire within. He didn't want it too dampened, though. He loved her heat. He wanted her hot. So he reached out and grabbed her, yanking her away from the rock and up against him. Against the hard-on she hadn't let die.

Pressed together, shoulders to knees, slippery and naked, one phrase played on a loop over and over in his mind:

I missed you.

I missed you.

I missed you.

The look in her eyes, the surrender drawn over her face, claimed the same. And this time she wasn't trying to cover it up or push it aside. Neither was he. Not now, with her in his arms again.

Three years spent poring over every minute detail of their time together. Three years of discovering that the moments that resonated loudest to him were those when she'd let emotion enhance how she used her body. Those moments when he'd opened himself up and allowed himself to feel something bigger than physical pleasure. They'd created promise together, and even though that promise had been severed, it had never truly died.

He meant to take her arms to bring them around his neck, but they were already sliding up his chest and into his hair. Her breasts were already pressed to his skin. She'd always seemed to know what he wanted, although at this moment he had conjured up no fantasies. No expectations. He just wanted her, in any way, shape, or form.

Keko held tightly to his neck and pulled herself up, wrapping her legs around his waist. She was so strong as she held him, as though he'd been the one trying to run away. All that skin, tying him up in a beautiful Chimeran ribbon.

His legs gave out, not from weight, but from the sheer force of desire that barreled into him. He sank into the water, taking her with him, shattering the magical stillness of the pool. Releasing his control over his element, little waves slapped over their bodies. There was a sharp dig in his scalp, her fingers grinding as she pulled his mouth to hers.

The word for what happened next wasn't *kiss*. No. A kiss was way too delicate, way too passionless.

Three years of frustration were built into this. Three years of missed chances and disconnected promise. Three years of continual longing, building and building despite the mind's orders to *let it go*.

She was trembling in his arms, and that might have been

the most startling and most fantastic discovery of all: to know for sure that he affected her as much as she affected him.

He'd missed the sweet smoke on her tongue. He'd missed the pressure of her lips and the way she opened so wide for him. He'd missed the power of her body and how she barely knew her own strength when it came to him, because that meant he'd made her lose control.

He wanted her experiences to mirror his, for her to know exactly what she did to him in the way he fed his reactions back to her.

He had to be inside her. Now. No finesse, no preamble. They needed to take the edge off right now before it sawed them both in half. Later, he would show her with his hands and mouth and cock that when he thought of her, Makaha and the Senatus and a close call war didn't exist. When he touched her, and claimed her mouth and body at this very moment, he wasn't thinking of that exchange of information they were both dreading and wanting.

It was only about her. Only about them.

"Keko."

He thought the name was only in his mind, but then it tumbled out with pure desperation and hard-driving need onto his tongue. He pressed the beautiful word back into her open mouth.

The water vibrated around them, their little liquid world gone to shaking. Desire rattled itself free from the cage in which he'd tossed it these long, long years, and his body joined hers in its trembling.

Keko's body rolled, her spine rippling beneath his hands as she rubbed herself against him. Even in the water he could feel how wet she'd gotten for him.

Releasing his mouth, she pressed damp lips to his ear and whispered, "Get inside me."

He didn't need to be told twice. Holding her tightly, he pushed to his feet, the water making them buoyant at first, then giving them up to the air with massive resistance. He completely forgot he was supposed to be physically wiped out and mentally fatigued from lack of sleep. At that moment he was as strong as a tsunami. Keko was still wrapped around him, her tongue licking up his neck, making him see his beloved stars when she got to the shell of his ear. Legs pushing hard through the water, he veered them toward the rock ledge and sat her perfect ass on the wet stone.

Slowly she peeled away from him, her hands loosening from around his neck, the separation of their chests giving him a lovely display of water trickling over her skin. He watched the trails of his element as they made curved lines across her flesh. Watched how his blatant, hungry stare made her breath quicken and her back arch.

Leaning back on her hands, she made for a brilliant image. A light tease of flame crossed her lust-blackened eyes. Slightly dangerous, completely sexy. He touched her face just below her left eye, drawn by the flame. She pressed into his touch.

Unlocking her ankles from around his back, she slowly spread her legs, the muscles in her abdomen flexing magnificently. Everything about her movements was as graceful as a dancer. Her heels came to rest on the lip of the rock.

She looked up at him, his hand still pressed to her cheek. "Please."

That was all she said. It was all she had to.

The hand on her cheek now curled around her head, past her ear, to clutch at the back of her skull. Pure possession. He came forward so the tops of his thighs grazed rock and the tip of his hard-on finally touched the hot, lovely place she was giving him.

Keeping a grip on the back of her neck—keeping her eyes on his—he used his other hand to draw a finger up the seam of her body, between her legs. Watched her shudder while trying to hold still, to be strong and resistant. She was beyond swollen, more slick than he ever thought possible.

He started to slowly push inside. Every centimeter made her eyelids flicker. Every centimeter coated him with surmounting pleasure. Then, as he finally drove all the way in, her eyelids fluttered closed and her inner muscles clenched him in the fist of heaven.

He gave her neck a soft squeeze and swirled a finger under her hair. "Open your eyes," he whispered. "Look at me."

When she did, warrior ferocity had replaced the feminine surrender. No fire magic dancing across her irises this time. Just Keko, connecting with him.

He withdrew a little, the grip and slide of her body making it exquisite, making it deliciously painful. But drawing back was the best, in his mind, because it just meant he got to go back in. That's what he loved most. Entering her. Claiming her. Watching her control be dismantled piece by piece. It was the most freeing sensation when the world disappeared and all he knew was her.

As he drove back inside, they made twin gasps. When she arched back, pushing herself onto him, he'd been a fool to think that she'd ever been at his mercy, to think that she would willingly give up any measure of control. Because with just that little movement she'd turned the tables and made him hers.

Had it really been so long since they'd done this? Been together like this? How come he remembered everything so clearly and still felt like she was brand new?

Digging his fingers into the base of her neck, using her as leverage, he took her in the hard way he knew she liked. The way he'd been dying to . . . this time.

Because even as he was driving hard into the most stunning, most desirable, most frightening woman he'd ever met, his thoughts of her were soft. Next time—next time, he vowed—he would touch her and have her in a way that echoed how he'd never stopped feeling this whole time apart.

She was growing warmer, the Chimeran blood reacting to the animalistic, human part of her that responded to sex. Which meant she was getting closer to the wonderful place they both wanted her to be.

Keko dug her heels into the stone and lifted her ass. With only her feet and hands for balance, her body took on an incredible roll and swing as he thrust into it, a free, breathtaking thing that alternately swallowed him and rocked him away. The heat in her was building to a point he'd been craving for years—a point that had scared the shit out of him the very first time, but which had quickly transformed into a dangerous kind of high.

A blast of heat emanated out from her core—a sharp shard of pain that licked along him, then instantly shifted to a rippling, searing form of pleasure the likes of which he would never be able to describe in either English or Ofarian. His water people from the stars didn't have words to adequately relate how it felt to be inside a Chimeran woman when she came.

He remembered not to stop as her fire and her orgasm crested, her body trembling madly. Her pleasure lasted for a long time, and he wanted to drain out every drop, to know fully what he'd given her. To watch her.

Still on hands and heels, her body made shaking, colliding undulations that reminded him of waves on the most tortured, lovely, storm-addled sea. Through the slit of her eyelids he saw the brilliant spark of her orgasm.

The sounds she made were completely unlike anything he'd ever heard. Soft and high and broken free from the toughness she was so good at portraying. It was those sounds, the unchained moans and feminine pleas, that undid him in the end. Set in time to his thrusts, to the collapse of her hips and the quivering of her thighs, the end of her orgasm brought on the beginning of his.

Her body refused to let him go. Her spine resumed its delicate and deadly arch, pulling out the intensity of his pleasure. The sight of her—the sound and scent and feel—scraped out every last molecule of lust inhabiting his body and sent them all shooting toward the scorching, wonderful place where they were joined.

Her body started to sag but he loved—needed—the position so much he couldn't let that happen, so he slipped a hand under her ass and lifted her up. Kept her body in perfect alignment to his. Let the wet slap of their bodies take over everything.

He couldn't see her anymore behind the black of his closed eyelids. Couldn't think about anything but *this*.

When he came, it was with a force that rivaled their first time, when sheer surprise and the thrill of discovery and the allure of forbidden fruit had heightened everything. That moment when he'd first realized that he wanted this woman in a way that he'd never wanted anyone else. He could hear his own gasps, but they were mere echoes of the pulsing euphoria that surged through his body.

The whole world shifted, and when it realigned he realized he'd collapsed against her body, pressing her into the rock. Her ankles were locked around him again, his face against the soft slope of her neck. His skin had pebbled with a chill, and he could feel the tender waves of heat she was doling out. Warming his body. And his heart.

TWELVE

A Chimeran should never take happiness from warming someone who was not one of their own, least of all an Ofarian, but as Keko wrapped her arms and legs around Griffin's body and sent a steady, low stream of heat into him, she couldn't help but love how it made her feel in return. To give that gift to someone. To him.

He didn't lift himself off her and she refused to unwrap him. Until all of a sudden it got to be too much. His breath on her neck, the light sifting of his fingers through her hair, the precious weight of him . . . everything in opposition to the urgency they had just given in to.

Sex changed everything. And nothing.

They were still the same two people who had formed an undeniable connection three years ago. Today that connection had been cemented, tied up tight with lock and chain, and tossed into a safe with six-feet-thick walls. Absolutely unbreakable, no matter the tool or weapon.

They were still the same two people with vastly different, conflicting goals.

Keko needed space. More time to think. Control over her emotions.

"Well. Now that we got that out of the way." She nudged his shoulders, and after a pause, he pushed up over her. She wriggled out from underneath him and rolled away. The space between them was invigorating. The space between them was empty and useless.

"Ah." He blinked, his insanely thick lashes clumped together with wet. "I see."

He pulled himself out of the pool with impressive strength, water streaming off his body.

She got to her feet. "What exactly do you see?"

He waved a vague hand in her direction. "How it is with you. I'm still not going anywhere."

"Not trying to drive you away. Just need to think. To process all this."

"Like I said, I get it."

She opened her mouth for a retort, for argument, but he watched her serenely and there was no fight in him. No challenge. He was letting her make her choice and giving her every means to do so.

The vow he'd made rang in her ears. The speed with which he'd given it still made her reel, pressing her to believe that he truly wasn't here for the Senatus. That she should just tell him about the Chimeran disease and get the Source's location.

Sex changed everything. And nothing.

It was dumb to stand there and moon about it. She was a woman of action, and if she stood next to this waterfall too much longer with Griffin, she'd be tempted to persuade him to get back into it with her.

She cranked up her inner fire and let the heat take care of the water droplets still clinging to her skin. A thin layer of steam coiled off her body, swirling around her limbs. As she pulled her hair over one shoulder, wrung the water from the mass, and then raked heated fingers through it to get it dry, Griffin watched.

The weight of his stare struck her hard in the heart, right where she couldn't afford to feel him. But she couldn't look away from him either.

Holding her gaze, his lovely mouth filled with even lovelier Ofarian words. Water wicked away from his skin, the droplets pulling away as though tugged by invisible strings. They grew fainter and fainter the farther they drew away from his body, until they dissolved altogether and he was standing there, naked and dry.

It was then she realized he'd managed to uphold the veil of mist above and around them the whole time they'd had sex. How much power and control he must have, to divide his magic like that and still make her feel like she was his sole focus when he'd been inside her.

Space, Keko. You need space.

The old tank top and shorts were beyond useless now, but she had a new gray tank and a pair of jeans left in her pack, and she pulled those out. Griffin watched her the whole time.

"Got any more of that soup?" she asked.

"Yeah, a couple more," he replied. When he bent over for his own pack, his body listed to one side and he had to catch himself on a rock.

"Whoa there, big guy. You okay?"

"Fine." He tossed her his last two cups of dried soup and yanked out a black T-shirt and black shorts from his own pack. She loved him in black.

The whole exchange was surreal and awkwardly domestic, making her feel like what they'd just shared hadn't happened. That was what she'd wanted, right? This space?

She went to the pool, scooped up water into her hands, made it boil, and dumped it into the cups. Above, the mist veil flickered, winking in and out like the static that often came through on the Chimeran radio that connected the convenience store gateway to the valley. Fear made a little slice through her mind. She turned around, worried, only to find that Griffin had propped his back against a rock, and had fallen soundly asleep. The mist disappeared entirely.

With the veil no longer hiding them, they were exposed to potential tracking by the Children. Griffin had held on as long as he could, probably assuming they'd have found their way back into an inhabited area by now so he could crash in relative safety. He hadn't counted on her seduction dragging out his energy, but then again, neither had she.

A day ago she would have seized this opportunity of his unconsciousness and scrambled out of this ravine and as far away from him as possible. How much had changed. Technically she could backtrack to the Queen's prayer and carve a new one again. She could stand there and stare at the star map until she thought she could decipher it. But there was too good a chance the Son of Earth would come back for her, and an even greater chance she'd never understand the angles in that mass of stars.

She needed Griffin. She hated to admit it, but she did. And

he'd shielded her from spying eyes after the attack. It was her turn to stand watch over him.

Keko dragged his vest over and slid out the giant knife strapped to the back. Then she settled against her own rock a quiet distance away and let Griffin have his much-needed rest. She kept one eye on the ravine that extended out to the ocean and the other on the Ofarian.

He twitched in his sleep. A tense, sharp concentration of his stomach muscles, as though he'd been punched. He didn't wake, but a harsh grimace twisted his face. For a moment she considered shaking him, but then his body stilled and the deep grooves between his eyebrows smoothed.

He'd given her his vow. Made upon his people's most sacred objects. She couldn't get past that and, really, that had been his point, hadn't it? Ever since he'd found her here on the island, he'd been denying his involvement with the Senatus and trying to convince her he was here of his accord. Had he succeeded? She laid the knife across her knees and considered him.

Griffin's conviction ran as deep as the legendary Source. He wasn't one to half ass anything. He wouldn't go after something unless he could do so with absolute concentration and one hundred percent effort. And he sure as hell never went after anything if he didn't believe in it whole-heartedly. In that they were too much alike.

He'd only ever wanted the Senatus. He'd only ever wanted Ofarian advantage. If she told him about the Chimeran disease she would give him such a weapon to wield, but through his oath he'd turned that down, sight unseen. He denied his presence had any involvement with the Senatus and she was . . . daring to believe him.

What had changed for him, this shift in objectives? Did it even matter? He had what she needed and she had his word.

Out of nowhere, Griffin's body gave a violent jerk. His big arm sliced awkwardly through the air to land across his chest. His hand made a fist. No, wait. The curl of fingers held a phantom gun.

"Griffin?" She moved to a crouch.

He convulsed, his body twisting to one side, one knee coming up as if to protect himself from a blow. A groan shot out of his throat, followed by a string of unintelligible mumbles, but then she distinctly heard something about "orders."

She started to crawl toward him, wary but worried, unsure what to do. This time the bodily twitching did not stop, but instead got more pronounced and intense second by second. The sounds that came out of his mouth were like garbled one-way conversations trying to patch through a spotty communication device. His closed-eye expressions shifted from fear to rage to cold fury to sadness.

Setting the knife down, she knelt before him and gave his shoulder a gentle shake. "Griffin, wake up."

It happened too fast. Too fast for even her reflexes. Griffin snapped awake, coming instantly alert. With a snarl he snatched her around her waist, flipping her up and around his body. She landed on her back and he came down on her, all his weight pressing her into the rock. The knife handle was in his hand, the blade tip at her throat. How the hell did he—

"I have my orders!" Spit hit her cheek. The fierce, hoarse cry ricocheted through the leaves.

In her warrior's heart, Keko knew she could throw him off. Knew she could inhale and draw her fire out, and either blast him far away or knock him out with its force. But that same heart realized that the Griffin she knew was not the Griffin with the wild, murderous eyes who loomed over her now. This was not Griffin the Ofarian attacking Keko the Chimeran, intent on preventing her from getting to the Source. He was panting, sweating, the knife tip trembling against her skin.

"What orders?" she whispered.

Griffin blinked, clarity and reality rolling back into his eyes. He crumpled, shoulders collapsing, the knife falling from slack fingers. The crushing weight on her arms and torso lessened, but he didn't get off her, instead just pushing back to sit on his heels, his chest heaving, spasms jerking his limbs.

He searched her face. "Keko?"

She raised her arms and showed him her empty palms. "What orders, Griffin?"

"Oh *fuck*." He rolled off her, going into a heap, his back to her, and tried to catch his breath.

She sat up and carefully nudged away the knife. "You were dreaming."

"Haven't had that one in a long time." He dropped his head into a hand. "A long time."

This was crossing over into unmapped territory for them, but she'd never been afraid of a little exploration. Like her, he didn't want pity or attention because of something personal, but she simply had to ask. "Why now, do you think?"

"I don't think. I know."

It wasn't the sex. "Orders" had nothing to do with that. Attacking her with a knife had never followed sex before. But they'd been in a pretty harrowing battle yesterday, and she suddenly recalled his reaction after it had all ended, the haunted look when he'd touched the tree after the earth elemental had left it.

"The earth elemental. The fight," she said. He agreed by not answering.

She rose and moved the few steps over to face him. He didn't look up as she lowered herself back to the ground, but he also didn't flinch away when her knees brushed his.

"Was it about someone you killed?"

"No." Now he looked up, met her eyes. And in them she saw a shattered soul. "It was about all of them."

They were more alike than she ever would have guessed.

"I see all of them," he said, and his voice sounded like it had dropped off the edge into a bottomless chasm. "One after the other. In the same order, first to last. Each of them playing out exactly as they happened. Every detail, the same as what I saw. What I heard and smelled. What I felt."

She made herself sit perfectly still because she knew he didn't want to be touched. "How many?"

"Twelve." His voice was utterly flat. "Twelve Primaries."

Her eyes widened, even more pieces completing the picture of this man. "Why them?"

"Because it used to be my . . . job."

She thought back to what he'd told her in the Utah hotel room. "I thought you were Gwen's protector."

"I was. But when her dad, the former Chairman, wanted a Primary taken out—a Primary who found out about us who wasn't supposed to know, or a Primary who violated terms of our contracts—he used me."

She couldn't breathe. For all her body was made for, she

couldn't take even a simple breath to power the human lungs of her existence. Suddenly she was back around a bonfire in the Utah mountains surrounded by anxiety and threats.

"That's what that was about," she was finally able to say. "When the premier ordered that Primary scholar's mind scrambled and you got upset. Because that's what you had to do once."

His expression hardened. "I had to kill. What they've been doing is worse."

"But that's what put you on edge. What might have made you mistake Makaha—" She cut herself off when his glare turned to blades, because she was more than aware that part of the blame belonged to her. "I mean, I understand now why you were so angry. You'd been poked hard in a wound, and then rubbed raw. It didn't make sense to me before. Now it does."

He didn't like her knowing this, she could tell. He wasn't ashamed or embarrassed by having her witness the nightmare, but he was pissed off he'd had to reveal it at all. He'd been trying to bury it for all these years, keeping himself behind a desk and surrounding himself with politics so he wouldn't have to go out into the field and risk resurrecting old ghosts.

"I've killed, too." When he looked at her in a silent way that said he was listening, she added, "More than twelve."

"When. Who."

"About five years ago the Chimeran clan from Molokai came over. They invaded our valley, wanted to take down our *ali'i*. Wanted to raise themselves up and make us all their lesser."

"What happened?"

She shrugged. "We destroyed them. They had small numbers. Their clan was dwindling and that was their last effort to make a name for themselves."

"Did they kill a lot of your clan?"

"Yes. My parents among them. They were excellent fighters but they were older. A lot of our younger, untried warriors died, too."

He took a deep breath she recognized as one meant to calm himself. The mark of a leader trying to keep his head. "The difference is, Keko, you were protecting your people against a clear threat. Someone tries to kill you or your family, take your home, you fight back. I get that. But that secretary in Toronto who walked in on her boss as he was using *Mendacia*, just as the illusionary magic was kicking in? That completely innocent woman who opened the door at the one wrong second out of the entire day? She deserved to die because of that?"

Keko sat there, transfixed, listening to this from an entirely new perspective, one she hadn't ever considered because her training had never allowed her to think that way.

"The Chairman sent me after her," Griffin went on bitterly, his face nearly unrecognizable, "and I went because I fucking had to. I had a clean kill planned out, but I must have made a noise she didn't recognize because she turned and saw me. Saw a strange man coming after her in her own house. I saw her fear. I saw her awful confusion. She had absolutely no idea who I was or why I was there. Only that I was there to kill her."

He popped to his feet and she had to tilt her head back to look at him. The muscle in his jaw did that clenching thing again, the thing that made him look mean even as his eyes softened. "When the Son of Earth came after you and I knew you were having trouble accessing your fire, that you were probably seconds away from dying, I went after him. I attacked and went for the kill even though I knew it would trigger the nightmare. I just have to deal with what I've done." He bent down, snatched his vest from the ground, stuffed the knife into the back holder, and zipped the thing over his chest.

She got the signal. He was done talking and they were moving out. She rose, a little unsteady from the shock.

"You know what?"

It was his tender tone, completely flipped around from what she'd just heard, that stopped her, made her look up. "What?"

"Fuck the nightmare. If the Son of Earth comes after you, I'll do it all over again."

Another couple hours' hiking to get out of the green tangle and across the main highway, and then they turned down a long, winding road high above the ocean. It was right at the line when day started to curve toward dusk, and the light had a golden quality to it.

A row of modest one-story homes with overflowing garages

and rusting cars in their driveways stretched up ahead, their front doors opening to one hell of a view of sparkling blue water. A hand-painted sign out on Route 19 pointed to a B and B and Griffin steered them toward it. Keko had tried to protest—she'd refused to hitch a ride, too—but they both needed food and a good rest. And he needed a phone.

Even in their dirty states, they didn't stand out. The island was crawling with people walking along the roadsides, thumbs jutting out, their whole lives contained in their backpacks. He didn't worry about being noticed as they trudged down the road—not from Primaries who puttered around their front yards and not from the Children of Earth. If their theory was correct, they'd left the Children's territory the moment they'd left the wild.

The B and B was a Victorian-era house with a wraparound front porch, moist from the humidity. The owners lived in the mid-twentieth-century home set farther back on the slope, and they accepted cash from Griffin, no ID required.

Griffin and Keko were the only guests, but he only booked one room.

Key in hand, he unlocked the heavy wooden door and let it swing inward. The room was clean but basic, done in faux bamboo furniture and draped in tropical prints. He stepped inside, noting the single queen bed, and didn't hear Keko's footsteps following. When he turned around, she'd backed up against the porch railing, her face slightly pale as she peered into the room. It had started to rain. Again.

"I'm hungry," she said. "Are you? I'll find us some food."

He didn't know what she'd brought with her when she'd set out from the valley. "Need money?"

She patted her pack awkwardly. "I've got a little." She backed down the porch, avoiding his eyes. Before bounding down the steps, she added, "I'll be back."

Something in her eyes told him she wasn't even sure that was true. Two things kept him from going after her right then and there: One, she didn't know how to read the star map; and two, he was finally alone.

Propping open the door with his boot, he snatched the phone sitting on the table by the bed, dialed quickly, and stretched the curling, tangled cord toward the porch. Standing in the open doorway, watching Keko walk barefoot in the rain toward a dense row of connected shops done in the same old Victorian style, he listened impatiently to the ringing on the other end of the line.

A man picked up, sounding skeptical. "Yes?"

"This is Griffin Aames. Get me the premier." The Air's hesitation pissed him off. "Don't even think about giving me the runaround. If he's there and alive, I need to speak with him."

"One moment." There was shuffling, and muffled voices.

Keko disappeared from view, taking the awareness of her signature with it. He tried not to let it worry or bother him, but he found himself mumbling into the receiver, "Come on. Come on."

Night descended, the steadily falling rain making the evening grayer and drearier. Minutes passed. He paced in the doorway, the phone cord stretched to its maximum as he went out onto the porch, trying to see if Keko had gone through one of the doors in that line of shops, or if she'd just kept walking.

A fumbling of the phone on the other end, then a familiar voice, resigned and tired. "Griffin."

With the time change, it would be after midnight at the air elemental compound in Canada. Griffin didn't care.

"What the *fuck*." To hell with propriety and diplomacy. "We had a deal, Premier. I come after Keko *alone*. The Children agreed to this. Keko is theirs only if she gets to the Source."

"Whoa, whoa." The premier sniffed and sounded like he took a drink of something. "Slow down. I have no idea what you're talking about."

"Really." Griffin gripped the slick porch railing, holding back a biting laugh and a shout of rage-induced frustration. "A Son of Earth attacked us and you're telling me you had no clue."

"Us?"

Griffin bowed his head, letting the rain hit his neck and run through his hair. "I found Keko. I'm with her. And this fucking earth elemental turns into a tree or possesses one or something, and almost kills us both."

The premier sucked in a breath. "Is the Source safe?"

"Heard of any natural disasters lately?"

"So our deal is still on." It wasn't a question.

Griffin squeezed his eyes shut. "Look, I'm upholding my end. You sure as fuck better honor yours."

The premier inhaled as though he had a cigarette between his lips. "I sanctioned no attack, authorized no breach of the deal. I gave you my word. Aya gave hers, too. I'll bring this up with her immediately."

"Tell her to leave us the hell alone. If you want the Source safe, I need more time."

"If all I wanted was for the Source to be safe"—another smoke-filled inhale—"I would just let Aya and the Children do their thing. Let them take care of it themselves. This is about giving you your chance."

A sick feeling twisted Griffin's gut, like he'd finally gotten a bite after nearly starving and the food had gone rancid. He stalked back into the room. "I'm handling this," he snarled, and slammed down the receiver. It felt good to do that. You didn't get to do that with cell phones anymore.

He stared at the phone for a long time, wondering exactly what he'd just done. By warning off the Children of Earth, he'd bought himself much-needed time with Keko—time to find out what secret she was protecting and what she was going to do with the map that was in his head. More time just to be with her.

And yet he'd also basically reconfirmed with the premier that he'd trade Keko for a Senatus seat.

But would he?

THIRTEEN

Aya broke through the hard, cold crust of earth and rolled herself onto the windswept prairie of southern Alberta. This spot was a few hours from the U.S. border, though that sort of delineation meant little to her kind. What did matter was that the land here had been worked over so much with plow and seed that there were very few purely natural, untouched areas left for her use as travel and entry/exit points. Except for this one spot where a great tree stood twisted like an old soldier standing sentry by the gravel road.

An icy, blustery night out here, where not much lived besides crops and the few farmers who tended them. And the Airs.

Spring ran cold here, and yellowed late-March grass poked up through the remaining patches of snow around the tree. She pushed her human body into being as quickly as the painful, awkward shift allowed. She magically fashioned clothing from the grass and the nearby dead husks of corn: a soft, woven suit that conformed to her body from neck to ankles. It looked strange, she knew, but she had no human clothing of her own yet.

Someday. Soon.

She started walking west under the blue-black sky made in the hours past midnight, the moon casting shadows and the stars guiding her way. On all sides she sensed the great space of central Canada extending out. She felt the unbroken rush of wind as it crossed the land and whipped across her body, and it made her smile to herself. Made her breathe in deeply the sweet scent of fresh air. Made her revel in what she could not get Within.

She'd been here before. Two months ago the premier had summoned her, wanting her counsel, when the Chimerans had been on the verge of declaring war on the Ofarians. And then one month ago, when she'd been informed that Madeline was no longer the Airs' mind-wiper, and that her position had been filled by her brother.

A similar summons had arrived barely an hour earlier, its urgency just as potent. She'd been sitting in her cave, human eyes closed, trying not to think about the walls closing in, when the little glowing root had pushed through a crack and unfurled the premier's message, written on a leaf in the way she'd only told him and the Chimeran chief to contact her. *My compound. As soon as possible.*

Her immediate thought? Griffin. Keko.

Now she trudged through the crunchy, barren aisles of dead corn, heading toward the massive white walls that loomed in the distance. When the crops gave way to the grass of the meadows that surrounded the Air compound, she passed several wooden signs staked into the ground.

HAVE YOU REPENTED?

WALK WITH THE LORD AND YOU'LL NEVER NEED TO RUN FROM ANYTHING AGAIN.

JESUS SAVES.

The white walls were two stories tall, impenetrable except for the iron doors big enough to admit a semitruck and stamped with a giant white cross. Razor wire coiled over the top of the wall. Security cameras covered all angles of the enclosure and the surrounding meadow.

As Aya approached, one side of the iron doors opened and a woman in a parka and hat and mittens appeared. She eyed Aya's body, tightly clad in the woven suit, unable to disguise her shock and wariness. Peering out into the cold, dark night, and then returning her stare back to Aya, she said, "You can only be . . ."

"I am." Though the female Air was taller than her by a head, Aya proudly lifted her chin and looked the Air directly in the eye. "Aya, Daughter of Earth. The premier is expecting me."

The Air shuffled back to admit Aya, and Aya felt the Air's

awe pass over her like the wind. Aya could not wait to blend in better, to not draw such stares.

"This way." The female hurried ahead, snaking through a vaguely familiar set of dark alleyways between narrowly placed buildings. The whole compound was like that, she remembered, a maze packed tightly with boxy, nondescript structures meant to hold and house the largest density of air elementals.

Aya could not keep track of their path. Just when she was sure she'd seen this particular corner or doorway more than once, and that the female was steering her back out the way they came, they popped out into a small square. Ahead rose a giant, ornate church topped with the massive silver cross she'd glimpsed from the other side of the wall. The other woman pulled open the heavy wood doors of the church and the two of them entered.

The inside looked nothing like the few other churches Aya had wandered into, but the interior didn't matter, as long as anyone flying over or trying to spy inside the compound thought this place was dedicated to a Primary religion and inhabited by isolationist zealots. Each Secondary race had its own way of hiding in plain sight, so it was rather an important thing to have been invited into another elemental world.

And this marked the third time. This excited her. She needed stronger eyes on the Airs. Aya's growing friendship with Keko had given her hope that she'd be allowed a peek into the Chimeran culture, and she knew Griffin would openly welcome a chance to meet with her eventually, but had both those opportunities been destroyed now? What then?

"Wait in here." The female Air directed Aya into a windowless room in the center of the false church but did not enter herself. She nodded toward a closed door on the opposite wall, set with a mottled glass window that gave the vague impression of bodies moving behind it. "He'll let you know when he's ready."

She left, closing the door, and Aya heard a subsequent click. On her last visit, they hadn't locked her in. There was no place to sit.

A burst of raised voices, all male, maybe three in number, made her jump, her head swiveling in the direction of the mottled glass door. The voices ramped up to overlapping shouts, their words indistinct but the anger very, very clear. Something crashed to the ground, followed by a heavy thump against a wall. More crashes, more shouts, then the door flew open.

A male Air stomped out, and not just any Air. *Him.* The one with the curly hair and pale blue eyes. The one she saw last time she'd been called here. The one Nem had mentioned.

Inside the office, the premier and Aaron stood in the middle of a disaster. A bookcase had been overturned and something glass lay in shards on the wood floor.

"Go do your penance, Jase," the premier growled.

The curly-haired Air halted in the center of the room, his back to the door. Fists balled at his sides, he closed his eyes and snarled back, "The name's Jason now."

"Ha. Changing your damn name doesn't absolve you. You still owe me. You still need to pay for *her.*"

Jase—Jason's—eyes opened, the intense stare spearing straight ahead, straight through Aya, even though she stood not three feet away.

"Fuck you." Razors laced his whisper. Aya felt them slice across her human skin.

"Reno," said the premier, his cowboy boots crunching on glass as he went to the door and gripped its edge. "Get it done." The door slammed with such force the entire wall vibrated.

Jason drew a deep breath, his chest rattling as it expanded and collapsed. Then he blinked at Aya, shook his head, blinked again. "Who the hell are you?"

An earthquake of odd sensations shook Aya's body and mind as she stood under Jason's powerful scrutiny, anger flushing his skin and a terrible loss clouding his eyes. She did not understand what she was feeling, how to parse the peaks and valleys of the effects of such direct attention.

"We've met before," she said.

His eyes narrowed. "No, we haven't."

She shook her head as a strange heat crept up from her chest, traveling the length of her neck to settle in her cheeks. "I'm sorry. You're right. Last time I was here I merely . . . saw you."

Last time he'd been standing, dead-eyed, just behind the premier, looking like he'd been sentenced to prison. That was when he'd taken over for Madeline, so perhaps that's exactly what had happened. Aya had never realized before that the Airs used their mind-wipers as a form of punishment.

Jason inched closer, and though most people were larger than her, right then he seemed impossibly tall, as wide as a mountain. His gaze traveled over her face and hair, the corners of his mouth turned down. "Who *are* you?"

Clearing her throat, she lifted her chin and looked right at him. "I am Aya, Daughter of Earth, here to see the premier on Senatus matters."

"I see." He nodded, the back of his teeth making a terrible grinding noise. "You don't look how I thought you would."

"What do you mean? What were you expecting?"

He let out a hollow laugh. His eyes made a general sweep of her body. Different than how Nem had looked at her, however. Jason's study was critical and detached. Still, standing there wrapped in the suit of woven grass that suddenly felt too constrictive, a new kind of warmth spread out to her extremities. Never one to cower, though, confident in her decision to evolve, she stared back.

"A Child of Earth?" he finally said with a faint snort. "Dreadlocks. Hairy legs. Bells on your wrists and ankles."

None of that made sense to her and she made a mental note to look it up.

"But you're none of that. Are you?" As his voice turned distant, his wandering gaze settled on her hair—still not entirely human, she knew, with its color, or lack thereof, and the way it tended to move on its own—growing, curling, wrapping around her neck and body.

With another sudden jerk and shake of his head, he threw off whatever ghosts clung to his thoughts and leaned closer. Filling her vision with his face.

"Don't worry, *Senatus*," he spit, "I'll do what you fucking want me to."

Aya opened her mouth—to ask what he meant or to defend herself or to deny she had anything to do with whatever it was the premier wanted of him—but Jason kept talking, his tone spiraling into the same ugly one he'd used on the premier.

"I'll do it," he said, "but you tell him that after this one, I'm done. This is the last mind I fuck with." Swerving around her with the force of a gale, Jason lunged for the exterior door, rattling the knob so hard Aya thought he might rip it off. "Nancy." He pounded on the wood. "Let me the fuck out."

Aya only stood there, knowing she could not reveal herself to this man. Knowing she could not tell him that she was just as abhorred by the Senatus practice of mind scrambling as he was.

Jason glared at her and she had to clamp her lips shut to keep from begging him to give her time. To hold on until Griffin succeeded and the two of them could start to steer Senatus thinking and practices in different, better directions.

Nancy, the Air who'd met her at the gate, unlocked the door and Jason fled the waiting room so fast Aya wondered if he'd used his magic to ride the wind. In his wake, she stared at the space he'd once consumed, still able to see his shape. Still able to sense the force of his emotion. Evolution had brought that to her, that blessing and that curse of being finely in tune with what others—Primary or Secondary—felt. And there was no doubt over what she'd just experienced.

Jason *hated* her.

How much time passed before the door to the premier's office opened, Aya couldn't say. The hole in her gut had eaten much of her present awareness. Her mind was spinning away, thinking about the human who would suffer so terribly at Jason's will because they probably inadvertently saw something they shouldn't have. Hating how, yet again, all she could do was stand here and watch it happen.

Was that what this was about? This midnight summons? Did the premier want to see her about Jason or a new threat coming out of Reno?

"Aya." The premier's voice hadn't lost its snarl.

She turned, giving him a slight inclination of her head and noticing with consternation how his icy eyes pierced her. "Premier."

Aaron stepped out of the office, beckoning her inside. Too late she remembered how human skin was susceptible to sharp edges. She stepped on a small shard of broken glass and hissed. A sliver of red leaked out from her sole.

The premier didn't notice. In fact, he stood in front of his desk, arms crossed, hair dented by the cowboy hat now lying upside down in a corner. Staring.

"I know a lot more about you now," he said, his voice chilly, "don't I?"

She swept a long look around his office, glancing pointedly at the ceiling where the huge Christian cross sat atop the false church. "And I you."

He didn't seem to hear her, or if he did, he chose to ignore her. "How you move about under the earth. How you can change your shape. Quite unusual. Quite fascinating. It's why you always insisted the Senatus meet outside. In the dark. In remote places."

There'd been reasons why the Children had kept their true nature and their history secret since the dawn of man: to avoid reactions like this one.

So this was what the summons was about, to confront her about the Children. Maybe to use her indiscretion—done in heat and haste—against her like Nem had done. Worry started to worm its way into her consciousness. Worry that the Father would learn what she'd done, and worry that the premier would feel threatened and cut her loose from the Senatus when she was so close to finally putting her plan into motion.

"Yes, that's why," she replied, because it would be disadvantageous to admit otherwise, or to give him any further information.

"But what I don't get"—he rubbed his forehead in a way that even she knew to be exaggerated—"is why the *fuck* you would go against your own directive."

Give away nothing. "Why do you think I did that?"

His hand came away from his face, one finger stabbing into the air between them. "Why make such a grand, dramatic entrance the other night, put massive demands on the Senatus, outline your own terms, and then blow everything to pieces?"

A strange, buzzing sensation filled her head, making her feel dizzy and nauseous. "I think you need to explain yourself."

"*I* need to explain?" He was shouting now. "There is one thing the Senatus is about, and that's solidarity. Consensus. You know this. And yet you rise up out of the ground and declare the Earth in danger if Keko so much as breathes on this Fire Source. You cut a deal to allow us to go after her and hopefully keep the peace with the Chimerans. You know you'll have a chance at her if Griffin fails. And you attack her anyway."

Dread and rage twisted through her, but she drew herself up as tall as the diminutive body would allow. "I did no such thing."

The premier shook his head in disbelief and turned to rest both palms on the edge of his desk. "Trust is a tenuous thing, Aya. Especially among Secondaries."

All this human emotion warred inside her—fear and anger, concern and confusion—and she didn't know how to keep them separate. Or even if she should. "You forget. The Children of Earth are the ones who approached the Airs and the Chimerans to begin the Senatus many centuries ago. We are invested in its success and don't want to compromise it. Now tell me what happened."

He inhaled long and slow through his nose as he regarded her. "Got a call from Griffin a couple hours ago. Pissed off as all hell. Said a Child of Earth attacked them when they were nowhere near the Source. Something about a tree coming to life."

"Keko. Is she—"

"Alive."

Aya held in the massive sigh she desperately wanted to release.

The premier pushed off the desk. "Griffin wants assurances he'll have his chance. Then you can have yours. As you originally agreed."

She raised her voice, indignant. "Absolutely. I gave no other orders to contradict what was said around the bonfire. I've kept my word."

The premier eyed her hard. "Then which one of you diggers didn't?"

She was just starting to get a hold on the concept of Aboveground insults, but she was pretty sure the premier had just handed her one. There was no time to dwell on it now. Fix the problem in Hawaii first, or else smoothing over a little namecalling would be the least of her issues.

There were two possibilities behind the attack on Griffin and Keko. The Father, who could have given an order to another

Child of Earth behind her back. Or Nem, guardian of the Source, who'd been so clearly angry with her on the Aran Islands.

The Father wasn't that crafty.

She had to find Nem. Fast.

FOURTEEN

An hour later and Keko still hadn't come back. It was all the time Griffin was willing to allow before he knew he had to go after her. Before he began to think that maybe she actually had memorized enough of the star map to try to find her own way. Before he started to fear that the Son of Earth had found a way to come back.

Which scared him more? Her trying to give him the slip again? Or another threat to her safety?

Locking up the room, he pounded down the porch steps and headed for the row of connected shops a quarter mile up the road. The rain had transformed into giant drops that hit him like bombs.

At home in San Francisco, when he listened to Ofarian issues, he had to be prudent about which emotions he displayed, and when and how. But here, alone and worrying about Keko after all that had happened between them—and all that had shifted and changed in the last few days—he threw away his guards and let himself *feel*.

She tended to do that to him.

The row of shops were lined with a boardwalk out front, a closed ice cream parlor capping one end, a long-shuttered theater in the middle, and a bar at the far end. A tourist trinket shop and an artist's studio were dark for the evening. The pub was open, however, acoustic guitar music trickling out to mix with the rain, and Griffin headed toward it.

A blast of heat and fire and magic assaulted his mind and took over his senses.

The whole front and one side of the bar were windows, all

thrown open to the salty air, the eaves long and deep enough to keep out the wet. The place was small, the short bar to the right with a glaringly lit kitchen just behind it, a ledge and stools lining the two walls of windows. Three old men sat at the bar with glasses of beer.

Keko sat at the ledge overlooking the ocean, bare feet hooked over the rungs of her stool, one finger toying with the straw in her can of ginger ale, and two wrapped hamburgers sitting untouched at her elbow.

She'd told him once, sitting in that hotel room bed, that she didn't drink. She didn't like how it stole her awareness. That said a great deal about her, now that he thought about it. The watchful warrior, always at the ready.

She hadn't ditched him again. And she was safe.

Keko didn't even notice him until he slid a hand onto the ledge near the burgers and said, "Hey."

She blinked up at him in surprise. "Hey." Peering into the corner where a neon clock hung above a faded, curling nineties-era beer poster, she asked, "What time is it?"

"Not that late. But you left over an hour ago. I didn't know what to think."

"Sorry." She nudged the hamburger closer to him.

He pulled out the stool next to her and perched on the edge, not taking the food. The wind off the ocean felt nice. Fragrant flowering bushes just outside filled the bar with a sweet scent. Beyond the ever-present line of clouds that clung to the shoreline, he could see the stars trying to inch closer to land.

"No, you're not," he said.

"You thought I'd taken off."

"I worried you might try."

She turned her face to the ocean and the breeze pushed her hair in a long stream behind her. "I've been sitting here considering it. Considering a lot of things."

He was dumbstruck by her profile, how so fucking beautiful and so completely strong it was. "Like?"

"How I don't like this."

"Don't like what?"

"This . . . this . . ." Her hand hovered over her chest, her fingers wiggling. "Doubt. Wondering. Questioning."

"Ah, I see. That's what most people call 'thinking things through.'"

"It sucks."

"You're used to just acting. Making a quick decision and going for it. Balls out. All in. No turning back."

Her almond eyes assessed him but she did not deny any of that, because she knew he was right.

"The stars are out," she said, still looking only at his face.

"They are."

"Does your vow still hold?"

He tried not to let his—trepidation? Curiosity?—show. "Always."

She inhaled but it wasn't of the Chimeran kind. She ran the heels of her hands up and down her thighs. "None of this is about my honor. At least, not anymore."

"That's what you said before, that it wasn't about you."

"It started out that way, partly. I wanted to restore my status and rise above the *ali'i*. I thought I could get back at Chief. But there's another reason—a bigger reason—and it's become the only thing that matters to me now. If I tell you, it's because I want what you can give me. If I tell you, it's because you can help me help my people."

"Your people?"

She ignored him. "I don't know how to sort this all out on my own, so I'm asking my faith to carry one hell of a burden."

"Faith means a lot to you. It won't let you down."

Neither will I, he longed to say but didn't. Because how could he be sure that he wouldn't? How could he finally learn her true goal, give her the location of the Source as he'd vowed, and then prevent her from reaching it?

He had to physically bite back his anguish, the burn of it making his chest feel hot and tight.

Tell me, he silently begged. *Don't tell me.*

Keko inhaled again. "Chief has lost his magic."

The words blurted out of her mouth and hit the ledge between them, leaving him as cold as the hamburger sitting there. The rain stopped suddenly, as if someone had turned off a faucet.

"What?" he finally managed to sputter out.

As she chewed her lip, he realized he'd never seen her

struggle with words this much. Like her actions, she'd always just . . . spoken. "It's some sort of disease. It stole his magic. He can feel it inside but he can't bring it out. And I guess he's not alone. Apparently it's hit other Chimerans, too. I don't know who exactly, but it doesn't matter. Our magic is everything. Fire means honor and life. You know that."

"Jesus, Keko—"

"If I can get to the Source, if I can tap into the pure, raw magic there and bring it back to the valley, I can cure them. I know I can."

Griffin had to hold fast to the ledge to keep from tipping sideways. The whole island seemed like it was flipping end over end.

"So you see," she was saying, "it truly isn't about me. I almost brought them to war, Griffin. Over my own stupid fucking broken heart. I shamed them when I shamed myself. I made a mess, and I need to clean it up. I owe this to them, to bring back what they've lost. And if I die trying, well, then that's what the Queen wills. At least I tried. At least I tried to make it right with them."

He just sat there, feeling carved hollow, pulled inside out. This changed . . . *everything.*

He rubbed his chin. "You made me think—"

"I had to," she said. "If it were just Chief, I would have shouted his weakness across the valley and challenged him right then and there. But this disease is affecting others, innocents. I couldn't tell anyone else in the clan where I was going or why, or it would've compromised the infected and brought them dishonor when they've been so good at hiding their disability." She shook her head. "When I left the valley I had power on my mind. I wanted to be followed and respected again, and the only way to do that was to become *ali'i.* Bigger than the Queen, even. Now . . ."

He edged closer. "You still want that, Keko. You've always wanted it, but now your motives are *truly* honorable. Before, it was just a name."

She searched his face for a long moment, and he heard her unspoken question.

"Yes." He nodded ardently. "Yes. Your purpose, what you just told me, is honorable. It might be the most honorable thing I've ever heard."

It hurt to say, because barely an hour ago he'd reassured the premier he'd still bring Keko in.

So much of what had happened at the Senatus and later in the chief's house now clicked into place. And so little of it he could actually tell her. With a growl of frustration, he shoved his hands into his hair. "I thought that the chief was acting weird. Like his mouth was telling me one thing—to go after you and stop you—but his eyes were saying just the opposite. I couldn't figure it out."

Her laugh was tinged with disgust. "I don't think he's figured it out either. He wants desperately to be cured, but he also doesn't want to be shamed and deposed, which he thinks will happen if I return to the valley with the Source. He knows he can't have his magic back and still be *ali'i*. He's constantly looking over his shoulder, I bet, wondering when and how he'll be called out."

Griffin had seen all of that in the chief's demeanor.

"If I go back with the Source," Keko continued, "he's cured but I've also proved myself above him. There's a greater chance I won't make it, but he knows me too well, knows what kind of Chimeran I am. That I don't accept failure. He's more scared of my success, so that's why he's having me stopped. Because he also knows I won't say anything about the disease if it compromises innocents. This is his way of winning, of holding me down and keeping his own lying ass out of the Common House."

Yeah, all that seemed correct. There was something else, of course, something Griffin couldn't tell Keko: that the chief had been all but forced to agree with the Senatus. There was no way Chief could've gone against Aya when she'd burst from the ground spouting doomsday predictions. There was no way he could've gone against the premier either. Revealing his illness and Keko's true cause would have compromised his position within his clan and also around the bonfire.

Griffin suspected that deep down the chief really did want Keko to succeed *because* she would cure him and *because* she wouldn't ever expose the blameless Chimerans or him. He thought he would win either way.

No longer, though. Not with the Senatus behind her retrieval. *That* had been the origin of the anguish Griffin had detected.

Fuck, it wasn't supposed to be this complicated.

Then he remembered a certain detail. "You know, I thought the chief's signature felt weak, but I just assumed it was because he was standing next to Bane. Your brother and you, I think you both have some serious power."

She eyed him strangely. "Why do you say that?"

"Because Bane was with this other Chimeran—a shorter guy with a tattoo covering one shoulder?—and Bane's signature almost knocked me out, but the other guy's was barely more than a whisper."

One hand covered her mouth. Her obsidian eyes went wide as she, too, realized what he'd just inadvertently revealed. "Ikaika. Holy shit. Ikaika, too."

"Yeah, that was his name. He's one of the sick ones?"

She shoved off the stool and it clattered to the tile behind her. One thumb went into her mouth and she chewed on the nail, her eyes on the floor. "He's got to be. And Bane must know about it."

Griffin rubbed his forehead. "But if Bane doesn't know about the chief—"

Keko waved a frustrated hand. "Bane doesn't give a shit about Chief. He's general. He's Chimeran and he's like me. He wants to be *ali'i* so he wants our uncle gone."

"So that's why he told me to help you."

Her head snapped up. "He . . . what?"

Griffin leaned down and righted her stool, patting the seat, though she didn't take it. "I told you the truth, that he wanted me to come after you, but there's more. He pulled me aside separately, told me he didn't care what the chief or the Senatus said, that he wanted me to help you get to the Source and bring back the magic. I get it now. He wanted me to help him throw over your *ali'i*."

"No." She sat slowly, her eyes dancing back and forth in thought. "He's doing it for Ikaika. He wants me to cure Ikaika."

"Why—*oh*."

The embrace of the two men, the way they'd touched, witnessed through the grimy window of that convenience store, came back to Griffin.

"I think he wanted me to do it for you, too," Griffin added. "To make sure you're safe."

Keko shook her head at the ceiling. "That's not how the

Chimeran world works, Griffin. I'm a threat to him. I always have been."

"I wouldn't be so sure about that. Look how you've changed."

She recoiled at that, like personal change was evil.

"You have," he asserted. "And yeah, maybe Bane wants his lover cured and maybe he wants to see the chief go down in the process, but he's still your brother. I saw his face. He wants you to succeed and he wants you back in the valley alive."

Hands on her knees, she took a breath and leaned forward. "Now do you understand what I have to do? And why?"

He did. Oh, how he did. Because it was exactly the same thing he would have done for his own people. And she wasn't even their leader.

A surge of emotion washed over him, took him under. He was helpless against it, flailing, gasping for air. Drowning in her.

He must have been wearing an odd expression, because Keko suddenly flared with rage, a wave of heat exploding out of her. "You gave me your word, Griffin. You use this against me or the Chimerans and this time I *will* come after you."

Reaching out, he took her face in his hands. She tried to fight him off at first, but he dug into her hair, finding the back of her skull, and brought her to him for a kiss. A tender, swift meeting of the lips that had less to do with passion and more with promise. She stiffened, understanding.

When he drew back, a profound look of shock transformed her face.

"You are amazing," he whispered.

Not a day ago, he'd thought her foolish and suicidal and selfish. Beautiful and desirable and . . . his . . . but still all of those things.

She blinked under the shadow of those words, then cleared her throat. "And you have something I need."

He did, didn't he? Going to the bar, he asked the bartender for a piece of paper and pen, and a map of Hawaii. The silver-haired, leather-faced man handed him a ratty tourist map marred by brown coffee cup circles.

"Come with me," he told Keko. "And bring those burgers. I'm starving."

They walked in silence away from the lights of the bar and the tiny town center, chowing on the cold burgers that tasted like ambrosia, heading down to the edge of the land where a rickety fence half-heartedly kept people from falling over the side. He could hear the ocean far below but could not see it.

The stars threw a billowing blanket over their heads, and he knew each and every one. Kneeling before a bench, he spread out the Hawaiian island map and took up the pen and paper.

Keko crowded him on one side, peering over his shoulder. Her breathing quickened.

An image of Aya came to him, of her emerging from the ground, horror on her humanlike face and words of doom and destruction on her tongue.

Great stars, what had he done, making these bargains with Aya and then with Keko? What the hell was he about to do by giving Keko the key to triggering a potential natural disaster? Why was he about to send her right back into the violent arms of the Children of Earth?

Because of her purpose. That damned honorable purpose that he understood so well.

His mind reeled with doubt and confusion. Then he realized that by deciphering the map tonight she wouldn't be waltzing into the Source right at that very moment. It was far away and it would take some finagling to reach it. That would give him some time to work shit out. And he would. He would figure everything out—how to let Keko heal her people, how to appease Aya and the Senatus, how to protect the Earth—but right now . . .

Twisting his head to the sky, he scanned the beautiful map of stars, instantly knowing his position below them. Pen in hand, he made a series of dots on the paper as he remembered them from the star map, taking into account the three-dimensional nature of it and adjusting it accordingly. A square marked the location the stone prayer had showed to be the Source, that glowing circle in the center of the carved figure's chest. Then he turned to the map of the Hawaiian Islands and marked where he and Keko currently stood.

In his head he overlaid the current pattern of stars above with how they would change from the vantage point of the

Source. His pen flew over the map, the angles and dimensions automatically shifting in his mind, pen lines mimicking his thought processes. Primaries would use equations and fancy tools and computers, but the stars were part of his Ofarian blood, and he just *knew*.

"There." A swish of the pen out in the open blue part of the ocean northwest of Nihau, the last main Hawaiian island past Kauai. Keko bent close to the circle and the X he'd drawn. "Are you sure? There's nothing out there."

He sat back on his heels, ignoring the sick feeling starting in his stomach. "The islands are an archipelago. Thousands of uninhabited little land masses stretching for thousands of miles into the Pacific. Your Source is on one of them. That one. Way out there." He tapped his circle.

She straightened and gazed off into the dark inland. "I thought it might be a—"

"Volcano? Like Kīlauea?"

"Yeah."

He frowned. "Maybe it is. I don't know what's there."

She faced him in her confident way that turned him on like nothing else. "Are you still going to try to stop me?"

Oh, that answer? He still didn't know it. Still didn't know which truth he would speak.

He could tell her now what Aya said, what she'd warned the entire Senatus about, but Keko wouldn't believe him. She would still see it as manipulation, and he wouldn't blame her.

Time. He had some time. And neither of them was going anywhere tonight.

Closing the space between them, he slid his hands around her body, loving how her arms came around his neck almost instantly. Brushing his mouth against hers, he murmured, "Not at this moment, no."

He might have to, though. And he didn't want to think about it. Didn't want to think what that might mean to the Chimeran people. To her.

Didn't want to admit that stopping her would annihilate every last thread of connection he and Keko had ever formed. And that hurt most of all.

She tilted her head back, her dark eyes simmering. "But tomorrow?"

"Tomorrow, I will think about tomorrow."

A long, slow blink. "And tonight?"

Like his vision, his very existence at that moment narrowed down to her. He stole a page from her book of honesty and forthrightness and made every word count, let her see everything he felt inside. "Tonight? Be with me."

It would be a long, cold hike across the fields to the natural, protected area by the tree at the edge of air elemental property. If only she could get out of the compound first.

The premier had dismissed Aya from his office, then locked the door in her face. Through the mottled glass she watched his shape righting the toppled bookcase and replacing the objects and books upon the shelves. He got a broom and swept up the broken glass, all but erasing the confrontation with Jason. Who was, chances were, already heading for Reno to destroy a human mind.

Aya went to the door leading out into the false church and knocked. A few minutes later the door swung open and fresher air rushed into the tiny, gray-painted room that was beginning to close in on her like the caves Within.

"You done?" Nancy asked, her forehead wrinkled.

Aya nodded. "Take me to the gate."

Nancy took her on a completely different path to the outer walls. Aya could never track her way through the maze of alleys and narrow streets and strategically placed dead ends, but of course, that was the whole idea. When they reached the gate, a guard came out of a little hut whose windows glowed blue-green with computer screens. He unlocked the exit door and Aya peered out into the vast, windy fields beyond.

"Wait."

Aya pivoted at the sound of the familiar voice. Aaron peeled himself away from the interior shadows and approached her. The guard fell back into his little hut and Nancy, with a respectful nod to Aaron, melted back into the city labyrinth.

Though Aya longed to make a run for the field, she folded her hands and looked up at the approaching Air, who wore a different expression—owned a separate demeanor altogether, actually—than that of the premier.

Aaron was older than his leader, somewhere in his fifties, Aya guessed, and his coloring was much paler than the premier's tanned, worn appearance. He cocked his head as he regarded her.

"Yes?" she prompted.

"How can you look so human," he murmured, "when you are so clearly not?"

She did not move and kept her features as still as stone. Evolution was the Children's greatest secret—even greater than their hidden domain and their means of travel across the planet. No Primary or Secondary knew of the choice presented to each Child. None knew that some humans who now walked Aboveground had been born Within.

"What you did with the earth," he went on, staring at her with bald curiosity, "seems impossible. For you to have been . . . that. And now you are . . . this. I have never seen a Secondary do anything like that."

She sensed her hair respond to him, the long white tendrils coiling around her wrists like vines. His eyes dropped to the motion, then widened with wonder. Not with fear or mistrust or doubt.

Perhaps in this man she might find an ally. Perhaps someone more sympathetic and less leery than the premier.

"We are not Secondary," she replied. It had never been declared a secret, that statement about her people's history.

Aaron crossed his arms. "What do you mean?"

Aya laced her fingers. "Children are actually Primaries. We are sisters and brothers to humanity, born as one being at the dawn of time, and then separated as life changed with the earth."

A heavy pause followed. "How come no scientists or archaeologists ever found skeletons or evidence of you, like they did early humans?"

"Because we die Within." Or, if a Child had already evolved, they died Aboveground and no one was the wiser.

"Fascinating," Aaron breathed.

She lifted her shoulders in a movement she'd copied from

Keko. "So you see, we are not truly Secondary. We've always been here. And we will always be—"

A klaxon roared throughout the compound, the small device sitting on top of the guard hut throwing out the terrible, shrieking, repetitive alarm. She doubled forward, hands over her ringing ears. When she straightened, she watched with dread as the guard yanked shut the iron exit doors to the compound, locking her inside the walls.

After screaming something to her she could not hear over the cacophony, Aaron took off running back through the tangle of buildings. That guard had a phone pressed to his ear, his hands flying over various keyboards. She could stand here and wait to see when they'd actually let her go . . . or she could follow Aaron and find out the reason behind the horror in his eyes.

His feet disappeared around the first left corner and she sprinted after him before he could take another turn and be lost to the labyrinth.

They ran and ran, this path far more linear and shorter than the other two she'd been pulled along. Very soon she and Aaron burst into the tiny square in front of the church she'd just left. Air elementals spilled from the bland, narrow buildings, streaming toward the church, their hands to their mouths and eyes turned up to another alarm blaring on top of the steeple.

Aaron sliced through the growing crowd, pushing up the steps and toward the doors. Aya followed, taking advantage of the space his people afforded him.

The church doors gave way under Aaron's mighty push, and only after Aya tumbled in after him did he realize she'd followed. But if he meant to shout at her or kick her out, there was no time because Nancy was running down the back hall toward them, panic making her face white and her eyes impossibly wide.

It was then Aya heard the screaming.

A woman's scream, a piercing wail that shot down from somewhere on the second floor. It never ended. Just kept running on a terrified, intensifying loop.

"Is that Hillary?" Aaron demanded of Nancy when she finally reached them.

Out of breath, Nancy replied, "Yes. Are the gates secured?"

Aaron nodded, ashen face turned to the stairs.

Footsteps pounded on the floor above, how many sets Aya couldn't say. At least three, maybe more. An explosion of shouting and the distinct sounds of a fight, fists and kicks and more things breaking. It was a violent one that made the scene she'd witnessed earlier through the premier's office door feel like a child's temper tantrum. Men shouted and grunted, cried out in pain or in threat. She could make sense of none of it.

A million emotions sailed through the building, bombarding her, wreaking havoc with her human senses. None of them were good.

"The premier!" Aaron had his hand on the railing, one foot poised on the bottom step.

Nancy grabbed his arm, pulled him back. "Already dead. Hillary found him in his bathroom. Throat slit."

Aya felt like the earth was taking her under while locked in this human body.

The fight upstairs rolled closer, the walls practically bowing out from the force of multiple bodies repeatedly striking them. The sounds were almost as deafening as the klaxon that still blared outside.

Then all of a sudden it stopped, the air charged with dread. There was a different struggle above, this one more focused, less intense. The muffled sounds of men's terse voices drifted down.

Two males appeared at the top of the stairs, each clamping hard to one of Jason's arms. Jason. Who was covered in blood.

FIFTEEN

By the time they got back to the B and B, the rain had started up again. A teasing spatter this time, thrown about in the wind. They walked side by side along the quiet road—the first time one of them had not led or been chased. They did not speak. Keko fought the urge to reach for his hand.

Griffin opened the door to their room, and this time the slow inward swing of the door didn't scare her. Didn't confuse her. Because she'd made her decision and got what she needed from him.

And now she just had *him*. For tonight, at least.

Still standing on the porch, she peered inside. "It's nice. A bed and everything." Her laugh was quiet and nervous, and she didn't recognize the sound of it. Hated it, even. "Haven't slept on one of those in a while."

Slowly, so slowly, he pulled the key out of the lock and turned around to face her. She loved the way he moved, had loved it from the first moment she'd seen him in that parking garage. Loved it even more as she remembered how he'd selflessly vaulted himself off that rock to attack the treeman.

She'd gotten spooked when she'd stood in this exact spot earlier, weighted down by choices and feeling buried in her revived feelings for him. So she'd headed down to that bar, ordered two burgers to go, and sat down to have a good think. A small part of her had hoped he wouldn't come looking for her.

But the vast majority of her was glad he did.

Brave Queen, she wanted him. In ways wholly different than she was used to. In ways that challenged her reasoning and her culture and the rules laid out by the Senatus. It felt okay to admit that now, standing there on a rainy porch in Hawaii with him staring expectantly at her. They'd each surrendered something. They'd each received something in return. They were going into tonight carrying a tenuous link of trust. It was something new for them, and like a bulky item of clothing she was unused to wearing, she was still shifting around in it, trying to get the fit right.

"When was the last time?" Under the sprinkle of rain his voice was as rich as coffee.

She blinked. "Sorry?"

As he quirked the tiniest of smiles, his expression turned soft and sublime. *That* was what she'd glimpsed in him years ago, that wonderful, brief moment when he'd told her he thought they should try to be together. She wanted more of that.

"The last time you slept in a bed," he added.

A vision of crumpled hotel sheets, throw pillows kicked all over the floor, the bedspread stuffed somewhere in a corner, came to her with vivid clarity. "With you."

A lift of those eyebrows. "Three years? And before that?"

"Never."

"Never?"

"In my house, the one that Bane lives in now up on the bluff, I put in a hammock so I could sleep and feel the breeze all around me. When I lay in it I could see the whole Chimeran valley through the front door. I used to sneer down at the Common House, thankful I didn't have to sleep on dirt and grass mats like them." She ran her hand down the door jamb. "And then I was made to."

He was still standing just inside the room, a hand on the doorknob, as she lingered out on the damp porch. Everything about him screamed an invitation to sex. It unnerved her, this role reversal. She should be the one beckoning him inside. She should be the one with the salacious glint in her eye. Shockingly, for the first time ever, she couldn't deny enjoying being on the receiving end.

Griffin, the beautiful man, gave a gentle nod for her to enter. She did, and he softly shut the door behind her. The sound of the rain shifted from wet plops on wood to a light drum on the roof. The smell of cotton and cleaning disinfectant replaced that of the rain. Darkness enveloped them, the only light coming from the balcony sconces that shone through the lighter colored pattern pieces on the tropical-themed drapes. Yet she saw him—oh, how she saw him—standing there in the center of their rented, temporary world for however long they could keep it wrapped around themselves.

She would not think about what she didn't or couldn't have, but instead vowed to take joy in who and what she had with her now.

His hands were in his pockets, stretching the T-shirt across his flat abdomen. She went to him.

Not a lunge. Not a physical body throw. Not an attack. A careful, deliberate advancement.

She felt everything, listened to the song of every sensation. The rough nap of the throw rug beneath the soles of her feet. The steady pound of her heart. The pull of his stare as his eyes locked with hers, dark upon dark, matched in desire.

As she came to within inches of him, his body this incredible magnet to her senses, his absolute attention on her a sensual potion she was absorbing through her pores, nothing else existed in the whole world.

He removed his hands from his pockets, a soft shush of fabric.

She pressed him against the door. No, he was pulling her. It was impossible to tell. All she knew was that his hands—those things that wielded an element she'd been taught to hate, to fight—had closed around her waist, pulling up her tank top and sliding over her skin. All she knew was that their mouths were together again, and it was the slowest, softest, wettest kiss she'd ever experienced.

She'd never known that you could kiss like this. That the slower you did it, the more you wanted it. The more you wanted it, the deeper the need rooted in your system. And the deeper the need, the more desperate you felt to have him *now*. Only it was the holding back that made everything that much more brilliant.

All she could taste was Griffin. He invaded her, surrounded her, and she knew, without a doubt, that she'd been waiting for this moment, to find this level of connection. With anyone. It wasn't something she could force with Chimeran-taught brash words or bold actions, or by opening her legs for whomever she desired back in the valley. This is what her soul had needed, and it had been waiting for Griffin.

And here he was. Touching her, pulling her into him with such exquisite, nearly painful gentleness.

Slipping her hands between their bodies, her palms rested on his chest. There was something about the cool, smooth cotton stretched over him, that delicate divider between her fingers and his skin, that made a starburst of longing explode in her mind. The force of it pressed thought and rationalization into the deepest recesses. Filled her only with the awareness of him and the various places they were connected.

Lips.

Hips.

Hands.

Hearts.

They'd never shared this kind of innocent, covered, slow touch. Why did it drive her this crazy when she'd already seen him naked, when she knew firsthand what beauty was underneath?

Time had never been in their favor, but now it seemed like they had forever. The clock and all the minutes and seconds in the world belonged to them. She'd bundle them inside her and keep them always, every single one of them packed with memories of their mouths together, the wet press of their tongues, and the low sounds that echoed the movement of their bodies.

Beneath her palms his pecs tightened, and she lost control of the tenderness of her touch. Her fingers curled, her ragged nails digging into the cotton, searching for the skin underneath but only getting his heat. His hands gripped her tighter, sliding down from her waist to her hips to her ass. He hiked her body harder against him, and she could feel his restraint, the way he was holding back, too.

She wanted to stretch this out, wanted to know every single molecule of him. She wanted to learn everything her heart hadn't already felt. There was so much of it, she realized. So much she'd never opened herself up to. Because she'd never wanted to with anyone but him.

The realization made her shiver, and her skin pebbled. Such an alien feeling.

Griffin released her, his lips gently pulling away, his hands leaving her hips to skim lightly up her arms, trailing more gooseflesh in their wake. He was watching the path of his hands, his head tilted. "Am I doing that?" he murmured in wonder.

Pressing herself against him, she opened her mouth on the hard column of his throat, loving the way he sagged under her tongue. "Yes," she whispered into his hot, hot skin. "It's you."

The vulnerability of that admission scared her, but that fear turned out to be a potent aphrodisiac.

His big, graceful arms folded around her, and even though they were nearly the same height she felt enclosed and cherished, but also his equal. They merely held each other, her breath fanning warmly across the skin below his ear, his clutch on her intensifying with every second, a vise whose pressure was most welcome. Then his head drew back, her hands automatically sliding around his short, soft hair that felt so lovely in her fingers, and they were kissing again.

A pure sweep of lips and tongues. A trembling of bodies.

He pushed off the door, walking her backward. He led like a dancer, and her body followed without thought or stumbling, as though she'd anticipated his movements and already knew the steps. As though her desire had conjured them in her head moments before and he was reading her mind.

And then he did something entirely unexpected.

He bent down, wrapped one arm around the back of her knees, and picked her up. Cradled her.

The Keko who belonged to the Chimerans would have fought this instantly, this blatant overtaking. The Keko who'd been general, and before that the highest ranking warrior, would have squirmed and kicked out, maybe thrown the heel of one hand into his nose or an elbow into his throat. She would have swept out a leg to knock him to the ground. They'd tussle, and maybe she'd let him pin her eventually, let him take her on the tail end of the fake fight, just to let him know she could win . . . if she'd wanted the victory.

But the Keko who belonged to Griffin wanted none of that right now. She wanted to know how he would care for her, how he would tend to her on his own terms. She wanted to know what his control was like, what *he* desired from *her*. So she chose not to fight, and instead curled an arm around the back of his neck and stared into his eyes. Waiting. Issuing a challenge of the silent kind.

He walked her toward the bed and she tensed, waiting to be thrown over it, like she'd done to him their very first time together. Like he'd done to her on their second. The corners of his lips, gone all soft and swollen, ticked up, because he knew she was thinking of that. Expecting it. Instead, his strong legs bent and he sat her on top of the green tropical bedspread. The cool polyester felt strange and wonderful against her skin that burned under the gooseflesh.

A slow, soft hand passed over her shoulder to rest on her heaving breastbone. Just a shadow of the first time they'd touched, when she'd grabbed his hand and gave him no choice about how he was to touch her. Now the choice was all his, and her brain buzzed with this new kind of power—watching the way she affected him. And there was no mistaking it, because his hunger was sewn into his expression.

The concept of being wanted *that* much, and to witness it in person, was more than overwhelming. This wasn't just sex, a conquest, a physical need. For her, it was a kind of birth, and it was both painful and beautiful.

He gave her a slight push. "Lie down," he whispered.

Scooting back on the bed diagonally, she slowly let her body arch backward, watching his face the whole time—a searing focus that declared he'd found his goal and would go after it with everything he had.

She longed to ease the tortured expression that knitted his brow. With an arch of her spine, his lips parted and he came down to join her.

Crawling, his biceps bulging out of the sleeves of his T-shirt, he straddled her thighs, towering over her. Her hands rested by her head, and though she was dying to reach for his zipper, to yank it down and have what was inside, she told herself that knowing his mind and what he wanted at that moment was far, far more desirable. This would be a lesson for both of them.

His stare pinned her with an invisible strength. He sat on her legs, hands slowly rubbing up and down her thighs, then he reached forward. The tank top was a piece of crap and he had an easy time ripping it away from her body. Just shredded it down the center. Flipping back the halves, he stared down at her chest, his tongue making a slow sweep of his inner lower lip. With even less care, he swept his own T-shirt from his body.

There was something about being underneath a man she'd never truly appreciated before. Something about reducing such a warrior—because that's what he was, as she learned to redefine the title—to the wordless staring, to the mindless desire circling in those eyes, that made her feel more powerful than the Queen.

Then he moved, shifting back, bending at the waist. Coming down over her.

Closing her eyes, listening to her own breath rattle in anticipation, she awaited the lick on a nipple, the stroke of the generous curve underneath, maybe a full-on grab, tight and needy. She wasn't at all expecting the feel of his torso, all that hard muscle and skin that she'd touched through his shirt, slide up over hers. There was a different kind of sensation on her nipples as his chest and heavy body covered hers. And then a familiar sensation on her mouth as he kissed her.

Nothing what she'd expected, but everything she loved.

She felt his hands on her head, smoothing back her hair, kissing and kissing her, his body growing heavier and heavier. Then his fingers drifted away from her head and slid across the bedspread to take her waiting hands. Fingers intertwined, palm to palm, they clenched each other. Held on to one another. Kissed like the Earth had stopped rotating and the moon would hang forever where it was and the sun would wait patiently for them to finish before rising.

He pulled away with a groan and a great gasp. She exhaled with loss as his body lifted off hers, silently crying for his return. He was looking at her, his gaze dropping to her jaw and chin, then shoulders and chest. He dragged his hands down her arms, finally—*finally*—to her breasts. But it was a tease, just a light scrape across her nipples that had her arching up like she'd been zapped with beautiful electricity. Then he did the most incredible thing . . . he turned his touch to water.

A cool, delicate, sharp, wet drag of liquid, up and around and down and across her sensitive, heated flesh. Her body responded immediately, igniting her fire magic. Steam rose off her, circling him, enveloping him.

She knew she was wet before, but with their magic mixed, she got absolutely soaked. She felt almost too swollen and tuned up to be touched, gone shaking in her need for him.

The water swirled over her nipples again, and this time, with the shock gone, there was only intense pleasure. She cried out, chin thrown back. She thought she heard him chuckle, triumphant, and then the water was gone. He eased off her, the absence almost hurting, until she felt his hands at her jeans. Pulling them off, under her hips, sliding them down her legs.

Barely a second passed after the last piece of her clothes disappeared before he was on her again, this time with his knees pushing hers apart, and this time with him whispering against her mouth in light teases, "So beautiful. So fucking beautiful."

Her arms came away from the bed to wrap around his neck. Her legs lifted and entwined around his lower back. Her heels shoved at the loose waistband of his baggy shorts, and then they were off, too, his body twisting, his hands scrabbling to make himself naked. It was a short burst of energy, all frantic and desperate like so much of their sex had been before, but then, as he leaned back and she caught a glimpse of his hard stomach, tense thighs, and raging erection, he slowed. Covered her body again.

"Please."

Who had said that? Him? Her? Some ghost in the room or the very energy between them?

"What do you want?" His voice against her lips, tugging at the softness.

So it had been her to speak, to beg like that. How wonderfully freeing, to be able to do that and not to be judged or thought weak. On the contrary, energy raced through her, exploding out of her skin in ways the fire never had. The fire was part of her, yes, but the magic was something inside her body, something given to her, something she could manipulate. This desire that was making her crazy and blind and deaf . . . that was *hers*. She owned it. And she would give it all to Griffin of her own volition.

"Touch me," she whispered. "Make me come. Please."

With a low animalistic sound, he slid down her body. All that friction blazed through her from the outside in. An entirely new, reverse kind of heat—his heat, and he was giving it to her.

On a delay, she realized that he hadn't moved in order to penetrate her. Instead his head was between her legs, his eyes focused on where she was desperate for him, his intent so very clear.

"The fire . . ." she began.

He shook his head, his eyes flipping up to meet hers. "I want to feel it. On my lips, in my mouth. I'm not worried. You won't hurt me."

But you'll hurt me, she thought. *And not physically.*

He licked her, right there where all emotion and sensation had spiraled and made her aware of the entire universe. Her hips bucked off the bed, but he clamped his hands around her thighs. Held her down. She had no strength, no fight left. Had she ever truly had any when it came to him?

His mouth closed over her, a soft fastening of the lips and a deliberate swirl of the tongue. She got lost in it, in its aching pace, in the shivers he was drawing out from her again.

Then she did a dumb thing. She opened her eyes, lifted her head and looked down. Looked at the roll of his mouth over her flesh, the way he ate her as though he were savoring his last meal, the smooth, even bob of his head between her legs. It was dumb because she'd never be able to forget the squeeze of his eyelids, or the appearance of his tongue as he dragged it up the sensitive seam of her body. Dumb because she knew she would think of and want this every day up until the moment she died, and she had no idea what was going to happen to either of them after tomorrow.

A sob wracked out of her as she came. She was crying and coming, her chest heaving with sorrow and pleasure, and she didn't know which to trust in more.

When she came down, when her body ceased its tremors and there were paths of wetness from the corners of her eyes to the bedspread, Griffin still had his mouth on her, only this time it was everywhere: her inner thighs, her hip bones, the divots between her stomach muscles. When he clamped his lips over her nipple again, a strange heat coated his tongue. Spicy, zinging. Her own.

He rose up to fill her vision again. "Your fire is delicious."

On his elbows above her, staring into her face, he nudged his cock inside her at last. Her vision winked and blurred, and she blamed the look in his eyes, that pure bliss shooting back at her, that *something* she was so afraid to voice but could name with the snap of her fingers.

And then he was fully inside her. Griffin Aames was inside her. Filling her from spirit to heart, soul to mind. She felt she might split apart from all that consumed her, and she had no idea what to do about that. As his forehead came down to touch hers, she gripped his short hair. Right before she closed her eyes against the intensity of his nearness, she knew she was lost. And this new place—a state of mind she'd never known before and was wandering through with little to no direction— was truly blissful.

Then he withdrew and pushed back into her with renewed power. Somehow larger, somehow deeper. The sounds that flowed up and out of their throats gave voice to indescribable feeling. Fire and water, combining inside her body.

They'd done this before, but the frenzied nature of their previous sexual encounters had masked the intensity of the two elements truly coming together. Now, with every centimeter of movement creating a mile of sensation, she was wholly aware of how warm her body was growing, how it was taking him in and wrapping around his element, combining with it. Intensifying it. He was water and ice and steam, and she could almost see that steam rising from the mountains of his shoulders, trickling through the lines made by his flexing muscles.

Another thrust, slow and hard. She discovered she did not want to demand speed this time. She did not want a fuck like they'd already had. No, she wanted more of this—this protective, intense, claiming penetration that locked their eyes as firmly as it joined their bodies.

His hips were heavenly, the way they scooped up and into her. He moved like water itself, smooth and flowing, its power deceptively beautiful and innocent looking. And then . . . suddenly . . . just for a moment . . . it seemed like he *was* water.

His whole body went translucent and shimmering at the edges, like he was losing control of who he was and who his body longed to be. Then he was back again, his olive skin as solid and lovely and taut as it had always been. The thought that she might have sparked that in him made her insane with lust.

She wanted to carve a stone prayer to the Queen asking if she could keep this man inside her forever and ever. That she could just keep this man, period.

Griffin's chin jutted out, his face reddening, his teeth clenching. She could feel her inner fire starting to release, which meant that he could, too. Little pinpricks of orange and sparkling gold turned her vision into a dreamy wonderland, and she loved the way Griffin appeared to her through it. Her water elemental, overlaid by flames.

They'd been together enough for him to remember what got her off, and he did it without prompting. He shoved a hand under her ass and hoisted her up, tilting her into the delicious angle that had him stroking the most perfect place inside. He held tight to her, not letting her drop, driving into her with increased force. Increased speed.

She rode it out, arms thrust to the side, hips high in the air, legs holding on to the man driving into her. She felt utterly powerless, a slave to the fire and the man who held her body so perfectly . . . and it was the greatest feeling in the world.

When she came again, the fire rolled through her with such force she thought she might ignite. She'd take the bed and the B and B and all of the Big Island with her, and not even the great Fire Source could match the way he was making her feel.

Her throat went raw with the sounds she made. Fire licked behind her eyelids, because she couldn't keep them open any longer. The conflagration at last began to peter out, but the experience wasn't over, because Griffin roared as he came. She distinctly felt him tighten and swell, the stroke of him turning into a wonderful rhythm.

Then he was cool inside her, a splash of water. An ocean of peace and power.

When at last he withdrew and lowered her ass back to the bed, she was numb to everything but the gentle rub of his skin against hers. Maybe it was hours later—maybe it was minutes—but she was still lying there, held in his arms, one of his hands stroking down her hair, one leg thrown over her thighs, claiming her.

Despite her best intentions, despite her wishes and dreams and all that she knew she must do tomorrow, she let herself be taken.

SIXTEEN

Regrettably, the sun rose.

Griffin opened his eyes to find Keko already awake. She lay on her back naked, her long, strong legs crossed at the ankles, fingers interlaced over her belly. Her dark nipples rose and fell as she breathed, and he found that he could still taste them on his tongue.

Her head was turned on the pillow toward him, a thick chunk of black hair swooping over her ear and under her chin to make a dark line across her neck. Despite the new light coming through the curtains, her eyes were somber and shadowed, and they absorbed everything. No amount of water magic could save him from drowning in her fire, and it did not frighten him. He reached out and covered her hands with one of his, giving her a mild tug, a subtle hint that he wanted her arms around him. On him. It had the opposite effect.

Instead of Keko rolling into him, she yanked away from his touch. Throwing her legs over the edge of the bed, she pressed her hands to the mattress. He stared at her back and triceps, at the shadowed lines between her muscles, at the sexy dimples above her ass.

Then he noticed the way she was almost gasping for breath. "Keko?"

So many things had happened between them last night, many of which he'd never be able to name, nor would he ever want to. They were singular occurrences, precious seconds and moments that could never be repeated. He'd distinctly felt, in a triumphant instant, when all the walls between them had been completely demolished, crackling into a zillion pieces. Even that final wall had come down—the one he'd been trying to remove slowly, brick by brick—and he'd nearly shouted with relief. With her body surrounding his, he sensed that she'd decided to turn back from her quest. He'd drifted into sleep holding on to that final thought, that he'd succeeded in keeping her alive. Keeping her with him.

But now, with daylight striking the tension in her back, he knew she'd reconsidered. In her own sleep she'd rebuilt that last wall and had awakened with renewed purpose. No matter what had happened between them, she was going to head for that island. She was still going to try for the Source.

And he couldn't be the one to stop her.

Sitting up, he positioned himself behind her but didn't touch her rigid body. He feared what he might say, so he didn't speak.

When she finally opened her mouth, she spoke to the floor between her knees. "I don't want to be the Queen anymore. And I don't want to die."

He couldn't help it; his heart soared. The stars seemed to blink all around him, sparkling motes in the daylight, as though they'd answered his prayers to make her change her mind. They would figure out another way to both help her people and mollify the Children of Earth. They would—

"But if I don't make it," she added quietly, "I want you to know something first."

He gripped handfuls of bedspread. The air stilled around them. He could barely breathe. "What?"

"That I l—" She looked down, chin to chest. When she raised her head, he couldn't see her face. Only the generic painting of a breaching humpback whale on the opposite wall had that privilege.

She said, "I love you."

The words hit him like an arrow, slicing through skin and bone to reach his heart. He released the bedspread and lifted a hand, his palm hovering just above her shoulder blade, her heat a beacon.

His hand descended, wanting to tell her with a touch that he felt the same. Perhaps more, if that was even possible. But before he could make contact she bolted from the bed and lunged for the bathroom. The door slammed behind her, the click of the lock following two seconds later. The shower came on, full blast.

The euphoria died with her exit.

She loved him. He'd come here to stop her and had lied his way into her presence.

She loved him. He was withholding from her a terrible piece of information about the severity of the Source and its capability for destruction.

She loved him. He absolutely understood what she had to do to save her people.

She loved him. He loved her.

Nothing good could come of it.

Fuck.

Keko never spent this long underwater. She'd never wanted to. But her fingers and toes had gone pale and wrinkled, and she still made no effort to remove her hands from where they were braced on the shower wall. Still didn't want to duck out of the spray hitting her body and covering it in smooth sheets.

Her head dropped and the water shot over her skull, crawling over her shoulders and down her back. Between her legs. She imagined being back under the waterfall in the ravine. She imagined Griffin sliding all around her.

Mighty Queen, she prayed silently, *why didn't you tell me love was such a weakness? Why didn't you tell me it could be such a strength?*

Keko had nearly quit her quest last night. Griffin had been moving inside her and she'd looked up at him and actually thought to herself, *I can't do it. I can't leave him. I can't chance ending this.*

Then she realized that even though the distinct emotion she felt emanating from him was very real, it was all still part of his argument to get her to abandon her quest. It didn't matter that he knew her true reason for going after the Source, or even if he agreed with her; he hadn't made any vow to stop trying to get her to turn around. Last night he said he would think about tomorrow, tomorrow. Well, tomorrow was here, and she thought that when she stepped out of this bathroom he might use her confession of love against her. He might touch her and beg her not to chance death. For him.

She should hate him for that, but she didn't. She shouldn't love him, but she did.

And that was why love was a strength and a weakness. Because at that very moment she felt incredibly emboldened, like she could conquer and accomplish anything, yet it was her love for him that was holding her back. Making her doubt her own purpose and the inherent risks. She could not let doubt take over.

This morning she would give Griffin a choice: help her reach the Source without complaint or asking her to turn back, or return to the mainland and let her do what she must. Regardless of his decision, she would hunt for her people's cure. Either way, it would likely be the end of them.

First, however, she would bring him under the water with her. To feel close to him one last time in the presence of his element.

Leaving the spray on, she climbed out of the tub and stepped from the bathroom.

The outer door to their room was ajar and the long, kinked cord between the phone and the receiver stretched from the nightstand all the way to the front porch. Griffin was outside, shirtless, shorts back on, his ass against the railing, sunlight on his back. The receiver was to his ear. He was already pale, but when his unfocused eyes cleared and he finally noticed her standing in the middle of the room, soaking wet and naked, his olive skin lost even more color.

"I understand," he mumbled into the phone. "I have to go."

He came back inside, shutting out most of the light in the room when the door closed behind him. Going to the nightstand, he replaced the receiver on the cradle. Far too slowly.

Her heart felt like it had dropped into her feet, and she couldn't say why. "Who was that?"

His fingers dragged off the phone and he finally looked at her, taking his sweet time to answer. "The premier's been murdered."

All air punched out of her chest, but did not result in flame. "*What?*"

"His wife found him dead. Couple of hours ago. Throat slit."

Her hand flew to her neck in sympathetic horror. "My god. Who did it? Why?"

"Aaron said it was one of their own. Someone who didn't want to pay his debts. That's all I know."

"Is Aaron the new premier?"

He rubbed at his chin, then scratched fingers up and down his cheek. The gesture unsettled her even more.

"Ah, no," he said haltingly. "The other delegates haven't voted a new one in yet. They're . . . waiting."

"That doesn't make sense. Voting is usually immediate. I've been through two other premiers." She bent to pick up her shirt and saw only the tatters of the tank top he'd ripped apart last night, so she threw on his black T-shirt instead, pulling the bottom tight around her waist and tying it in a knot. Snagging her jeans from the floor, shoving her legs into them and yanking up the zipper, a sudden realization hit her with the speed and pain of a bullet. "Wait a second."

She looked up to find Griffin staring at her. Guilt made a single line of his eyebrows and she felt like the Queen had reached down from the sky and snatched the earth from under Keko's feet. "I didn't hear the phone ring."

"You were in the shower." It was nearly a whisper.

Though she couldn't move, her voice jumped up a couple of notches. "But I didn't hear the phone ring."

"It did." The words came out of his mouth sounding sticky-dry.

"How'd they know where to find you?"

He swallowed and it looked like it hurt. He even winced.

"How the *fuck* did they know where to find you?"

The curse emphasized the rage of blood in her ears and the crackle of the fire building underneath her skin. The last of the water from her shower evaporated, encasing her in wrath-induced vapor.

"Because I called the premier. Last night. When you went out."

Her blood turned to thousands of tiny knives, scraping her raw from the inside. It was like the treeman had come for her again and she was running for her life, unable to catch the breath that would give her flame.

"Why?"

His blink was a beat too long. "To confront him about sending an earth elemental to attack you."

The sweet ash and smoke from inside her body crept up onto her tongue, begging to be released. "And why would you ever think that the head of the Senatus would come after me? Why would he even know where I was?"

When he didn't answer, she took a Chimeran breath and spit fire into her hand. It was an involuntary reaction, that thing she'd tried to explain to Griffin years ago, when Makaha had used fire to express frustration and Griffin had read it as an attack.

"Talk," she said. "And don't fucking lie to me. You've already been caught. They sent you, didn't they? They sent you and you've been lying to my face this whole time."

"*No*." He came for her, arms raised as if to touch her face, his expression a fake seriousness that did nothing but mock her. "That's not what—"

"No more lies!" she screamed, the fire leaping from her hand. She snapped it back before it could hit the bed and do any damage, but her control was weak under the pressure of growing rage, and the odor of singed polyester clung to the air.

"Fine." He was the Ofarian leader now, all glower, his body set like a statue. "No more lies. Let me explain."

"Explain that the Senatus ordered you to stop me from going for the Source? Explain that you fucking *lied* to me about it? Over and over again? Explain that all this"—she waved her unlit arm at the bed, the sheets rumpled and twisted from the writhing of their bodies—"was to get me to turn away and satisfy *them*?"

"That's not true."

She laughed bitterly. "Which part?"

"The last part."

She wasn't dumb enough to fall again for the emotion in his eyes. "Bullshit!" He turned his face away from the blast of heat her word threw at him. When the heat died his eyelids flipped up, and there was such torture dancing across his brown irises. Oh, he was good. A real goddamn actor.

"The Senatus didn't send me," he said, his voice far too even. "I volunteered. And yes, I came to stop you. But you already knew that. I never lied about that."

The word "Senatus" sent an uncharacteristic icy shiver across her skin. "They promised you a seat if you brought me in. Didn't they?"

"Yes. They did." And by the way he answered without pause or expression, she knew he was telling the truth. "I didn't want you to find out like this."

"No, you didn't want me to find out, period."

"It was me or them coming after you, Keko. I sure as hell wasn't going to let it be them."

"Why you? And do *not* feed me some rancid meat story about how you care so much for me you didn't want to see me hurt."

He rolled his lips inward, slowly shaking his head. "I didn't want to see you dead. If the premier's team hunted you, you would've run twice as hard to get away. You would've found a way to get to the Source, I have no doubt about that. And when you got there, the Children would've had free rein to kill you. They said exactly that. I wasn't going to just stand there and let that happen. Not when I knew, deep down, that you would've paused for me. If anyone had a chance to get you to turn back and remain alive, it would've been me."

She felt like a worse fool than the day her *kapu* affair and her broken heart had been revealed to Bane and the chief. "Why do the Children care so much?"

He had the nerve to step closer. She blew more fire up her arm, the whole thing one giant, beautiful flame. She didn't care, as long as the traitor stayed away.

Griffin stopped and raised his palms. "Keko. The Fire Source is part of the earth. If it's disturbed, it has the power to move tectonic plates, make volcanoes erupt, cause massive earthquakes."

She narrowed her eyes at him. "I don't believe that. There's nothing in the legends or history that talk about that kind of destruction."

"Aya said it herself. She overheard Chief and Bane telling me privately about you and your quest, and she sprung up out of the earth, almost exactly like that treeman did, and she demanded in front of the whole Senatus that you be stopped, or else they would kill you."

Aya? No. Not quiet, inquisitive Aya. Not the strange woman whom Keko had dared to consider a friend. Keko felt disturbingly weak and painfully blind. Brave Queen, why was she so damn stupid sometimes?

Unless . . . unless Aya had placed faith in Griffin that he could stop Keko and prevent a Chimeran death at the hands of the Children. That tactical and political maneuver made more sense, but it still hurt—all this deception, all this manipulation, when Keko just wanted to make things right for her people.

"Do you see now?" Griffin said. "Do you get it? I couldn't let that happen, just let them hunt you. So, yes, I came to stop you, but it was to prevent massive destruction, too. I didn't tell you that part because I knew you'd think I was lying just to make you give it all up."

She stood there so long trying to process his words that the fire on her arm died. When it went out, he heaved a visible sigh.

"When I came here," he said, "I thought that you were about to destroy yourself in the name of a ridiculous, outdated bit of Chimeran culture. I continued to think that up until last night, when you told me the real reason why you're here. Your conviction and your purpose are stronger than anything I've ever known, stronger than any Source, touched or untouched. Something changed in me last night. *You* changed me." He placed a hand on his bare chest, the gesture infuriatingly sincere. "And I want to tell you that I no longer wish to stop you. I want to help you succeed."

The only sound in the room was the still-running shower. It created a drone in her mind, convoluting all these statements and stories he'd fed her. Messing with her emotions.

Water. Ruining everything.

"You don't want to help me."

"Yes. I do." Another step closer. "These last three years have been a waste. An absolute fucking waste. I believe in what you have to do for your people—this disease, this cure— because I would do exactly the same for mine. And I want to help you."

She squeezed her eyes shut so tightly she saw stars. Stars. His stars. The ones he swore on before she told him about the Chimeran disease.

What had she done?

Opening her eyes, she saw him inching closer. She showed him the fire in her irises and in the back of her throat, and he stopped coming forward.

Then he repeated, "I want to help you."

No. She would not fall for his words again. "Stop. Fucking. Saying that."

"It's the truth."

"There is no truth when it comes to you. Except maybe for this." Right as she said it, his game became entirely clear. The whole thing unfolded before her, taking on the color of fury. She formed a new fireball in her hand and went right up to him, teasing him with death and magic.

All he did was fold his arms and stare her down. "This should be good."

"What if *you* orchestrated the premier's death?"

He sputtered before finally ejecting a: "*What*?"

"It makes sense. I think you had no trouble at all trading me for your precious Senatus seat. I think the moment you heard about me running loose you saw your opportunity and grabbed it."

He vehemently shook his head but she wasn't buying it. "Wait a sec—"

"You come to Hawaii to bring me back and then you'll finally get your seat around the bonfire. Meanwhile, since you're nowhere near the mainland and the murder couldn't be traced to you, you hire this other rebel air elemental to off the premier. Since the Senatus is waiting on word of your success with me to admit you, they decide to postpone the election of a new premier."

His jaw clenched. "I thought you learned your lesson about jumping to conclusions. At least that's what you told me. You're paranoid and grasping for any explanation now. That's so fucking ridiculous."

She let out an ugly laugh. "Is it? Pardon me while I jump to a few more conclusions. How goddamn convenient for you, this timing. You'll show up at the next gathering having saved the day—no, wait, the whole entire *world*—and they'll have to be stupid not to vote you premier. Ta-da. You get everything you've ever wanted."

His chest pumped hard. "Not everything, Keko."

"And the killer part?" She choked on her voice, trying to stamp down the rising tears. "I told you my people's biggest weakness. Are you dying to exploit that?"

"You need to calm down." He stepped closer to her fire. "I swore on my stars. That secret stays in here." He tapped his forehead.

Flame crackled between them, the ball in her hand jumping and dancing.

"I never should've picked you up at the airport." Seconds later she realized she'd whispered it, but no amount of fire could burn the sentence from existence.

His shoulders dipped, his head sagging to one side. "It would've happened anyway. You and me. Don't you see that? Don't you get what's between us?"

That snapped her focus and anger back into place. "It was a mistake. All of it."

"You don't mean that. Keko, I've lied to you, yes. But I think you really know that I won't turn you over to them. It's just easier for you to be angry, to react to surprise. It's your nature and I get that, but you're thinking crazy. Listen to my words, to all that I've just told you right here, right now in this room. Because *that* is the truth."

"What are you going to do? Pray tell, oh mighty Ofarian leader. Tell me how you plan to heal my people and win their favor without ever disturbing the Source. Tell me how you'll get that Senatus seat and be voted premier, and everyone will gaze up at you in admiration. Tell me, oh fabulous Griffin, how you plan to trick me into never being able to let you go for the rest of my life. How you plan to conquer and trap my heart, but never let yours go."

"Keko . . ."

He reached for her then. For her face, where her flames didn't touch. He wasn't scared, didn't remotely flinch. And that scared *her*.

She stumbled backward, out of his reach. "God, I hate you. I hate you so much."

She had to get away from him. Immediately. Only one option remained.

Gathering all her fire—everything that she held in her palm and every little spark from deep inside her—she let it build and smolder, a great balloon of heat that turned her skin to shimmering white-hot red, like metal buried in coals.

Fear finally came to Griffin's expression and he backed away, but it was too late. Keko released her magic—a blast from a furnace, an invisible cloud of heat. It slammed into him, flipped his body backward, sent him sprawling. Keko let him lie there. No movement from his twisted limbs. She went over, toed his shoulder to roll his body onto his back, and saw that his chest still moved. The lights of consciousness, however, were completely out. Good.

She swallowed, looking down at his slack jaw and jelly limbs. "I'm leaving now," she said. "And I can't have you following me. Can't have you stopping me. This time, it's really over."

Before she could change her mind, she sprinted from the B and B, pausing only for a second at the bottom of the porch steps to consider her direction. Griffin knew the location of the Fire Source. So did she, and she'd need a boat to get there. Hilo was by far the biggest place to grab a charter on this side of the island, and that's where Griffin would expect her to go.

So she fled the opposite way.

When she'd made it up the steep, windy slope, she felt a profound tug on her conscience. Stopping, she turned around to see the B and B, a hundred yards below, nestled in a vee of green land. As she stood there, the door to their room banged open and Griffin stumbled out. Shirtless, holding his head and weaving on his feet, he leaned heavily against the railing. At this distance she couldn't make out his face, but she saw his head swing around. Looking for her. Quickly she ducked behind a tree. What was the range on his damn Ofarian bloodhound senses?

I can always feel you.

Her lungs suddenly felt clogged, like she'd been the one hit with that blast of heat. Running now might draw his attention, so she slid to the ground and carefully peeked around the trunk. Griffin stomped down the porch steps and took off on a wobbly jog toward Hilo.

Keko waited until he was out of sight . . . but waited for what? He was gone and she still couldn't move from that spot. Slowly coming to stand next to the tree trunk, she gazed down at the B and B, seeing the ghosts of her and Griffin walking in last night, and then both of them running away. Alone. Separate.

A strange movement in the window caught her eye. A flicker of yellow and orange, when the room had been done in greens and blues, and the drapes white. Then she smelled it. Smoke. The fluttering gold in the window dimmed as black smoke leaked out from underneath the door.

No. No, no, no!

She'd thrown too much magic, too much heat, at Griffin, and it had lingered. Festered. Ignited.

Merciful Queen, that wasn't what she'd intended at all. It wasn't what she wanted! The Source still pulled her out to sea, but her legs brought her back to the B and B, sprinting as fast as she'd ever run.

The smoke coming out of the room thickened, the dance of flames in the window taller, larger. She flung open the door and inhaled—a Chimeran breath of the greatest kind. The fire and smoke instantly obeyed, swirling back into her body. She took it all back in, every last flame of her mistake. For once, the fire tasted awful.

She stood there in the doorway, looking down at the charred black oval on the wood floor where Griffin had once lain, and the ashen, teetering remnants of the table that had been placed beneath the window. The bottom half of the drapes were gone, the ends now jagged and crisp with black.

Hand to her mouth, she whipped around and fled back into the hills to the northwest, guilt making her feet impossibly heavy.

SEVENTEEN

The Airs refused to let Aya leave until the funeral was over. She sat on the steps of the false church, arms wrapped around her knees, the cold air trying to bite through the impenetrable grass suit. The freeze barraged her face, however, and the sting of it pulled tears from her eyes.

Real tears. Human tears.

The wind shifted, bringing with it the stench of the funeral pyre being lit on the far end of the compound. When it was over, they would name a new leader. Though she hoped it would be Aaron, there were no guarantees. And she, as a Senatus delegate, was required to remain here until she'd been given the name of the new appointee.

Did it really matter? Aya longed to escape out to open space, to dive into the earth and search for Nem, to confront him about what he'd done to Keko and Griffin. To forget about what she'd witnessed here, and how she could have ever found someone like Jason so compelling.

Today marked the first day that she wore human skin but desperately wanted to strip out of it.

A group of Airs turned the corner and entered the square, a low mumble of voices preceding their appearance. Aaron marched at the head, talking and gesturing to Nancy, who walked closely beside him.

Aya rose as Aaron stopped at the foot of the stairs.

"It's me." He set one foot on the second step. "I'm officially the Air Senatus delegate. I may have jumped the gun a bit when I told Griffin by phone earlier that a new premier wouldn't be voted upon until he returned, but it's what the premier—" He cleared his throat and paused, glancing at his shoes. "It's what Charles would've wanted. He was coming around, with regard to Griffin, you know."

At least there was that, that Aaron would wait to see what happened with Griffin before making a motion to vote on the new premier.

She nodded to cover her despair and loss. "May I go now? There's a matter with my people I need to attend to."

He regarded her for a long moment. "That Son of Earth who went after Keko? Charles told me about it. Yes, you need to take care of that." He waved off Nancy, who started to come forward. "I'll take Aya to the gate myself."

As they approached the gate it opened for her again, this time onto a brilliantly sunlit field. Aya faced her new equal on the Senatus. "I'm so sorry about what's happened here."

Aaron pursed his lips, enhancing the wrinkles that radiated out from them. "And I'm sorry you had to witness it. But it concerns my people alone and you shouldn't think about it. The traitor will be dealt with. He's a repeat offender, and that is that."

Aya peered into the angular shadows lying down between the labyrinth of tightly knit buildings. Killers deserved their punishments, she told herself, and this was a Secondary matter dealing with an issue within a single race. It had nothing to do with humans, who were her utmost priority. Aaron was right; she shouldn't think on it anymore.

Yet as she bowed her head to Aaron and finally stalked out into the open field, striding for the tree in the distance whose bare, clacking branches whipped in the swift wind, she *did* think about Jason. How she'd apparently gotten him all wrong, and how disturbing that was to a human mind. How she'd been so terribly mistaken when she'd thought she'd seen personal pain and a deep regret in his troubled eyes when she'd first met him, and then his enraged defiance, vehement denial, and total confusion as he'd been shoved down the stairs in custody.

The frozen cornfield seemed to elongate with every step, so she took to running to erase the space quicker. When she finally crested the small rise before the dirt road that stretched one way to nowhere and the other way to nothing, her legs were tired and her lungs burned from inhaling so much cold air.

Normally she would have reveled in such human sensations, but now all she wanted was to merge with the crust, tap into the great web of the earth, and locate Nem.

Coming down the small hill to the patch of untouched ground between two of the tree's major roots, she froze—as suddenly and with as much terror as the moment when Griffin had destroyed half that Chimeran warrior's arm. For there, wedged underneath a layer of bark starting to peel itself away from the tree, flapped a tattered yellow sunflower petal.

She fell to her knees. The strength in her body just gave out and the earth shot up to meet her. To cradle her. Almost instantly, the smooth, pliable magic grass garment that had protected her body started to merge back with the dirt. She let it, because she could not focus on anything but the fact that Nem had been here.

He'd followed her again.

And she knew, without a doubt, that Nem had been the one to slit the premier's throat. Not Jason.

Days ago on the Aran Islands she'd witnessed a murderous intent cross Nem's face. Back then it had been directed at Keko, his duty as Source guardian sewn into his Children's blood. Even though he'd given his word, Nem had gone after Keko anyway. And he'd failed.

So he'd switched his focus and gone after the premier, whom Nem believed had given the no-kill order. The fact that Jason had been there—the very air elemental Nem had accused Aya of wanting more than him—had given him the perfect opportunity to escape. The perfect person to frame.

Aya shuddered. The cold wind of the great Canadian prairie finally seeped into the grass that was trying desperately to make root again around her. She started to shiver.

No, not from the cold. It was the fact that Nem, a Son of Earth, had chosen humanity for her, and humanity had turned on him. Twisted his mind. Disagreed with his choice. His descent was ugly and irreversible and she had to stop him before he hurt someone else. Before something even bigger and more devastating happened.

There was only punishment left for him, a lifetime of sunless days and gasping for thin air Within. She needed to find him. She needed to tell the Father what he'd done.

She needed to tell Aaron that Jason was innocent.

Ill and desperate, Aya yanked herself free from the restraining ground and pulled protective magic around her again. Coming to stand on wobbling legs, she started back up the rise, the expanse of field stretching far, far back to the white walls.

A terrible realization stopped her dead, erecting an invisible barricade that prevented her from taking another step.

The truth about the former premier's murder would bring war.

How could she run back into the compound and admit that one of her own people had somehow snuck beyond the walls and killed the air elemental leader?

Conversely, how could she let Jason take the fall for something she had had a distant hand in causing?

The earth reached up and grabbed her. Pulled her down and tried to embrace her. To tell her exactly what she had to do. Where her true loyalties lay.

It hurt so much, this choice. How could anyone live with this? Live through this and come out alive when it was over? It was a physical pain that inhabited the entire place where her organs should be. Her body curled into itself, but the position did nothing other than remind her how small she was, and how she had to fit so much into that little, evolving heart and mind.

A rumble started in the distance—the insistent whir of a car's engine getting louder and louder as it came down the dirt road. Aya had to reach deep for the earth's magic to camouflage her body where it lay on its side atop the rise. She was weak. Too far away from the untouched spot on the earth. And too human. But she managed to assume the disguise as the car rolled by, appearing as just another bump on the half-frozen, snow-dusted ground.

She lay there for a long time, watching the car become smaller and smaller until it finally disappeared. Though she did not believe in signs or omens, the appearance of the human's vehicle had seemed to make her choice, and it left her as lonely and empty as this very spot in the world.

If she told Aaron about Nem, the Children's position in the Senatus—carefully planned and positioned over centuries and centuries—would be annihilated. All the jockeying they'd done to keep the Secondaries together and under the Children's watch would disappear.

If she told Aaron about Nem, war between the Secondaries would seep into the human world. It would destroy parts of their planet and it would endanger innocents. In the end, everything had to come down to her sister race. Humanity's existence relied on peace.

With a dreadful tremor that shimmied from her crown to her toes, she let the earth take her back in. Swallow her. The rock and dirt and clay ground her up. She felt no better in tinier pieces.

She would hunt Nem, she decided. But the secret truth behind the murder would have to remain her own.

Griffin dragged his feet away from the B and B. Hilo. He had to get to Hilo. That's where she'd try to get a boat, but with what money? What was she thinking? If he could get there quickly, he could try to reason with her once she'd cooled off.

Except that she'd made it pretty damn clear that reasoning with her would be like slamming his head against a wall.

She hadn't killed him, but she'd thrown some serious, scary magic at him. Knocked him out so good he still heard the bells, and he was still trying to get his vision to realign.

He jogged as fast as he was able, but already he needed a bit of rest. Using his own magic was out of the question, at least until it had some time to regenerate. That heat she'd blasted at him had boiled his water to uselessness. Time. He just needed a little more time to recover, then he could hunt again.

Ahead stood a one-pump gas station that looked like it had been caught in a 1975 time warp. He snuck around to the back of it and collapsed against a cracked concrete wall. Exhausted, legs pulled to his chest, forehead resting on his knees, he fought for his equilibrium.

I love you.

Those words gave him the tiniest edge of hope to grab and hold. His fingers were worn and bloody, his muscles shorting out and his heart in tatters, but he'd fucking well cling to that edge.

"*Fuck.*" Griffin's arm flew out to the side, his fist hitting the concrete. A chunk of it, painted pale green, crumbled off and fell to the dirt.

On the front side of the gas station, a screen door opened

and slammed. Two voices—one male, one female—drifted back to where Griffin hid. They sounded worried, their tone clearer than their words. Griffin thought he heard the word *fire* tossed about. He couldn't be sure, but his stomach dropped anyway.

No, Keko wouldn't. He shook his head, choosing to believe she wouldn't have done anything to harm Primaries. She was many things, but not that kind of woman. She knew her battles, and right now her only opponent was him.

He peeked around the gas station corner and saw the rotund figures of a man and woman hurrying up the road in the direction from which he'd come.

Griffin pushed to his feet. He still needed time to recover, and if those two had been the only employees inside, they'd just given him a good opportunity. He slunk around to the front of the station. The place was empty, the door laughably locked. The screen in the door gave way under his fist, he undid the feeble latch meant to keep it locked, and the hinges screeched as he let himself in. A phone hung on the wall behind the cash register and he snatched it up, pulling the cord over the counter so he could stand in the aisle and keep an eye out for the returning couple.

He got an answer on the third ring. Gwen still picked up her phone even when she didn't recognize the number of the caller. She'd told him once that after all she'd been through, she never knew who might be calling, who might need her help. When Griffin heard his friend's voice answer with a terse "Hello," he'd never been so grateful for a practice he'd once chastised her for.

"It's Griffin."

Gwen exhaled. "Great stars, Griffin, it's been days. I thought I'd hear from you sooner. Or at least get word through the Senatus."

"Not from the premier you won't. He's dead. Bad situation I don't know much about. Things are a little . . . up in the air right now."

"Are you okay? You don't sound so good."

He glanced down at his body. "I'm alive."

By the way she paused, he knew she was about to say something she didn't want to. "I'm sure you don't want to hear this, but your cabinet is restless, and when they get like that, they talk. They hate not knowing where you are, what you're doing, and they're letting all Ofarians know it. You're going to have your own bad situation on your hands when you get back. You might . . . Griffin, I'll just say it. They're talking about deposing you."

That was a new one. Grinding a heel of one hand into his eye socket, he took pleasure from the burst of stars that came out behind his eyelid. He didn't want to hear about his cabinet or his office right now. There were bigger things to worry about.

"Listen, Gwen. Things have . . . changed."

"Did you find Keko? Are you with her?"

The ache in his chest burned with her absence.

"I was," he replied. "Then I lost her. And I think—oh God, Gwen—I think I might have to let her go. I think I might have to let her get to the Source."

Gwen's tone shifted from that of worried friend to concerned Ofarian. Which was exactly what he needed. "You can't. That's not why you went there."

"I know I *can't*. But . . . oh fuck, Gwen." The hand that didn't grip the phone tapped incessantly on the counter. "I think . . . I think I love her. And the only way she'll ever believe how I feel is if I let her go after the Source, let her do this one thing that means more to her than anything, far more than me. The one thing that she believes will make her whole."

"The Children will *kill* her before she ever gets it, Griffin."

"I know! You don't think I know that?"

The pause on the other end was interminable. "There's more you aren't telling me."

He barked a short, hard laugh. "A lot more. And if I could tell you, I'm pretty sure you'd agree with me."

"I probably would. You sure you can't say anything?"

"No. I really can't."

He could almost hear her nodding. "Okay, then. You called for a reason. What do you need from me?" This was the Gwen he knew and treasured—the Gwen who'd never backed down from a challenge and whose mind knew all too well how to parse the personal from the political, the heart from the head.

"I just need you to listen. I'm trying to work shit out in my head."

"I'm here."

Yes, she was. And he could trust her.

He scratched at his face and neck. "So I go after her. Stop her. Drag her back to the Senatus and get my seat. Save the fucking world from breaking apart or whatever it is the Children fear. Yay. I'll get everything I want by surrendering the one person I desire. Keko is alive but all her hate for me is validated. I'm nothing but a liar and a traitor, and in her eyes I'll never be able to climb out of that pit."

"Did she really say she hated you?"

"Yes. After she told me she loved me."

Gwen whistled. "Wow, all right."

"So I have to let her get killed to prove my honesty? To prove how I feel? That's such bullshit."

"You'll lose your chance at a Senatus seat if you do that."

"Fuck the Senatus. I want what's best for Ofarians, and if I have to find another way, I'll do it."

At length Gwen said, "You know what I think?"

"No. Please tell me. I'm flailing over here."

"I think you should talk to someone else."

"David?" Griffin could use a good slap in the face. David was much less diplomatic than Gwen.

"No, not David."

And she gave him a name he hadn't expected.

He hung up with Gwen and reached over the counter to dial a new number. As it rang, he pushed aside the flapping portion of the door screen to see if the gas station owners were returning. The coast was still clear.

As someone picked up, the explosion of chaos on the other end of the line—music and the TV and young voices—had Griffin pinching the bridge of his nose to stave off emotion.

"Hello?" A deep, skeptical voice.

"Pop, it's me."

"Griffin." He heard the familiar creak of the old couch as his father got off it.

"That's Griffin?" called his mother in the background. "Is he okay?"

"Where the hell are you?" Pop demanded. "Everyone's—"

"I'm sorry." The apology was as much for interrupting his father as it was for his unexplained disappearance. "I'm fine, I promise. Is Henry around?"

"Henry?" Griffin heard his dad's curiosity, but didn't want to add anything more. "Yeah, he's in his room. I'll get him. You sure you're okay?"

Griffin wasn't remotely sure, but he said he was anyway.

The door to Henry's room opened and a stream of really bad dance music tumbled out. "Turn that off," their father shouted over it. "Your brother's on the phone."

The music cut. "Which one?" Henry asked.

"Pop?" Griffin said before the phone was handed over.

"Yes?"

"You didn't hear from me today. No one in the family did. Okay?"

"I can't at least tell people you're all right?"

"No." Griffin hated to do this. "And that's an order. Please."

Pop sighed. "Absolutely." Then, "Come home safe."

There was shuffling as the phone traded hands.

"Hey, buddy," Griffin said.

"Griff!"

"How are you?"

"Good, I guess. Got a B on my math test yesterday. Thought you'd like to hear that." There was very little excitement in Henry's voice.

"I do. Wow, buddy, that's great."

Griffin's chest filled up so suddenly and sharply he had to brace himself against the counter to keep his balance.

"So, ah," Griffin said, "I was thinking that when I get back, I'd like to spend a little time with you at the gym. Help you out, like you asked."

Henry gasped. "For real?"

The boy's eagerness and excitement splintered Griffin's emotions and shifted some muddy areas of thinking back into alignment. Sometimes Gwen was a genius.

Henry wanted nothing more than to follow in his parents' and brothers' and sisters' footsteps, to become a soldier worthy of wearing the Ofarian black. To protect the race. To make his leader, and oldest brother, proud.

So who the hell was Griffin to deny him that? What gave Griffin the right to try to steer a boy into a life track he didn't want to enter in the first place? How did that make Griffin any better than the old Board? It was Henry's choice to make. It was Henry's heart and passion on the line, and it was Griffin's job to support him in whatever that was.

Griffin could, however, do exactly as he just professed to Gwen. He could still try to pave the way for other Ofarian kids who wanted to branch out. He could still focus on expanding their options, and that, in turn, would end up helping Henry.

There, in a dingy Hawaiian gas station, with Keko sprinting toward the first boat she saw, Griffin grinned at his baby brother through the phone.

"For real," he said. "I'll even help you with the formal training application if you want. But you gotta know I'm not going to pull any strings or anything. You want to do this, you do it with your own skills. You got that, soldier?"

"Aw, yeah!" The books and academic trophies on Henry's shelves rattled as the kid jumped up and down.

"You and me, bud," he added. "When I get back. I promise."

Griffin twisted his head to the side and had to focus hard on an old Camel cigarettes poster, because who knew what was going to happen to him or his leadership or his people when he left Hawaii.

Then he hung up the phone, punched out of the gas station, and started jogging down the road. *Away* from Hilo. Because he realized while talking to Gwen that if Keko was intending to throw him off the chase, she wouldn't have headed into the big town, toward the obvious source of boats. That's exactly what she'd assume Griffin would think. No, she would go for the hidden spot, the remote area with fewer craft . . . so that's exactly where Griffin went, too.

Because he couldn't help the future and current generations of Ofarians by standing on the sidelines, by just throwing away all that he'd worked toward for five long years.

He couldn't help Keko obtain a cure for her people if he didn't find her first.

And he sure as hell couldn't fight for the woman he loved if she went and got herself killed.

Keko would not cry. She would not fucking cry.

Enough water plagued her every step—it sat in her line of sight no matter where she looked, and it poisoned her heart with a slow drip. No tears. Anything but water. She turned up her inner heat, trying to burn away her emotions, but not nearly succeeding.

She concentrated on running, her legs pumping over the uneven ground as she clung to the edge of the Big Island, heading away from Hilo. The little enclave of homes and local shops and the B and B she'd burned fell behind. The land sloped hard upward, dense clumps of trees pointing inland, in the direction she did not want to go. The houses spread out and she slowed her steps, moving more carefully over private land, keeping to the cliff side draped in trees and greenery. Every now and then a large tour bus gave a high whine as it braked, and then gunned its way up and down the distant road.

The run refused to delete Griffin from her mind. He would come after her again. But he would be too late.

When he found her, she would be holding the whole of the Earth's fire in her hands, and it would be hers to command. The Queen had touched the Source once and there had been no devastation like Aya had claimed. The same would be for Keko; her prayer had been answered and she could feel it.

Now she *did* want to be Queen. Fuck what she'd told Griffin just that morning. She wanted to rise above everything . . . but most especially heartbreak.

She slipped from a wide swatch of private land into an area heavily forested with tall, skinny trees that permanently swept back and away from the coast like a woman's hair in the wind. The natural area climbed higher and higher, and at the very top the bluffs dove sharply downward. At the bottom and about a half mile to the northwest was a small community with a marina.

The air whistled as it tried to negotiate its way through the thick trees, and Keko had to slow down even more to get up and through the rocky, shaded area. She refused to listen to the moans and complaints of her body. It was how she'd been trained, and she was still Chimeran, above everything. She pushed and climbed until the sun went down, splashing into the ocean.

She wanted food. She craved water.

When Griffin's stars popped out, she knew she had to stop.

She could give herself fire to see by, yes, but it would also announce her presence to anyone peering out into the dark.

She found an outcrop of rock, a huge tree erupting from the top, its roots coiling down from the sides to form a black, moist, hidden cave, and she climbed into it. Thirty feet in front of her the bluff dropped off a scary distance into the roaring ocean. From her little hiding place she had a good vantage point to the left and right—high enough to see anyone approaching before they noticed her.

A distinct scent filled her nose, bringing with it an avalanche of unwanted emotion. It confused her until she remembered she was wearing Griffin's T-shirt. Grinding the back of her skull into the rock, she turned her face to the treetops, trying to get away from the smell she loved but didn't want to. If she could burn the black cotton like she'd burned his coat, she would. But she couldn't.

She choked back any and all sorrow. Choked it back hard enough the tightness in her jaw turned to pain. Bitterness and disappointment and heartbreak and determination clenched every muscle into a wiry, uncomfortable, shaking mass. Though her eyelids dragged down, the extreme physical discomfort did not allow her to sleep.

She would stay awake until daybreak, then, and meet her fate under the sun.

So when she actually did wake up, blinking into pockets of sunlight breaking through the shadowed morning trees, it was with great disbelief. She was lying on her side, knees tucked into her chest.

Not ten feet away, Griffin leaned against a tree, watching her.

EIGHTEEN

Keko rolled to her feet before the sleep had been fully shoved from her head. There was no weakness in her muscles, no lingering rest or stiffness from unexpected sleep. Just power. Only alertness. And a fierce, focused glare, sharp as a blade, on the Ofarian man who watched her with infuriating calmness.

She'd been right. For once in her life she didn't want to be, but Griffin's appearance here—following her after he'd admitted to colluding with the Senatus to bring her in—proved he was driven only by his political motives. He was a liar. Nothing more. And nothing he could say would ever prove otherwise.

With a great leap she pushed out of the little cave and jumped down to the flat space among the trees below. The ground was squishy, cushioning her landing. Lowering her center of gravity, she circled around Griffin, arms pulled in and ready to do her fire's bidding. Her chest filled with magic, her tongue and lips ready to unleash it.

A battle was coming, and this time she wasn't sure if the loser would survive.

Griffin came away from the tree far too slowly, far too easily. His crossed arms dropped to his sides. A hunter's gleam brightened his eyes. She knew that look well. He wore deadliness like invisible clothing.

Mist clung to the edges of his skin, blurring them against the early morning sky and the waving tree branches. It made him seem godlike, sprung from the atmosphere. She knew he'd dissolved his body and thrown himself to the wind, tracked her from the air. He carried nothing with him, wore nothing other than those black shorts with the side pockets. His chest

and arms and face gleamed with moisture and she didn't know
if it was sweat or his magic. She didn't care. It didn't matter.

He was real now. Corporeal. Threatening. And he was coming for her. His legs made long strides across the dirt and mat
of fallen foliage. The space between them halved.

Keko inhaled and showed the flame dancing at the back of
her throat. "I'll fucking burn you."

"You would've done that back at the B and B. You wouldn't
have just left me."

A pang of guilt hit her hard. It seemed he didn't know what
had happened after he'd left, how her residual magic had caused
damage. She chose to say nothing.

"You don't have to do this," he said, for the eighty millionth
time. "You don't have to fight me."

She could feel her body heating up with frustration, could
see the grass and bushes around her start to shimmer from the
terrible temperature she was throwing off. Just let Griffin try
to touch her. She'd singe him.

"My only other choice is to stop, to go back with you. That
isn't happening."

He took another step closer, his shoulders bunching up, fists
forming. "It's not your only choice. If you'd only—"

"I'm not perfect," she said, thinking about the fire in the B
and B. "Neither are you."

"Never said I was."

He started to circle around sideways, taking his back away
from the edge of the cliff . . . and trying to push her toward it.
Wouldn't work. Not on *her* island.

His fists released as he raised his palms to her. "Will you
please just listen to me?"

She blew a sheet of flame down her arm. "I already did and
I've heard enough. Now you listen to me."

After a great pause, in which he rolled and licked his lips
several times, swallowing whatever lying words he wanted to
spew out, he finally crossed his arms over his bare chest and
said, "Fine. I'm listening."

She pointed the flaming arm, a short spear of sparking fire
extending out to him in warning. "You won't take me back to
the Senatus. You will not deny me this chance to do one great

thing for my people. I believe that if the Source is what feeds my people our magic, it will grant me access to it. It will give me what I need without the destruction Aya tried to scare you with. You can chase me all you like, Griffin, but I won't be your trophy on your wall as you sit back and think about how you duped me. About how you used me to get what you want." She drew herself up. "I'm not yours. I won't ever be yours."

"But I," Griffin said, "am yours."

"Don't you dare say that again."

She released the fire, a great scarlet and gold bomb that barreled toward Griffin. She lost his face in it, her magic consuming her vision. Her will commanded her mind—her will and her anger, her determination and her love. And as the fireball swung toward him, the flames stretching tall, a tiny sliver of her wanted to pull it back. The rest of her, submerged in his lies and his so-called love, pushed the bomb toward him with renewed force.

The fireball imploded. It died midair, sucking into itself, before it could take down Griffin in a blaze of skin and hair and death.

As the fireball shrank and shrank, it changed. Shifted. The air around it blurred in a way she recognized as Ofarian power drawing moisture from the atmosphere, then the whole thing started to harden. Shards of silver and white formed in its center, spiking out. Blades of shimmering ice burst out from what had once been fire, her greatest weapon. Now rendered inert. Inconsequential.

Griffin stood behind the rotating ball of magically forming ice, his expression angry but not malicious. She didn't understand that. She'd just called his bluff, had just tried to destroy him. Where was his hate? His sense of justice?

Their eyes met over the hovering ball of ice. His wrist flicked and the ball shot toward her, breaking apart into a barrage of gleaming, sharp arrows. So fast, so deadly. She inhaled and sprayed flame across her body, melting what bolts she could, turning their water into harmless steam, but it wasn't quite fast enough. Some of the ice arrows got through, slicing and stinging across her upper arms.

Then all was still. Even the relentless ocean winds seemed

to have paused. Ofarian and Chimeran magic—fire and water, complete and utter opposites—crackled in the air. She didn't have that Ofarian ability to sniff it out, and she could still feel it.

Griffin's chest heaved, his arm still thrust out, his fingers curled into icy claws that thawed as she watched. His arm slapped to his side. "We are too evenly matched."

Keko looked down at the hairline stripes of blood across her upper arms.

"I didn't come here to fight you," he said.

"You were just planning to haul me back to the mainland in one of those boxes my old captor—your kinsman—had made."

"No. I want to help you, Keko. Somehow."

That again?

The fact that he'd even opened his mouth and said something that ridiculous pissed her off even more. Maybe they couldn't fight each other with magic because they'd just cancel each other out, but she sure as hell still had her body. She was a Chimeran warrior and this was *her* land. She knew where the Source was and she was physically stronger than the Queen had been when her time had come.

"You don't want a fight?" she growled. Then she charged. Head down, thighs burning and toes digging into the dirt. Arms flung out, she slammed her shoulder into his midsection. Took Griffin's lying ass down.

The sound of his surprise, just before his breath exploded from his lungs, was the greatest music she'd ever heard. She couldn't stop the grin from splitting her face, though it probably looked like something evil, something animal and violent. Good.

Pinning him to the ground with her knees, she whaled him. Fists and elbows coming down again and again. He threw up blocks but did not fight back, his face twisted in a grimace. After a flurry of punches, she landed one to his cheek . . . and then she was on her back, a rock grinding into her spine, her skin abraded by the dirt. Griffin held her down by her shoulders, the muscles in his arms and chest and neck popping out. If he was affected by her enhanced body heat, he didn't let it show, didn't wince or pull away. Adrenaline would do that to you, would erase those warnings you were supposed to feel.

He lowered his head, got right in her face. "If you need a fight, fine. I'll give you one."

"I'm not going to hold back this time," she gritted out.

He came even closer, and for a scary minute she thought he might try to kiss her. "Good. Neither will I."

Exactly what she wanted to hear.

Power pushed itself out from her core—not fire magic, but sheer physical strength. The strength given to Keko by the Queen and the ancestors she'd brought together from all over the South Pacific.

Keko wrenched one of her legs free and slammed it up between his. He groaned and closed his eyes against the searing pain. His grip on her loosened, just a little but enough for her to wriggle out from under him and get one elbow into his neck, then another into his side. She kicked him off, then flipped to her feet over him, daring him to recover, daring him to come after her. Because she was fucking ready.

She didn't get to be general for nothing. They hadn't just handed her the title. She'd fought her ass off, made challenge after challenge, and she'd won them all. Against men and women who were far bigger or older or had more wins under their belt. She'd beaten them all. And now she'd beat Griffin.

Skirting away from the edge of the cliff, going deeper into the open space between the trees, she wanted to give them enough safe room to go at it.

On his knees, Griffin's teeth were bared in pain, his hands cupping his injured junk, his eyes squeezed shut. Keko dove, going in for another attack, not wanting to miss this golden opportunity. Griffin popped alert, all show of pain instantly gone. She saw his trickery too late. His leg swept out, taking her down, smacking her skull against the ground and laying her out all over again. She saw his stars, winking there above her consciousness.

Then he was standing above her. She glimpsed a knee of his going back, a cocked foot ready to spring forward, ready to get her right in the ribs. With a jolt of power she rolled. Not away but into him, taking him out at the ankle he balanced on. He toppled forward, but true to his training, he didn't just fall. He used the momentum to drag her with him and they rolled together.

She took an elbow to her cheek. He absorbed a punch to the chin. A heel crunched into her knee.

"You done?" he gasped. "I'm not . . . taking . . . you . . . to the . . . Senatus."

The lies. The lies! She had to stop them, to make him choke on them. She thrust out her hand, preparing for another slam. The soreness fed her, the adrenaline kept her going. There was no weakness to succumb to. Only purpose. It's what she was born into, what she'd been given. And to turn her back on that was an insult to her people, to her Queen, to the very Source that pulsed somewhere beneath her feet.

She flipped on top of Griffin now, clamping his waist between her thighs, fist descending again to his face. Blood glistening from cuts beneath one of his eyes and his lower lip. She'd done that. She'd done that, giving him what he deserved.

He caught her fist in his crushing grip. Fuck. Despite her best efforts to stamp it down, the weariness was finally starting to eat at her. She couldn't give in. Not now. Not when she was so close to finishing him. Finishing this.

With a sharp twist of her arm that had her screaming, he wrenched her body down, her chest flush against his. Sweat and blood sealed them. Fire and water repelled. His closeness, the smell of him and everything he'd said and represented, made her fury burn brighter and hotter than the sun.

He spun her, rolling her again, encasing her in the vise of his legs and arms. He didn't stop. Just kept rolling her over and over. Body over body, pain over pain. Until she didn't know which way was the earth and which way was the sun. There was no leverage for her to go at him. There was no way to control the momentum he'd created. He just kept going and going, the ground eating at her body every time he rolled her over, his grunts coming out every time he threw her over his body.

And then there was no more ground.

It took her a mere second to realize what had happened. Where he had taken them. Their intertwined bodies had rolled off the edge of the cliff. Hundreds of feet down before the white, angry water far, far below. No safety net. Nothing but death.

Nothing her magic could ever save her from. Nothing she

could do but flail. Powerlessness was the worst kind of weakness.

They fell and fell and fell, her stomach trailing feet behind.

A terror like nothing she'd ever experienced ripped through her. She let go of Griffin out of pure fear. Nothing around her. Nothing but warm air. Nothing between her body and the ocean. She saw Griffin's face then, floating above hers, just inches away but feeling like miles, like universes, and he wore fear, too.

He was saying her name. She couldn't hear him but she saw the letters form on his tongue, the shape of her name on his lips. His fingers grabbed her, finding her waist and shoulders. Though they were still falling, falling, falling, wind whistling all around, he managed to pull her to him, wrap her up in his limbs.

Still she fought, because he'd trained her to do that. To push him away. To hate him for how he was killing them. How he was taking away her dreams even now. How he preferred death over letting her beat him.

"I am yours," came the whisper in her ear. But of course that was just the wind, pushing them toward the sea, into her death.

Death came with the implosion of the whole world against her skin, a great crush and wet suffocation, and the sound of a mountain being thrust into the sea. She went deaf with the power of that sound, and blind from the brightness of the dying sun. Then blackness took over her vision.

To her surprise, the crush lessened. She was being cushioned, bouncing in something unseen. Floating again amongst an undulating black.

Death was surprisingly peaceful. She waited for the Queen's greeting, for her forgiveness, for her welcome into the afterlife.

And then Keko breathed.

Her lungs contracted, gasping. There it was: Damp, sweet air flowed between her lips and into her throat. It filled her lungs and pumped her chest in and out, in and out.

What the—

Her eyelids flew open. She was floating in a bubbling, frothy world—a water world made of a million shades of blue and green. Water flowed all around—above, below, on all sides—but it did not touch her because she was balanced in the middle of some sort of giant bubble. Her limbs were weightless, her hair swirling around her head.

The foam and bubbles racing around her incredible cage of air popped and fizzled, clearing away the murk, finally giving her a view of the ocean below the waterline. The ocean, as far as she could see.

The water cage shivered, and she knew this was Griffin's doing. Indeed, the bubble itself *was* Griffin. Him. All around her.

She was alive but trapped.

The cage began to move. It pushed through the water, slowly at first, dragging her with it. Then it started to pick up speed. Unable to control anything, she panicked, trying to throw her fists against the walls, still wanting to fight the man who'd taken her, but her movements were waterlogged and ineffective.

He was pulling her back to the mainland. She just knew it. And she sure as hell wasn't going to allow it, to just let him throw her from a cliff into the ocean and drag her back to the Senatus in a cage made of fucking *water*.

She screamed at him, her voice sounding muffled and wimpy.

She squirmed, her limbs and threats coming off puny and slow.

She reached for her magic, but the fire died on her tongue the second she opened her lips. It was still there, not dead, not diminished, just unable to be released within Griffin's confines.

Fuck him. Just . . . fuck him.

The bubble cage was zooming now, the parting water churning past, rolling off the sides of Griffin's magic. Off Griffin himself. He shot them through the ocean, in and out of pockets of shadow and sun, light and dark. Schools of fish darted out of their way. Reefs stretched out their hard fingers, trying to pop the bubble, but Griffin deftly steered around them. The great looming shapes of migrating whales passed in the distance, their eerie, sorrowful sounds amplified in her watery prison.

Keko continued to fight. Her mistakes would haunt her forever, but perhaps no mistake bigger than the one holding her now.

Minutes, or maybe it was hours later, she felt them start to rise, to slant diagonally up through the water. Outside the rounded walls of her cage the shades of ocean blue paled. Rolling onto her back in sluggish, delayed movements, she watched the glitter of the sun lay itself over the top of the water. Long beams of light tried to make their way down to her. Then more and more. They pierced Griffin's magic, striking her, blinding her.

He was bringing her to land again, and when they popped out, she was sure they'd be surrounded by Ofarians. Griffin— and all of them—better be ready for one crazy fight. She steeled herself, preparing. She expanded her chest and took in all that godforsaken damp air. She liked that—using the very oxygen Griffin gave her to prepare the weapon she was about to use against him.

The light above, twinkling in the water between the bubble and the surface, grew and grew in intensity. The pressure in her ears and body lessened. She could see the waves now, tipped with choppy white.

The bubble cage burst free from the ocean. It tumbled across the surface, spinning and spinning. Land appeared below—a harsh, jagged shoreline. They sailed up and over it, then the cage was no longer water, but a fine mist, swirling all around her in a dizzying, solitary tornado. She was nauseous and disoriented, and when she felt that mist coalesce back into Griffin's body—his arms and legs still wrapped tightly around her—she felt furious.

They hit the ground, rolling again. With an "*oof*" and a moan, his clamp on her loosened, and then released her completely. When her body stopped jouncing over itchy dry grass and rocky soil, she somehow got her limbs to obey and pushed herself up to hands and knees. The world seemed determined to pitch her back into helplessness. All she could focus on without heaving was the spinning ground.

A large male hand rested on her back. It calmed her, though she didn't want it to. When the hand skated gently up her spine to hook her hair off her neck, and a smooth current of refreshing air hit her skin, it jolted her back into reality.

She shook Griffin off, scrambling away and shoving to her feet. He remained kneeling, letting her go, merely looking up at her with oddly resigned eyes.

"Get up," she snapped. "Fight."

He dabbed at his cut lip and flicked a glance off to one side. "Look around you first. If you still want it, then I'll give it to you."

It was difficult to look away from him, but that's exactly what she did. And took in a completely unexpected sight.

They were on a tiny island whose entire, uneven shoreline could be seen from their vantage point. Hard, pitted earth rolled in all directions, and beyond that, the vast, endless ocean. No other land in sight. In the center of the island jutted up a flat-topped rock, split raggedly down the middle, looking like a petrified giant clam. From that crack spewed a river of magic that Keko could feel in her chest and in her soul. She knew that magic. She'd wanted it and had made it her prey.

Griffin hadn't brought her to the mainland. He'd taken her right to the Source.

She swiveled back to him, her jaw working but no words coming out. Maybe there was nothing he could *say* that would prove his loyalty to her, but apparently there was something he could *do*.

Another dab at his split lip. "I tried to tell you. I—"

His pupils dilated. His eyebrows came together and he looked far past her shoulder. Just like the day in the canyon with the Queen's prayer.

And that's when the Son of Earth burst from the ground and attacked.

NINETEEN

No tree to possess this time. The Son of Earth unfurled from the ground in a tumble of lava rock, his black craggy body splitting away, reversing gravity as he grew taller and wider. The chunks of his arms shot out from his sides, his head coming together in a clatter of stones, fitting together in a horrifying puzzle. A small earthquake shook his lower half, and the massive chunk of rock severed down the middle, forming legs. The whole thing took less than two seconds.

He took a pounding step toward Keko and Griffin. Then another. And then the fight began.

Griffin had been warned. He knew this was coming. He'd even agreed to this, to letting the Children have Keko if she got within reach of the Source, but even as he'd taken both their bodies over the cliff on the Big Island and plunged them into the ocean, he'd clung to the belief that he'd somehow find a way around Aya's ultimatum.

He still believed he would, if only now because he had no other choice. It gave him something to fight for. Something worthy.

As Griffin rocked to his feet, Keko fanned out wide, wisely splitting the Son's attention. If she could maneuver to the stoneman's back, Griffin could attack from the front. Except that Keko never got that far, because the earth gave a giant lurch under the Son's rocky feet, levering him into the air and arrowing his massive body right at her. At the same time, the earth below Griffin belched, throwing him airborne in the completely opposite direction.

A point of lava rock got him in the shoulder as he came

down. No time for blood. No time for pain. He scrambled to his feet and found Keko across the minefield of upset earth.

She'd fallen, too, the roiling ground continually moving underneath her, and she couldn't find her feet. Her defensive position was terrible. Griffin could see her trying to stand, to get up and fight back, but her balance was being constantly tossed about. That said a lot, considering what Griffin knew her capable of. Fear for her grabbed hold of him with tight, shaking hands.

The Son went at her, obliterating the space between them, hitting her squarely on. The sound was ugly, terrifying. Rock on skin and muscle. She went down, blood spattering from where the rough edges of his body had snagged and stabbed at her.

As in the canyon with the prayer, the Son was intent on destroying Keko alone, Griffin nearly invisible. Griffin had to use that, so with a roar, he sprinted toward them.

A scream cleaved the daylight. Keko. The Son was winning and Griffin's heart nearly exploded with worry.

He hopped from tilted rock to tilted rock, coming around the mound formed from the Son's entrance. Griffin had no knife this time, but it didn't matter. The blade would only shatter against this body. And rock was not skin; he could not burn the Son with ice as he'd done to Makaha, and the Son's movement would break apart any freeze.

At last he reached Keko, and he realized he'd been a fool to ever doubt her ability or consider her lost. She was on her back, the Son above her. Her knees flexed between their bodies, her feet planted on his chest, strong thighs holding him at bay. She was pummeling his face with her elbows and fists, little rivers of silvery crimson trickling down his cheeks from the blows. The Son's exterior was more skin than rock now—a smooth, taut charcoal gray lined with veins of red, like lava rock that had been reignited and flowed again.

Keko screamed at her attacker, but not in defeat. No, his Keko was far from finished. She gritted her teeth, bent her knees just a tad more, and kicked the Son off with a mighty yell. All power, all strength, more than Griffin had ever witnessed in her. The Son's body flew to one side and he hit the ground with a yelp. He'd landed on his left leg—the leg bearing a giant, festering gash down the length of one thigh, the leg Griffin had injured once before. He gripped his thigh and snarled up at Keko, his agonized eyes a strange, haunting silvery gold.

As Griffin finally reached them, the Son released his leg and lumbered to his feet.

Keko rose, too, eschewing Griffin's helping hand. If she felt pain, it didn't show. With a nod he moved out wide, keeping their dual position strong. Her chest expanded, creating her fire. She lit both arms, holding them out toward the Son in a frighteningly beautiful warning.

The warning was not heeded.

The Son growled and lunged. Keko arrowed her fire at his feet, igniting the ground around his body in a tight circle, encasing him. Brilliant, his Keko.

The Son laughed at first, the sound half human, half gravel. Then he tried to power through the wall of fire surrounding him. The smell of burned skin and sulphur, and the shriek of unexpected pain filled the air. He looked down at his hands in shock and then in fury as though he hadn't known about the damage fire could do. His chin rose, his lip curled in a cocky sneer.

He went for Keko again. This time through the earth.

The Son's feet and shins shifted from skin to rock, his body shrinking as he tried to go under, to let the earth swallow him. It didn't work.

Keko's fire flared in the ragged piles of upturned rock on which the Son stood. Chunky, sharp lava rock cradled her element, spitting out flames under and around his feet—his own personal section of Hell. It rendered his escape and transformation impossible.

The sight of her beaten and bloody body, coated in waves of flame, made her fearsome. Made her invincible. She moved closer to the Son and asked in an eerily calm voice, "Who are you?"

The Son glared at her through the flames.

"Who are you?"

At great length he finally answered, "I am guardian of the Source. And you have violated our boundaries."

She took another step closer, increasing the blazing circle around him. He cringed, throwing up a useless arm.

"Your name," she demanded.

Though the lower half of him remained as rock, keeping him locked into the fire cage, the charcoal skin on his torso and arms ran with lava-red veins. His short hair glistened strangely silver. Half human in shape, but not anywhere near human in appearance.

"I am Nem." The pink of the inside of his mouth stood out in sharp contrast to his skin. "But my name doesn't matter. If you destroy me, another Child will come to take my place."

"Did Aya send you?" Keko's voice hiccuped over the Daughter's name.

Interestingly, Nem's face also darkened.

The fire circle crackled and hissed. His skin broke out in droplets of sweat that shone like quartz, and then plinked to the lava rock in solid form. "She didn't have to," Nem said. "This is the purpose of my line, to protect the Source."

Keko sighed in what Griffin understood to be relief. What didn't he know about Keko and Aya?

Griffin pushed forward and barked at Nem, "You went against Aya when you came after us on the Big Island. Why?"

Nem shifted his glare to Griffin, one hand grazing his leg with the gash. "I went after *her*. I didn't know she wasn't alone."

Keko had been his sole prey, his only mark.

Griffin's mind rolled back to the scene outside the Senatus bonfire, to Aya's words of warning: *If Kekona touches the Source, fire feeding fire, she could destroy continents.*

Fire feeding fire. Of course.

Griffin whirled on Keko and thrust a finger at the flaming cage. "Will that hold?"

"As long as I keep control over it. Or kill him." Her eyes narrowed. "Why?"

"Don't kill him." Over Keko's shoulder he caught sight of the massive, cracked rock jutting out of the center of the small island, and he nodded toward it.

"He tried to kill me," Keko said, frustrated arms flinging out to her sides. "Twice. Don't I owe him the same favor?" Then she noticed how Griffin was staring at the broken rock. "What? What're you thinking?"

He said nothing. He didn't have to. She understood.

Her beautiful dark skin paled. "No. Griffin, *no*."

Griffin looked long into her determined, blood-streaked face, then started to walk away. Toward the entrance of the Source.

"Wait. Stop." It was the Chimeran general talking now. "What the hell do you think you're doing?"

The split stone called to him, made his signature awareness light up in a way he'd never before experienced. "I'm going in."

Her grip on his arm was so powerful he felt the twinge of pain all the way to the bone. She spun him back around so hard he had to struggle for balance.

"This is *my* fight, Griffin. *My* purpose." No anger this time, as he'd expected, just a sadness. A disappointment. Devastation.

"You can't go in there, Keko. Look at the crack, how narrow it is. Even if you could drill for the next fifty years and get yourself inside there, what Aya said about triggering something massive and horrible *will* happen."

"It's no different if it's you or me. Why do you think you can?"

Griffin glanced at Nem. "Because of something Aya told the Senatus. Because I am water and you are fire. Think about it."

A tight shake of her head. A terrible crease across her brow. "I don't understand."

He couldn't help it. He had to touch her, had to chance it. One hand came to her cheek, thumb grazing lightly beneath her eye. She startled, killing the fire on her hands but still managing to maintain the circle around an increasingly agitated Nem. Through the sweat and blood, beneath the fire magic, Griffin could feel her true beauty—that gorgeous soul that had given her this quest.

"You're stronger here on this island," he said. "Aren't you? My senses are going crazy and it's more than just signatures I feel. I can see it's affecting you, too, in how easily you overpowered Nem. I can feel it in your body, see it in your magic. The Source is feeding you."

Her gaze turned inward, as though she just realized the truth of it. "Yes. I do feel stronger. And a little . . ."

"What?"

She flexed her fingers. "Unstable."

"Right. Because you're made of fire. Same as the Source.

Don't you see? You are too close as it is now, but if you actually find a way down there, if you actually touch it, it'll be like driving a gas truck into a burning building. Do you understand now?"

Keko's expression slackened, then she pulled away from him and stomped back to Nem. "Is it because I am fire," she demanded, "that you're not allowed to let me in."

"Fire feeds fire," Nem said, the truth in his gold-silver eyes. "Fire destroys."

She made a sound of frustration. "But the Queen found the Source. She touched it."

"No," Griffin said. "She never made it."

Keko gasped.

"No one's ever gone down there," Nem said, and Griffin noticed with a shudder that the Son did not ever blink. "My ancestor killed her when her boat landed right over there."

"No—" Keko looked unsteady as she glanced at the small beach thirty yards away.

"Think about it," Griffin said. "If she'd touched the Source, the world would've known. There would be stories or legends, or geological proof of such a huge disaster. Because she was fire." Taking her arms, Griffin turned her to face him. "And I'm water," he whispered.

Her sorrowful gaze dropped. Then her shoulders followed.

He cradled her face, lifting it back up to him. Pressing closer, her heat enveloped him.

"I know you want to do this yourself. Believe me, I know this very well." She stared at him with glittering, dark eyes. "But you can't, and I won't let you try. You will die down there. You'll trigger something huge, something deadly. You won't come back with any kind of cure. And your Chimerans will still lose their magic."

She shuddered within his grasp. "What will you do? How will you do it?"

He licked his lips. "I have an idea."

She took his forearms in that enhanced grip. "But . . . you've ruined your chance with the Senatus."

"Said it once before and I'll say it again: Fuck the Senatus. I came here for you, remember?" He touched his forehead to hers. "This will help you. And your people. Mine will be there when I get back, no worse off than how I left them. The good thing about the future is that it can always change."

He would think about the Ofarians later. For now, he belonged to Keko.

Her lips parted, a sweet little cloud of her magic smoke leaking out. He breathed it in gladly.

He released her, gently pushing away. Her arms hung in midair. He looked at the rock and its narrow crack, his intent clear.

"No!" screamed Nem, thrashing from inside the circle of fire. It sizzled and bit at his flailing limbs. "No! You don't know what will happen!"

Keko lowered her arms. "He's right. You don't know what's down there, what will happen. You're not Chimeran. How will you hold the magic?"

Griffin smiled sadly. "Why, Kekona. Are you worried about me?"

"I was willing to bargain my life." She slapped an angry hand to her chest. "I don't want to gamble with yours."

If he touched her again, he'd never want to let go, so he took a step backward instead. "This time," he said, "I'm going on faith. And I have to say that it feels pretty damn good."

A sound somewhat like a choke came out of her mouth. She turned her face to hide her emotion, but he wasn't fooled.

She murmured, "After all I've done to you, after all I've said, after how the Chimerans have acted against the Ofarians, I can't believe you'd do this for my people."

Griffin took one final look at her with his human eyes. Ofarian words rolled across his tongue and spilled out from between his lips, bringing up his magic, transforming his body to liquid.

He watched her eyes widen as she finally realized his plan. The humbled, overwhelmed woman disappeared. The confident, steadfast woman stood before him now, and he couldn't have asked for a better partner.

She came closer to his watery shape, blowing orange flame across one palm and holding it out to him. "Let me do it."

Griffin nodded his liquid head.

She touched him, her burning hand pressed to his wobbling, translucent chest. The heat from her fire, her magic, turned him to steam. It was a far different feeling, to have it done to him rather than doing it himself. It was an incredible feeling, one he wanted to experience again and again.

He gently entwined himself around her whole body. Curling his molecules next to her ear, he thought *I would do anything for you.* She sagged as though she'd actually heard him. Maybe she had.

Reluctant to leave, but resolved to help her, he peeled the steam away from her skin and floated toward the crack. Flattening himself into a long, thin stream, he slipped into the narrow fissure and instantly surrounded himself with dark. With earth and rock. With unadulterated magic. The world around him was shadowed and craggy, the lava rock slicing off at harsh angles, turning directions without sense, making his path crooked and dangerous. Even though he wanted to zoom ahead at full speed, he had to go slowly or else risk being drawn too thin or being broken apart. There were limits to his power; time was one of them, and the careful pace set him on edge, made him worry about how much energy he'd have left for the return trip.

From somewhere deep, deep down in the blackness, the Source sensed his presence. Maybe it knew he was water. It blasted against him. Intense heat and stormy magic sent out constant shocks. They pulsed against him like giant waves and he was the tiny minnow trying to swim against the riptide. He had to pull his steam body along as much as thrust it forward, and, like when he'd been tracking Keko across the Big Island, it drained his magic exponentially.

He kept going, kept driving on, without any indication of how far he had to burrow into the heart of the earth. He couldn't think about it because turning back wasn't an option. Every second brought increased heat, more treacherous maneuvering, and the dizzying counterstrength of pure, untouched fire magic.

All of a sudden, the narrow, twisting passage exploded into openness. A vast cavern yawned in the shape of a near perfect circle, a separate contained universe hidden deep in the bowels of the planet . . . complete with its own brilliant, pulsating, dangerous sun.

Only this was no sun. This was the Fire Source—a giant, blistering orb of white, with tongues and whips of blue and sparkling silver snapping out like poisonous snakes trapped behind wire. They left tiny floating flecks of flame in their wake, which flared on their own for a second or two, then died. The Source was a living thing, an amorphous beast contained in an elastic shape, constantly pushing against its constraints. It reeked of danger and power.

Griffin hovered at the circumference of the cavern, awed and petrified over what glowed before him. It was astounding that something like this existed in a human world, on the human plane. It had been born with this planet, not brought here like his own people. It would die when the Earth did. Or vice versa.

That was all the time he allowed himself to think. He had something else to do.

When he'd taken Keko beneath the ocean's surface and encapsulated her in magic water, he'd sensed her trying to release her fire. The water wouldn't let her. His element hadn't killed hers, it just . . . contained it.

He had to trust in that same principle here.

The Source pulsed in a great, uneven heartbeat. It seemed to grow more and more agitated by the second, Griffin's presence feeding and affecting it. It knew something had infiltrated its lair and it was merely biding its time before unleashing its weapons, waiting for the perfect moment to strike. It was a dragon—a chimera—stalking and teasing its prey.

Death churned inside that thing. Hope, too. And they were all tied together by faith.

Those blue and white flames continued to loop out from the surface of the Source like the solar flares in the Earth's sun. They stretched and bowed then snapped back, leaving remnant flecks floating in the air, glowing in their wake. Griffin watched them greedily.

Then he saw his opportunity. Perhaps his only one. He prayed—to the stars, to Keko's Queen, to whomever might be listening—that it would be enough.

A bolt of crackling blue flame shot out—straight for where he'd flattened his particles against the wall. It wanted to dissolve him. To destroy him. The whip of fire snapped before it reached him, leaving behind a web of tiny blue-white motes— pure specks of magic no longer attached to the Source itself. Residual fire just lingering in space.

His for the taking.

Before another flare could stretch for him, he ballooned his steam out from the wall. Sent it looping around a flickering blue remnant no larger than a pebble. He grabbed it, encased it as he had Keko's body. Stole it.

Here in this cavern of extreme heat and elemental fire, Griffin fought for control of his own magic. Digging deeper into his power than he'd ever dug before, he forced the steam immediately surrounding the live spark into liquid, wrapping it in a dense bubble cage.

The fire sputtered but held. Weakened but did not die.

There was no time to worry or think or do anything else other than run. He gathered up the floating, translucent particles of himself, cradled and cushioned the speck of the Source inside his magic, and fled back through the crack.

The Source did not like that at all.

The cavern and passage walls vibrated, throwing Griffin's already tenuous form against the rocks, threatening to break him apart and loose the treasure he carried. A great cloud of heat and smoke screamed at his back, the soundless voice of a mother who'd had one of her many children ripped from her bosom.

He would not be deterred. He would not let it go. This thing he stole belonged to Keko—this infinitesimal bit of fire—and she would use it for the noblest of purposes.

Tightening the hold on the fire speck, he pushed harder. Raced up through the quaking, narrow passages. The planet felt ripped off its axis, gravity and direction meaning absolutely nothing. Still, he flew. Zoomed. Faster and faster.

Hot fire consumed his trail. Not just heat or threats anymore, but actual liquid lava, scorching rock, and attacking flame. They all chased him down. He may not be made of fire, but he had still caused an eruption.

He zigged and zagged, concentrating hard on keeping his magic whole, on keeping the fleck safe and alive. Tremors hunted him, wielding the Source's weapons, but he could feel the air getting fresher up ahead. It fed him energy. He pushed on. And then . . . light.

It refracted off the rock lining the sides of the fissure. It pierced his vapor and the bubble and struck the fire fragment, making it come alive, turning it into a starburst. He clutched it, feeling the magic trying to get out but unable to release through his water.

It seemed to call to the Source, too—a child to its mother—and the Source answered with a burst of heat and flame that actually pushed Griffin the final few yards up and out of the entrance, sending him soaring between the halves of the great split rock, shooting high above the island.

The sky was a dazzling, blinding sheet of blue above, and the island below was a quivering black mass of lava rock, crumbling and cracking like an egg from the force of the Source's expulsion. The ocean immediately surrounding the island rippled, billowing blooms of white rising up from underneath.

He saw Keko, a dark figure being thrown about on the small, quaking mound of land in the middle of the water, trying to keep her balance as the rock shifted. Nem was still there, screaming death threats, but only for a moment longer. The island gave a great heave and Keko tumbled to the side, thrown to the ground. She must have lost control of her magic because the circle of fire around and below Nem suddenly died. And then, barely a second later, he was gone. Sunk back into the shaking, breaking earth.

Griffin made sure the fire speck was still safe and zoomed down to Keko. Ash belched from the bowels of the earth, the distinct odor of sulfur and the tang of hidden fire consuming everything. Steam and black smoke poured out of the fissure now, and he shot through it. Even in the growing murk he could find her. He would always be able to find her.

As he drew closer, Keko pulled herself to her feet, but the ground fought back, continually trying to throw her down. He'd seen many emotions cross her face in their time together, but panic had never, ever been one of them. Her wide eyes darted around, looking for escape, for answers. For an enemy to fight. But this time the attacker, the Source, was made of her own element and her weapons would never be strong enough to win.

Griffin swirled around her in a misty ribbon, gently pressing against her, letting himself go more liquid. When she realized it was him, he felt her body shiver, her slight exhalation of relief. He rolled the bubble containing the fire spark up through his being, aligning it with her sight. Her eyes turned glassy when she saw what he carried.

Now to figure out how to give her the pure bit of magic. If he released the bubble, the fleck would likely sputter and die as it had within the cavern. If he assumed human form, the result would probably be the same.

Another lurch of the earth. Keko's mouth dropped open . . . and he saw his answer.

Without thinking, without allowing himself doubt, he opened a space in the mist, released the bubble, and shoved the blue-white spark free. It arced out and away, shooting straight for Keko's mouth. Her jaw jutted out and she caught the tiny flame between her lips. It disappeared into the dark behind her teeth, then her mouth closed around it.

She swallowed, then gulped and gasped, both hands flying to her throat, fingers scratching at her skin. Her eyes rolled back in her head and her body convulsed.

The island lost all stability. The rock that had been the gateway to the Source exploded, hot shards flying, the first bubbles of red and gold lava erupting out of the split in the earth. A molten river rushed toward them.

Keko's eyes had gone wholly white, one hand still at her throat, the other pressed to her chest. Her body was tilting sideways and she did not put out her arms to stop her fall. If she collapsed here the encroaching lava would consume her.

Though weary, his strength and magic nearly gone, Griffin wrapped his mist tightly around Keko, cushioning her fall. Catching a gust of hot, sulphuric wind, he swept them both up and away from the ground as a surging roll of lava consumed the spot in which they'd just stood.

He spun around her as he carried her away, smashing his molecules together to form another, larger bubble around her limp form. He took them away from the broken island and the angry magic that was burying it in fire, and plunged them back into the churning ocean.

The water had gone cloudy with agitation. Within the waves the volcanic eruption felt entirely different—muffled and distant, but no less deadly. He shot through the water, Keko's inert body bouncing around weightless and powerless inside his protection. He pushed on, back toward the Big Island, sensing the eruption fade and dim the farther away they got, until they were well away from its threat altogether.

At last the ocean floor started to slant upward, forming the base of the giant, ancient volcanoes of the Big Island. Griffin speared through the water, rising up, fighting and then using the mighty push and pull of the waves as they neared the shore. The surface was in sight, a sparkling invitation. He'd reached the dregs of his power, but even that wasn't a good enough excuse to give up.

He gave one last push and propelled himself up and out of the water, spitting them over the waves and onto land. He lost all water magic in midair, his human body coming to him straight from vapor, making every muscle and bone and last bit of his spirit scream in pain. He still clung to Keko, though, managing to roll himself under her, so when they hit the shelf of serrated black lava rock strewn with chunks of loose white coral, it was he who took the brunt.

The jagged points of the rock dug into his skin but he barely felt them, for the drain of his energy stole all sensation as it pulled away his consciousness. He would feel it later. He would feel it all.

Vaguely, he was aware of Keko sliding off his body in a tangle of brown, limp limbs. With his last bit of effort, he blindly reached out and found the pulse on her neck, which was thready but present. His last thought before passing out was that she was warm.

Wonderfully, frighteningly warm.

TWENTY

Keko awoke on a bed of nails, a thousand sharp points gouging into her skin, the pain both extreme and welcome. It forced her back into awareness when she knew she couldn't afford to be in the black any longer.

The sun was setting, and she awoke a different person. Only she didn't know why. Or how.

Rolling her head, she winced at the scrape against her scalp. Her fingers flew to the back of her skull and brushed what she knew to be the rough and blocky 'a'ā kind of lava rock. The stuff had been borne of fire, deep within the earth, but it was wicked on the body, Chimeran or not.

The sound of waves filled her ears. Easy, insistent waves.

The earth was still, free of smoke and fire.

How did she get here? And where was here? The last thing she remembered was the island rumbling beneath her feet, the anger of the Source bubbling up from below, throwing her down. The force and shock of the quake had jarred loose her control over her magic. She'd watched Nem's fire cage collapse, then witnessed him clawing his way back into the enraged earth. Then . . .

Keko gasped as panic consumed her.

Griffin. Griffin had turned to vapor and disappeared into the fissure, and then a long time later the world had exploded around her.

"Keko."

Maybe she was only hearing her name in his voice because she wanted to so badly. And maybe, after she turned her head on the spiky rock and found the Ofarian stretched out beside her, his normally olive skin gone pale, his lips colorless, it was only a vision her desperate mind had created.

But then the vision struggled to sit up, and she knew he was real. Griffin was real and alive. And he was weak.

"Are you okay?" he asked, his voice as torn up as his body.

She peeled herself off the rock, grimacing at the way it had punched divots and cuts into her skin. Glancing around, she knew immediately that they were back on the Big Island, on the remote coast south of Hilo, close to the Chimeran valley.

She could not answer Griffin. She could only look at him, take him all in. And wonder.

Then she sensed it again, that clear difference in her body and being. Her skin felt the same, familiar, but everything inside—from the darkest reaches of her brain to the smallest, most insignificant muscle—pulsed to a tune she'd never heard before. Her inner fire burned with a permanent light, a never-ending source of energy.

Like she'd never have to take a Chimeran breath ever again.

"What happened?" she said.

Her voice sounded odd. Deeper and more resonant. She put a palm to her chest, where it felt strange.

Griffin's stare dropped to where her hand lay and his eyes widened. Then she looked down and saw what he did. She still wore his black T-shirt, and through the fibers glowed a light, outlining her fingers and beating in time with her heart.

Keko scrambled to her feet, her hands slipping into the neckline of the T-shirt and ripping it down the center, exposing the skin just above her breasts, now possessed of a soft, blue-white light.

"What is it?" she cried, even though she knew. "What *is* it?"

Griffin stood and lifted a hand toward the glow, but did not touch her. "The Source," he said, meeting her eyes. "A tiny part of it anyway."

Each pulse of the muted light sent a new bit of magic into her system. Its purity was undeniable, its beauty almost able to be tasted. Sweet like the smoke she loved, but a sweetness no one before had ever had the pleasure of rolling on her tongue. Unlike Chimeran blood that had been diluted by history or mixed breeding with Primaries, this magic was uncontaminated and whole. And even though that tiny part was now inside her, it was still the Source, and it would never die.

It was the Queen's *mana*, her spiritual power incarnate.

Griffin had done it. But . . . how?

Another bit of memory came back to her. Him, in mist form, feeding her the little blue-white spark he'd brought up from below. Her swallowing the fire magic, how it had burned going down. How it had felt like death.

Turning, she looked toward the setting sun, the lowering light calling out the thick plume of smoke far, far on the horizon.

"Brave, mighty Queen," she murmured, the name scratching at her throat. She swallowed, gathering strength and moisture, and faced Griffin, who watched her with overwhelming intensity. "What happened?"

"You wouldn't've survived," he said, shaking his head, "if you'd gone down there."

And then he told her the most incredible story that ended with a volcanic eruption out in the middle of the ocean, and a piece of the Fire Source inside Keko Kalani.

Griffin had succeeded. In the end, he'd told her the truth. And he'd helped her.

She honestly did not know what to do in the face of that remarkable sacrifice—him giving up his dreams of the Senatus and risking his life to hand her the resolution to her own goals. Her very first thought was one of shame, that even though she'd found the Source and now carried a bit of it inside her, Griffin had been the one to retrieve it. She was Chimeran through and through, and her blood told her that Griffin's actions on her behalf called out a weakness.

She did not know if she'd ever be able to erase or appease that feeling. Or even if she wanted to.

"Do you think you can cure them?" he asked.

She looked deep into his eyes and drew a Chimeran breath. With the inrush of air, the burgeoning new power inside accelerated and bloomed with a force she could barely control. It wanted to scream out of her throat and dance all over everything. She just barely yanked it back before it loosed itself upon Griffin.

"Keko." He still didn't touch her, his hand hovering between them. "What is it?"

For the first time in her life, she feared her own fire.

"It's so . . . different. Scary."

She opened her palm to the sky and pursed her lips, intending to blow flame into the cup of her hand. It was the very first trick a Chimeran child learned when they came into their power, something any fire elemental knew and could control with barely a thought.

Keko had meant to create a tiny flame, a flicker of the red and orange and gold she knew so well.

What came out was a fireball as large as her head. Beautiful and wondrous and deadly in a whole new sense of the word. And it shimmered in a sparkling, searing blue-white.

"Yes," she murmured, transfixed by the color and power that had come from her body. "Yes, I believe I can cure them."

They stood in the misting rain, far enough inland that she'd lost sight of the ocean. Far enough away that she could not watch the sun setting behind the massive smear of smoke and lava she'd created. At first she did not recognize the sentiments that tangled in her gut, because regret and doubt had never kept space in the limited emotional arsenal the Chimeran culture allowed, but as she and Griffin stared at each other, what she felt now became all too clear.

The Keko who'd hiked out of the Chimeran valley, intent on taking the Source at any cost, would have simply turned her back on the damage she'd done to the B and B, and the chaos she'd caused out in the ocean. But the Keko who now held pure fire magic within her body worried about who and what she'd affected, and how badly.

She had Griffin to thank for that, and she did not hate him for it. In fact, she found that she did not hate him at all.

He stood close but did not touch her, eyeing her carefully. Lovingly. That's how it had been the whole time as they'd stumbled off the coastal lava rock and hiked inland. Bloodied, weary, dirty, they'd stopped only when they'd found a phone and she'd made her call to the stronghold.

Now they waited for a specific Chimeran to bring the car.

The rain cleansed her, rinsing her skin, trickling into her mouth. She licked at it gratefully. Griffin had to cup his hands to drink from a puddle. That alone told her that his magic was depleted.

Her black T-shirt was thoroughly soaked, enabling her to fold the ripped section over her gently glowing chest and hide what made her eternally different. She would have to do this, she realized, for the rest of her days.

She gripped a fistful of the fabric, feeling the pulse of new magic through her skin, and looked deep into Griffin's eyes. "Why?" she whispered.

He reached for her, hands peeling off his wet torso where he'd tucked them underneath his arms, but she quickly stepped back with a warning look. If she felt this different inside, she had no idea what her skin might do to him. That distance—the idea that she might never be able to touch him again—hurt more than the gashes on her back or the bruises dotting her arms.

Griffin didn't look worried, but he let his arms drop without argument. "I've never told you about my brother," he said.

She looked at him quizzically. "No. I don't know anything about your family. Other than what you told me in the hotel, about being born a soldier."

"I have this brother—well, I have five of them, but I'm talking about the youngest, Henry. He's twelve and he's . . ." Griffin finally looked away from her, off toward the great slopes of the old, dead volcanoes rising in the distance, long since gone green. He turned his face up to the rain and ran a hand through his wet hair, making it gleam black. "Henry's mine. My heart. *My* reason. I didn't know it before the Board fell, but since then . . ."

It suddenly made sense. Everything he'd done—it all made sense. "You see yourself in him."

He still didn't look at her, his focus somewhere distant. "I *saw* myself in him. I saw chances for him—and all Ofarian kids, really—that I never had. And it frustrated the hell out of me that he didn't see what I did, that he wasn't chasing down this new life. But the thing is, he's *not* me. He's Henry." At last his eyes trailed back to hers and she saw in them a love and devotion that existed on a plane she'd never personally known.

"I can give him what I can," Griffin said with a shrug, "but the rest is up to him. All I can do is help him along his own way."

And Keko thought, with a bloom in her heart that had nothing to do with fire magic, *You will make an amazing father someday.*

"The Senatus," she said, "and all the stuff with the Primaries—"

"To me, my kid brother wore every Ofarian child's face, and I stopped seeing what Henry truly looked like. I pushed the Primaries and my dreams on him and everyone else, because of what my birthright made me do. Because of what the old Chairman made me do. All I want is something better for Henry and the other kids, and I want to give them those chances. I thought the Senatus was the way. Now? I don't know."

She released the clutch on her shirt, suddenly feeling hollow. "I have only ever lived for me."

Then Griffin was there, as close as he could get without touching her. "That's not true."

She shook her head. "It is. I went for the Source to get the cure, yeah, but in my heart I wanted to be bigger than I was. To lead, to be the Queen. I've never known how to be selfless."

"Stop it. It's not the same thing as being selfish. Which you aren't."

Long moments of silence passed. "I admire you," she finally said. The admission surprised her. "So much. I need to figure out what to do now, what I can do . . . after I go back."

He rubbed at his jaw, and she was starting to figure out that he did that when there were many things he wanted to say but couldn't. Or wouldn't. Like he was massaging the words on his tongue to keep them calm, to keep them from escaping on their own. Finally, very slowly, he said, "You will figure it out. I can help you. If you'll have me."

She had to close her eyes, because the tenderness and understanding on his face was simply overwhelming. "You've already done so much. This"—her hand hovered over her chest—"is difficult for me to accept. That you got to the Source and I did not."

"I know."

And when she opened her eyes, she saw that he really did know.

"I'm sorry it went down like that," he said. "If I could erase my presence here and let you have that, I would. If you wanted, I would take away all that happened between us in the waterfall and the B and B and . . . in here"—he touched his heart—"to give that to you."

Is that what she wanted? Could she ever do that? Trade this precious, exciting, beautiful connection with him for the ability to walk into the Chimeran valley and say she'd succeeded where the Queen had not?

Griffin was too good. Too sacrificial. She'd grown up believing she was deserving of the best, that she was worthy of fighting for what she wanted, but this man had been touched by the stars and the Queen alike, and his light was so very bright. It chased away her shadows, and she'd always relied on those shadows to guide her. To remind her of her bad decisions and past experiences.

"Griffin—"

The whine and grind of an approaching Jeep cut her off, and she turned to watch the familiar yellow vehicle jouncing over the dirt road. It stopped between two white flowering trees and the driver got out.

Bane slid from behind the wheel. He just stood there holding the door open, staring over the top of it, his gaze bouncing between Keko and Griffin. At last he slammed shut the door and stalked toward them, his bare feet pounding through puddles.

As he drew closer, Keko could barely believe what she was seeing. Bane, the Chimeran general, looked like he was on the verge of tears. He pulled up ten feet away and repressed his emotion in a most Chimeran way.

"You're alive," he said, and she heard the unmistakable relief in his voice. "The sky went dark . . . we knew there was an eruption somewhere . . . I thought . . ."

"You knew about Aya's warning," Keko interrupted, "about the danger to the Earth and myself if I touched the Source?"

Bane nodded once, thin rivers of rainwater swooping down his neck and bare chest.

"And yet," she went on, "you still asked Griffin to help me."

Bane looked to Griffin, but the Ofarian was standing slightly behind her so she couldn't see Griffin's reaction.

"Because you knew that if I came back bearing the power of the Source, I could cure Ikaika. You could stop covering for his loss of magic."

Bane paled but, to his credit and training, did not otherwise react. He'd always been so good at hiding the true depth of his feelings for the other Chimeran warrior. "How did you know about that?"

"Because the chief is afflicted, too." She had no qualms in saying it now. She needed her brother's help and it required his knowledge.

"Holy shit." Bane blew out a breath and raised his arms, locking his hands around the back of his skull. "That changes everything," he muttered, his dark eyes darting from puddle to puddle. She knew he was already considering his formal challenge. Plotting the *ali'i's* downfall, just as she'd done only days earlier.

"No." She advanced on her brother, one hand coming up to pull back the flap of her ripped T-shirt. "This does."

Now Bane reacted. And not at all in the way she'd expected.

His attention immediately dropped to the soft white glow beneath her breastbone. He rubbed his own chest, as though able to sense what did not reside there, and then his stare snapped back up to her face. His eyes went impossibly wide. He breathed hard. His massive shoulders sagged.

And then he fell to his knees, hitting the mud with a splat. He gazed up at her in what she could only describe as divine awe.

"My Queen . . ." he murmured.

Behind her, Griffin sucked in a breath.

She should have known this might happen. She should have realized that it was not for her to determine how others might view her when she stumbled back into the valley.

Keko stood over her brother, whose tears were now very real. The dark orbs of his eyes shone with them, even in the deepening twilight.

"I am not your Queen," she said. "But I am a cure. And I want you to bring me to Chief. In secret."

Bane blinked, finally looking again like the general she knew. "But . . . why? You should enter the valley in the darkness and let everyone see what you've done. What you have inside you. They'll want to know you. They'll want to follow you." He pounded a hearty fist on his chest. "You should take what you've earned."

Now Keko finally looked to Griffin, who watched her with his lips flattened in assessment. If she wanted, he would tell the story of how he'd actually been the one to face the Source, but she did not will it.

"No," she told Bane. "I won't do that."

Because she had not earned it. At least, not in the Chimeran way. A gift alone did not merit such praise. What she did with that gift, however, just might. She had some proving to do.

She met Griffin's eyes. He gave her the faintest of smiles and a small nod, and she knew he understood. Because he was extraordinary like that.

"What I will do," Keko said, focusing again on her brother, "is cure the diseased. One by one, starting with the *ali'i*. To reveal myself and my true reason for going after the Source would compromise all of the victims, and I won't have any of them looked down upon because of a weakness they were powerless to fight. It is their secret to reveal. Not mine to use against them. I will give the same order to the chief."

Bane, still on his knees before her, looked like he might try to throw another argument her way.

"You say nothing," she said. "Understand?"

He rose to his feet and bowed with a speed she'd never before witnessed. Not even when he'd responded to the *ali'i*.

TWENTY-ONE

Once again, Keko found herself on the back terrace of the *ali'i*'**s** house, staring through the closed glass door at the thick silhouette of the man standing inside. It had been nearly a week since the last time she'd done this. It was night again, the sound of the birds gradually fading and the wind picking up, tossing about the trees. The whole scene was freakishly familiar.

Only now, instead of harboring threats and pleas, the Queen's treasure burned inside her body. And she had Griffin at her back.

"Do you want me to wait out here?" His voice was feather soft near her ear, and it took all her effort not to lean into him.

She turned, and the shadows loved him. Made him appear mysterious and serious and lovely. She owed him so much—so much she'd never be able to repay.

"No," she replied. "Come with me."

The inside of the small house was as cool and damp as she remembered. Candles burned on various tables scattered about the dim room, their pillars low, and wax dripping around their bases. Underneath the scent of their lit wicks lingered the odor of phosphorous, the remnants of matches—even though the candles clearly had been burning for quite some time.

Sneaking through the shadows of the valley to arrive here in secret, she'd been able to pick out the various kinds of fire being wielded by Chimerans, whether she could see the people or not. Each and every instance of flame called to her in a different voice, and she wondered if this was what it felt like to be Griffin with his sense of signatures. And was this a blessing or a curse from the Source? She did not yet know.

Chief stood in front of the couch, almost exactly where she'd left him. Maybe he'd been standing there for days and days, continually praying for her success. Or her failure. She no longer knew which he valued more.

As she moved deeper into the room, she tugged aside a flap of her T-shirt. The Source released a serene glow, bright enough to mark her as different. Enough to proclaim her victory.

Chief gasped. Stumbled back. But he couldn't go very far because of the couch, and then he wasn't moving backward at all. He revised his steps, coming forward. Coming for her with wide, unblinking eyes and an outstretched hand.

Griffin closed in tighter at her back. Bane moved around to one side.

Keko threw out a hand, and even without inhaling or calling up or commanding her fire, her fingers rippled with a blue-white flame that appeared almost liquid. Chief stopped as suddenly as if he'd hit a wall.

"You did it," he murmured, his eyes clear and wet.

She willed the fire to die, and it obeyed. "I did. Even though you agreed with the Senatus to stop me. Even though you sent Griffin after me."

Chief's eyes closed, and it seemed that in the past few days his wrinkles had deepened, elongated. He looked like he'd aged more since she'd last left here than in the past twenty years combined.

"I had to," he said. "Aya overheard me and Bane, and she told us what could happen. I had to agree with her or—"

"Risk exposing yourself," Keko snapped. "Yeah, I get it. You'd never dream of compromising your name, but you'd gladly let mine be dragged through the shit. You'd never dream of telling the truth to the Senatus about my reasons for searching for the Source, but you'd let them think that I was this crazed, jilted, selfish Chimeran willing to destroy part of the world just to get a little respect."

Chief's breath hissed through his nose. "I was secretly glad Griffin went after you and not the large company the premier wanted to send. I thought that you'd be able to escape one man. That you'd find a way to survive and succeed."

"And heal you." She let out an ugly, short laugh. "I should let you live without your fire. I should heal all the others and let your shame come out on its own. Watch you go down the way you watched me."

Chief blanched. "I gave you that chance before and you didn't take it. You're too honorable for that, Kekona."

She hated him for saying that. She hated him because he was right.

"Here's the thing." She moved closer, into the candlelight. "I'm not entirely sure I can heal you. It was all a wild gamble to begin with. But if you want your fire back so badly—if you want to protect your name and status—I think you should be the guinea pig, dear uncle. I think I should test out my new power on you first. What do you say to that?"

Chief looked to Bane, but Bane only stared expectantly at Keko.

"And if it doesn't work?" asked the *ali'i*.

She shrugged. "Nothing lost, as far as I can see." Except that she was playing a part, because the thought of not being able to cure Ikaika and the others yet to be named made her nauseous with disappointment.

If this didn't work, all of Griffin's sacrifices would be for nothing.

"There is great power inside me," she said. "Even I fear it. Control is a flimsy thing and I have to fight for it constantly. I have no idea what will happen when I touch you."

Chief's hands turned to fists at his sides, but that was the extent of his visible reaction.

"Come here," she said, and the *ali'i* approached after only a moment's hesitation.

She could feel the Source stretching out to him the closer he got. As though it knew this man had the magic deep inside but could no longer command it. Maybe all the chief needed was a kick-start, a charge. Maybe if she opened up the conduit between the spark inside her and his body, she could feed him enough power to get through whatever blocks the disease had built.

No time to wonder. No time to doubt.

Calling the blue-white flame to her hand again without taking a breath, she slapped her palm over Chief's right pectoral. The little chunk of lava rock—the symbol of the Queen she'd once coveted—bounced on his chest.

He cried out, his face instantly contorting in pain. His legs buckled. He went down, knees hitting the tile, but she bent forward and held on. Source flame, intense and blue-silver like the dusk, rolled down her arm in waves and sank into the chief's body, like he was the shore and her power was high tide.

She had to battle for control of it. It kicked and fought, and wanted free rein to explode into him, but she knew if she did that—if she let it take control—he'd die. She could also feel it working. Could feel the fire pumping back into him, restarting his system, cracking through invisible barriers, and feeding back to him what had been withering inside.

A long, low moan streamed up out of his throat. His whole body shook with violent tremors. She'd never witnessed such agony—on his face or the face of any Chimeran—but he didn't resist. Didn't try to pull away. Despite everything he was, everything he had said or done to her, she had to commend him for that.

The pain and power grew and grew. It got so bad that he ceased making any sound or movement at all.

In the end, it was not Chief who stopped the flow. Of their own accord, the flames pulled out of his chest and retreated back up her arm, then flickered and died. The second she removed her hand from his skin, he pitched forward, just barely catching himself on his hands before striking the floor.

A fine line ran between healing and death.

Bane rushed forward, taking Chief by his shoulders and helping him to sit back on his heels. The *ali'i*'s head lolled on his neck, his arms limp at his sides, and his chest . . . Bane saw it the exact moment Keko did, and her brother looked up at her in panic.

Griffin came to her side. "Is that . . . ?"

It was. Her handprint, charred and black, embedded in Chief's flesh. Proof that he'd needed healing. Proof that he'd needed *her*.

Chief looked down and saw it, too. Bane released him and the *ali'i* scrambled to his feet, his shaking fingers picking at the edges of her mark like a scab, his face ashen.

"Did it work?" Bane demanded, the desperate tone of his voice clearly speaking for another diseased Chimeran male. "Are you healed?"

Chief finally stopped staring down at the permanent charcoal reminder, and lifted his chin to meet Keko's eyes.

"Reach for your fire," she told him.

Chief drew a Chimeran breath. Upon the exhale, he raised a hand to his lips and blew out a thin stream of gold and orange flame. The tips of each finger danced with gorgeous fire and he watched them with a childlike glee.

He started to cry. The venerated *ali'i* of the Big Island Chimerans was *crying*.

Between his sobs he inhaled, sucking the fire back into his body. Then he relit his fingers with a laugh, rolled the flame into a ball, and passed it from hand to hand. Holding it before him like an offering, he gazed over its flickering top and said to Keko, "Thank you."

She hadn't done this for *him*. She did it for all Chimerans, whether they'd lost their magic or not. She did it for the fire itself, the element that wanted to be used by her people. And she did it for the Queen whose dream was finally realized.

No, she hadn't done it for her uncle . . . but she couldn't help but be moved by his reaction. By this reunification. It gave her a tremendous joy and satisfaction to see the same on his face.

It made her feel completely selfless.

She sensed Griffin edge even closer, and when she turned her face to him he was watching her carefully.

"Are you okay?" he asked.

The Source sent white-hot waves of power and strength and excitement shooting through every vein in her body. She tried to think of something to compare it to. Maybe sex, if every time could be like that last time with Griffin in the coastal B and B. Perhaps love, if it was absolute and unshakeable. If it were perfect. If it were undeniably mutual.

But unfortunately, love was none of those things.

Griffin looked at her with grave concern. She wanted desperately to share this feeling with him, for him to experience the power, the healing, the giving of something to help another in need—but then, it was entirely possible he already knew.

She didn't know if she could love him any more than she did at that very moment.

"Keko." His voice was a breath, a small, invisible container of emotion she could not dare herself to believe in.

The brush of air by her ear was his hand as he raised it to touch her. How she wanted that! But she could not chance it. Not when he had no loss of fire magic to cure. Not when she'd seen the great pain she'd caused the chief—and the resulting mark. She ducked out of Griffin's touch. Not a big movement, but enough to warn him off.

He sighed and let his hand fall yet again.

"I'm fine," she said to Griffin. Then she turned to the *ali'i* who was still playing at his flame as though he were a child just come into his powers.

Bane had locked his hands around the back of his skull again, and he stared with undisguised horror at the askew black handprint on Chief's chest.

Keko went to her brother and said low, "They'll all be marked. If they want to be cured, they'll have to wear shirts to hide it." No other way to keep it secret, not in their culture of bared skin. "They'll have to make the choice. No magic or a scar."

Bane unlaced his fingers and turned to her. "But *you* will get no choice. If the people find out about the disease, they'll know about the cure. They'll have to know about you."

She saw the devotion in his eyes, what she'd seen when he'd fallen to his knees once before. "I'm still no Queen."

He tightly shook his head. "That's not for you to decide."

But it was for her to believe.

"Bring me Ikaika," she said, deliberately changing the subject, "and let him be the first to make his choice."

Bane pressed both fists to his chest, a gesture of worship usually meant only for ceremonies involving legends of the Queen. The *ali'i*, seeing this, stiffened but said nothing. He could not, after all. Not when he was no longer the most powerful in the valley.

Bane hurried out. Keko moved to stand before Griffin.

"You know about Ikaika," she said, "but not the others. I think, for the sake of their privacy and the sanctity of our culture, because you are Ofarian—"

"I'll go." Griffin glanced at the *ali'i*. "My oath still stands, Keko. My word and my stars are yours." Then he turned and left, the latch in the glass door making a soft click that sounded far too loud in the dense, silent room.

A short while later, Bane returned with Ikaika through the

shadowed and secret back entrance, both men slightly out of breath. Bane's eyes glimmered in anticipation. Ikaika's brow furrowed in confusion when he finally saw Keko.

"I know about your fire," she told Ikaika without preamble. When the warrior threw a harsh look at Bane and then a fearful look at Chief sitting on the darkened corner of the couch, Keko held up a hand. "Your general said nothing. It doesn't matter how I know. You've lost your magic. But I can give it back."

Ikaika sucked in a breath. His eyes kept darting toward the *ali'i*, and Keko gestured for Chief to come out of the shadows.

"I can give you back your fire," Keko said, beckoning Chief even closer, "but you will be marked. As the *ali'i* is."

Ikaika gaped in horror at the handprint, and then in clear shock at the face of the man who wore it. "What then? Will I be sent to the Common House?"

Chief replied quickly. "No. I'll think of something to explain the mark, but in the meantime, you have to hide it."

Keko could not think about honesty or shame or pride or worthiness just then. Those were for Chief to weigh and live with, and if he could roll over and sleep soundly at night knowing he was covering up something he would have easily used against any other Chimeran just a year ago, then that was his issue. He would never admit to the weakness himself, and she chose to be grateful that it meant she would not be called out as Queen.

She just wanted to make her people whole again. It was not about the power. Not anymore. She was not marking her subjects or declaring herself above them. She was giving back what was rightfully theirs.

"Do it." Ikaika stomped to Keko, looking every bit the fierce warrior he'd proven himself to be. "Do it now."

He grabbed Keko's arm and slapped it to his bare chest, just below the band of white beads around his neck. The Source fire responded immediately, blue-white flame surging from her body to his. Only this man did not fall to his knees as Chief had done. Ikaika remained standing, fists balled tightly at his sides, veins and sweat popping out all over his body. His head dropped forward and his jaw shook, but he never faltered. Not even when it was finished and Keko fell back.

Bane came free from the granite stance he'd assumed in the

corner, stalked across the room, and grabbed Ikaika's shoulders, forcing him to look up. The two men stared at one another, Bane's fingers digging into the slick brown skin where Ikaika's tattooed shoulder sloped up to his neck. Then Bane softened, leaning forward. Their foreheads and noses touched in a delicate *honi*—the sharing of each other's breath and well-being. The exchange of life.

When they exhaled, a flicker of flame escaped each of their lips, mingling in midair, and then their mouths came together. Brief, but full of passion.

Chief turned away, but Keko could not. She'd never seen such naked emotion in her brother, had never known him—or any Chimeran, really—capable of such stirring intensity. And that had always included herself.

Until she'd met Griffin.

It was Ikaika who stepped back first, even though Bane did not seem to want to let him go. Ikaika looked to Keko with such awestruck gratefulness that she could not help but smile in return.

"Bring me the others," Keko ordered Bane gently, before Ikaika could name her Queen. "One by one."

Twenty-two afflicted Chimerans. Twenty-two of her people— from all status levels and born into every major family— walked shaking into the *ali'i*'s home believing their ultimate secret had been exposed and that they were being delivered to him for punishment. Twenty-two made their choice. And all twenty-two Chimerans stumbled away from Chief's house bearing the handprint of their cure beneath a shirt.

She had not allowed one of them to call her Queen, though she'd seen the name shining in their eyes and dancing in the restored fire on their tongues.

Bright sunlight now lit up the scraggly garden out back. She'd been channeling the Source all night without sleep or pause, yet she'd never felt more awake, more alive.

Movement out in the garden, and she realized it was Griffin sitting on the crooked steps of the terrace. He leaned back on his hands, stretching his neck, then cracking his back. The small burn mark on his temple, the one she'd given him during Nem's first attack, drew her attention. The sight of it made her heart twist. Such a tiny thing, but it was a reminder of all that he'd done for her and her people—and what he'd given up for his own. Like the handprints, he would wear her mark forever. The cuts and bruises from their cliffside brawl and the battle with Nem would fade, but that burn would remain.

She exited the house, the sound of the door opening bringing Griffin to his feet. As she approached him, she marveled at how every time she thought she looked upon a beautiful god in human form, he managed to somehow look even better the next time she laid eyes on him. Even now, when he was as dirty and ragged as she.

He held his breath as she went up to him.

"Will you come with me?" she asked.

He smiled. "Always."

She skirted around the morning meadow that was filling with Chimeran warriors preparing for their drills, a shouting Bane and a shirted Ikaika at the front.

She brought Griffin to her hidden spot high up on the cliff, the one that had views of the valley and the ocean. The place where she'd incinerated his coat when she believed herself cured of his presence in her mind and heart. Who had she been kidding? Even back then?

He climbed without complaint, though he must have been exhausted. There was no place else to take him, however, since she could not bring him to the Common House in broad daylight, and she had no other home. If she'd demanded Bane vacate her old house he would have done so, but that would draw unwanted attention.

"Griffin." She turned to him, a million things to say on her tongue, but the two words that mattered most came out. "Thank you."

Then he was on her. Pushing her against a rock.

Touching her.

She tried to scramble out of his grip, to save him. The Source . . . who knew what it would do to him?

"It's okay," he whispered, his hands firmly wrapped around her arms, the hard length of his body pressing against hers. "I am water."

And when he kissed her, she sensed his smile. His joy. His pride.

Inside she felt the Source reacting, trying to get out, flinging itself against her skin and coming up against a sparkling, formidable barrier in the man she never wanted to stop touching. Because she *could* touch him. Deep down she knew that she would never be able to touch another Chimeran man in this way again, but Griffin . . . he was water.

Her opposite. Her complement.

She kissed him back, eyes squeezed shut in near pain. Because they floated in a dream of a future she was sure they would never be able to have. He lead his people. They depended on him, and he would return to San Francisco with a slate wiped clean—all that he'd worked for, all that he'd promised the Ofarians, gone—thanks to what he'd done for her here. The amount of work ahead of him was astronomical. He could not be tethered to a Chimeran woman, not if he hoped to focus on strengthening future Ofarian generations.

And the Chimerans needed her. This was still her home, still her culture, and she could not simply walk away. Maybe she could not allow herself to be Queen, but she was still a cure, and the disease might strike again. Maybe that's what the Queen had intended for her original quest all along: to discover the illness's origin and eradicate it forever. *That* was a noble purpose and one Keko could easily dedicate herself to in this day and age.

She did not want to walk away from Griffin, but she just might have to.

The realization ripped a sob from her throat. She had not cried before when she believed he'd double-crossed her, but she did right then with his mouth on hers, the tears pricking at the corners of her eyes. She cried for what she'd learned and discovered and unearthed inside herself. She cried because she chose to believe that he really did love her, even though he had not spoken it.

This belief she grasped tightly and wrapped around her heart. She channeled it into a deeper, more frantic kiss, an almost frightening urgency to her motions. She let herself be ground into the rock at her back, not feeling any of her injuries, only feeling Griffin. Tasting him. Loving him.

His spirit was his own Source. His selflessness gave him a purpose she'd always found foreign but now accepted with a profound understanding. His fair, considerate concern for the well-being of anyone other than himself was a bottomless well that would never run dry. It was counter to the Chimerans' way of life and it humbled her greatly. But it also gave her something to strive for, and a gift she could slowly feed to her own people.

Griffin pulled away, leaving her breathless not from the broken kiss, but from the depth of the emotion on his face. His hands slid up her arms and shoulders, and the Source fire traced his fingers' path underneath her skin, making her shiver with awareness, kicking up the pleasure of his touch. Taking the flaps of her ripped T-shirt—*his* T-shirt—he parted them gently, exposing her chest but not her breasts.

The Source glowed, a tranquil spot of light, until Griffin bent his head and kissed her skin. Right over the gift he'd given to her people.

This time the Source did break free in a flash of blue-white. Keko gasped, but Griffin only smiled with his lips and hands on her as a cool sheen of Ofarian water trickled over her skin. Rising in equal challenge to the fire inside her. Claiming her.

Deep inside her mind and body, fire and water magic clashed together. They tangled briefly, a sexy tussle, then they found a way to interlock. To accommodate one another without losing what made their element unique and powerful.

When Griffin released her, his lips were moist with magic and his eyes were dark and filled with understanding, and she knew that he'd experienced exactly what she just had.

He took her mouth again with a deep groan, eliciting from her a bone-deep shiver, heightened by the dual, opposing bits of magic. Heightened by him. Indeed, the whole world seemed to vibrate.

And then the world actually *did* vibrate. Tiny stones somersaulted down on them from above. Nearby, the tree branches, covered with giant, waxy leaves, trembled. The ground shook under their feet.

Griffin shoved away the same moment Keko felt the rock shift at her back. Instantly she knew what it was. Instantly she knew that the Child of Earth had returned.

Keko knew no fear.

She spun toward the rock as it folded and clinked and rolled

back in ways that seemed to dissolve and eat itself and transform all at the same time. Shoving Griffin behind her, she
called Source fire to her hand, more than she'd ever dared
before, ready for Nem's newest attack.

But it was not Nem who appeared.

Keko watched, wide-eyed, as Aya's familiar, diminutive
human body and pale, streaming hair gradually replaced the
elements of earth. When her transformation was complete, she
merely stood there, taking in Griffin and Keko with sad green
eyes.

Keko could feel Griffin behind her, his chest pressed to her
back, the way his heart beat faster, the struggle of his lungs.
He was afraid.

"I've come to demand punishment," said the Daughter of
Earth, her attention shifting solely to Griffin.

If Keko had held on to any doubt that Griffin had told her
the absolute truth about his reasons for coming to Hawaii, she
regretfully let it go now. Aya's presence and demand confirmed
everything.

Griffin asked, "Were any Primaries hurt?"

Aya briefly closed her eyes. "No."

He pressed on. "And did the eruption cause any other damage that might put Primaries in danger?"

Aya's glare hardened. "No. The new volcano, relatively small
as it is, is far enough away from civilization to not have a direct
effect, though it's caused a slight sea level rise. But no loss of
life, no." She lifted a graceful hand. "That was not our agreement, Griffin, and you know it. The terms were for you to make
sure the Source remained untouched or Keko is ours. The Father
is aware of what's happened and he demands retribution."

"No. I won't let you." Griffin tried to push out from behind
Keko, but she steeled her arms and legs and refused to let him
pass on the narrow path. He took a breath as if to say something
more, and Keko sensed he was about to tell Aya the true reason
behind her quest. Then he went still, and she knew that he was
holding true to his vow. Even though it killed him not to
defend her.

Aya stepped closer, having to lift her chin to look up at
Keko. Before, during their talks outside the Senatus gatherings,
Aya had always seemed somewhat childlike. Now she was

decidedly adult. Eerily composed. And perhaps a little regretful.

"Can I tell you a secret?" Aya said.

"Yes," Keko replied, blinking back surprise but not letting down her guard.

"I don't want you to be punished any more than Griffin does. I am trapped between my heart and my duty, but, in the end, my race and the Primaries we protect must come first."

That didn't make much sense to Keko, but behind her Griffin gasped. "You protect them?"

Aya nodded. "It's why I wanted you to go after Keko. It's why I wanted you on the Senatus. Because you and I, Griffin, we want more for the elementals and more for humanity than our races believe in, and I see in you many good things. I would've sided with you, and we could have made so many changes, but now you've destroyed your chance. And since Keko touched the Source, I have to take her Within."

"She didn't—" Griffin began.

Keko wouldn't let him finish. She couldn't allow him to sacrifice any more.

"The volcano was my doing," Keko blurted, because it truly was, when it came down to it.

"There was a man," Griffin growled, "a Son of Earth who attacked us twice and escaped through the earth both times. Did he tell you what happened on that island?"

Aya looked disturbed and mournful. "No. Nem never returned. We don't believe he got away from the island before the volcano destroyed it. Not even a Child can survive something like that. He was . . ." She shook her head, trying to compose herself. "He wasn't supposed to go after you, but something about him isn't—wasn't—right."

"Am I being blamed for his death?" Keko asked.

The tension in Aya's expression told her *yes*. Keko looked to the sky.

So the only two people alive who knew that Griffin had been the one to go down to the Source were standing right here. It was another secret she would make him carry. There was no way she would let him take the fall for her actions. There was no way she could allow herself to be more indebted to him than she already was.

A calm settled through her. Maybe this was what she'd known was coming when he'd kissed her. Maybe her mind had already realized her punishment and their separation were imminent, and it had to convince her heart that it must happen to protect them both.

This way, the Chimerans would never learn about the Queen's treasure and the Source, and the afflicted's secret would never get out. This was better, the only way.

Keko raised her hand, the one still rippling with the Source flame. She used it to tug aside the T-shirt so Aya could see what she bore, and part of the black fabric burned away before she willed the white fire to die. She pulled away from Griffin, away from his touch.

"A part of the Source is in me," she told Aya. "I own the magic. And I will pay for it."

Keko cast a long gaze over the valley, seeing each and every face of the Chimerans she'd healed. They had fire again. They could smile, and that brought her a profound sense of peace.

"I argued against death," Aya said, "because you, Keko, changed me. Helped me to see the Aboveground world in a way I'd never imagined. I want you to know that you made me want to become human."

Keko could not say anything for the shock, unaware she'd affected Aya in such a way. Unaware that the Children even had such a choice.

Griffin exhaled.

"But you disturbed something you should not have," Aya went on, her face darkening, "and caused offense to the Earth. My people will not kill you, but you will serve us Within. Your magic will not work down there and there is no sun. It was the will of the Father, who rules us. I am truly sorry."

Keko finally turned to face Griffin, and she was nearly knocked over by the fierce protest in his eyes and the terrible tension in the coil of his muscles. She saw everything on his face—their entire tumultuous history and the future that would never be. She saw it all, and couldn't help but be grateful for ever having experienced and known him, for however brief a time.

"No," he said. The single word of defiance came out harshly, though the look in his eyes was tender and soft. Then he reached out and yanked her to him, enveloping her in his arms. She had to concentrate very hard on keeping her fire under her control. When she went Within, she wouldn't have to worry about that struggle anymore.

"Let me," he whispered in her ear, low enough that Aya couldn't hear. "Let me tell her the truth."

Keko merely shook her head, her face against his neck. "Before you," she said, just as softly, just for him, "I thought love a weakness. Before you, I thought only fire and fists mattered. I was wrong."

She pushed away, and he reluctantly let her go. Though his hands were at his sides, she could still feel him reaching for her.

"I love you," he said between gritted teeth, his eyes filling. And then again, "I love you."

Those words—the ones she feared and longed to hear, finally spoken in his voice—painted themselves over her skin. She would never be able to wash them away, nor would she ever want to.

She touched Griffin's face with great sadness and aching loss and all the love she'd been gathering and storing her whole life, awaiting the appearance of this man. She could not look upon those three years apart from him as a waste. Instead she chose to look on the time they were given as a blessing.

She kissed him, quick and chaste. "And I love your stars."

With the reminder of his vow, his head dropped forward on his neck, his chest heaving. One hand came up to dig his thumb and forefinger into his eyes.

This was her time.

Keko turned to Aya. "It's done."

Without hesitation, Aya snatched her in arms made of skin and stone, and whipped Keko's body around. The Source fire wanted to be let out, to fight, but Keko kept it in check. She would not oppose this.

Griffin's head snapped up, his face a mask of terror and despair, his arms reaching for Keko, his feet grinding up dirt as he lunged. Keko saw her name on his lips but could not hear him for the roar in her ears.

Aya threw Keko against the rock, and she braced herself

for impact, for pain. But there was none. There was only the vision of a hopeless Griffin charging after her, and a sickly, strange sensation of a hard world going spongy all around her.

Then all went black and silent as Aya took them both deep into the earth.

TWENTY-TWO

The rock bit and ripped at Griffin's fingertips as he futilely tried to scrape his way Within. The blood didn't matter, the pain was inconsequential. Aya had taken Keko into the earth because of Griffin's actions, and nothing he could physically do would ever dig her out.

Something he could *say* might bring her back, might allow him to trade his life for hers, but she'd carefully reminded him of his vow and he was forced to hold true to his stars, as ever. Just as he would hold true to Keko, because in the end he believed wholeheartedly in what she'd done for her people, even though it felt like his soul had been buried along with her.

Great stars, she was gone. Inside this wall before him. Hidden. Taken.

She'd called him selfless. She'd told him she admired him, but she'd been the one to anonymously give such a gift to her people.

Her disappearance would likely be explained—and her whole existence therefore diminished—by Chief telling everyone that she'd thrown herself into the ocean. Keko had told Griffin back in Utah that in the eyes of Chimerans, dying purposely by water was the ultimate cowardice. And yet it was one she was willing to live with if it meant peace for innocents.

And *he* was the selfless one?

With a great bellow of anguish wrenched from the bottom of his diaphragm, he smashed a final fist into the rock. The shock of agony rippled up his arm. His body collapsed right there on the path, his back against Keko's invisible prison door.

He'd dislocated two fingers on his right hand, and with a grim numbness he popped them back into place.

He refused to do nothing. He refused to just allow this to happen. Once upon a time Griffin Aames had been the shadowy guy who lingered along the back wall and took orders. He'd had to either live with their consequences or watch, helpless, as the appalling results of his actions unfolded. No more.

He was no longer peripheral. He was the goddamn Ofarian leader and he believed in action when a purpose called to him. For the past five years that action had come through politics, but this could not be fixed through the Senatus. Magic would bring no solution. Neither would brute force or a personal plea to the Children.

Below, in the valley meadow, the Chimeran world came alive. A beautiful, intimidating chorus rose up. Hundreds of Chimerans chanted in sharp, harsh voices. Griffin got to his feet and peered over the tangle of lush, drooping greenery at what was laid out before him.

Row upon row of Chimeran warriors filled the meadow in perfect lines. Bane stood alone, front and center, facing his fierce men and women, leading them in the synchronized movements that were half dance, half challenge. Their brown skin gleamed in the new sunlight, their faces chilling masks of open lips and bared tongues. Timed with some unheard tune, they stomped their feet and slapped their arms and legs. Their deep warrior rallying cries echoed throughout the valley.

Even at this distance, Griffin saw Keko in every movement. He could see her standing in Bane's place, her body strong and commanding, her voice imperious, her fire awe-inspiring. He saw everything Chimeran that she loved and fought for, all that she'd lost when she'd taken such a risk all those years ago and had given herself to him.

Kapu. That was him to her. Forbidden. Taboo.

With a rousing shout, the warriors' dance of intimidation ended. Bane roared something to them, the words lost to Griffin at this distance, and the warriors' lines broke apart. They started to spar with one another, using arms and legs and fire. They possessed such tremendous fighting skill, using techniques he'd never seen and movements he appreciated.

The chief's house loomed over it all.

When Cat Heddig had come here months earlier to beg for peace on Griffin's behalf, she'd described the balcony on the second floor where the chief had watched his people train. That balcony was empty now. Chief—likely clothed and ashamed—hid in the confines of his walls.

His absence revealed to Griffin exactly what he must do to try to get Keko back.

He scrambled back down the steep slope into the thick foliage surrounding the meadow. If he could, he'd march right through those Chimeran lines, but he had to think of Keko, what she would want. What was best for her survival and rescue. Revealing his presence was not part of that.

He jogged over the uneven terrain his feet and legs were starting to become accustomed to, ducking under giant leaves and passing through clouds of fragrant blooms, until he came again to the back garden of the chief's house. He stomped right across it—culture and diplomacy be damned—and threw open the glass door.

The chief still watched his warriors, but now from behind the small kitchen window. He whirled when Griffin came barreling through the door. For a brief moment, fear flashed across Chief's face, but then the Chimeran seemed to remember he wielded his greatest weapon again, and his chest expanded ever so slightly. Griffin wasn't scared.

He wore a shirt, the tips of Keko's handprint peeking out from behind the top two open buttons.

"You are a coward," Griffin said.

The worst name one could call a Chimeran. A tiny yellow spark lit the chief's eyes, but he said nothing, because he knew he'd been called out.

Griffin advanced, the kitchen far too small for two men of such size. The chief retreated, his heel catching the cabinet below the sink. His gaze darted into the shadows of the house at Griffin's back.

"Where's Keko?" asked the chief.

Griffin sneered. "Do you care? Now that she's given you everything you wanted?" Another step forward. "Your fire. Your power. Your leadership."

The chief reached up and wrapped a protective hand around the Queen's black rock that dangled around his neck. "I . . . I am grateful to her."

"No, you're not. You think she owed you this. After how she got involved with me. After the almost war. This all worked out so very well for you, didn't it?"

Chief's fingers tightened around the rock as if Griffin might snatch the stupid thing away.

"I came back here to tell you two things."

"I don't have to listen," Chief said.

Griffin laughed. "True. You could leave, but I would follow, and then you'd have to explain to your people why an Ofarian is in the valley. Or you could call out to one of them right now to have me removed, but I get the feeling that neither Bane nor Ikaika would comply. And to any other warrior you'd have to explain my presence."

Chief knew he was trapped. His hand released the rock.

"Point number one." Griffin circled around closer to the counter near the ancient refrigerator. "I gave my word to Keko that I would never speak of this disease, and I intend to uphold it. So even though you think your secret is safe, that you can sit up here on your false throne with the majority of your people gazing up at you in ignorance, *I* know your shame. An Ofarian. And that shame does not lie with a sickness you had no control over, but the fact that you hid it from your own people while banishing others, and let a brave woman take your fall."

"You don't understand our culture."

"No, I understand it very well. And I learned about it from someone who loves it far more than you."

Chief's hard glare shifted to barely veiled guilt, but it was still just a shade of the vulnerability he'd worn when Keko had placed her hand on him.

"My second point," Griffin went on, "is that Keko could have easily become Queen. You know this. She knows this. But she wanted to protect innocents from the same kind of scorn you threw down upon her. It amazes me that you lump in people who were stricken with such a terrible thing along with someone who broke *kapu* and tried to start a war. Keko knew what she did was wrong and tried to help her people to make up for it, and you treated them exactly the same. You're lucky, you're so goddamn lucky, that she is as forgiving and noble as she is."

Griffin hated the chief's unwavering silence almost as much as he hated replaying the image of Keko disappearing into the earth.

"You were there," Griffin said, "when Aya made the threats against Keko, about hunting her. About punishing her. You should know that Aya's made good on those threats."

The Chimeran's body sagged. "What?"

"Aya came here and took Keko. Into the earth. So your dirty little secret is safe forever and you won't ever have to worry about Keko becoming Queen. Though you may want to pray that the disease doesn't come back. Hope you're happy. And fuck you."

Chief's hands came to his hips and his head bowed low. "What do you want me to do?"

But it wasn't a pure, honest question. Chief didn't really want to know what he could do. He just wanted to ask for the sake of asking, so he could look like he had no other choice but to stand behind what he'd already done.

"I don't care what *you* do. I just want Keko back. So that's what *I'm* going to do." Griffin started for the back door, because he said what he'd had to say and standing there staring at the chief wouldn't get anything done. He had to get back to San Francisco, clear his head, *think*. There was an answer somewhere—

A rumble started outside, low and consistent enough that Griffin assumed it to be approaching thunder, growing louder and more intense with every passing second. Except that the day was cloudless and the sun shone brightly on the valley.

With a sense of foreboding and a thick tug on his signature awareness, he went back into the kitchen because the sound seemed to be coming from the front of the house. The chief had heard it, too, and was leaning on the counter looking out the smudged window over the sink. Griffin joined him.

Not thunder, but movement out on the meadow. A mass of Chimeran bodies shifting and marching in a mob way that was not militaristic or orderly. The warriors surged across the grass toward the chief's house, strong arms raised, mouths open, little bursts of fire and the resultant plumes of smoke lifting to the sky. They were following someone. A big Chimeran male strode at point, determination and confidence in his step. And it was not Bane.

This man's right arm ended at the elbow.

Makaha led the Chimeran crowd, whose fervor Griffin couldn't distinguish as mocking or encouraging. Makaha stalked toward the house, chin down, legs strong, shoulder-length hair flapping behind him. He stopped just beyond the front terrace and stared hard into the kitchen window. The Chimerans fanned out on both sides. Though half of Makaha's arm was gone, he was no less massive, no less formidable. His eyes were nearly consumed with threatening flame, so much so Griffin only saw gold and orange, no black or white. When Makaha opened his mouth, it was not fire that screamed out from his throat.

"Griffin Aames!" bellowed Makaha. "Leader of the Ofarians! I know you are inside."

At mention of the Ofarians, a great murmur erupted from the Chimeran crowd. Anger mixed with confusion over discovering one of their opposing race to be in the valley.

Beside Griffin, the chief gasped.

"What's going on?" Griffin asked, mystified as to how Makaha could have possibly known he was here.

It was Makaha, not the chief, who responded, lifting his severed arm and screaming at the house. "Griffin Aames! I, Makaha, of Chimeran descent and born of fire, challenge you!"

Griffin's hesitation was not made of fear. The moment between the issue of the challenge and the movement of his feet toward the front door was packed with everything Keko had told him or intimated about the Chimeran way of life—and so much that she had not. Everything had to be earned, she'd said, through physical challenge. Respect, one's position in society, redemption . . . everything.

Makaha—like Keko—had been banished to the Common House. The Chimeran warrior's only way out would be to challenge the man who'd disfigured him and caused the shame in the first place. But what were the chances of that man ever actually entering this hidden valley? Practically none. Until now.

As Griffin exited out onto the front terrace, in plain view of the meadow crowded with muscular, fire-wielding Chimerans, he understood. He got why Keko had seized her opportunity to go after the Source when she did. When a Chimeran's chance came along, they grabbed it with fists or fire, and did not let go until they'd given it their all.

Makaha had lived in shame for three years and this was his sole chance for redemption.

Griffin slowly descended the stone steps to the worn grass. He was beaten down physically and emotionally. Keko was trapped somewhere in a prison beneath his feet, in desperate need of help. And now he had to fight this man? Who had two inches and at least thirty pounds on him?

"How did you know I was here?"

Makaha separated from the pack, speaking low enough for only Griffin to hear. At least there was that. "I saw movement up on the slope. That's Keko's spot. I hoped it was her since I've been worried, so I went to look. I saw you coming down."

This man had once been Keko's friend, as Griffin recalled. If only he could tell Makaha about Keko—why she'd left the valley in the first place, all that she'd done and sacrificed, and the danger she was in now—there was the slight chance the warrior might stand down. But Griffin couldn't, and Makaha had his Chimeran pride.

Makaha pointed the stump of his arm at Griffin and raised his voice. "It's been a long time since I've felt any pain in this." He made a fist with his one hand. "Or this."

"Soldier to warrior," Griffin said, "I thought you were attacking me. I am truly sorry."

The Chimerans murmured.

Makaha grinned, but not in pleasure. "Apologies mean nothing in this valley."

Griffin longed to shout, *I can't fight you now. She needs help. We are wasting time.*

The faces of the other Chimerans were not mocking, but intensely curious. Perhaps even a bit excited. He did not know if that was because Makaha had challenged an Ofarian who'd inexplicably infiltrated their valley, or if their warrior natures just wanted to see a fight.

"You don't have to take it."

Griffin looked up to find Bane had come silently to his side. Makaha said nothing. Because he couldn't in front of the general, his superior.

"Makaha is lower than you," Bane said, his eyes on the warrior. "The challenge is yours to accept or deny."

"What will happen if I don't?"

"Nothing."

Nothing. Exactly. Makaha would remain where he was. Where he'd been stuck for the past three years.

Griffin knew, without a doubt, that if Keko were here, she would approve of this challenge. She'd likely stand with the crowd and cheer on her friend instead of her lover—because Griffin had nothing to lose and Makaha had everything to gain.

Griffin nodded at Bane to come over to the side. "The Children have taken Keko," he murmured to the general, and he watched Bane struggle to hide his anger and sadness. "It was her choice, but we don't have to accept it. There's no time for this."

Bane crossed his arms over his chest, jaw clenching around the questions he couldn't ask and the heartfelt reaction he couldn't give. "I can't interfere with the old ways. The challenge has been made to you. It's your decision."

Griffin started to walk back to Makaha, ready to accept. Ready to throw the fight and get it done within record time. Bane, however, snatched Griffin's arm, fingers biting in. He bent his head, leaned in close to Griffin. His voice was rough as a thundercloud. "If you accept, you accept it all. You will insult him if you do not fight to the best of your ability." A heavy pause. "You will insult her, too."

Makaha stood, proud and fierce. As Griffin approached him, the crowd of Chimerans shifted, widening out to make space. Preparing.

"When does it end?" Griffin asked.

Makaha shrugged. "When it ends."

Griffin drew a breath, shoring up his strength, grateful he hadn't used magic in well over a day and that he'd drifted off for a time on the back terrace of the chief's house waiting for Keko to heal her people.

She hadn't slept at all, he thought numbly. She must be exhausted . . .

He shook thoughts of her from his head, because if he was to give Makaha his all, he had to focus. "No magic," Griffin said.

Another ripple of murmurs from the Chimerans. In the distance, he could see more folk flowing from their homes up on the slopes, coming down to the meadow to watch.

Makaha glanced meaningfully down at his half arm. "No magic."

Griffin nodded. "So what—"

The fist that smashed into his face took away words and replaced them with blinding agony. Griffin stumbled backward, knocked off balance. The Chimerans scurried out of his way, enlarging the circle. Letting him trip and fall to the ground.

No cheers for Makaha. Just silence, the intermittent nod of a head as the Chimerans seemed to be assessing what was going on, evaluating.

The only sounds were of Makaha's breathing and the final fade of Griffin's pained moan. Then Makaha's bare feet on the earth as he rushed forward again.

So that's how this fight was going to be.

Griffin pushed to his feet, righting his vision and shoving aside the humiliation over having fallen to a sucker punch. He faced Makaha's charge, forgetting about any weakness still lingering, forgetting about the stars that blinked at his periphery, forgetting about anything but giving this challenge his all.

Griffin ducked another left throw and didn't hesitate to slam a one-two into Makaha's midsection, knowing that the other guy couldn't do the same. But Bane had told him not to pull up, and if Keko were here she'd tell him the same thing.

Makaha couldn't punch with his right, but he could, however, pummel Griffin with his half arm, the strikes coming down in between kicks and jabs.

The fight seemed to go on forever, but then, that's usually how they felt even when they lasted only a few minutes. Makaha was brutal and relentless, so that's exactly how Griffin retaliated. Each punch thrown stole as much energy as the advantage it gained. Each blow received sapped more of his strength, until nothing but sheer will kept him upright.

Griffin was fading, all his tumultuous days in Hawaii throwing him into a tornado until he no longer knew which way was up. He could feel the swelling of his face and body, the blood oozing, the muscles aching, the strength seeping out.

The last thing Griffin felt was Makaha's great left fist

driving an uppercut into his chin. And the last thing he saw was the brilliant blue Hawaiian sky before it zoomed down and suddenly, instantly, transformed into night.

Aya did not know how to process all that she'd just witnessed and the barrage of strange, new human emotions that came with it. The Ofarian man, the one in which she saw such great promise, had just attacked that Chimeran warrior, freezing off half his arm.

The whole thing was wretched. Ugly. No one seemed to want to listen to anyone else. There was shouting and physical fighting. She did not understand any of it. She just knew she wanted to scream.

Then the Ofarian had been driven away, dragging many of her hopes behind him in the mud.

Aya plunged deeper into the Utah woods, wrapping her cloak of twigs tighter around her body. The night was black and moonless, as she always insisted upon for a gathering, and she still had a short distance to walk before she was well enough away from the Senatus to return Within. All she had to do was cross that frozen stream and she'd find her secluded spot.

Someone was sitting on a boulder next to the iced-over water.

Aya almost ran into her, her clothing and skin and hair were so dark. The woman spun, coming to her feet remarkably fast in a defensive pose, then settled when she saw it was only Aya.

"You are Kekona?" Aya asked. "The Chimeran general?"

Kekona eyed her, then nodded.

"Why are you out here?"

"Why am I out here?" Kekona wrapped her bare arms around her waist. The Chimerans were so fascinating, being able to withstand such bitter cold without protective layers. "Why am I out here—good question. Because I don't want to go back yet."

Aya looked down the hill toward the bonfire, which was a speck of dying orange through the trees. "I am sorry about what happened to your warrior. I saw that you went after Griffin. Did you hurt him?"

Kekona made an odd sound that was difficult to decipher. Aya thought it might have been a laugh, but it also could have been a sob. Emotions had such blurred lines. So much to learn.

"I did," Kekona said. "And he hurt me, too."

By the haunted look in Kekona's eyes, Aya thought she understood what the Chimeran meant. She had observed interaction between human men and women who were interested in mating, and Secondaries were not any different. There was a benefit to being the quiet one, the observant one, the one others seemed to forget was there. Over the past few days, she'd thought she'd witnessed a change in the way Griffin and Kekona had acted toward each other. They tried very hard to hide it under the veil of the Senatus rules, but Aya had noticed little things here and there. Little things that signaled their interest was growing, deepening. The scene around the fire, Griffin's reaction, and now the pain of Kekona's aftermath, confirmed it.

Only, to Aya's eyes, their connection meant far more than simple mating. It reached much deeper into their souls than just the base need to reproduce. It was beautiful and overwhelming, and it spoke to Aya on a level she'd yet to personally experience Aboveground. Perhaps something as powerful as this kind of desire was worth living a life for. Perhaps it was what would make death palatable.

"Wounds will heal," Aya told her. "Even those you can't see."

The Chimeran woman's shoulders lost some of their tension. She looked at Aya for a long time, then shook her head as if to clear it. "It doesn't feel like that now. It feels like I'm going to be in pain forever."

Aya thought of the vast difference between Within and Aboveground, when it came to time. "Forever is just a word. It will have a new definition tomorrow."

Keko's brow furrowed as she dropped her gaze to the frozen stream.

Something told Aya that perhaps she should feel awkward in this silence, but strangely, she didn't. There was something about this scene that made her heart feel warm. Like keeping Kekona's secret about her feelings for Griffin and offering support was the right thing to do. The human thing to do.

And right then and there, Aya knew that she had made the most important choice of her existence.

"When I left the fire," she finally said, "your chief was looking for you. The other warrior, the taller man, took the injured one back to your car."

At the words "injured one," Kekona's eyes teared up, but then she immediately blinked the moisture away.

"Okay," Kekona said. "So, uh, thanks. This made me feel better."

"It did?"

Hands on her hips, Kekona nudged some muddy snow with her bare toe. "Yeah. I think it did. Listen, will you be here again? At the next Senatus?"

"Of course."

Kekona gave a stiff wave and started back for the bonfire. "I guess I'll see you then."

Here, Within, Aya clung to the shadows of the dim cave, a painful ache in her all-too-human heart, and watched Keko work with her brush and bucket.

Keko swept up dirt and pebbles, the remnants of the Children's travel through the earth, her movements sluggish, her eyes dead. The blue-white glow of her Source flame had gone out, as had her spirit.

Aya watched her a lot, remembering every single one of their private conversations outside of the Senatus. Remembering Griffin's reaction as Aya had pulled his love away.

She had yet to approach Keko, her sympathy too great, her sorrow too infectious. Keko needed hope, and Aya had none to give.

She trudged through the caverns until she reached their end, then she threw herself into the earth and tunneled toward her private cave, thankful for its distance and solitude and secrecy. But when she finally pushed out of the wall and assumed human form, she wanted to scream all over again.

There on the clay floor lay a single, pristine sunflower petal.

So this was how a Chimeran fight ended, Griffin thought. There was pain even in the afterlife. How strange. And unfortunate.

The light that leaked through his cracked eyelids was incredibly bright and not remotely holy, so he shut them again.

"Welcome back."

At the sound of the oddly familiar male voice, Griffin pried open his eyes fully. One aching arm rose to try to block the harsh light, but a lance of pain pierced his shoulder, and he had to drop it.

Someone walked across his blurry vision, followed by the sound of drapes being drawn closed. In the softer, easier light, Griffin recognized Bane's silhouette.

"That better?" asked the general.

Griffin nodded. On his whole body, his head hurt the most.

Bane came to the side of the bed Griffin was lying on. A woman sat on a chair, her Chimeran face round, her black hair cut unusually short. A long swatch of fabric had been unrolled on the sheets in front of her, and on it rested little sachets and pots of powders and herbs. Dirty bandage strips spotted with a rusty color sat in a pile to the side. She gathered everything up, stuffed them all into a bag, drew one long, assessing look down Griffin's body, and nodded firmly. He, too, glanced downward, noting that he was naked and covered in newly white bandages over a patchwork of wounds. The medicine woman tugged a sheet over him, then left without a word.

"You lost," Bane said.

No shit. "And Makaha?"

"He won." Bane gave Griffin a small smile. "You've been out for two days."

Two days?

"Keko?" Griffin asked.

Bane's smile died. "No word. I want to know what happened."

Griffin's eyes stung, but it hurt too much to reach up and wipe away the liquid emotion that leaked from them. All he was able to say was "She is trapped."

Bane turned and said, toneless, "Chief? He's awake."

A chair creaked somewhere Griffin couldn't see. Then the sound of bare feet padding across a tiled floor, coming closer. The chief appeared, bending over the bed. He still wore a shirt, this time fully buttoned to cover the handprint. The Queen's rock hung perfectly framed in the V, and it looked dull and unassuming.

He frowned down at Griffin, his eyes deeply troubled. "Can you walk?"

Griffin didn't think he could even sit up at this point, but he wasn't about to admit that, so he nodded.

"Then get up," said the chief, "and come outside. I need to talk to you."

TWENTY-THREE

Griffin hobbled out of bed, testing the ability of his body and finding nothing broken, though the stiffness made it difficult to walk. The shorts he'd been wearing on his days running through the Hawaiian backcountry had been washed and placed on a chair, though they were so stained and ragged they hardly looked any better. It didn't matter. He pulled them on and left the room, having to duck beneath the low ceiling beams in the hallway.

He'd been lying in the chief's bedroom, apparently, because it was the only bedroom in the tiny house. Griffin wondered where the Chimeran had slept the past two nights. Maybe he hadn't slept at all, which gave Griffin a grim satisfaction.

The bedroom was on the second floor, the lone window facing the back garden. Griffin caught his reflection in a foggy mirror hanging near the narrow, twisting staircase: bruised and beaten and sunbaked. A thousand other injuries marred his body, but it was the sight of the narrow stripe of burn on his temple that made his stomach flip. He abandoned the mirror.

Every step down the stairs made him wince, but as he exited onto the main floor, he wiped any evidence of pain from his face. Seeing no one, he started for the back door.

"Griffin." Bane's voice behind him. "This way. Out front."

Griffin turned to see the general standing in the dim little foyer with his hand on the knob of the arched front door. A sinking feeling settled into Griffin's gut as he walked toward Bane. Meeting out back meant in secret. Going out front meant something else entirely.

"What's going on?"

Bane shook his head, his dark eyes swimming with doubt. "I don't know, but it's something. And I'm worried. I shouldn't say that to you, but so much has changed . . ." He started to turn the knob, then stopped and looked back at Griffin. "What is Keko to you?"

She is my Queen, too, Griffin wanted to say, but somehow didn't feel it appropriate, like it would diminish the title in her brother's eyes.

"So much," he replied. "It's hard to put into words."

At that, the skin around Bane's eyes and mouth tightened as his gaze dropped to the tile. "Then I understand."

Before Griffin could ask about Ikaika, Bane threw open the front door. When the chief had said "talk," he had not meant a quiet chat alone.

Griffin slowly exited the front door of the chief's house onto a wide stone terrace lit with brilliant sunlight . . . and came face to face with the entire Chimeran population, easily three times the number that had watched the challenge two days ago. Dusky-skinned, black haired people filled the meadow, their expectant faces turned up to the terrace. Many had the carriage of a warrior; most did not. This was every Big Island Chimeran, from every status level, and they all stared curiously at Griffin.

Another fight? Griffin wondered. Another challenge?

The heavy muscle aches lingered. So did the stiffness and fatigue—and the soul-deep crush of loss and guilt over having to watch Keko disappear. But he would fight again if he had to, if it came down to that. For her.

Lengthening his stride, shoving aside his weakness, he crossed the terrace to come even with the chief standing at the balustrade. At the foot of the steps below, the Chimerans spread out far into the distance, a sea of shifting bodies and hushed, speculative voices. The buzz of their massed signatures tingled in Griffin's mind and he realized, with a heartsick feeling, that the chief's had been restored.

The Chimeran leader, however, had not removed his shirt.

Griffin assessed the crowd, noting others whose chests and shoulders were covered. Far more than the twenty-two Keko had healed, so maybe the chief and the others she'd cured wouldn't stand out as much as they'd feared. In the front row stood Ikaika, his T-shirt bright white against his skin. He met Griffin's eyes in solemnity, giving away nothing.

Makaha was nowhere to be seen. Of course. The warrior was likely still stationed at the back, because even though he'd challenged and defeated the man who'd maimed him, he was still considered disabled.

Chief faced his people and raised a thick arm. The entire valley went instantly silent. And then it erupted in a shout worthy of a volcano.

A single word, spoken as one great voice—as dazzling as fire, as intimidating as war, and as reverent as all the Earth's religions combined. Griffin didn't have to speak old Chimeran to know it was a name. The chief's name. *Ali'i* in a language that predated their people's great migration across the sea.

Never, not once, had a former Ofarian Chairman been greeted in such a manner, with his people saturating the atmosphere with admiration and love. It was the stuff of stories, of fairy tales, of faraway lands, the way people might have bowed to a king. The major difference was, the title of king and Ofarian Chairman had been bestowed because of birth and blood. The title of Chimeran *ali'i* also came by blood, but that of the drawn, battled kind. No matter what poor, unfair decisions Chief had made with regard to Keko, he had undoubtedly earned this position time and time again, and his people worshipped him for it.

Such devotion was beyond humbling.

Chief slammed a fist against his chest in a show of mutual adoration toward his people. The fist remained pressed against the light blue of his button-down shirt. A sheen coated his black eyes. The sun reflected off the moisture, making them spark.

The Chimerans responded. A simultaneous pounding of their chests—men and women and children, warrior and common folk alike.

Griffin shivered under the force of it. And then he shivered because he still did not know why he'd been called out here.

"You are wondering," Chief said, his booming voice carrying across the field that had again fallen obediently and rapturously silent, "why Griffin Aames, the Ofarian leader, is in our valley."

Griffin stood as still as the stone balustrade beneath his

fingertips, keeping his eyes on the chief, and carefully managing the pound of his heart and the pace of his breathing.

Chief, however, looked only at his people. "He did not come here to face and be challenged by the Chimeran he disfigured, as some of you have speculated."

Pockets of Chimerans shifted on their feet, looking over their shoulders, trying to pick out Makaha in the crowd. Griffin felt his blood begin to boil, the deep heat starting around his neck and ears. Not embarrassment, but a slow, simmering anger aimed at the chief.

"He did not come here to ask for peace or to beg for an alliance," Chief said. "He came here because of Kekona Kalani."

More movement, a few murmurs.

"A few months ago we were ready to go to war against the Ofarians," Chief intoned. "Our general had been taken hostage by one of the water wielders, in what was then believed to be a hostile grab for power."

Now Griffin moved. A slight tightening of his fists. A little bend of the knees, firming his stance. Readying himself for whatever was to come.

"Our attack was called off when it was proven to us that Kekona was taken by a rogue Ofarian. That part you do know. What you don't know"—Chief finally slid a glance over to Griffin—"is that Kekona defied the rules of the elementals and the *kapu* laws of her clan when she chose to be with Griffin Aames."

That garnered a response, a widespread wave of surprise that raked like nails over Griffin's skin. Out of the corner of his eye he noticed several warriors edging toward the terrace, ready to take him down if he made a move toward their leader. Griffin couldn't be certain that he wouldn't.

"Kekona was dishonored because she was dishonorable. Her war mongering was falsely based, stemming specifically from her relationship with that Ofarian."

Discontented, defensive rustling rippled through the crowd.

"Chief," Griffin growled, because he couldn't stay silent any longer.

But the chief deepened his voice and upped the volume. "Three years ago, Griffin disobeyed the most sacred Senatus rule and used his magic to attack one of our own during a gathering, disgracing the great warrior Makaha. He has spent nearly every moment since trying to convince me and the rest of the elementals that we are flawed and he is eternally right."

The rustling intensified. Whispers changed to questions, accusatory sentences, and dark looks.

Chief lifted both hands, calling for silence. "But he is not here because of what Kekona did wrong. He is not here because of what he did wrong." When he drew a breath it was not Chimeran, but still one that shook and rattled in his chest. "He is here because of what *I* did wrong."

Griffin gasped, but the sound of it was lost in the wave of confusion wrinkling the blanket of rapt devotion the chief had cast over the valley.

Chief shouted something in Chimeran, and his people went quiet and still, though it was no longer instant, the unrest lingering. They watched him intently. Griffin noticed Bane inching closer to the steps leading down to the meadow.

The chief's fingers gripped the balustrade. He leaned heavily into his arms, his head bent—the first time Griffin had ever witnessed him not looking directly at his people. The whole valley seemed to be holding its breath, including Griffin and Ikaika, whose face had gone ashen with shock and worry. Would the chief actually—

"I lost my fire."

He would. Oh great stars, he did. That resonant, authoritative voice, speaking the truth. At last.

"My fire died without reason or warning. I have been hiding it from all of you for a very long time."

Griffin's fists released at the same moment the Chimerans erupted again. This time the burst of sound was decidedly less joyous than the earlier greeting, one made of fear and panic instead. Some Chimerans tried to push closer to the house, but Bane hopped down the steps and positioned himself at their base, the glare of the general warning everyone off. The outraged voices did not quiet.

The chief finally lifted his head. Finally took in the extent of the disruption he'd caused. The buzz gradually faded as the people stared at him. And then, before everyone, he drew a true Chimeran breath and set a line of red-gold flame scorching above his people's heads.

Some shrank back, as though they weren't made of fire themselves. Some cried out in shock, others in a reaction that seemed to come less from the fear of death than the fear of oppression. But everyone watched the chief in utter puzzlement.

"As you can see, the fire has been returned to me. *That* is why I have gathered all of you here this morning. And *that* is why Griffin Aames has come to Hawaii. Because Kekona discovered my secret and risked her life to find a cure. Griffin thought she would die in her quest and came here to stop her out of worry, but he ended up helping her instead." Chief lifted his voice even higher. "Kekona Kalani has found the Fire Source. She has used it to heal me, and I willingly bear her mark as proof."

Chief wrapped his fingers around the collar of his shirt and ripped it open. Buttons flying, light blue fabric fluttering in the island breeze, he stood bare-chested before every Chimeran on the Big Island.

Keko's handprint stood out black and stark for all to see.

Chaos flared on the meadow. Surges of Chimerans rushed for the terrace. Bane stood with massive legs spread, arms up and out to ward off the mob. Ikaika came to his side, standing shoulder to shoulder, prepared to help. The people were terribly confused, unsure whether they had the right to break through the general and one of his top warriors, or whether the chief's revelation over his ultimate weakness made the military order of things null and void.

Griffin could feel the sense of betrayal poison the air that had so recently been plump with pride, and such a sudden shift made him scared for too many lives on that field.

Chief released the grip on his shirt and let the wind flap it away to a leaf-strewn corner. With one hand he yanked off the Queen's lava rock necklace and held it in a tight fist, the black stone dangling over the heads of the angry crowd. "I abdicate!" he screamed.

Bane's head wrenched around to look at the chief. Griffin jumped down the steps two at a time to take the other side of the general, holding back the crowd who demanded answers by shouting Keko's name.

"I abdicate!" Chief thundered. "Be calm!"

Even in the melee, the chief's words carried. They took several minutes to sink in as they were relayed back through the crowd. A few more minutes passed before the Chimerans actually did calm, the waves of people gradually settling down like the sea after a storm. The storm clouds lingered, however, as all eyes again shifted to the terrace where the chief looked down upon them.

All Griffin could see was Keko's handprint, and he knew he wasn't alone.

"You're saying that Kekona Kalani has touched the Source?" a woman somewhere off to the left cried out.

Chief dropped his arm, the lava rock hitting his leg, though he didn't let it go. "Yes. She has."

A new murmur traveled through the Chimeran crowd, this one filled with wonder and positivity. So similar to the reaction Keko had received from Bane and Ikaika and every other one of the Chimerans she'd cured—the reaction she'd shut down and refused to acknowledge for the sake of keeping their secret.

"Where is she?" another voice called out. And then another. And another. Because of course no one would have realized before that she—a disgraced untouchable—was not among them.

"She is . . ." Chief gathered himself. "She has left the valley."

Someone else, someone daring, cried out, "How can we believe you, if she's not here?"

Griffin's throat dried up. He wondered what the chief would tell them, if he'd tell the truth about agreeing to give up Keko to the Children.

Chief abandoned looking at his people and instead turned his head to find Griffin. The Chimeran opened his mouth, his chest expanding. Griffin thought he might be reaching for his fire—and by the depth of the breath, perhaps *all* his fire—but instead only sound came out.

A single name—an intense plea in the deepest bass register—reverberated across the valley: "*Aya!*"

The Chimerans glanced at each other in confusion, having no context or knowledge of that name.

But Griffin gasped, the pump of his blood stopping completely, then slamming back into motion so fast he went lightheaded. Hope and trepidation and disappointment and love filled his being.

Way out in the grass, past the very last line of fire elementals, came a rumble—a distinct rumble he knew came from within the earth. That sound and this feeling inside him had always preceded an attack. Or devastating heartache.

Griffin peeled away from Bane and bounced back up the steps, skidding to a halt next to the chief again. He whirled around to face the sea of Chimerans and stared far into the distance, over their heads, to where a flat patch of field churned as though being dug up from underneath.

One by one, the whole Chimeran clan responded to the strange noise and vibration, turning around to watch. They fanned out, warriors jogging toward the scene, fire flowing to their fingertips in preparation for the unknown.

"Please," the chief called, but no one seemed to hear him except Griffin.

To the soundtrack of Chimeran exclamations, Aya's compact human body morphed from the rising mound of rock, dirt, and grass. She made no threatening gestures and did not speak, and when the Chimerans realized that she was one small woman against thousands of fire-wielding warriors, they started to settle. Their sounds of fear switched to those of surprise and awe, for it was clear no one had ever seen an earth elemental.

And then Keko appeared behind Aya.

The black haired beauty slowly unfolded herself from a crouch, standing a foot taller than the Daughter of Earth. A rising chorus of recognition saturated the air. Keko set her body in a position of power—legs apart, shoulders back, arms ending in loose fists. This far away, Griffin could not make out her features. Could not tell what expression she wore, how well she'd been cared for, what she'd experienced Within.

He could, though, see the peaceful white glow of the Source emanating from her chest. And so could every other Chimeran.

Keko stepped out from behind Aya, and the Daughter let her go. Keko no longer wore the shredded jeans and ripped black T-shirt from the moment of her disappearance, but, oddly, a long, sleeveless, charcoal colored dress with an iridescent shimmer. She lifted her gaze above the openmouthed mass of Chimerans and shot a stare straight to the terrace. To where the chief and Griffin stood side by side. With long, purposeful strides, she came forward, gliding right into the crowd of her people without pause. They parted hurriedly, creating a seam for her to pass through. Some reached for her, their hands dropping or pulling back just before their fingers could skim her skin. Others pressed hands to their mouths and watched her go by with glistening obsidian eyes.

Many others touched their own chests, just as Bane had done when he'd first witnessed the visual proof of Keko's ethereal power.

The crowd opened before Keko and closed behind Aya as the Daughter followed. As the two women advanced toward the house, the name *Kekona* created a series of waves across the meadow.

When Keko neared the front, one Chimeran actually did dare to touch her, a palm upon her shoulder, a simple, non-threatening contact. But the Source responded, a sizzle of blue-white zapping the man's hand. He cried out, his face contorted in pain. When he wrenched his hand away, his palm smoked in a way that Chimeran skin should not.

Keko turned to him in concern. Though Griffin could not hear what she said to the injured man, he could see the compassion in her eyes and the clench of her fingers as she wanted to reach out and comfort him, but could not. At last she continued on through the crowd, the people giving her a wider berth.

"Don't touch her." "You can't touch her," floated the whispers all around.

Griffin could not believe she was here, Aboveground. He could not believe that the woman he looked at was flesh and magic and *real*. He'd watched the earth snatch her body and could not believe that anyone not a Son or Daughter would be able to survive below the surface. Yet here she was, a glittering image coming toward him. Did she see the way his chest lurched with every beat of his heart? Could she tell how his fingers were very nearly crumbling the stone balustrade in his attempt to remain still and not rush for her?

She could not, he realized, because she was not looking at him. Her black stare was focused solely on the chief.

The people pressed forward, quieting, as Keko neared the steps. When she reached the bottom step, a tight half-circle formed behind her. With astonishment, Griffin saw that her dress was made of thousands of tiny black lava rocks, all strung together in some invisible manner. All magically reflective. It swung about her legs and grazed the tops of her bare feet. The neck dipped low, openly displaying the magic behind her breastbone.

Ikaika and Bane stepped aside to let her pass. At last she turned her attention to Griffin and his breath caught. Time stopped.

In broad daylight, amidst her entire clan—even under the heavy weight of *kapu*—he saw what she felt for him. The whole of it, the depth of it, the sheer power of it.

And in that moment he stripped away all of his own restrictions, all his own doubt, and finally let her see his emotion in its entirety, as raw as the magic she carried inside her, far more potent than three little words. She responded with the tiniest of nods—such a testament to her strength and confidence—and turned again to the chief.

"Come here," she told him.

To Griffin's amazement—and to the verbal shock of everyone else in the meadow—the chief obeyed. He skirted around Griffin and descended the stairs. When he came off the last step to stand before Keko on the grass—on even ground with her, at her order—the murmurs of speculation and disorder grew.

Aya came forward, her garment of Hawaiian flowers and greenery flowing in the breeze.

The chief lifted his voice to address the crowd again, though he did not remove his eyes from his niece. "Of her own volition, her own strength, Kekona Kalani hunted and found the Source. She took the magic, the Queen's treasure, and returned to our valley in secret to heal me. She refused to be acknowledged as Queen because she did not want to compromise me, and when the Children of Earth rose up to demand punishment for her causing a volcanic eruption where the Source was located, Keko accepted the sentence. Even though I am the one who should serve it."

Keko's lips parted, her eyes widening ever so slightly.

"Aya, Daughter of Earth," Chief intoned, "because of my deception and selfishness, because of all that Kekona has done for me and all Chimerans, for her bravery and courage, I demand that I take Kekona's place."

A roar went up among the crowd, although Griffin couldn't tell whether it was in protest or agreement because he was already bounding down the steps. At first his target had been Keko. For a moment it seemed like she might faint, but then at the last second he realized that his Keko was about as far from a fainting woman as one could possibly be, and he shifted his target to Bane and Ikaika. Both men looked ready to spark an uprising, to charge at the chief and throw him into the ground themselves.

Griffin pushed a palm into the general's chest, holding him back. "This is Keko's. Let her have this."

Bane blinked down at Griffin and finally settled back, Ikaika following suit.

"Uncle," Keko said, her voice as clear as a bell. The sound of it heralded silence across the field.

With a firm nod and the tiniest of smiles—a mixture of pride and resignation and sadness—Chief reached out, took Keko's hand, and coiled the Queen's necklace into her palm.

"Thank you," he said. "One final time."

Griffin looked to Aya who, inexplicably, was looking back at *him*. Her green eyes were positively shining with unmistakable satisfaction.

Aya ducked behind the chief. The vines and leaves of her dress snapped out to snake around the chief's body, covering him foot by foot, masking his dusky skin in waxy green. The last part of him to be covered was Keko's handprint, the black symbol there for every Chimeran to see.

With a spin of white hair and a great yawning of the earth beneath her feet, Aya dragged the former Chimeran *ali'i* Within.

TWENTY-FOUR

Keko had to shut her eyes when Aya enveloped her uncle with her magic and the earth swallowed them both. She knew all too well how paralyzing a feeling it was—of being smothered and crushed and blinded without actually dying. You had no control over your body or your movements. You could not scream.

Come to think of it, it was similar to being encased in Griffin's water bubble beneath the ocean, except when Aya's magic had released Keko, she'd not been on an island beneath the sun with Griffin fighting at her side. With Aya, she'd been spit out into a deep, dank cave lit only by scant glowing rocks and filled with only the thinnest amount of air. Sight without true seeing, breathing without truly living. Down there, the sounds were unnervingly foreign, the comings and goings of the half-formed Children even more so. Sustenance had been a chalky block of tasteless nothing, meant to keep her body functional but nothing more.

What had been almost three days Aboveground had felt like three years Within.

Keko had endured it because she believed she deserved it. She'd endured it because she'd resigned herself to her fate and wanted to spare Griffin the blame.

Until the moment when Aya had finally come to her, after being left so long alone in the dark, and told her that the chief wished to take Keko's place.

At first Keko had refused, but then Aya had told her something extraordinary and confidential. "I want nothing more than for Griffin to lead the Senatus," Aya had said, "and he needs you by his side to gain his seat."

"He doesn't need me for that," Keko had replied. "He told me his goals have changed, that he wants to rethink things." That had been difficult to realize, even harder to say. "And they won't let him in now anyway."

"The new Air delegate is progressive and open. I belong to humanity above the Children now, and I support Griffin's ideas for integration. If your uncle is no longer the chief, if you return Aboveground and take his place, you will send him to serve his own punishment for the way he sabotaged you. You will also be able to help Griffin achieve what he wants by you leading the Chimerans, which you've always wanted to do anyway. As Senatus delegate you can vote Griffin in. Can't you see? He needs what you can do for your people, Keko. He needs *you*."

So with Griffin as the carrot, and her uncle's shocking turnaround, Keko had finally agreed to the exchange.

Coming back to the surface, she didn't know which was harder: the physical, claustrophobic travel within the Children's magic; walking through the sea of her kinsmen and sensing their awe and wonder; or witnessing her once-beloved uncle being dragged Within, into hellish imprisonment.

She wondered if she'd ever find the strength to enter an enclosed space again.

When the sounds of the earth magic silenced and the shocked cries of the Chimerans died off, Keko finally opened her eyes. Her uncle was gone. So was Aya.

Griffin stood at the top of the terrace steps, his love in his eyes. He bore many new injuries, and she wondered and feared what had happened. She longed to go to him, but there were greater things she had to address first, and she reluctantly gave him her back.

Every single one of her kinsmen stared at her. Expectant. Unsure. Frightened. Hopeful. Wonderstruck.

When she'd risen from the earth, the Source magic had been returned to her, and again burned lovely and hot and immense in her chest. She'd missed it, and now it seemed to be responding to the gathered presence of her people.

The string attached to the Queen's rock dug into her fingers, though the thing was not remotely heavy. She'd only ever looked at the rock, had never touched it, instead waiting for the day when she could wrap her hand around it as *ali'i* and feel its little sharp edges scrape the skin on her chest.

Lifting the necklace now to eye level, she let it dangle, looking into the cause and price and reward of her quest. Her day had finally come.

A Chimeran man, buried somewhere in the crush of the crowd, called out, "*Ali'i*! My *ali'i*!"

Someone else picked up the cry, then another, until it was one big long word being volleyed about from one end of the field to the other—a demand from her people to drape the necklace around her head and take what was hers. A unanimous show of support. She had not issued a formal challenge in the Chimeran sense, but in their eyes she'd already earned the position.

The necklace had been granted to her, her uncle had admitted to his wrongdoings, and she was Aboveground again. With Griffin.

Turning, she slowly went up the steps, the gown swaying against her lower legs. She trapped Griffin's eyes with her own as she ascended toward him. She saw the pure emotion on his face and heard the echo of the three massive words he'd said before the earth and Aya had taken her away.

Stretching out a hand, she touched his face, fire against water. Her power sparked blue-white against his skin, and the crowd gasped. Griffin gave her a beautiful smile and reached out to touch her in return.

His cool palm pressed over the glow on her chest, and the Source inside her hummed from the counterpresence of his magic. She smiled back at him, for all her people to see.

Then she stepped away and went to the balustrade, to the spot in which her uncle had stood so many times over the years to address the people. The cries of "*ali'i*" only got stronger. She had expected this. And since she'd been eleven years old, she'd *wanted* this.

So it was in a sort of dreamlike state that she raised both palms to the crowd and said into the ensuing silence, "I am Kekona Kalani. And I am not your *ali'i*."

A rumble of confusion swept through the Chimerans, which

quickly shifted to a thunder of near outrage. Griffin stood too far to one side and she couldn't see his reaction, but she knew without having to witness it how those thick eyebrows she loved so much were drawn together. How he was probably positioning himself closer to protect her from an angry mob.

There would be no need.

Lifting her palms and voice even higher, she added, "I am Kekona Kalani. And I . . . am your *Queen*!"

This time the response came on a delay. A delay filled with a great gush of air, the collective intake of breath, followed by a rousing, deafening roar. The space above the Chimeran heads became dotted with bursts of jubilant flame, and the earth seemed to vibrate again, this time from the force of thousands of stamping feet.

One person remained still, however, and it was to her brother she turned. Bane wore the same reverent look he'd given her on that rainy coastal road when he'd first seen the Source inside her. Only now it was paired with a smile. When she nodded to him, he gave her a deep bow in response.

"I bear the Queen's treasure," she said when the whoops and flames had died down, "and I share it with you. I am Chimeran, made of powerful blood from across the sea and magic gifted from the heavens. I am Chimeran, and I know honor, for I've lived under its rules all my life. I know what it means to be worthy, and I know why we fight for such recognition every day."

A new set of cheers went up.

"I can picture myself standing among you, either in the front line as your former general, and also at the far back, as someone who once misled you and had to pay the price. I have been in every place within Chimeran society. I know what it means to abuse power, to fight for yourself, to accept punishment, and also to learn from it. That is what I bring you. An eye and a mind shaped and formed by each and every one of you, and I promise you that because of this, I will forever be accessible."

Another cheer, this one loudest in the far back. She looked but could not find Makaha.

"The truth is," she went on, "we all have weaknesses. We all have strengths. But our mistakes are our own. It's my wish that as I take you into a new age of Chimeran culture that we accept that, and try to find new ways to evaluate how we judge others." She lowered her arms at last.

"I can picture myself standing among you right now," she repeated, "staring up at this house at someone who challenged death by going after the Source and returning with such ancient, pure magic. I know what I would feel. I would look up here with the same awe as you are now. I would shout in the same way. And even though I would look upon the glow of magic with a stab of jealousy, I would recognize that that Chimeran is not a deity. Not infallible. I would know that she was given this gift to help her people grow, not to snatch governmental power and take over the running of this valley."

A few people glanced at each other questioningly. Bane folded his arms across his chest.

"I said that I am not *ali'i*, because I am not. But I do think we need one. I think we need someone to lead this particular clan and make important decisions I cannot or will not. My goal is to help *all* Chimerans, to bring the islands together and better our way of life, and I can't be the Big Island's *ali'i* for that. We need someone to guide our warriors and be the emissary between clans on the other islands. Someone to counsel me, and someone I can counsel in turn." She thrust out the lava rock necklace over the balustrade, the stone swaying in the wind. "Who wants it?" she cried, scanning the crowd. "Who is worthy of it?"

Two men came forward.

Bane immediately pulled out of the front line, shoulders thrown back, to the chorus of enthusiastic support from his warriors and most of the population. That was to be expected, though Keko had deliberately not looked at him as she'd made the call.

Then, from his place all the way in the back, parting the crowd with a gentle hand so he could get through, came Makaha.

He looked beaten up, but also empowered and confident, and she finally figured out the reasons behind Griffin's new cuts and bruises. It had been a fair challenge, it seemed, and her Chimeran friend now felt vindicated for his disfigurement.

Keko let her lip quiver, let her eyes glimmer with happiness and pride for the friend she'd once been forbidden to talk to—the disgraced friend now vying to be *ali'i.*

Bane and Makaha came to stand side by side just below the terrace, and Keko looked down on them without judgment. She knew the people were expecting her to choose one, that as Queen she held that kind of authority. Maybe she did, but there was something to be said for upholding the old culture while adapting it to new thinking and modern ways. She had every right, for instance, to send the unworthy Makaha back into the crowd.

Instead she lifted the necklace high into the air and declared, "There shall be a challenge!"

The people's voices surged in support. Bane and Makaha turned to one another, Makaha looking pumped and ready, Bane perhaps even more so. When Makaha thumped his chest in a salute to his competitor, he used his stump of an arm. Bane gave it the sparest of glances, as if to say he would give no quarter for a disabled warrior. Makaha smiled as if to say he was glad for that.

Keko raised her arm to call for silence and the Chimerans obeyed almost immediately. "Tomorrow," she said. "Tomorrow at sunrise on the meadow the challenge to be *ali'i* will take place."

Bane and Makaha separated and went back into the crowd.

Keko entwined the stone necklace around her fingers and moved slowly to the staircase opening, pondering her next words. She could not look at Griffin. Not yet. There was so much to say to him, and just as much for her to hear. But not here. Not now.

When she got to the top of the steps, the whole of the population could see her, head to foot, wearing the strange, enchanted gown Keko had insisted upon and that Aya had created Within. The gown made of not one, but *thousands* of little lava rocks.

She stood there, silent, until she commanded the attention of every single Chimeran on that field. With a meaningful glance at the bulge in the dirt where her uncle had last been seen, she lifted her chin and began a speech she hadn't realized she'd needed or wanted to give.

"If I am to be your Queen, there will be no lies. No disguises. No cover-ups. I give you myself, faults and all. I want to tell you something, and if after I tell you it changes how you feel, whether or not you want me as your Queen, I will accept it. Because I am Chimeran above all and I understand you."

At last she turned her head to find Griffin. His eyes were filled with such high regard she was sure that even if her people physically threw her out of this valley, she would find a refuge with him, a place where she would always be welcome.

He gave her a barely perceptible nod and it infused her with confidence.

"I carry a part of the Source within me," she said, facing her people again, "but I did not go alone. Griffin Aames was with me. Though I found the Queen's prayer as told in the legends, I am not the one who deciphered the Source's location. Griffin's knowledge of the stars guided us there." She licked her lips. "And I am not the one who dove into the earth and touched the Source itself. Griffin did, using his water magic. He risked his life to bring me the power that would cure my uncle. Because if I'd gone in—if any Chimeran had gone in—that volcano would have been a thousand times worse. And I would not have come out."

Complete silence fell over the crowd. Absolute stillness. No one so much as blinked or glanced at their neighbor. All eyes were upon her and she couldn't read a single one of them.

"I am telling you this," she said, "because I see the way you look up at me, like I am the old Queen incarnate. I am not. I am not perfect, and I did not complete a perfect quest. I did not challenge the earth and the Source, and I did not win a terrible battle with my own two hands. I had help from someone who believed in me and my purpose, and I could not have found the cure without him. I am not ashamed of this, because I think to admit you need someone else and accept their help is the greatest vulnerability and the most admirable trait to have." She cleared her throat and edged her toes toward the very top step. "If you do not find me worthy to lead anymore, if you do not want me to be Queen after knowing this, I will understand."

She knew her people, and she fully expected that to happen. So she held her breath and waited.

A man in the very front row went to one knee. He was an

older warrior, one aged out of the ranks but still well respected, and it took him a little while to do so, but he finally got his other knee to bend and shift behind his body. When he was on both knees, he thumped two fists to his chest and spoke the old Chimeran word for *Queen*.

The name hovered over the meadow, glittering like diamond smoke.

Keko stared at this man, blinking over and over, until the vision of that one man shifted to a hallucination of hundreds more Chimerans doing exactly the same thing. With a shake of her head she realized it was no hallucination. It was real. Thousands of her people followed suit, their knees hitting the ground and *Queen* a reverent whisper on their lips. An ocean of Chimerans rolled away from the *ali'i*'s house as they all kneeled.

Every single one of them devoted themselves to her. Every single one stated their belief in her . . . and her connection to her Ofarian.

Then Griffin was behind her, his hands sliding up the length of her arms. He pressed a kiss to the top of her shoulder. Forget the sight of thousands of Chimerans showing their fealty, that kiss was true love.

TWENTY-FIVE

The center of the meadow was on fire. Sheets of gold and orange flames blazed in a perfect circle and stretched for the stars, contained by the collective magic of the people who feasted and danced and kissed around it. Tonight the lights in the homes along the slopes were all dark, as every Chimeran on the Big Island filled the valley floor, all trying to have their moment with their new Queen. To hear her story again and again.

For many, a glimpse was enough to fill themselves with the wonder of her, of the sight of their pure magic living inside her. Griffin did not understand that. A glimpse would never be enough for him.

As he stood by her side and observed her people celebrating in her name, he knew that she and this place had become a part of him—a part he was not willing to give up.

They'd both cleaned themselves up as much as possible, though the removal of several layers of dirt and dried blood just called out the extent of their injuries and wounds. As they'd dressed, they'd told the stories behind each one. She'd listened, enraptured, as he'd recounted, blow by blow, the challenge with Makaha.

Keko's back was a mess of scratches and bruises, and the small wrap top that covered only her breasts bared without shame the deep, slanted wound Nem had given her.

Griffin thought she'd never looked more beautiful.

The bonfire raged without fuel or attendance, and Keko led him around it, introducing him to families and warriors, kids and cooks. No one wore anything fancier than shorts and

T-shirts, the only adornment being fresh flowers around necks and tucked behind ears. The food was remarkably fresh and simple—all raised and grown in the valley—and Griffin continued to eat long after he was uncomfortable.

Well into the night, he realized that Bane had been lingering behind them, far enough away that it wasn't immediately obvious, but close enough to make it clear that he was watching out for his sister. That he was guarding his Queen.

Griffin itched to talk to him, to pull him aside and have an hours-long conversation about being a Chimeran male and warrior, about the culture. About Keko and their young life together. Then Keko would touch Griffin's hand or back, magnetizing him to her again, and Griffin knew that he would have plenty of time for Bane later.

The party was at its height, a jubilant scene filled with drink and dance, set to the beat of drums and the laughter of half-naked children, when the bonfire suddenly diminished. It didn't die but the top of the flames collapsed, shrinking, and when the crowd swiveled toward the center to see who had killed part of the sustaining magic, Ikaika was standing on a picnic table.

Beside Griffin, Keko stiffened, sliding away from his touch.

Ikaika found Keko—she was difficult to miss in the dark now—and gave her a long, warm look of clear gratitude. Once he'd captured every Chimeran's attention, their murmurs of curiosity arrowing up to him, Ikaika reached behind his neck, grabbed the back of his shirt, and pulled it forward over his head.

The dance of the fire played across his bare chest. The black mark of Keko's hand was unmistakable.

The Chimerans reacted, surprise in their sounds, their hands covering their mouths.

"The Queen cured me, too," Ikaika said, his voice carrying easily in the hush. He stood on the bench of the table, one leg propped on the top. "Tonight I've been hearing many of you curse our former *ali'i*, discrediting all he's done because he lied. Because he lost his fire."

Griffin glanced at Keko, who was watching Ikaika with shining pride in her eyes.

"The *ali'i* did not tell you that he was not the only one struck by this disease because he wanted to protect Chimerans like me from dishonor, but I'm here to say—even though I have no right, I know—that I feel no shame. I once lost my fire, but then the Queen brought it back and I am not disgraced. I consider myself blessed. And nothing any of you will do or say against me will change that."

Keko's breath hitched.

Someone moved within the crowd. Griffin turned his head, expecting to see Bane heading for Ikaika. But it wasn't. It was a woman Griffin didn't know, a woman younger than he, with a baby on her hip. She went right up to the picnic table and lifted her face to Ikaika. He blinked down at her, unsure, then she extended her hand to him in silence. After a moment, he tugged her up to stand on the bench beside him. The baby gurgled in her arms.

Slowly, one-handed, the woman unbuttoned her shirt and folded it back, revealing Keko's handprint.

"I, too, am blessed," she said.

Amazement rippled through the crowd—amazement that only increased as more and more Chimerans approached the table. Twenty-two of them covered the table, surrounded it, exposing their marks that, mere days ago, would have brought them scorn.

They stood there, of all ages and abilities, daring with their resolute expressions any Chimeran to knock them down. None did.

Though Griffin was not Chimeran he sensed the distinct shift in their thoughts. In the building blocks of their culture. It was powerful stuff, made of something more than magic, more than history. It was change and progress, and it was scary and necessary and uplifting all at once.

He wanted to touch Keko, to tell her with his hands and mouth that he was proud of her, that he would stand next to or behind her—wherever she wanted—as she guided her people.

Every Chimeran looked to her now. They were expecting her to make a grand speech like she had on the steps of the old chief's house, to rouse them with words, but instead she just placed a hand over her own chest, her fingers a dark silhouette against the gentle blue-white of her skin, and simply said, "You are."

The entire valley took a joyful breath.

Then Keko snatched a cup of something she'd otherwise avoided her whole life, and took a grand swig that made her cough and sputter in a most human, self-deprecating way.

"Stop staring at me," she said through a watery smile, "and drink!"

The drums started up again but were quickly drowned out by a stirring cheer. The clan spun back into motion, and it seemed as though couples paired off quickly and easily. Mouths and bodies came together in passionate kisses and embraces, firelight dancing over the movement. Joy and release permeated everything, so sweet Griffin could taste it.

At the picnic table, the man who'd begun this scene stepped down. A curvy woman with black hair brushing her hips was waiting for him, watching him with revelation. Ikaika opened his arms and she came into them. When he broke the clutch, he tilted her head back and kissed her.

Griffin, surprised and confused, touched Keko's arm and nodded toward Ikaika. Keko saw the male and female couple and sighed. "Yeah," she said. "It's a little complicated."

Bane stood nearby, pointedly *not* watching Ikaika, his jaw tense, his eyes dark.

"They came together one night a couple of years ago. Everyone knew about that. It's not unusual here. But it kept going on in secret, even though Ikaika is partnered. I only know because I caught them. I don't know how Bane deals with it."

Not well, apparently.

She threaded her fingers through his and the simple touch ignited him. He didn't have to think about the countermagic. His water and her fire knew each other now. Instinctual. Complementary. Spellbinding.

"Come with me." As she tugged at him her voice was soft, her expression full of meaning.

"Shouldn't you stay?" He was thinking of the Ofarians, of course, how he was expected to do certain things at certain times. How he was supposed to act in a very specific, formal way and offend no one by neither speech nor action.

With a playful wrinkle of her nose, she grinned at the crowd. "I think they'll be just fine on their own."

Griffin did a double take as he caught sight of a man who'd backed a woman against a tree and had his hand beneath her skirt, right in front of everyone. "Wow. Turned sexual pretty quick."

"And you're surprised? Considering how we met?"

The scene in the parking garage, how she'd practically eaten him with her eyes. Her sexuality right there for him to feast upon. It had scared him at first, that openness. Then it had fascinated him.

She chuckled, another tug on his arm. "This is nothing. It's not even an *ume*."

"A . . . what?"

"So much to teach you. Picture this, a hundred times more sexual. A lot of people. Out in the open. Sharing. It's how Bane and Ikaika first met."

All he could do was blink at her.

"I'm going to break open that stiff and proper Ofarian mind of yours yet." Her chuckle rolled into a full-on laugh and at last he allowed himself to be pulled away from the party.

"Where are we going?" It was dark outside the fire circle and he'd lost his bearings. "I want to see your house. The one you told me about with the hammock and the door that looks out over the valley."

Her fingers tightened in his but she didn't reply. She found a narrow dirt path that cut through an overgrown sweep of some sort of native Hawaiian plant, and led him up a small rise. When they came out of the brush and the moonlight struck the long, low white building, Griffin understood where she'd brought him.

"That house I told you about?" she said. "It's not really mine anymore. But neither is this place. I want to tear it down, send the people who live here back to their families. Where they belong."

Griffin pulled her into him, her whole length flush with his body. The Source was a second heartbeat against him and he loved it.

"I think you're amazing," he said, touching her face. She reached up to mirror his movement, her fingers skating over the small burn on his temple. "So where are we sleeping tonight?"

"I never said anything about sleeping."

In the morning, under a rolling, cloudy sky and amidst the remnants of last night's celebration, Bane and Makaha faced off.

Keko stood far to the side, well away from the action,

knowing that the *ali'i* position at stake was going to make this a challenge for the ages. Her baser Chimeran instincts longed for this, to see what the warriors would bring. Bane, always aggressive, always skillful, would be a force. And just last night he'd been forced to watch his lover with another. He'd always successfully used emotion to enhance his battles. But Makaha owned his namesake ferocity; he had something serious to prove and was coming fresh off a defeat of Griffin.

Earlier, at sunrise, Griffin had reached for her, sliding a hand over the bare skin on her hip. It was still astonishing to her that he could fuck her with such biting passion and then touch her with such tenderness. She hoped that he would continue to astonish her for a very, very long time.

"Who do you want to win?" he'd asked.

She'd just looked at him, confused. "It's not about what I want."

"Ah." His favorite word, when it came to things Chimeran. His brow furrowed. "So all that you said last night about worthiness and weakness doesn't apply here?"

"They both want to lead the clan. They have to prove themselves to the people. They aren't being judged on what they don't have, or something out of their control. They're being measured by their actual abilities. Makes perfect sense to me."

He sat up, flinging aside the blanket they'd used when they finally passed out naked under the stars—because she couldn't yet stand to be enclosed after having endured being Within. The early morning light was very kind to his body.

"Makaha is at a distinct disadvantage against Bane," he said.

"Seemed to do just fine against you." Keko poked him. "You just don't want him to win because he kicked your ass."

He snorted. "Anything I might say in my defense would come off as weak to you, I'm sure. But yes, he did kick my ass."

Later, with Griffin standing next to her on the grass, they watched Makaha defeat Bane.

The valley roared its approval over Makaha's valiant fight and his ability to overcome. The clan swarmed around their new *ali'i* as Keko went to her brother.

Bane stood tall and strong despite looking like he wanted

to collapse to the ground in fatigue and disappointment. She wanted to hug him—a strange, non-Chimeran urge—but knew she could not. Not ever, not without hurting him. So she said, "I'm proud of you."

Breathing heavily, he bowed with two fists across his chest.

Then she went to Makaha. The people parted to let her through. The *ali'i*'s chest pumped with the last bits of adrenaline and a powerful air of dignity she hadn't witnessed in him in years.

"It's good to have you back, my friend," she told him.

He pushed back his long, sweat-soaked hair. The smile he gave her was huge and honest and full of a happiness she'd never witnessed in an *ali'i*.

She found Griffin perched on top of a picnic table, his feet set on the bench, twirling a long yellow flower between his palms.

"That's who you wanted to win," he said as she fit her body between his knees.

"Maybe." She glanced all around, taking in her valley. Her home.

He set down the flower and turned serious. "I have to go back. To San Francisco."

She nodded, but it must have come too slowly or she must have done a crappy job of disguising her disappointment, because he quickly added, "I'm not leaving you."

"I know. I know you aren't."

"I have to get back to my people. Gwen said things are getting testy, probably the worst they've ever been. I'm going to have a fight on my hands."

"Shit, really?"

He nodded, lips tightly pressed together. "I owe the Ofarians an explanation for my absence. They need to know what's happened with you and the Chimerans and the Senatus straight from me, and it needs to be sooner rather than later. And I really, really want to see Henry."

"Griffin, you don't have to explain. You're a leader."

"And now you are, too." He swept a hand over her hair and her scalp tingled. "I'm coming back. In fact I'm sort of looking forward to sleeping with you on the dirt again. Unless you want to find us an actual bed while I'm away."

He meant it to be funny, but it struck hard in her heart, mixing with all the things she still needed to tell him. All the things she'd been straightening out in her head.

"What is it?" he asked, because he was starting to know her so well.

"Can I drive you to the Hilo airport?"

"You want to be my chauffeur again? Talk about coming full circle."

That pulled a small smile out of her. "I'm still going to make you carry your own bag. But I want to take you someplace else first. And, yes, I'm driving."

Several hours later, after speeding northwest along the coastal highway straightaways and swerving daringly around the turns, she pulled the battered yellow Jeep into the gravel along the side of the road.

Griffin gaped at the scene out the windshield, motionless. Finally they climbed out and met in front of the car's grille. They were back in the rainy part of Hawaii, and the water droplets made hollow *splooshes* on the car hood and quieter splashes in the puddles at their feet.

"What are we doing back here?" he asked.

Keko gazed up at the B and B in which more than their goals had changed. Boards had been hammered over the window and door of their former room. The sight of it made her throat tight.

Griffin finally noticed and gasped. "What happened? It was fine when I left."

"My magic. It was too much, contained in too tight a space. It must've combusted and started a fire. I was watching. I saw you run off, and then the fire broke out. I ran back here, put it out, but it had already done some damage." She shook her head and finally had to look away. "*I* did that. I didn't mean to, but it's someone's business, someone's life. And now it's unusable because of me. But you know the worst part about it?"

"What?"

"I desperately want to make it up to the people who own this place. I want to help them, pay them back for what I did, but I can't."

Griffin took her arm and turned her to face him. "Sure you can."

"No, I mean like I *can't*." She pointed a finger back down the highway, in the direction of the valley from which they'd come. "You see how we live. How little we have. Even if I wanted to pay for damages or a whole new B and B—which I do—I can't because I literally don't have a cent of my own."

"Keko . . ." He ran a hand below his jaw and glanced out toward the ocean. "I can—"

"No, Griffin. Don't even say it. I'm not taking your money. I'm not letting you step in and do this for me. I just can't. And it has nothing to do with being Queen or whatever. You understand that, right?"

He did, because she saw it in the warmth of his eyes and the easy bob of his head. "Okay, so what are you thinking? Why did you really bring me here?"

She took a deep breath, felt the reassuring fire within. "To tell you that I want to come with you. To San Francisco."

His eyes brightened, widened. "Yes. *Yes*. Absolutely come with me."

She pressed a hand to the wet shirt on his chest. "Not solely to be with you. Like you, I have to be here for my people, so my going to the mainland can't be forever."

"I get that, sure. So what do you want to do?"

"I'm thinking"—she licked her lips and tasted the delicious water of her island, the stuff that would always, always remind her of Griffin and their days spent slugging through it—"that I want to ask for the Ofarians' help."

He opened his mouth, made some sort of odd sound, then finally got out, "What do you mean?"

"I am Chimeran Queen. I assumed and accepted the name only if I knew I could bring change for the better. You know how my people have been living. It is poverty. In this day and age, it is nothing more, and the clans on the other islands are the same way, maybe even worse off. Why does it have to be like that? I'm not saying we have to be rich and live in ocean-front condos on the Kohala Coast, but we have no prospects and no skills applicable to the real world. Ofarians do."

He drew a sharp breath in realization, but she went on.

"I've been thinking about this ever since Aya brought me back from Within. How I was the first Secondary other than their own kind to see that realm. How Cat and now you have been the only Ofarians to visit the Chimeran valley. How no one knows anything about the Airs, or Sean and Michael, those spirit elementals who were with me in Colorado. How is this good? How can we possibly help each other if we're peering at each other through teeny tiny holes?"

"Wow." He sank onto the bumper of the Jeep. "I guess I never thought of it like that. I was too set with the whole Primary/Secondary thing, trying to figure out ways for us to fit in better to *their* world."

"But that's the thing. You already have such a leg up on that. Ofarians know so much and Chimerans know nothing except what we've been looking at for centuries. Education and technology and the ways of business—I want your people to teach my people all of that. I don't even know how to turn on a damn computer. No Chimeran does. You can help us."

He nodded enthusiastically. "We can. Absolutely we can."

"And that could just be the beginning. We could start to organize diplomatic tours between all the races, learn as much about each other as possible—"

He snaked his arms around her waist and pulled her into him. "We?"

His hair was wet and shiny and silky between her fingers. "We. You and me. Start a whole new thing. 'Fuck the Senatus,' if I can steal your words. You said yourself you're going to have a fight on your hands when you get back. Let me stand next to you when you face them. Let me help you tell them all that you've done. Let me help you present something new and wonderful, this collaboration, that they could help birth. Give them ownership, you know?"

"Fuck the Senatus," he whispered. "Oh God, Keko."

And then she was crushed in his embrace. Water, water everywhere.

"You can help us, too," he said into her skin.

She peeled herself away and raised an eyebrow at him. "We can?"

"Henry would just about kill to learn some of the fighting maneuvers I saw your warriors do out on the field the other day. So would most Ofarian kids."

"Bring in the newer generations," she said. "I like it."

His expression turned grim. "I should warn you, not everyone will. It's been the story of my life for the past five years."

Didn't he get it yet? "Battles are virtuous only when there's a prize worth fighting for."

He framed her face in his hands. "This is just a thought so feel free to shoot it down, but we have this doctor, Kelsey Evans. She's brilliant and eager and has done so much for us. What would you say to her and her staff coming to take a look at your people who contracted the wasting disease?"

Hope and love soared within her, making her nearly buoyant. "You think she could find a cause?"

Griffin shrugged. "Don't know, but it's worth a shot, don't you think? I know she'd be up to the task and her husband, David, would jump at the chance for a free trip to Hawaii."

He kissed her neck, the lick of him mixing with the moisture from the sky, and she shivered even with the Source thundering through her body. Then her mouth found his, and the kiss drowned her in a flood that no longer scared her.

"And guess what?" she said against his lips. "You're not *kapu* anymore. That's my first declaration as Queen." She struck a fist on his chest. "There. Done."

He sighed, but it came out like a shudder. She thought he might kiss her again, but instead his liquid brown eyes stared into hers as he said, "I am never going to be able to hold you tight enough. I will never get tired of the feel of you. I will never take you for granted. And I will fight for you until the end of my days."

"Good." She drew back, planted fists on her hips in an echo of her trademark defiant stance, and smiled mischievously. "Because it's going to be one wonderful war."

Turn the page for a preview of Hanna Martine's next

HIGHLAND
GAMES NOVEL

Coming from Sensation in December 2014

I need a hot guy in a kilt.

Shea Montgomery was standing in the middle of a sea of whiskey bottles when her best friend Willa's text buzzed through. Smiling, Shea thumbed back: *Funny, exactly what I'm looking at right now.*

Through the folded-back flaps of the white tent dedicated to the Amber Lounge's whiskey tasting station, Shea could see the group of two-hundred-plus-pound kilted men milling about the sprawling athletic field. The first throw of the day's Scottish Highland Games would go off in about two hours.

Bring one back to the city for me, texted Willa.

Shea peered hard at the field. *Lots of kilts. None hot. Sorry.*

Take a pic. Let me decide.

Shea laughed, shaking her head. *I'm working. And it's 8 am. You are dead to me.*

Shea tucked her phone into the back pocket of her black pants and went back to inventory. She was fingering the necks of the bottles she'd curated for the day's tasting, mentally matching them up with what she'd shipped out to the Hamptons from her cellar in SoHo's Amber Lounge.

If she were able, she actually would march out to the field and snap a stealth pic of the hugely muscled men in kilts for Willa, but Shea would have no such free time today. Truth be told, there was very little Shea wouldn't do for Willa, considering Willa had been the only friend to stand by her when she'd cut loose her former life and taken that giant leap of faith into freedom.

The beautiful white tent rippled and flapped around Shea on this gorgeous, crisp, early May morning. High circular tables draped with white linen and tied with blue bows peppered the center, with squatter tables and cushioned chairs set outside under a canopy. An honest-to-god velvet rope corralled the whiskey drinkers in this private space, setting them apart from the general masses who would gather in a few hours when the gates opened to the NYC Scottish Highland Games.

It was a perfect day for it—for the sun and the laughter, for watching powerful kilted athletes compete by throwing ridiculously heavy implements like the hammer and caber around the grass. For lying back on your elbows and surrounding yourself with the heartbreaking, beautiful bagpipe and drum sounds telling history through song.

It was a perfect day for Shea to remember the moments when she actually began to *live*.

Even if this particular games had its nose in the air as opposed to right down in the peat and heather where it should be, the tip of the hat to her Scottish ancestry warmed her heart.

Fifteen minutes before ten, Shea and Dean, the middle-aged bartender she'd coerced into working with her all day after closing the Amber at midnight the night before, skillfully pulled out short-stemmed tasting glasses and made artistic towers along the back table. The bottles of Scotch whiskey she'd already set out caught the yellow morning light as it shot into the tent, making flickering shapes on the fabric ceiling.

Dean tossed his empty cardboard box out of sight behind the tent and ran his fingers across the labels of the portwood and the twenty-seven-year blend and the eighteen-year-old single malt from the only distillery to still use their iconic peat towers in their distillation process.

He whistled in a high arc. "Nice choices. Not exactly starting at the bottom, are you?"

Shea got rid of her empty box, too. "Yeah, well, you have to pay a hundred dollars extra to come in here to taste. It was made very clear to me that I had to make it special."

Dean's eyes bugged. "A hundred bucks? No shit?"

Hands on hips, she surveyed her "special" setup and glanced with chagrin out at the blue velvet rope. She sighed. "No shit."

Her phone chimed again, which reminded her to shut off the text sound before the work day started.

Still in bed. Willa again. *Dying for a kilted man to bring me Gatorade and ibuprofen.*

An unwitting laugh bubbled out of Shea's mouth. *Still working.*

Still hungover.

A figure appeared at the still-roped-off tent entrance, fuzzy and indistinct in Shea's peripheral vision. Funny and horrible how Shea recognized the shape and stance and just general oily presence of the man she deliberately hadn't seen in five years. She looked up, her eyes confirming what the shiver down her spine had foretold.

Oh fuckity fuck, she typed to Willa.

She swears while working!

It's Nathan. He's here. FUSCKK.

Quickly, she shoved the phone into her back pocket like she was in high school, not thirty-two years old, and had just run into the guy she'd once been obsessed with who'd dumped her out of the blue.

Maybe she'd once been obsessed with Nathan, but it hadn't been he who'd done the dumping.

Stepping over the velvet rope—because such rules had *never* applied to him, oh no—he took his sweet time crossing the empty tent. Dean must have sensed the impending awkwardness and made himself scarce. Shea came around from behind the bar. No need to hide from Nathan anymore.

"Hi, Shea." His smile was brilliantly, falsely white.

"Hello." She would be civil, cordial. Though she was standing in her place of work, where it was easy to become who she needed to be, her ex-husband's unexpected presence threw everything all out of whack and she hated it. "You look"—*orange*—"tan."

He seemed so pleased she noticed. Gross.

"Greece," he replied. "Remember that yacht off the coast of Santorini?"

Yes, she did remember. And no, she didn't want to. She crossed her arms. "What are you doing here?"

He did that thing she hated—cocking his head and making a face like *she'd* been the one to do the confusing thing, that *her* emotions and actions were wrong and *how dare she* not realize this. He opened his arms, gesturing to the tent. In one hand he waved a program for the games.

"Saw your picture in here. Came to do the gentlemanly thing and say hello."

"No, I meant what are you doing *here*, at the Highland Games? You never used to let me be involved in stuff like this."

He made an indignant sound. "That's ridiculous."

It was very true. Every time something with the NYC Scottish Society had come up and she'd expressed interest in going, he'd book something else for them to do. Something obnoxious and lavish on the opposite side of the globe. And she'd gone with him without argument. Stupid girl. Stupid, spineless, clueless girl.

But she wasn't that person anymore, and she supposed, when it came down to it, she had Nathan to thank for that.

"You know," he said, "I really did just come in here to say hello, see what you're up to." He swept his eyes toward the apex of the tent, then brought his stare back to her—the one that had leveled her that very first night so long ago, when he'd picked up a twenty-two-year-old Shea as she'd been bartending. "Surprised to see you here. You don't belong behind the bar anymore. Don't you have employees?"

He would never understand her, what she truly wanted, why she'd left him. She sighed and uncrossed her arms. "Why did you come in here, Nathan?"

"Uh." He actually had the acting chops to look sheepish. "I miss you?"

"No, you don't."

"It's been a few years. Maybe I went about things the wrong way. Maybe things have changed."

"Nothing's changed. Believe me." At least not with him. The man had sprung from humble beginnings, but his sprint up the New York City real estate ladder had wrung out his humanity.

"Shea." He shook his head, looked at the ground, and she saw he had a heck of a lot of silver in his hair. He would be approaching fifty by now. "Listen, when you're done here tonight, why don't you come over? We could have a quiet drink as old friends. I built a new house over on the beach—"

"Ah, I get it now. You got dumped."

"No. That's not it."

But the slack of his mouth told the truth.

"She's coming back," he added hastily, after she raised an eyebrow at him.

Shea laughed and turned around to her precious bottles, the lovely things that had given her courage and purpose, and had finally allowed her to ask for the divorce. "New houses on the beach. Yachts in Greece. Those things don't impress me, Nathan."

"They used to."

Boy, he climbed all over that one fast.

She faced him, stared him down. "I was young and dumb."

The sheepishness and humble pie died. Just vanished from his face. His posture straightened and tightened.

"You know," he said, "Shea Montgomery served on ice doesn't taste very good."

"You don't like strong drinks. You like them all watered down."

He considered her with that flat stare she recalled too well. "I'll never get why you changed."

"I know, Nathan. And that's the sad part. Enjoy your new house."

His nostrils flared. "I will. Enjoy your . . . *bar.*"

Bar said, of course, like she owned a whorehouse.

"I will. Because it's *mine.* And it's more than you ever let me have."

He opened his mouth to defend himself, to say something awful like "I let you have everything. I gave you everything," but she held up a hand to inform him of its senselessness. Because when she'd left him, she'd made it a point not to take a dime from him; he had nothing to throw in her face.

"Have fun at the games," she said as pleasantly as possible, knowing he wasn't going to stick around now that she'd shut him down. He'd come here specifically to hunt. She was a conquest, a trophy. Today, like all those years ago, he'd been hoping to tranquilize her, chain her to his side again, maybe strip off her personality and free will like he'd cut the skin off of his prey. Once again, he hoped to hang her in his new house for people he didn't care about to look at and make comments about how well she reflected on him.

As expected, Nathan turned and left.

Whiskey shouldn't be untouchable, relegated only to a certain social level of drinker, but that's exactly what Shea and her bottles were today, hidden away in this too-fancy tent. No one could enter the velvet rope who wasn't wearing the yellow one-hundred-dollar wristband. Ridiculous for a Scottish festival.

Shea just wanted to talk whiskey. Just wanted to serve what she loved.

Two couples ducked out of the bright sun and came in laughing. The taller husband, the one in a plaid, short-sleeved, button-down shirt, was holding a set of stacked, empty beer cups. A Drinker, Shea pegged him, coming in here to chase the buzz. The other man, the one in a blue T-shirt, headed right for Shea, nodding as though they already knew each other. He was either a Hot Air—someone who *thought* he knew a lot about the good stuff—or a Brown Vein—someone who really *did* know.

Of the women, one wore a red visor that parked itself around her ears and extended far over her face. The other had a short blond ponytail. Neither woman looked particularly interested in why they'd come in here, though all four people sported wristbands.

Shea spread her arms across the table and gave them all a welcoming smile. Didn't matter why anyone came in, when it came down to it. They were giving the drink a chance, and educating newcomers was one of the favorite parts of her job. Sometimes that was the best kind of challenge, to win over someone who'd been skeptical—a Squinter—or someone who had cut their teeth on whiskey by sneaking their parents' ten-dollar plastic-bottled swill bought at the corner bodega.

"So what do these get us?" Drinker waved his yellow wrist.

Always genial, always polite. "Tastes of three amazing whiskeys and a walk-through of each, by yours truly."

"That's a big deal, my friend," added the other man. To Shea he gave a deep nod, lips pursed. "Saw you on the History Channel the other night." He didn't mention which special.

"Yeah? That's always great to hear. Glad you came by." She

turned to her artful setup of bottles placed under the large banner with the Amber Lounge logo, and swung back around holding a tray of glasses. She flipped over each to slide across the white tablecloth with smooth, practiced ease. One glass, two, three, four—

A fifth yellow wristband appeared at the elbow of the blue-shirted man she was leaning toward pegging as a Brown Vein. This new wristband wrapped around an arm that was crusty with caked mud. The newcomer's fingers and palm looked like he'd tried to wipe them somewhat clean, but black still clung under his nails. Shea followed that arm upward, which widened out significantly at the biceps. He wore a red-and-black-striped rugby jersey, soaked with the efforts of a recently completed match. His short dark hair was sweat damp and stuck out all over the place, his cheeks sunburned.

Out of the corner of her eye, she saw one of the wives nudge the other.

"Hi," Rugby said. "Do you remember me?"

His eye contact was so strong she swore it might have been the source of gravity.

She blinked at him. She remembered regular faces, especially those who repeatedly came in to the Amber, but with so many tastings and traveling events and interviews these days, transient people tended to dissipate from her memory.

Yet there was something . . . familiar about him. Something about his off-center, bright smile set against the tanned skin layered with sweat and specks of dirt. But she couldn't place it right away, and there were four other customers who had paid nicely for her attention.

"I'm sorry, I don't." She was careful to hold on to her genial smile.

"I'm Byrne."

A little cocky of him—but not quite obnoxious—to assume that she'd remember him based on one name. She didn't.

"Just Byrne?"

"Just Byrne." The smile widened, tilting even more to one side. Holy crap.

"Shea Montgomery," she replied, using the moment to swivel around and choose the first bottle.

"Yes. I know," said Just Byrne to her back.

The sound of his laugh, soft and low, slid an invisible hand around the nape of her neck, took a light hold, then dragged itself down her back. A delicious shiver. This did *not* happen to her while she was pouring.

People laughed in her bar every day, in tones exactly like Byrne's, and it never elicited this severe a reaction. She shook it off because she had to, and turned back around to face her tasters, holding the eighteen-year-old single malt. She poured a shallow tasting amount in each glass, starting at the far end with plaid-shirted Drinker and ending with Byrne, who pushed his glass a few inches closer to her.

"Last summer?" he prompted.

She made the mistake of lifting her gaze, of getting a good, long look at his eyes. Almost powder blue with a navy blue ring around the rim.

"Up in Gleann, New Hampshire," he continued. "That cow wiped out your tent. Me and my team helped you clean it up."

The bottle slipped from her fingers. Just a few inches, but it made a graceless clink on the table.

That damn crooked smile layered a boyish tint over his confident, intense focus on her. He pressed his hipbones right up against the bar. She guessed he was just over six feet, and built exactly like a rugby player should be.

And that was far longer a personal assessment of any taster she'd ever allowed herself. Time to move on.

"Oh, yeah." Cool as the breeze, that was Shea. "Didn't you guys win the tug-of-war?"

"So you do remember." Spoken all drawn out, packed with suggestion.

He was acting way too encouraged, so she shrugged. "That's about all. Did you win the rugby tourney, too?"

"Nah. The tug-of-war must've gone to our heads."

"Or maybe it was the whiskey," called Drinker, way too loudly, with an obnoxious eyeball at Shea. Drinker's wife poked him.

Time to shut down the personal angle.

She purposely left Byrne, stepped to the middle of her set of tasters, and poured herself her own tiny glass. "Are we ready, folks?"

Drinker held up the small, squat-stemmed glass. "Why not the flat-bottom glasses? What do you call those again?"

"These are better for nosing the whiskey. Here, hold the base like—"

She didn't mean to look over at Byrne again. Habit, really, to take in everyone at the tasting table, to make sure she had their attention and that they each knew they were important to her.

Hot Air—for that's what she knew the second husband to be now—was grasping the glass underneath, holding it in his palm like a medieval goblet. But Byrne had the round base balanced lightly in his fingertips. Correctly. As he bent forward to set his elbow on the bar, the whiskey in his glass remained as still as a windless, hidden lake.

She ripped her gaze from him and focused on the couples. "Hold it like this." She showed them how to hold the base of the glass and not grip the bowl like a Viking. "What we're going to do first is nose the whiskey three times, each time slightly longer than the last. One second, two seconds, three seconds. I'm going to count. Why don't you all watch me as you do it?"

The women shared a glance and laughed, and Shea wondered how many of those empty plastic beer cups had been theirs.

"One."

Shea lifted the glass to her face, inserted her nose, and inhaled.

The couples followed suit, and displayed pretty much the range of reaction she'd expected. Everything from I-Don't-Give-A-Shit-Let's-Drink, to Ew-This-Is-Disgusting, to dramatic, chest-pounding coughing because she'd inhaled too deeply and too long. Hot Air's expression said that this was nothing he hadn't already known.

And then there was Byrne. Nose in his glass for about a quarter second longer than was necessary. Powder blue eyes lifted just over the rim. Set solely on her.

Shouldn't a rugby player be exhausted after being on the field? Because he was feeding her some serious energy. And shouldn't a rugby player be able to read the defense? Because she was throwing up some big blocks and he was trying to charge right through them. Did he think he was the first guy to give her The Eye from the other side of the bar? This flat surface in front of her was No Man's Land. Quite literally.

One mistake in that regard had been enough for a lifetime, thank you very much.

"Should be different the second time, now that you got the shock of the alcohol out of the way," she heard herself saying. "It should be sweeter."

The corner of Byrne's mouth twitched, a hint of that crooked smile, then he buried his nose in the glass again, exactly matching her movements. Concentrating. This time *not* looking at her. Black lines of dirt had settled into the deep grooves of concentration along his forehead. Damn it. Why had she noticed?

And what position did he play?

On cue, Hot Air started spouting off to his companions a list of all the things he smelled in the whiskey, and while there were never any right or wrong suggestions to specific scents—whiskey was an entirely personal experience—he was messing with Shea's rhythm.

"And the third?" Byrne asked Shea, cutting into Hot Air's thesaurus recitation. Hot Air shut up.

"On the third nose," Shea said, "you should smell some fruit, going deeper into the intricacies of the glass."

Her tasters followed her actions.

"Byrne! You done in there yet? Come on, let's go!"

Byrne swiveled to the sound of the chorus of male voices. Outside in the sun, the rest of his team, muddy and disheveled in red-and-black, beckoned to him, laughing. No other rugby players wore yellow wristbands.

Byrne acknowledged them with his glass, then took a perfect taste of what Shea had poured.

The brown liquid disappeared slowly into his mouth. His jaw worked it over for a good four or five seconds. Biting it, chewing it. Savoring it, as it should be done. Then he swallowed it back, his throat working.

Exactly like how she was about to instruct her newbies.

Byrne lifted his eyes to Shea without a hint of pretentiousness or flirting. "Excellent, thank you." Then, with a nod to the other four people, he left her tent.

She watched him go. In her mind she was holding one of those giant cartoon mallets and was racking herself on the head, but she watched him anyway.

He had a long stride, masculine but oddly graceful. A leisurely confidence to his gait. He also had ridiculous legs, and she was annoyed with herself for noticing. They were tanned and thick and strong, with a distinct pronunciation of his quads. Might as well have *rugby player* tattooed down the side of them.

God*damn* it.

Outside, she watched him wiggle off the yellow wristband in a way that might have the organizers rethinking their purchase next year. But instead of rejoining his team, Byrne went over to a group of middle-aged adults spreading out a blanket next to the flag rope surrounding the athletic field. Out in the grass, the sheaf toss was starting. Byrne tapped a woman on the shoulder, said something to her, then when she smiled and nodded enthusiastically, he offered her his hundred-dollar wristband.

Then he pulled three more brand-new bands out of his shorts pocket and passed them out to the others. As one of the men reached for his wallet, Byrne waved off any sort of compensation.

The four recipients of the new wristbands slapped them on, and Byrne went over to his team.

As he passed by the roped-off outdoor seating of the whiskey tent, he turned his head and immediately, instantly found Shea. Found her staring.

She quickly ducked her head and wiped off an already-clean section of her makeshift bar. But not before she caught a final glimpse of that crooked smile, far too bright in the sunshine.

That smile promised a lot. Things she hadn't allowed herself—or been afforded—to think about in a long, long time. Things that hit her right where she hadn't been touched in an embarrassing number of months.

It disturbed her, to be disarmed while in uniform, so to speak. It disturbed her even more that the man who'd done it was a taster, and quite possibly a Brown Vein. An absolute no-no.

He wouldn't win, though.

He had to know that even though he'd caught her staring, and even though she'd looked away like a shy virgin at a bachelor auction, it didn't mean he'd won, or that he'd gained any sort of ground with her. She had rules to uphold, a hard-won reputation to maintain, and a business to keep at the top of the New York scene.

But when she looked up to tell him all that with her cool, disinterested expression and Stay Back eyes, Byrne was gone.

FROM *USA TODAY* BESTSELLING AUTHOR
THEA HARRISON

Rising Darkness
A Game of Shadows Novel

In the ER where she works, Mary is used to chaos. But lately, every aspect of her life seems adrift and the vivid, disturbing dreams she's had all her life are becoming more intense. Then she meets Michael. He's handsome, enigmatic and knows more than he can say. In his company, she slowly remembers the truth about herself...

Thousands of years ago, there were eight of them. The one called the Deceiver came to destroy the world, and the other seven followed to stop him. Reincarnated over and over, they carry on—and Mary finds herself drawn into the battle once again. And the more she learns, the more she realizes that Michael will go to any lengths to destroy the Deceiver.

Then she remembers who killed her during her last life, nine hundred years ago...*Michael*.

theaharrison.com
pcnguin.com

FROM *NEW YORK TIMES* BESTSELLING AUTHOR

NALINI SINGH

Heart of Obsidian

A PSY-CHANGELING NOVEL

A dangerous, volatile rebel, hands stained bloodred.
A woman whose very existence has been erased.
A love story so dark, it may shatter the world itself.
A deadly price that must be paid.

The day of reckoning is here.

PRAISE FOR THE PSY-CHANGELING SERIES:

"A phenomenal series."
—*Joyfully Reviewed*

"I don't think there is a single paranormal series as well
planned, well written, and downright fantabulous
as Ms. Singh's Psy-Changeling series."
—*All About Romance*

nalinisingh.com
facebook.com/AuthorNaliniSingh
facebook.com/ProjectParanormalBooks
penguin.com

M1331T0613